The gr_____
all over the world. In the Great American Desert,
aka the Bloodlands, a band of refugees found
evidence of far less selective murder.

Jessie nodded. Minutes later she found a small pelvic bone—a child's most likely—that looked like it had been shattered.

"They were slaughtered," Burned Fingers said in the same careful voice.

Jessie realized that she could be crouching over scores of bodies, a veritable warren of bones that could extend for miles. Everything before her could be a massive unmarked grave. They'd already come upon almost fifty bodies—and ample proof of murder.

Who did this?

Burned Fingers stood slowly, his only obvious sign of age, eyes once more fixed on the all-encompassing emptiness. She rose beside him, noticing most of the caravaners staring into the void of the great desert, as silent and solemn as they'd been at Augustus's camp.

Why were these people killed? And why here?

Why not *here?* she countered herself. *People are killed every~~~*

Her eyes _____ he saw that the dead m___

Like us.

By James Jaros

Carry the Flame
Burn Down the Sky

CARRY THE FLAME

JAMES JAROS

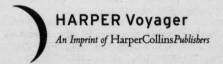

HARPER Voyager
An Imprint of HarperCollins Publishers

HARPER Voyager
An Imprint of HarperCollins*Publishers*
10 East 53rd Street
New York, New York 10022–5299

Copyright © 2012 by Mark Nykanen
Cover art by Getty Images/Stockbyte
ISBN 978–0–06–201631–7
www.harpervoyagerbooks.com

First Harper Voyager mass market printing: August 2012

Harper Voyager and ❯ is a trademark of HCP LLC.

Printed in the U.S.A.

10 9 8 7 6 5 4 3 2 1

For the wayward

Acknowledgments

I'm honored to have a group of friends who read for me, point out my errors, make fruitful suggestions, and do so in the most supportive manner possible. With that in mind, many thanks to Dale Dauten, Darryl Santano, Monte Ferraro, and my lovely sister, Kim Nykanen.

I have a huge thank you for Mark Feldstein, an author who pulls out an especially sharp editor's pen and marks up my pages with insight and great diligence. We've been doing this for each other for a long time. May it ever be so.

Likewise, I want to thank Ed Stackler, who has provided a precise editor's eye for five books now. Ed is a marvel to work with and a pleasure to know.

This book wouldn't have appeared without Harper Voyager editor Will Hinton's ongoing and enthusiastic support. Will championed both this book and *Burn Down the Sky*. He's made many helpful suggestions en route to their publication, and I'm thankful for them.

I also want to direct lots of gratitude toward my agent, Howard Morhaim, for his redoubtable efforts on my behalf.

CARRY THE FLAME

Chapter One

The horizon darkened by midday. Jessie watched black clouds boil from a ridge in the Great Smokies, mountains once verdant and lushly green. Thunderheads, most likely, but she knew the charred forests would offer little fuel for lightning. Wildfires had long scorched the southern high country, and the drought-stricken land had not recovered. The trees and brush had turned to cinders and ash, and the ash—the final mute testimony of life, and the eternally empty echo of death—had been cast by the wind to the desolate valleys below. But what turned Jessie away from the raging clouds wasn't the bleak vision of final ruin, or the potentially lethal force of a crackling sky. It was an elusively subtle scent that tormented her with the darkest, most wrenching memories, and threatened everyone on the caravan with a merciless demise.

Burned Fingers joined her. Despite his age—she guessed late fifties, giving him a good fifteen years on her—he walked nimbly uphill for a better view, leaving her in the shade of a hijacked tanker truck filled with gasoline. It baked in the sun near an armor-clad van packed with looted food, water, and gunpowder.

Nearby, adults and even the youngest children scrambled

to chip off sharp lengths of an obsidian wall for knives, traps, and spear tips.

Like hunter-gatherers, Jessie thought without irony as she looked from the collection in her hand to the imposing size of the tanker. She saw Bliss, soon to turn fifteen, holding up a flat, slivery rock. The girl reared back to test it as a weapon, like baseball pitchers had once wound up to deliver a strike. But Bliss didn't let it fly, saving the black glassy stone for when she might need to kill. She caught her mom's glance and smiled, suddenly a child again. Both of them were tall and lean with braided black hair and skin frightfully bronzed by the harsh, unrelenting rays.

Burned Fingers slipped past Jessie so quietly that she found it unsettling. Then he took the disk-shaped rock from Bliss, rubbing the razor edge against his chin; he was one of the few men Jessie had ever seen who still made an effort to shave. After inspecting his salt and pepper stubble, he hefted the rock's weight to check its balance. "It'll throw fast and true. And this," he thumbed the edge, "will split a man wide open."

Words like the blessing of a brimstone prophet. Burned Fingers looked the part with a bone-drawn face that flaunted an unnerving geometry of unforgiving features; raked back, shale-gray hair, and the burned index and middle digits of his shooting hand that had given rise to his nickname. Not unhandsome, his steely looks complemented his manner as much as his fused, arced fingers suited the curved trigger of his sawed-off shotgun, like they'd been burned to bear arms above all else. He could have been stained red, for all the blood he'd spilled, including the blood of Jessie's husband. She could not look at Burned Fingers without seeing Eden lying by the gate to their camp, bludgeoned, bleeding, dying. The path that had brought the marauder to her side remained grim, enigmatic, haunting.

He handed Bliss back a weapon old as the Pleistocene and turned again to the blackening horizon.

Augustus moved up beside Jessie and stared at the erupting sky. "It's over my camp," the missionary said slowly, "whatever it is." The first spoken suggestion that the midday darkness whirling toward them might not be a rainstorm or gales of gritty dust, but a far deadlier force.

Jessie closed her eyes, no longer able to deny the scent of seared flesh or the hateful weight it carried. Not a strong stench, not so sickeningly sweet as the smells she'd known only three weeks ago when they burned down the fortress of the religious zealots who'd kidnapped their daughters; but in these stark and pressing seconds the scent felt as real as the soot that colored those clouds.

She said nothing about the haunting odor. Maybe Augustus hadn't noticed. Or maybe she was wrong, though her sense of smell had sharpened during these long decades of deprivation, like hearing honed by blindness. They would learn the answer soon enough because the pacifist preacher had shown real heroism during the rescue of the girls, earning him a ride to his settlement. It sat along what had once been the border of Tennessee and Kentucky—the path Jessie and Burned Fingers planned for the caravan's long, perilous journey north.

Burned Fingers had warned that their attack on the fortress would be seen as an attack on the Alliance, a shadowy network of heavily armed outposts across North America. Augustus brought that up to Jessie as he stood by her side, but he also reminded her—maybe himself, too—that the Alliance had stayed away from his settlement. "Called us the curse of Cain, and never came around, like being black was contagious." But moments later the sweet smell thickened and he shook his head wordlessly, and she remembered him once adding that the men in the Alliance never left you alone for good, "not if you've got so much as a flint knife worth stealing."

We've got a lot more than that, she thought, eyeing the tanker brimming with gasoline. We've got the Holy Grail of the new Dark Ages, and *maybe* the only way to get to the new Jerusalem—arctic Canada, where land was said to be green, and palm trees and crops grew, as well as dates and Kamut and oranges.

That "maybe" worried her ceaselessly, kept her looking back as much as she plowed ahead. Made her feel watched by hidden eyes, knowing the Alliance would rake the very coals of hell to retake the tanker and reassert control of the region.

Burned Fingers had likened the truck to a "rolling gas station," and Jessie knew they'd never caravan to the Arctic without it; but she also feared that it would get them massacred.

She looked over the adults and children scrambling to add to their cache of weapons, and found it inconceivable that all thirty of them would survive this trip. Far easier to imagine them lifeless as the land they planned to cross. Far worse for Augustus, who might have reason to worry that his people already had been slaughtered, their homes and bodies burned.

He had left a wife and twin girls in the settlement, now roundly cloaked by those black clouds rolling ever closer. But the believer had spoken of his twins only of late, and said little else about them, simply that they were "of age," which meant they were about to start their menses—prime targets for the ruthless zealots who claimed a God-given right to abduct them for procreation.

"Grab your stuff and get on board," Burned Fingers ordered. "We've got to get moving."

"But that thing's coming right at us." Ananda, Jessie's twelve-year-old, backed up as she stared at the massive wall of clouds marching toward them. With plaited black hair and darkly tanned skin, she was another pea in the family pod.

"And if it's rain, it could disappear," her mother replied. "If it doesn't, we'll stop when it hits." Whatever *it* was, she thought, keeping her gruesome concerns to herself so the caravan could stay ahead of the Alliance—or the mercenaries its secretive leadership had sent after them. Might even be marauders from Burned Fingers' old gang.

Jessie watched everyone gather up their rock shards, hoping that turning them into knives and spear points would keep them busy enough to spare her any cries of "Are we there yet?" from the younger children, a complaint as common now as it had once been in cars and on wagon trains. Cassie's mourning came to mind immediately; the smallest, frailest girl's father had been shotgunned to death trying to take control of the tanker. Since then she'd been cared for by her father's old friend, Maul, a big, bald, fierce-looking man who captained the truck with a shotgun by his side and pistol and butcher knife in his belt—but who'd wept openly when he knelt next to Cassie to tell her the news about her dad.

Similar grief haunted other children climbing aboard the vehicles, including nine-year-old Imagi, a Down syndrome girl, and Mia and Kluani, eleven-year-old twins who took turns wearing a twine necklace they'd macraméd for their father, who bled to death after leading the attack that netted them the van; Jessie had taken the necklace off his body to give to his daughters.

She placed her hand on Kluani's back, guiding her to a berth under the belly of the tanker near her darker-haired sister. Throughout the day, the most fidgety children changed positions with one another, shifting along the sides of the trailer or down below the tanker.

Maul, behind the wheel, handed his twelve-gauge to Erik. At thirteen Erik had been given the weighty role of riding shotgun, though the dark-freckled boy recognized that he was mostly an extra pair of eyes for the large man beside him, who handled his weapons as naturally as his forbearers had used utensils. Maul started the truck, and thick plumes of oily black smoke streamed from twin exhaust pipes that rose like horns above either side of the armored cab.

In front of them the van started to roll away, carrying three teenage girls blinded by the zealots, but who still cared for three female babies who'd been in their care since birth.

Brindle drove the smaller vehicle. He was short, wiry,

and suffered from a stammer that disappeared only when he swore. He swore a lot. Tow-headed Jaya, fifteen, rode shotgun for Brindle. Jessie had assigned him to the van, and Bliss to a guard post on the tanker, to try to keep them apart, at least during the day. She hadn't been entirely successful: during a break yesterday, she chanced upon them clutching passionately; though their hands were busy, their clothes had been on.

Bliss took her position at the front of a narrow metal walkway that ran along the top of the tanker and studied the territory ahead with the sharp vision of youth. She pumped her shotgun as her mother climbed up the trailer's rear, facing backward on the same narrow grating to watch for creatures that might stalk them. Not all the animals were human. Some, like the playfully named Pixie-bobs, had four legs and fur, beguiling faces, and shocking ferocity. They'd been bred from domestic felines and bobcats, or *Lynx rufus,* as the wildlife biologist called them when she still had use for Latin. The Pixie-bobs had turned voraciously feral, proliferated in the Appalachians, and hunted in packs of a hundred or more. With little fear of humans, these piranhas of the apocalypse could strip a good-sized man to bone in sixty seconds, a child in less time than it took her to scream, turn, and start to run.

After scanning the wretched landscape they were quitting, Jessie waved her arm. Bliss relayed the go-ahead to Maul, and the truck rolled out behind the van, keeping enough distance that a single gas bomb, often poisoned with human waste, would be unlikely to blow up both vehicles and all the children.

Jessie lifted her eyes to the blanched sky, noting the contrast with the black clouds several miles ahead. The caravan would have to stop when the storm hit, assuming that's what it was. If the blackness vanished—and they'd seen the most violent looking thunderstorms abscond with the sweetest promise of rain—they'd continue so Augustus could return to his family by nightfall, or see to their remains.

Who are you kidding? Jesse shook her head, understanding for the first time that hope and grief were death's only real ghosts. *It'll be their remains, if there are any left.*

Minutes later the smell of burning bodies turned as suffocating as the memory of the pyres that had blazed near their marauded camp, flames that granted her murdered friends and loved ones their only leave.

She turned to order a halt so they could scout the danger, when Bliss yelled and pointed to the suddenly accelerating advance of the black horizon. Close enough that Jessie startled at the towering wall of clouds scouring the earth and spitting it to the ethers. In the same instant, she grabbed the grating against a powerful gust that whipped past the vehicles, darkening the air.

She ordered the truck to halt, and saw the van stopping too. Jaya sprang from the front passenger door.

How much time do we have? she asked herself. *A minute?*

"Get under the tanker and cover up," she shouted to the children clinging to the vehicle. They looked frozen with fear. "Go. Hurry! *Move!*" she bellowed, stepping down onto a metal ladder.

The temperature jumped twenty degrees in ten seconds, a heat wave that gave lie to the original, pallid meaning when her long dead relatives could open fire hydrants or lounge in pools to cool off. These were like siroccos, come to life in the last half century and fueled by higher temperatures than the Sahara of old had ever known. The hot winds funneled across the hugely expanded Great American Desert, raising inestimable tons of dust; and when they swept over isolated bands of humans, they could choke a child to death and leave her parents gasping.

Computer models of the collapse had never predicted such explosive heat, or comprehended chaos theory well enough to explain the mysterious physics of temperature spikes—much less anticipate the vast waves of hot wind that would charge wantonly across the planet, turning it into a laboratory for meteorological uproar. Jessie had only heard of such torrid winds, and had no idea how long they could last or how many lives they could claim.

Grit tore at her skin as she climbed off the truck and children cried out around her. She peered through the slits of her eyes and saw the black clouds surge over them like the monstrous surf of an oceanwide tsunami foaming over the length and breadth of the foothills.

Struggling to duck under the trailer, she watched the wind rip away a blanket of dust, revealing deep, caterpillar tracks. A *tank*? She dropped to her knees, like she'd taken a blow to the gut, disbelief in her eyes, dread at her fingertips. An armored tank in this world could crown its owner king. But that's what it was—a trail of armored murder. No one bothered with bulldozers or other earthmovers with metal treads, not with gas so precious, and slaves to dig and haul away rocks and dirt. Only tanks, with their turrets and flame-throwers, got to guzzle fuel. In the dark realm of weapons, they had become the one-eyed man in the land of the blind.

She looked up, terrified that she'd see the beastly creation barreling through the blackened air, crushing everything in its path; but she couldn't even make out the child beside her, and knew that she would have to try to save the girls from the immediate threat of the storm.

She joined their huddle under the truck and demanded a roll call, relieved when everyone—including Ananda and moon-faced Imagi—offered their names, barks muffled by the clothes they breathed through and the siren of wind lashing the trailer's struts and ladders.

Then Jessie remembered Bliss and called for her, too. The girl didn't answer.

"Bliss?" she wailed.

Another gust blasted the tanker truck, and the girls in the tight circle gripped one another and drew closer, each one instinctively trying to burrow her way to the center, where she would be less likely to find herself ripped loose by the wind.

To Jessie's horror, the truck screeched, like metal shearing. She reached up and felt a wild shudder, sickening with fear that it had been smashed by the armored tank, whose tracks lay so near, and that gas would spill down and an inferno would engulf them. But her hand couldn't remain on the metal long: the child she'd been holding blindly to her left screamed above the howling and started to slide away. Jessie pulled her back with enormous effort.

The metallic screeching ceased a beat before another gust slammed them, and the group shifted en masse toward the rear of the trailer. The wind was agonizing, like a wall of tornados drilling them with dirt, dust, and pebbles hard as buckshot. But it brought no gas, no fumes, and they pressed ever closer together, their every breath suffused by the now sulfurous smell of the dead.

Jessie's hold on the girl who'd almost been swept away made her hand ache and the child cry, but she never relented as shrieking wind slammed the group backward again and again, eternal seconds of biting terror. She feared the pummeling would drive them out from under the trailer's narrow cover and tumble them like weeds through the charred forest.

Instead, her back struck one of the big rear tires. Arms throbbing, she held three or four girls—she couldn't tell exactly—and felt others forced against the hard axle. She pitied them, heard their agony, but as much as she could tell, the hellacious wind had not yet torn apart the group.

But where's Bliss?

Jessie moaned when she remembered Jaya jumping out of the van, sensing right away that back at the obsidian wall the two of them had planned a rendezvous in what they hoped would be rain.

To dance in it?

She rolled her head in despair. *They* know *better.* Every child in the camp had been warned about heat storms. And this one had uncovered the tank's tracks, and brought the stench of burning bodies.

She could smell the dead, taste the bitter waste, and then

her ears filled with the harsh clanging of metal tread and the deep rumble of an engine powerful enough to move the armored tank's massive weight and howl louder than the screaming wind. The earth itself began to shake beneath her, and she knew the machine that had laid those tracks was only feet away, rolling closer with every second.

Chapter Two

Every living element—and every slab of steel that surrounded Jessie—vibrated violently. The air itself rang with bedlam. Another screech rose from the gasoline tanker, right above her head; and she thought surely this time the armored tank would rip the trailer in two and that she and the girls would be smashed or burned to death in the next instant.

She jammed her back against the big tire, as if a sudden stiffening of muscle and bone could thwart 100,000 pounds of cannon and guns, flamethrowers and grisly murder.

But the metallic screech stopped, fast as a wince in the overriding darkness. The earth and tanker truck still shook, but not as severely, and in seconds that played against an infinity of fear, the harrowing engine noise of the armored tank was swallowed by the wind and soot still lashing the trailer's struts and ladders.

She stayed bunched-up with the girls between the rear wheels, ears ever alert for the tank.

In a daze of dread and fatigue she noticed three lulls in the storm, gazing at a night sky brilliant with a band of chalk-white stars burning with grace notes of unseen mercy. But three times the wind wiped the heavens from her eyes, leaving her with a renewed fear of the tank: Where was it? What were they doing? *Waiting for daylight so they can murder us without blowing up the gas?*

At dawn the storm lifted and the sky blazed blue as the oceans at the dawn of the century, when the most tranquil turquoise waters masked the bleached rot of coral reefs.

She uncurled herself from the girls' sleepy limbs and found a strip of freshly chewed-up earth alongside the gasoline tanker. Above the tracks she saw two deep horizontal scrapes, one near the front and one that passed right above where she'd huddled. The latter extended to the end of the tanker and explained the abrupt silencing of the screech. She figured the cannon had gouged the side, swung away from it, then gouged it again as the crew tried to outrun the storm. Rolling through blackness, it would have been easy enough for them to think they'd struck a rock wall—if they even noticed the impact in the blinding, deafening chaos.

The scrapes also indicated the direction taken by the armored tank. Her eyes quickly trailed the tread pattern down the same slope the caravan had traveled yesterday. The tracks ran near or over the ones she had spotted as the storm descended. The memory turned her toward a thin gray curtain of smoke still hanging over where Augustus said his camp stood.

But where was the tank now? Over a ridge? Hiding behind a hill? It would have been forced to stop, too. She couldn't imagine that it had kept blundering blindly through a land pitted with deep gaps and steep drop-offs.

She looked around again. Not a soul. Only a preternaturally bright and silent dawn after a terrifying night. The wind that forced them to find immediate shelter had flattened even the hill's brittle, charred forest. Boulders had ceded to gusts and rolled into gullies or were piled against larger rocks, forming huddles likely to last eons. Yet all around her she saw a desert forming rapidly, a thousand years of parching compressed to hours by grinding heat and wind.

In a coruscating flash, the blue sky blanched, as if incinerated. She rubbed her eyes to see if her vision had failed, but the atmosphere—*poof*—had simply returned to its most pallid appearance. Then she worried that the tank cannon had come alive; but no, it wasn't that, either.

Bewildered by what she'd witnessed, and uneasy over what it might mean, she checked on the sleeping children before rushing to peer inside the cab. Maul and Erik were still resting in their tight, protected hub.

No sign of Bliss.

She searched all around the truck, then hurried to the van, about a hundred feet away. Augustus was crawling out from under the engine, dark skin paled by dust.

"We've got to get moving," he said, glancing behind him, to the sides, everywhere at once. "Something's still burning." He raised his eyes to the pale smoke about five miles away. "My wife, my girls. Dear God, let me find them. *Alive*."

Jessie put her hand on his broad shoulder. "Didn't you hear the tank last night? It came right through—"

"Tank? No, I never heard that. The storm was so loud I could hardly hear myself think. Was it coming from there?" He pointed to the gray smoke.

"I'm not sure," she hedged. "We won't know till—"

"Oh, God." He dropped to his knees and hung his head; in prayer, she guessed.

"We'll go there," she said. "I promise. But I've got to find Bliss."

He looked up. "Your girl's missing? In this?" His eyes widened, but looked emptier for the effort, like he'd seen a holocaust—or imagined one coming.

A nod was all Jessie managed before she turned and threw open the van's driver door, shaking Brindle. "Where's Jaya?"

The scrawny, bearded stammerer opened his eyes on the empty seat beside him. Then he swung around, as if puzzled by the blind girls and babies crowded among the crates of dried fruit, produce, and smoked meats.

"He's not back there," Jessie said.

"Goddamn h-h-him. H-H-H-He jumped out b-b-b-before I—I could st-st-stop h-him."

"Bliss is gone, too."

She gazed at the hills, noticing that dust had collected in scores of uniform lumps against a sharp slope; but her eyes dropped at once to the tank tracks. Burned Fingers ran up, pointing to them.

"That was close. Very close," he said.

"You see the side of the tanker?" she asked him.

He looked over and swore in surprise.

"It couldn't have been more than three feet from me and the kids."

"I thought I heard one but I wasn't sure till I saw the tracks."

"They could have taken Bliss and Jaya," she said. "They're gone."

He nodded. "But I doubt the tank took them. That crew couldn't see any better than us. The electronics in those things are shot to hell. They don't have any night vision, but they do have firepower that could blow us all to hell." He spoke from experience: his hand had been burned decades ago after commandeering an M4 Sherman. "No, those kids are out there. That's my thinking."

"You been out looking?"

"Yup, and they could have been sucked up to the sky for the tracks I could find, except for those things." He snorted at the tread marks. "You can bet that tank's looking all over for us, blasting their flamethrowers every chance they get. You smell those bodies?" He glanced at the smoke above Augustus's camp. The black missionary kept his eyes averted.

"You sure that's what it is?" Jessie asked. The scent, like the smoke, had thinned; and she couldn't stop herself from hoping.

"Are you kidding? You never forget it." Burned Fingers held up his scarred hand.

She forced herself to rally: "We're going to search for Bliss, Jaya. They would have tried to escape the storm some-how." She looked at Augustus. "You know this area, right?"

"Sure, but if my people are still there," he raised his eyes to the pall, "they'll know who's around."

"That's a big 'if,'" Burned Fingers said.

"We're not leaving here without my daughter," Jessie asserted.

"It might be revenge," Augustus said, as if he'd never heard her; his eyes were emptier than ever. "They saw me with you." He meant at the battle to rescue the girls. "They couldn't miss me, and they're looking everywhere for us. My camp would have been a target. If they took that thing—" He stopped talking when his eyes landed on the tank tracks. Sorrow never sounded deeper.

"Sorry, Augustus," Burned Fingers said, "but my guess is that they did their burning and were heading back when they passed this way. It's the most obvious route, right? But if I were doing this . . ."

Meaning, *when* you were doing this, Jessie thought, roiled by the abrupt reminder of the man he had been.

". . . I would have left the sickest fuck I had behind, in case whatever I was looking for showed up. There are only so many places you can drive with a truck full of gas, and they know that. And I'd tell that sick fuck to get word to me right away. So the longer we stand around here, the worse it could get." Burned Fingers leveled his eyes on Jessie. "I'd also be picking off stragglers. You can use them in all kinds of ways. Our best option is to move on, the sooner the better."

"No way. We're searching."

"Every minute we stay gives them more time."

"We don't even know if there's a 'sick fuck' out there. We might have some time."

"You smelled it. No sick fuck? Are you kidding? I wouldn't go betting any farm in the Arctic on that." Burned Finger's voice rose, and a baby in the van began to wail. "The Alliance is doing everything they can to get that tanker back. Look at that." He pointed his sawed-off at the tracks. "They sent a *tank* after us. Me, you, him?" He glanced at Augustus. "They *might* give up on us, but not a truck full of gas. They might not see the likes of that for another year. Two. I knew we never should have stopped once we had that thing."

"And what? Leave my friends behind? The ones who survived your attack, so maybe they could be slaughtered by other madmen?" Some grief you couldn't put aside, but Burned Fingers never even blinked.

"Everyone will get slaughtered if we don't move. What are we going to do? Spend days looking while they're looking for us? We've got to get out of here."

"I'm not talking days."

"Would someone shut that kid up," Burned Fingers shouted into the van. He looked back at Jessie. "You want an hour to find those two horn dogs? Fine, take an hour. I'll even go with you, but I won't be party to any more than that. We leave everyone else to fight off the hordes. We're risking everybody for those two."

The baby's cries grew louder.

Jessie said nothing. She'd take the hour and go from there—alone if she had to.

Burned Fingers turned away and yelled, "Oh shit," before slamming the door on Brindle and pulling Jessie to the ground next to the van. Augustus dropped beside them.

A single gust swept the scalded hillsides and barreled into the caravan, shaking the armor by Jessie's head. She, Burned Fingers, and Augustus grabbed the plating to keep from being swept away. Then she looked over and saw the girls still clinging to one another under the trailer.

Sky quake. She had seen one years ago. A storm's after-shocks, land and sky sharing the same affliction: the two poisoned as one by heat.

The gust passed, and they looked up to see the atmosphere turn purely orange. Not tinged with mauve or purple or red—the orange of soot-stained skies in evening verse. *Orange.* Like the citrus supposedly growing in the far north. Jessie had never seen the sky color so quickly or completely. Pale? Yes, but not this. Then the orange vanished as fast as a wraith, and the sky lightened again, casting a thin screen over a fuzzy urinous sun.

"What was *that*?" Jessie asked.

"You're the scientist," Burned Fingers said. "You tell me. It's been a crazy morning up there." He stood and startled her by extending his scarred hand. She took it.

"I'm a biologist, not a climatologist, but it could be methane." Jessie brushed herself off. "There was always a big worry that if enough of it came up out of the oceans, it would start drifting over land. Doesn't matter, we've got to get going."

"Doesn't matter as long as it doesn't blow *us* up," Burned Fingers said. "That or the tanker."

He threw open the door on Brindle finger-combing his long beard. "How fastidious. I hate to interrupt your grooming, but did pretty boy happen to say where he was going? Or were you too busy primping to ask?"

"Ass-h-h-hole." Jessie wasn't sure whom Brindle insulted: the marauder with the sawed-off or Jaya, who'd been riding shotgun. "H-H-He j-just j-jumped out and r-ran off."

Burned Fingers whistled to the dogs. Hansel hopped over on his three legs. The marauder elbowed Jessie. "Tell me, can Stumpy the Wonder Dog actually track?"

She nodded, but looking at Hansel's eager face gave her little hope. "I don't have a scrap of her clothes to get him started. Everything she owns is on her back."

"Yeah, well Jaya's ass was on that seat." Burned Fingers pointed past Brindle. "Let's give him a good sniff. It's a dog's life anyway."

In the first sweep of the storm, Soul Hunter watched the boy and girl stumble toward a ravine that had once been part of a bird sanctuary. The wind had forced them far from their vehicles, and pressed their clothes against their privates, offering hints that would fever his imagination—and torment his soul—through the night.

The pair ducked into the rugged, rocky depression, passing within feet of where he hid. Though the air darkened and the gusts screamed, Hunt, as his brothers in the Alliance called him, didn't let his eyes stray; and he saw the wind whip her shirt up around her neck before the boy's hands could stake their own claim on her godless skin.

But the two of them hid their other filthy secrets behind the scrim of darkened air. Hunt glimpsed only their desperate lunge into a U-shaped boulder pile on the far side of the ravine. He would have liked it for himself, but couldn't risk confronting them in blinding conditions. So he'd hunched down, back against the leeward side of a broad rock, and endured the onslaught of grit and bits of burned branches till he sat buried to his waist.

In the darkest hours, he heard moans that might have been the wind; but as the night passed he grew certain that he was listening to their obscene, open-mouthed orgy—gasps and outcries that filled him with the same animalistic urges that had brought his Lord's merciful vengeance upon the stained peoples of the earth.

As first light grayed the sky, he prayed to God Almighty to deliver him from the burden of temptation. And he took solace in knowing that only he and God had witnessed her bold display, and that nothing—*nothing*—happened that wasn't part of His plan. The Lord Thy God had granted *him,* Hunt, a full second of her naked heathen chest. Not the boy's naked parts—hers. *For a reason. A reason.* God the Father wanted him to desire the woman in the girl's budding body. To draw his eyes to her. His attention—to her. His *needs*—to her.

She *was* a beauty. Hunt had seen that, been moved by it, too; but he was always wary of the evil that could afflict him in an unguarded moment, when his thoughts turned to nakedness and tantalized him with the lone temptation that above all others must be resisted—the apple of Eden that hung low and hard and heavy on a strong young tree with smooth firm limbs.

A beauty, a beauty, a beauty, he repeated to himself, as if these fraught words were the blunt instrument of prayer itself.

But even insistence of the most desperate kind couldn't hold off his most disturbing voice, the one that hailed from Satan. It appeared like a boa and swallowed her beauty whole: *But so is the boy. So . . . is . . . the . . . boy.*

Hunt's mouth narrowed with thirst. He drank water, as if to wash away his incipient sins. Then he offered God His most hallowed prayer—*Forgive us our trespasses as we forgive those who trespass against us*—to no greater effect.

Rueful and unnerved, he unwrapped a Colt .45, a venerable revolver at least a hundred years old. An heirloom long worshipped with gun oil and bore brushes, and prized above all other bequests by ancestors wise to the wickedness of the world. He was delivered of their loins and heavenly beliefs, and gave thanks every day that he hadn't been born to Pagans, Jews, Catholics, Muslims, or any other smutty faith that visited the stains of the father upon the sons—and warred with good men born again of God-given grace.

Generations had handed down the Colt to Hunt, yet it still gleamed in the strange stirrings of the coming day and the last leavings of starlight, catching glimmers of both on a blue steel barrel. Hunt had fired it fourteen times, always at close range, harvesting the sweet fruit of death. The Lord had commanded him so, and he was a vassal of the Almighty, never more than on the day when he'd tracked down the stolen wares of the Alliance, and he would savage two more of the unforgiven. The tank with its big gun had searched for the gas and failed—and was reduced to simple retribution against the compound cursed by Cain—while he, Hunt, with only a motorcycle and the revered Colt, had succeeded. The "Supreme Soul Catcher," His Piety once called him. And so he was.

He stepped from behind the broad rock, gaining ground silently in the dust that had blown into the ravine. But he didn't head toward the sinners. He retreated about seventy feet to an old wagon road that wound down the gap's widest wall. Grotesque doings back there, the worst that he had ever seen; but he had to attend to the evil—or whatever scourge it might be—as much as he had to unmuzzle his hound for the strict commands of the day.

A beauty. A beauty. A beauty.

So . . . is . . . the—

Hunt refused to reckon with the boy, but the more he fought the arresting allure—hairless face and hidden genitalia—the more he imagined the worst that can befall a man of True Belief.

Breathless even more, he turned and stared at them one more time. Still sleeping. Easy to take unawares. But she'd carried a shotgun—the boy nothing but his raggedy shirt and chopped-off pants, which made Hunt weak to consider. Half his age and burning with sin, a child of heathendom, a child of hate.

Hunt thought of the long line of imperatives stretching from heaven to him. And then he imagined all manner of unraveling. He warned himself that a struggle over their flesh would mean another struggle over his soul, for he had often gleaned what he would do, and begged forgiveness from God—before plunging ahead with foul demands on His most fallen. Alone, then, in the vastness of his pure grieving conscience, he'd punished his seducers with knives and hungry vermin. And as they lay as waste, bound and gnawed and suffering still, how many times had he—of his own accord, no other—dropped to the broiling earth and crawled till his knees bled and his hands boiled with blisters, purging his guilt and giving thanks to the one merciful Lord?

Only to be tested today.

No. He would spare nothing of himself for these two. He had to take them back to the old military base, to the stone chapel where the iniquitous were baptized with the blood of their confessions, and dangled as ransom when they could utter no more answers.

When the tanker and van were retaken, the last of the unholy herd carefully slain, he would walk the boy and girl to the most sacred killing field. There he would claim his final earthly reward for keeping watch on the path to Cain's children, where fire had burned the accursed—and now drew the murderous plunderers to their pending destruction. Richer rewards still would await him in heaven.

So he swore off the girl's bare chest and the boy's punishing appeal. He would not force them to commit the obscenities that had spared him Wicca disease—and ravaged so many of the sodomites who'd ended their lives in his hands. The righteous had named the virus after the demon females—witches all—who had set the sickness loose on a world full of unsuspecting men. These were good fathers and brothers of faith, though females were the first to fall, as God in His infinite wisdom had so justly decreed. The Lord had granted immunity to only a tiny percentage of men. Most of the others, even believers rich with prayer and constant pleading, were cursed with the plague and seethed with vicious hallucinations—grotesque visions that triggered murderous and suicidal impulses before the stricken killed others, themselves, or perished in the agonizing grip of the disease.

The only way to have sex and appease God Almighty was to wed girls right after menarche. For their first twelve periods, they knew their own immunity—and the only purity of their otherwise damnable lives. Or—and now Hunt breathed audibly and gave himself pause—he could pierce his own soul by having sex with boys, yes, *boys,* who had not known the deadly pulse of penetration, who had kept themselves clean for the likes of him.

No, you won't. Promise me you won't.

Resolve precious and slippery as semen, he hurried the last few steps to the wagon trail and untied a tarp that covered the old Harley 74 and a side car, and a rattly trailer with five gallon gas cans lining the outside like an ammo belt. Rising behind the battered red cans on one side was a faded picture of a fly fisherman defaced by black graffiti.

The trailer's roof had been cut off with a blowtorch, the top of each side sculpted into pikes. The rear was open, the bed almost filled with matching, century-old aluminum and Plexiglas telephone booths laid next to each other.

Hunt had just enough room to edge between the booths. Even with the tarp, thick dust had coated the glass. He swept it away with his hand, feeling contaminated by the nearness of his touch to the twins. They were conscious, but he wasn't sure whether one could be awake and the other asleep.

He reviled the very sight of them. Not just the devil's black skin or the burns on their body. No, he reviled far worse than skin color or scars or identical dark eyes. He reviled a fact so fearsomely present at first glance that he'd known in the same repulsive instant they had to be resurrected from their near death—and the imminence of hell ever after—so he could take them to the base and parade them before His Piety.

Parade what? He studied them. *The Devil's own seed?*

So many mysteries with these two, beginning with their number.

Bliss awoke with an arm wrapped around Jaya, the other resting as peaceably on her shotgun. The storm had forced them to seek cover in a ravine or canyon, visibility horrid by the time they stumbled down there.

A thick layer of dust coated their bodies, but she figured it had kept them safely hidden. Even so, she listened intently before lifting her head and brushing off her face. Carefully opening her eyes, she spied the day's first light, faint and swift, stealing across the sky.

A dun layer draped the boulders that rose around them on three sides, softening their appearance. She realized with a start that they were lucky to have found a trail and not stepped off the edge.

She lifted her shotgun knowing that she didn't dare work the action till she'd blown away every last particle of dust. *I'll huff and I'll puff,* she smiled, *and I'll blow your house in.*

Thinking of candles, she counted fingers on her hand and realized it was her birthday. *Fifteen! You made it.* How many times in just the past few weeks had she thought she'd be killed? And here she was—more alive than ever—with a boyfriend.

She eyed Jaya resting under the powdery blanket, prizing him as the most joyous gift of her life. The hard length of him still felt hot in her hand, and his presence lingered from the long glorious minutes when her mouth, full and heavy and rich with want, made her so crazy that she'd almost ripped off their clothes in the dust and dirt and sweat and stones. But Wicca had stopped her as surely as it had shut down procreative sex among the tiny percentage of the world's population that had been spared the pandemic.

Only after she and Jaya had settled last night, satisfied by touch and taste, had she begun to feel watched. So eerie a sensation that she'd stared into the blackness and scolded herself. *No one can see you. You can't see two feet in this.*

But the grim feeling returned now. She looked at a rock wall rising right behind them, and knew that anyone could spot them from above. She wasn't thinking of her mom, but Jessie came to mind immediately.

You've got to get back. She'll go nuts if she finds out you're gone.

Gone where? The question scared Bliss. How long had they stumbled around, oblivious and aroused, seeking a refuge for touch—and her first intimations of love—in a land of blood and fire?

Bliss looked up again, searching for a familiar marker, and saw orange blaze everywhere at once. She sat silent and astonished, an ancient eyeing an eclipse, a child of storms and stony seas.

The forbidding sky had come alive with ghosts and spirits and strange colors. Evil doings all. His Piety would know their foul portent, but Hunt rose from the dust, spitting its filthy taste from his lips, already certain that Satan's fiery breath had gripped the air he breathed, like the dark one's madness gripped the soul and twisted it into a raging fist of sin.

Eyes retreating from the sky, he returned to the twins, fearful and clinging to each other, and looked at the dog locked in the booth beside them. The beast's eyes lit up, so ready to do his duty that there could have been two of *him*.

The metal muzzle would have to remain on the creature till his bark posed no threat. A "hound of Hades," His Piety had described the dog. "We have dominion over the beasts, and we rule their animal ways."

It was true, it was in the Bible, like God Himself, and he knew it was a fool's damnation to think otherwise. To deviate from scripture was to be a *de-vi-ant*. To suffer as one. *Look at the world. Look at it.* There could be no disagreement. True Belief protected him from himself, made him turn from temptation. *Yes, you will. Do not doubt it.*

The boy and others no less despicable were the reason for the "Sealing of Sight." The tainted ones looked right at you, so boldly, so *coldly,* it was like they could read your secret thoughts, making the plucking of eyes essential for the saving of souls.

No less had been claimed for the "Deformation of Faces," a sacrament conducted on the Risen Day of Easter for all the women who flaunted their beauty by enticing worthy, reverent men from the greater glory of God.

Hunt had long believed it unfair to disfigure only females; surely, from what he'd known, the faces of the boy and his conniving lot deserved far worse for the abominations they caused among God-fearing men. But he'd never spoken of extending the sacrament. Not a word to anyone. Only to God Almighty in the fever clasp of his most private prayers.

He unlocked the booth and gripped Damocles by the muzzle, shaking the hound's long pointy snout, then slipping his finger through the cage to check his teeth, white as right. "Getting excited, boy? Huh? You got a mission, too."

The sleek leggy beast stood and bristled with pleasure, muscles rippling down his long dark back and flanks. "I'll take this off," he said, and gave the muzzle another hard tug, "when we've got them good and ready."

What else are you going to take off?

Shaking off Satan in the day's first sun, he chained the dog to the trailer. From a corner pike he took down a ball of rusty barbed wire and cut a length long enough to bind the boy's hands. He repeated the effort three times, for feet and hands must be bound on both of them, as they were on the twins.

He checked the lengths again, and considered cutting them to give the boy and girl crowns. The twins had worn theirs well, pretend crowns for their pretend Jesus. That's whom they'd been praying to when he'd found them in the smolder. True spawn of the Devil, they'd been hard to burn.

"You have no claim on the Son of God," he'd bellowed as he'd wrapped wire around the twins' heads, a coronation that did not end until their brows bore the same red streaks as the One True Son. "So you must pray for forgiveness."

Damocles pulled hard on his chain. The dog wanted to do his duty. His master stared at the telephone booth that had kenneled him, and now waited to be filled.

Like you, the most disturbing demonic voice taunted. *Just like you. Filled with the red heat of your animal dreams.*

Hunt cocked the Colt's hammer.

Chapter Three

Hansel pointed his nose skyward and sniffed hungrily at the broiling air. Jessie snapped her fingers, signaling the brindle back down to the dust. He was a mastiff-bloodhound mix, with the latter's keen sense of smell, though she doubted any creature could snag Bliss or Jaya's scent from air scoured by the brutal gusts that had buffeted the region. Even the nauseating odor of burning bodies had grown faint.

She and Burned Fingers were guiding the gimpy dog down a slope where the storm had heaved aside countless tons of dust as if they were no more weighty than weed pollen. She couldn't fathom how the teens could have moved into the hellish wind. Augustus knew the area, and he agreed; but human reasoning wasn't helping Hansel, whose frustrated snout seesawed right back up, signaling a message of his own—that he hadn't picked up the scent.

Sudden gaps in the earth also slowed their search, forcing them to climb or crawl around sheared-off sections of blistered roadway that rose like crumbly cliffs or sank like the proverbial stone. Heat had burned-up so much water—entire rivers, lakes, and inland seas had evaporated, only to dump back down in ruinous, raging storms—that the planet's friable crust was rising and falling "like some fat lady on a fucking trampoline," in Burned Fingers's prickly account.

But even the three-legged Hansel appeared fleet-footed compared to yesterday's pace when they'd maneuvered the gasoline tanker, with its 50,000 pound payload, around these geological disturbances. The truck had inched up the ridge like a marooned mollusk, giving Jessie ample time to note all the shadowy recesses where they could be ambushed. No less aware of her surroundings now as they worked their way back down the ravaged road. The same crushing concern for security had them assign Maul, the big bald truck driver, to organize all the adults and children into a defense of the caravan.

Defense against what exactly?

Against anything. Jessie answered herself with the worst sense of certainty—the kind born of known threats, like the tank and unforeseen enemies, human *and* animal.

Maul had broken out the RPG immediately, and he enlisted the children's help in making gas bombs. In the right hands, the RPG could be effective against a tank; but Jessie remained openly dubious about the homemade bombs.

"You better believe they'll work," Burned Fingers snapped, stepping around a gaping hole. "The Germans used to call our tanks 'Ronsons' because they burned up so fast."

" 'Ronsons'? What are you talking—"

"Old cigarette lighter. 'Lights the first time every time.' Remember?"

"No. And I doubt we're looking at some vintage World War Two tank."

Burned Fingers snorted, swore. "You wouldn't believe what I've seen rolling around. I almost got flash-fried in one of them."

"I've heard."

Hansel still hadn't picked up a trail. The only tracks that hadn't been scrubbed away by the storm were the deep, knifelike cuts of the tank tread, which they'd veered from minutes ago. Even so, with every step Jessie worried that it would roar over a hilltop and storm toward them, flame-thrower blazing.

She found little relief in turning her thoughts back to Bliss, imagining her daughter and Jaya lying broken-boned—or worse—at the bottom of a "road failure." That was a term, she realized with a wince, much too quaint for the grotesque conditions.

When she and Burned Fingers did step through patches of dust, it felt light as spider silk on their feet—but carried useless scents from miles off.

Burned Fingers jabbed his sawed-off at Hansel. "Looks like Stumpy the Wonder Dog can't buy a break."

She rubbed his ruff. "I doubt he's hearing much, either." Though given the rapacious creatures that had survived the collapse, she didn't find the silence entirely unwelcome. But she did wonder aloud whether firing off a round was advisable. "Bliss might hear it and at least know—"

"No, *don't* do that," he said, glancing everywhere at once. "The critters will think it's a dinner bell and we're the buffet."

His warning had her looking around, too—and switching the M–16 to full auto with the first thought of panther packs and Pixie-bobs.

To spare herself another surge of anxiety, she seized on how hard it would be for any animal to hide after the winds had flattened the charred forest in a swath so wide that she could see no end to the destruction. Extreme weather? Her ancestors hadn't a clue.

On the broad hills bookending the ridge, only nine tree trunks had been stout enough to survive the windstorm. To Jessie, the limb-stripped basswoods, buckeyes, and maples looked like lonely black sentinels, aggrieved and tormented by the devastation surrounding them. She missed autumn so suddenly she ached. That she'd once driven rural highways splashed with color was nothing less than astonishing to her. That her girls would never see such simple wonder—the beauty of an astonishingly vibrant world—made her eyes pool with helplessness.

With a blink and a wipe she turned from the niggardly stand and saw that they'd dropped about a hundred feet of elevation. At this remove, the rear of the tanker truck could have been a tarnished oval hovering in space.

Burned Fingers put out his hand to stop her and pointed to another oval—a large shadowing on the land at two o'clock on the directional dial. "See the sun? That shadow makes no sense unless it's a depression of some kind. And you know what else? That would be a good place to duck into."

"Then why aren't they on their way back?"

"Cause they might have fallen into that thing. It's got to be deep, or we'd be able to see the bottom of it. Maybe it was a lake, or maybe the earth just yawned and opened up. No telling. But I'll tell you one thing, we're not coming at it head-on. Anything could be waiting down there. You see those hills?" He pointed to his left. "We'll take the valley running through there. We can climb out when we get close and get a good look down. See what's stirring."

"**W**ake up, dear heart," Bliss whispered to Jaya. Only then did she remember her dad waking her mom with the same endearment on the day of the massacre. She tried not to think about her dead father because the memory that haunted her most—and made her feel murderous every day—was of her dad chained like a wounded animal to the front of Burned Fingers's truck.

She took a breath, hoping to wipe away the ravening image, and rubbed Jaya's smooth tummy, feeling a trail of down that lured pleasing sensations back to life. Briskly, she withdrew her hand and grabbed her shotgun. "We've got to get moving."

"What's going on?" He sat up quickly, brushing dust from his face and hair.

She shushed him and whispered, "It's morning. We've got to get back. They're going to be really worried."

They stood, Bliss with her hand on his shoulder to keep

his sleepy head below the rocks that had provided them sparse shelter. She saw the ravine walls clearly now. Higher than she'd thought. The area was larger, too, about a quarter mile wide and a good half mile long, with boulders big enough to hide man or beast. And so quiet that she worried that even her whispered words had been overheard.

She put her finger to Jaya's lips. He nodded, and silence encircled them, sudden and chilling as a shriek. Then she pointed her shotgun to the top of the barrier, all but saying, *We're going out there*.

Jaya nodded again, this time fully awake.

Hunt crept soundlessly in the dust outside the U-shaped rise that hid the boy and girl—and all the deviltry they'd committed before God and man. *God and man*. So holy, so true. In those few biblically blessed words he knew that there could never be any question of his importance to the Almighty. If God knew the movement of every ant—*And he does,* never *doubt it*—then what of a lone man who served Him with such devotion?

Smite me, Lord, if I am wrong.

He and the Almighty shared the kinship of divine retribution, for he was a sharply tuned instrument of the Lord, a silvery flute in the land of the fallen. A deadly weapon in the hand of a God-given man.

Now and always, bless me, Lord, in Thy name.

Hellfire and hallelujahs rang in his ears, lit up his eyes, blue as unscarred sky. He coiled like a serpent and waited for the harlot who'd bared her chest—and for the boy who'd made him burn. In seconds too precious for temporal time alone, they would expose all their weaknesses of the flesh to him. Of the *flesh*. He relished the mysterious rising sap of that word, of a world so forbidden that he felt like Adam in the Garden, Satan casting spells with the beaming apple of sex. Hunt felt it warm and hard and—beneath its wild scarlet skin—teeming with the sweetest juice a man could ever taste.

After all the brazen sins of the boy and girl, committed in the presence of God the Father—and in the unslakable sight of his own mind's eye—their surrender felt as ordained as finding the twins in the cindery ash. He would take the violators into the Lord's custody, and the hound would do his swift duty. Then he would bear the heathens to the base, adding legend to his name.

Trophies of a sacred war. Tributes to the One True Son.

God and man, beating on his breath like the wings of heaven's dove.

The blood of ages to bleed the blood of man.

Jessie and Burned Fingers avoided a damaged road that ran through the valley, walking down a riverbed of smooth round stones instead. Dust softened their steps; but their sandals, cobbled together from old treadless tires and lizard skin leather, left clear tracks.

She welcomed the shade of the hill. The valley was narrow enough to shelter them from the stark morning light, sunrise and sunset the only earthly constants that hadn't been mangled by the reckless generations that had left them this ragged world.

Goddamn them.

Nothing but scorn for the louts who ruled her country at the turn of the century. Those feckless politicians and their big money backers—and the supine media that exalted them all—could have saved billions of lives and millions of species; but in those first fifteen, twenty years, when simple steps could have averted this tragedy, they did worse than nothing—they created an illusion of safety and comfort while the world spun inexorably toward collapse.

Goddamn them.

The signs had been everywhere—oceans dying, Arctic melting, killer heat waves, massive crop failures, freakishly strong storms, the list went on and on—but her grandparents and most everyone else pranced about so childishly, so narcissistically, that they'd made Nero seem like an alarmist.

Goddamn them.

She could scarcely imagine the courage, the unerring instincts of those who did try to stop the genocidal consump-
tion, who bombed and struggled for years to try to shut the
maw of that beast—and were hunted and tortured and executed for their fearlessness.

Kids, mostly. Nineteen-, twenty-year-olds. Some even
younger. A few older. Veterans, too. The first leaders of
the rebel forces. They'd fought back, and Christ, they were
killed with a ferociousness that exposed both the cruelty and
underlying fear of those in power.

She wished the wastrels who'd persecuted them—who
were so busy pointing their fingers and guns at others—had
done the planet a favor and aimed at themselves instead.

"Ready to start up there?"

She had to ask Burned Fingers to repeat himself; but she
didn't hear him a second time, because her eyes were drawn
to dust-laden lumps on the slope to their left, like the ones
she'd seen on another hillside less than an hour ago. And
then she realized with a start that the protrusions were too
precisely uniform for any boulder field that she'd ever seen.

"Does that look right to you? It looks too perfect."

"Not *them*," Burned Fingers said as the first Pixie-bob
rose to its feet, kittenishly pawing silt from its face before
turning its eerie yellow eyes on them.

In seconds the entire slope shifted.

Bliss failed to account for the sun's blinding strength, nar-
rowing her eyes as she eased from the shadow of the boulder
wall.

The instant she shaded them, a gun barrel pressed into the
base of her skull. Another hand jerked away her shotgun,
then clutched her throat with fingers so dry and callused
they could have been covered in scales.

Choking violently, she glimpsed Jaya looking around
wildly. He had no means of retreat, no firearm.

"You become a bully boy," the man said to Jaya in a voice quieter than his threats might have allowed, "and I'll kill her. Then it'll just be me and you." He lowered his eyes to the boy's chopped-off pants. "Then I'll kill you, too. I'll have to," he added cryptically. "Be a good boy," his tone softened, scaring Bliss even more, "and I'll let you live."

He marched them about fifty feet to a motorcycle and trailer and pushed them away. She felt shade and looked back at him still in the sharp light, squinting hard. The lines around his cavernous blue eyes were deep, and drew his cheeks and nose up, as if the whole of him were fighting the harsh rays. But long ago he'd lost whatever battle he might have fought with the sun: his blond hair was bleached almost white, and his skin was dark and leathery. His voice sounded worn as well.

"Get on the ground, on your bellies. You have no cause for the heavens." But that wasn't the only reason he wanted them facedown.

He kicked apart their legs and ordered their arms outstretched till they looked like they were trying to hold back the earth from committing another grievous crime. Keeping his gun on them, he edged over to the motorcycle and placed her shotgun in the side car. He looked pleased by his coup and prospects. Always alert, he led the chained hound to his prisoners and fed out the links slowly, building the beast's desire.

"You going to have fun now, boy? You gonna have fun?"

"Don't do this," the girl said. Shaky voice.

The dog issued a deep growl, not loud but marked by an urge for savagery.

"You hear my hound? He knows your words."

The dog clawed the earth and jammed the metal muzzle against her smooth skin, like he was trying to bite through the brittle looking cage.

She cried out once. Hunt didn't care. Eyes fixed on her and the dog.

Oh, he wants them so bad. Hunt raised his eyes skyward. *Should I, Lord? Should I?*

Penance was always the burden of belief, the sweet reprise of victory over the fallen.

Yes, my son, you should.

Hansel whined.

"Shut him up," Burned Fingers hissed.

Jessie signaled the dog and returned her attention to the Pixie-bobs, now a teeming mass of brown and gray and black fur. One hundred of them? Two hundred? No idea. And she also didn't know whether to start shooting—or hope that the notoriously ravenous creatures would awaken slowly to the needs of their bellies.

"Let's keep going," Burned Fingers said in a calmer voice. "High ground never hurts."

Jessie heard her breath quicken as the hill steepened. Slow going, but the cats were starting to stretch, familiar feline behavior that made them appear slightly less nightmarish.

She eyed the crest about two hundred yards away, hoping that if they could slip over the top, the P-bobs would forget about them. Out of sight, out of mind? Something like that. But mostly she hoped to see Bliss and Jaya alive and unbroken down below.

And if they're not there?

Then she'd take her rations and stay behind. But she'd make Ananda go with the others. If she found Bliss and Jaya, even days from now, the three of them would trek after the lumbering caravan, and trust that it was hampered by uphills all the way to arctic Canada—and that they themselves would not be set upon by Pixie-bobs, panther packs, or roving bands of brain-fevered men.

But the gathering P-bobs looked like they could break any promise of survival.

"Good dog. Yes-yes, good boy." Hunt fed out the chain so Damocles could root at the boy's pretty features. Almost girlish, but not, which made them even better. A fair-haired boy. *That's what they call them, the blond ones with skin so pure you could just tear it apart with your teeth. And him trying to turn away, like that's gonna stop Damocles.*

"His muzzle's coming off. It's what has to be. You don't understand but I do. We're part of something here, and it's bigger than you or me."

Speaking softly, but there was no point in explaining. Still, he'd tried. His conscience would allow no less.

"If you're smart, and I mean smarter than you've been in your whole heathen lives, you'll do nothing but pray. Damocles knows. He *knows* a true soul. But no matter what *he* does, you better do nothing but pray because if you try to fight the Lord's will, Damocles will go crazy with vengeance. It's only right and just. You'll see."

He bent over his dog. "You want me to take that off, boy? Do you? Do you?" His master's touch incited the beast. Sinewy muscles rippled in the sun. Froth speckled his flews. And another fine growl—deep and rich and deadly—unsettled the air.

"What you gonna do now, Damocles? You gonna help me? You gonna help the Lord?" He worked the muzzle's leather straps, tight knots he couldn't tear apart fast enough, fingers mean as fever sores.

The girl's eyes were on them. *She's got herself a pretty face, too. Yes, she does.* "And don't you forget it," he said to the dog.

When he undid the first knot, he could have sung a thousand hosannas. Only one slipped from his mouth. The boy looked at him and closed his eyes.

Living in your own world. Can't take this one, can you? And you don't even know the half of it. Do you? But you sure will. I keep my promises. God above knows it's true, and so will you.

He yanked off the metal cage and slapped the dog's snout with the meat of his hand. The animal growled louder.

"No, Damocles." A sharp, whispered command. The dog quieted, shuddered.

Then he slapped him again. "You like that? You want some more, do you?" Slapping him two more times. Getting him all worked up. *Got to do your duty. God's watching. God's watching.*

The dog knew about pain and pleasure, sin and grace. *More than they'll ever know.* How you had to keep the balance true. The whole universe, every dark corner of it, teetered on a point so fine that the eyes could never see it. Only the soul, and only in God's heavenly grasp. Right where the blinding blackness met the infinite burning brightness of the Almighty, Satan warred with the Lord over a golden throne that could never be shared. And it came down to every man, woman, even babies—*Yes, girl babies, special ones. Guardians from God, but real as saints and miracle wonder*—to keep the fiery claws of hell from raking out the eyes of angels, the light of kings.

It came down to him.

He looked at the two of them stretched out on the ground. His role was clear. It had always been so.

God and man.

He squeezed Damocles's head to his breastbone, felt the dog's moist heat, his squirming animal hide, and spoke sacred words to him that no demon could bear.

Then he fed out the chain, faster this time.

Sunlight now coated the whole hillside, gnawing Jessie like a parasite. She and Burned Fingers were only feet from the summit. He lowered himself to his hands and knees, and she settled next to him. No telling what might be crawling up the other side, but could it be any worse than the Pixie-bobs? They'd stopped their stretching, and at least forty of the cats were studying them openly.

"Hurry," she whispered to Burned Fingers.

He unwrapped his field glasses, raised it to his eyes and looked down. "It's a good-sized ravine." He glassed the periphery. "But I don't see a goddamn track."

She peeled her eyes from the cats and peered over the hill-top. "Wouldn't be any with all that wind."

"But no one's come out since it stopped blowing."

"Can you see down into it?" She had decent vision—good enough to keep one eye on the brightly lit P-bobs, but not strong enough to see into those shadows.

"Nope." He shifted his elbows for a different angle. "I can make out some rocks, but it's too deep to see anything below the wall closest to us."

She swore softly. She could march down there fully exposed or wait to be eaten by those cats. All their creepy yellow eyes were fixed on them, making her decision easy: she stood with the full intention of heading toward the ravine, but Burned Fingers pulled her back down.

"Not so fast," he said in a hushed voice. "Let's give it a few minutes and watch."

"A few minutes! Look behind you."

"I'm seeing a section that's catching some sun now," he said, ignoring her panic. "It looks like a motorcycle hauling a trailer, but the goddamn thing's open in the back, and it's got a couple of those old telephone booths crammed inside. One's open, the other's chained up."

"Oh, Jesus, did you hear that? And would you *look* at what I'm saying."

The first yowls rose up the hill. Like a baby crying.

Damocles lunged at the boy. Fair skin, fair hair, fair game.

"Temptation, temptation," Hunt whispered, sunlight spilling into the ravine, more every minute. He fancied them nude on the ground, hot sun moving over them like a big warm hand, patting their fine round fannies, heating them up, turning them pink as pink can be. Getting them ready.

The hound strained so hard on his chain that the links snapped as loud as his jaw.

He wants a piece of him. Don't I know.

"He's getting closer, boy. Better take off your old shorts or

I'm going to let him do it for you." Saw his dog shaking, the boy shaking in his clothes. "He'll take your skin, you don't do what I say." *More than skin, God's will be done.* "Yeah, Damocles, you like him. Don't you, boy? I can tell. You do."

Oh, dear Jesus, not that.

Damocles tearing into the boy's back, ripping at it, lifting the weight of him off the ground.

"Stop him! Please."

Boy begging, moaning bad, hiding a scream. Hunt needed the hound worked up, fever frenzy, but not biting crazy. Boy blood made his dog mad. He looked it now, with pink foam dripping down. And trying to break the chain, digging up deep lines of dirt.

He worked hard to hold him back. Dog's claws caught the girl's leg and tore it down to her ankle, sure as a razor. But she lay still. No shaking from her. No moans. Not even now. Nothing moving but the blood curling around her toes.

Hunt yearned for more, just like the hound, but dragged him to the girl. The boy was driving the beast insane. *Blood on his back. Blood on his back.* He kept repeating those words. Exorcism or incantation? Wasn't sure. Couldn't say. Medieval and wrong, but wicked strong. The whole of the sun spilled in, a curtain rising, and he saw bone through the bite, and red rivers running to the boy's armpit, ribs.

He forced the dog's sniffer to the girl. "She smells *good.* You want her? You want her? You," he wheeled on the boy, fast as a lash, "take them off."

But Damocles didn't much care about the boy now, sniffing all the way up her baggy pants.

There he goes, snuffling, rooting at her, raising dust between her legs, motes spinning madly in sunbeams. The hound wouldn't hardly let her go. And the boy, newly naked in the sun, fanny warm and pink as he'd hoped.

"You, too," he said to her, voice reedy with all kinds of need. *"Take them off."*

He pulled the beast off her, man and dog jerking like flames in rain, and grabbed a green cloth collar. *Green for go. Green for I found them. Bring guns, men. Bring back the tank.*

The beast drooled, strained to see the girl. Hunt snapped his fingers so hard the air rang for seconds, sharp sound keeling on stone.

But the dog's eyes stayed on her. Hunt grabbed his jowls, got his stare.

"Home," he commanded.

Damocles sprang loose, unburdened by desire, racing around boulders, never looking back. Up the road, still sprinting.

Hunt watched him vanish, then looked back at the naked boy and girl, arms and legs open to the earth. A magnitude of filth.

He would offer them the blessings of True Belief.

But first he would favor himself, as he had the hound, with release from the only chain that bound him.

Hansel could not take his eyes off the Pixie-bobs. The spectacle must have been shocking to the canine: scores of cats stretching their open mouths into the air, yowling louder with every passing second. As Jessie reached over to make sure he stayed close to the ground, she spied a sleek white and gray dog bolting from the ravine.

"Over there," she said to Burned Fingers, pointing to a shockingly fast sight hound tracking up dust. Looked like a Borzoi. Or a saluki or whippet. More likely a mix, maybe of all three.

"Your rifle," Burned Fingers said, urgent as a heartbeat.

She handed it over. He aimed the M–16, but the dog sprinted into shadows and reappeared only in ghostly sporadic movements.

"I can't get a fucking fix on him."

"Why kill him? What's the point?"

"Because he's a messenger dog. Like the pigeons. Heard of them? And there's only one message anyone's sending."

"Holy shit." The truth of it slammed her. "Is there any way to catch him?"

"Nope, not even if I had that bike down there. Those dogs can move around this country faster than anything."

Burned Fingers grabbed his field glasses, but the dog had disappeared. "We've got to get down there and find out what's going on. That trailer's cutting off my line of sight. All we can do is get our asses in place and hope to hell we're not spotted."

It can't be any worse than them. She'd returned her eyes to the cats, and they greeted her attention by starting up the hill. Not fast, not in piranha mode, but with unmistakable intention.

"You see that?" She nodded at them.

"Sure do, and it doesn't make me want to hang around." He turned back to the bare hillside that loomed over the ravine. "We've got to separate, not for them but for who-ever's down there. And we've got to run," he said, standing. "No straight lines. Keep them guessing the whole time."

She dragged herself to her feet and commanded Hansel to heel. Burned Fingers was already barreling down the hill. She glanced back one more time at the advancing Pixie-bobs and took off, bearing right before cutting back sharply after the first few steps—running poorly because of a gun-shot wound to her thigh. It caused her serious pain for the first time in days, but mostly she felt as exposed as the sun, the land, the sorry plight of humankind.

Chapter Four

Hunt stared at the boy's pinkening rump, trembling. Blood from Damocles's bites pooled at the base of the kid's spine, brimming as if it might spill into the cleft, the only shadow that still defied the sun.

His mouth moistened, longing even the brute heat couldn't burn to ash.

He didn't looked closely at the girl. Not once. His refusal marked his penance, eagerness to show the Lord strength and resolve, his true spirit soul. And he'd seen all he wanted of her clawed leg and foot, her horrible body.

He kneeled behind the naked boy, talking of sin and absolution. Then he waited, holding his breath for a minute at a time—penance, *penance*—and prayed.

When his resistance proved his faith yet again—when he had no doubt of his strength and consecrated these moments in the name of the Lord—he drew his knife and held the blade between his teeth. "You'll know God, I promise," he whispered. "In a minute."

Time corporal, time eternal.

Time to taste the boy's blood. He slipped his tongue past the steel blade, stirred the red pool, round as the sun at dusk, when it seared the horizon and raised monkey ruins of hell to the wicked imagination of man.

The boy flattened, boring into earth.

"No," Hunt whispered again, but vow had been replaced by threat: "Don't move."

He licked an ear, licked it again, shifted his head to the side so the sharp tip could thread through the boy's light hair, score the back of his skull. *You feel that? Sure you do. You'll feel more, just you see.* "That's my mouth," he said without removing the blade. "Think about that." But the boy said nothing, quaking beneath him.

A red line swelled. Hunt tasted that, too.

Still trembling, he slipped his knife from his mouth and sat on his heels—blood on his teeth, copper on his tongue. His head rose to the sun and he closed his eyes, every cell alive. In the crystal light he knew the most sanctioned moment of his life, for God and all that He inspired spoke to him, and the message was as clear as it was reassuring: He must cast aside kindness—and sacrifice even his own righteousness here on earth—to confirm the boy's depravity, his deserving of punishments most severe. But what stunned him most—what made him suddenly hang his head in eternal gratitude—was the understanding that he'd been doing this all along. Every act he'd ever committed with sodomites and heathens and errant brothers of True Belief had been part of the Lord's plan. He was a spy in the realm of sin, an infiltrator of flesh, and need not have begged the Lord's forgiveness for actions that He ordained.

That's right, My son. All that has passed was pure. All that will come is promised.

From high above, Burned Fingers spotted a man hunched over Jaya. He would have gunned him down if the lead shot would have spared the kid, but at this distance his sawed-off was no more sure than his pistol.

And he wanted so much more than the man's simple

death. With a single glimpse, he wanted to savage him with his hands, his blade, gut him like a gamecock because the rapist's back revealed what his imagination had spared him—the final limning of his young son's horrific sexual assault and murder by soldiers in Baltimore. Till this moment, Burned Fingers's memory had moved no further than the gruesome scene's dishabille: Cody's torn clothes and naked, rumpled form lying near his slain, partially dismembered mother in a burned-out basement. But now the tense, predatory hunch of the man down below fleshed out the earlier, archetypal violence—and sparked a hell storm in Burned Fingers.

He screamed "No," which echoed off the rock walls, and ran toward an old wagon road that ended in the ravine.

The rapist jumped to his feet and spun around, as if the fury were charging him from everywhere at once. Then he bolted to the motorcycle, bigger than Burned Fingers had thought looking through his field glasses. Large as an old Harley. The blond, darkly tanned man leaped on it, kick-started the engine, and hunched over the tank like he'd hunched over the boy.

But he wouldn't be moving anywhere fast, not dragging that trailer and side car up the steep road.

Even as Burned Fingers placed the odds in his favor, the biker sprang off the seat and unhitched the ungainly trailer. Less than twenty feet away, Bliss, naked and standing, rummaged *through* her pants instead of putting the goddamn things on—or running away.

Get down. If the guy turned, he could shoot her; Burned Fingers saw a pistol in his belt. But the fiend threw himself back on the loudly idling bike without ever seeing Bliss.

Burned Fingers ran along the edge of the ravine, closing the distance to the road, warning himself not to blow up the gas tank when he shot the rapist.

You want that bike.

Did he ever. Nothing better for scouting, and nothing rarer. He was still riding big bikes about thirty years ago, and knew what they could do and how fast they could do it.

He heard the engine growl, saw black smoke and dust rise behind the rear wheel, yet thought he'd have time to set up for a kill shot. He might even catch the hog before it crashed riderless into a boulder.

But while racing up the road, the biker jerked a metal bar, cutting the side car loose, accelerating even faster. At the same time, Bliss pulled something from her pants and startled Burned Fingers by chasing the bike. He tried to shout a warning but the engine noise drowned him out.

She stopped anyway, only to rear back and throw the sharp rock that she'd shown him at the obsidian wall, burying it in the biker's lower back. Blood burst from the crude wound.

But the believer never slowed, leaving a dense funnel of oily exhaust in his wake.

Burned Fingers, breathing hard, smelling fumes, neared the road as the bike rose from the ravine. He didn't spot the rider immediately because the guy had flattened his dark torso against the tarnished tank and propped his chin on the front of it, making a clean kill shot all but impossible.

As the bike raced for the open space ahead, Burned Fingers dropped his sawed-off and yanked his bone handle knife from its sheath. Then he launched himself at the man, hacking murderously at his back, striking bone—hoping it was spine—before embedding the blade in flesh and spilling to the ground.

The motorcycle wobbled. Burned Fingers jumped up and gave chase, hoping the frame wouldn't bend or the precious wheels collapse when it crashed.

But the rider pulled himself upright and sped away—with the knife stuck in his thick trapezius only inches from his neck.

What the fuck!

Burned Fingers pulled out his revolver and shot at him, the bike, tires—any target that would dump the rider on the ground. But the guy was racing through a series of boulders, showing less of himself with every second. Jessie opened up with her M–16 from a few hundred feet away—with no more success.

In the ravine, Bliss grabbed her shotgun from the jettisoned side car and, still naked, started running up the road.

"Put your clothes on!" Burned Fingers shouted. "Bastard's gone!"

He dusted off, second-guessing himself furiously. He should have unloaded the sawed-off on him. *Fuck the bike.* But he hadn't been able to resist its allure—or its great promise. It would have been a tremendous help to have a fast, nimble two-wheeler for guiding the caravan. He'd made the wrong call for all the right reasons.

And he'd forgotten about the Pixie-bobs.

Hunt roared down a paved road gapped enough to scuttle the motorcycle and swallow it whole, leave him mangled, dying, eaten by carrion birds. The sun-clawed surface wound past a second boulder field before curving behind the hill that rose above the ravine.

The agony in his back wrapped around to his chest and groin, like the rock and knife were eating their way right through him. A *rock*. They were savages. He didn't dare pull it out—too close to vertebrae—any more than he'd yank on the blade. The doctor would see to the weapons, the Lord to his well-being.

He took the shoulder of a road through a valley formed by steep, drought-stricken hills. The pavement itself was another wasteland, but the side looked mostly unriven. He rode the cycle faster than he'd ever dared, gripping the throttle tightly, gritting his teeth, anything to escape the sharpening pain.

He didn't notice Pixie-bobs until they rampaged down the slope to his left, trailing streaks of silt so fine that they hung in the air like smoke.

His pain fled, body triaging threats, veins fat with adrenaline. He pushed the Harley harder, risking sudden splits in the crumbly surface and rocks that could condemn him to a gruesome death. But better to die from a crash than to be taken down by this pack. Even the screaming engine couldn't drown out the death call of the cats.

In a blur he did come upon a hole so deep that he caught no sight of the bottom as he launched over the void at a harrowing speed, the shadow of man and bike disappearing into blackness. Clearing the threat, he gave thanks, but a terrifying yowl tore his eyes from the sky to the cats now springing off the eroded remains of a retaining wall. Two of them lunged at him from feet away, fell short and were trampled.

A numbed memory reminded him they were sprinters, good only for the predatory pounce; but they'd sustained their charge for a minute at least—though terror always wound a tight clock—and were *still* exploding at him.

The one in the lead, ears pinned back like all the rest, bounded over a chasm and landed on his shoulder, bit off his ear, clawed his cheek, and tore open his neck—and in such rapid succession that he almost dumped the bike.

He pulled the beast from his flesh and threw it aside, flinching as another one jumped for his leg. He jerked his boot off the foot peg and watched the Pixie-bob flail before it fell under the rear wheel with an audible *thump*.

"Oh, God" was all he allowed of prayer or imprecation before two more landed on his back, ripping at his bloody skin, and a third clamped its claws around his left arm and sank its needle teeth into his elbow. The onslaught almost drove him off the shoulder into a dry riverbed to his right.

In a fearsome effort he tore the Pixie-bob from his arm and hurled it to the dirt. Wind whipped blood from his eviscerated elbow as he registered the full savagery of the cats on his back.

A series of fast, furious bites by his shoulder blade made him risk another lunge; but when he grabbed the creature's head, it bit the meaty base of his thumb, boiling pain through the whole of his hand.

He tried to release the animal but it bit down harder. Frantically, he shook his hand till a chunk of palm started tearing loose. Sensing release, he beat the beast against the side of the Harley till the flesh tore away completely and the cat fell off, still gulping pulpy tissue.

He throttled hard despite the cat feeding on the muscle next to his spine. Then the claws climbed higher, and he knew the P-bob was trenching up his back, *ripping* him open.

He told himself he could take the pain. Just thirty more seconds and the pack would have to give up and he could kill the cat eating him alive. But the beast was wrapping its legs around his skull, clawing his scalp, brow, temples, and lips. With its warm belly pressed to the back of his head, its musk ripening the fast flowing air, the Pixie-bob ripped his face from the corner of his eye to his bloody nub of ear.

When it tried to claw him again, he turned to the side, fearing the loss of sight above all else, and spotted the mass of Pixie-bobs slowing, watching, as if waiting for the cat shredding his skull to bring him down. Then the creature's hind leg jammed the knife handle, driving the blade sideways in his wound. A scalding agony erupted, and he violated all precaution by braking. The bike swung around, tires smoking, till it left him facing the pack a hundred yards away.

In a blazing panic he dragged the cat off his head, peeling its claws from his face. Holding it away from his body, suffering it still, he yanked the blade from his trapezius and stabbed the beast repeatedly, finally impaling it on the knife. He raised the squirming, squalling feline high above his head and shook it violently, torturing *it*. The creature's piercing screams formed an unearthly chorus with the idling bike.

He flung the body from the blade and watched it fall hard on decayed pavement twenty feet away. It clawed the ground with one paw, couldn't rise up, lay writhing on the pebbly remains of asphalt, a seizure-gripped clump of bloody fur.

The pack stared, winded as one. He jammed the knife in his belt and raced off, wounds burning and throbbing as adrenaline drained away in the red sweat of passing miles.

He thanked the Father with prayer, mumbling the words over and over, spit and blood spilling from his lacerated lips—along with a stark earthly injunction: *Hold on. Hold on.* To the bike. To life. To the supreme knowledge that the Lord would not let him die after he'd unveiled—and chained—unshakable evidence that the fallen angel Lucifer had staked his claim to the abiding sun.

His Piety had warned of the coming signs, this one above all others, when the Curse of Cain would appear as beast and griffin, cruel grotesqueries and demon seeds. When the signs would herald Holy War.

There would be no Rapture, no hand of God plucking believers from the scourged earth to His heavenly abode. Not yet. Not with hell's creations crawling from ash.

Jessie ran down into the ravine, Hansel hopping gamely behind her. Bliss was pulling on her pants, blood crusting her foot. Jaya sat naked and unmoving on the ground. He looked drugged or concussed. Then she saw blood on his back, a lot of it, and skin that looked grated.

"What happened?" she asked Bliss.

"That asshole put a dog on him. Pretty much said we were dead if we moved. And he prayed a bunch of mumbo-jumbo." She cinched her belt and kneeled next to Jaya, stroking his cheek, handing him his chopped-off pants.

"And you?" Jessie asked pointedly.

"He clawed my leg. Jaya got the worst of it."

"Forget the dog," Burned Fingers said as he raced up. "Where the hell are those cats?"

Jessie studied the top half of the hillside—all she could see from the ravine—but spotted only a few cat tracks, and the footprints that she, Burned Fingers, and Hansel had left. "Where *did* they go?"

"Long as they're gone," Burned Fingers said without conviction. "Let's move."

"Wait a second. Can't you see?" She put her hand on Jaya's shoulder. "We'll have Hannah take a look at those bites," she said to the boy. "Come on, get dressed."

Burned Fingers reached down, offering his scarred hand. Jaya took it without expression and pulled himself up.

"You'll survive," Burned Fingers told him. "People have dogs licking their wounds all the time to get better."

And a lot of them get sepsis, Jessie almost said, checking herself because Burned Fingers was trying to give Jaya hope. At least he wasn't giving him grief.

"Mom," Bliss said uneasily as she backed away from the trailer, "there's something in that thing." Her eyes were on the telephone booth wrapped in chains.

"Some *thing*?" Burned Fingers said, drawing his sawed-off and advancing slowly.

Jessie raised her rifle and watched him lift up on his toes to look through the Plexiglas from a few feet away. He holstered his gun.

"What?" she asked, lowering her own weapon. She heard something shift inside the booth. It's alive, she thought. Whatever it is.

"You might want to prepare yourself," Burned Fingers said as he hurried to strip off the chains.

"For what?" she asked.

"Just a sec, and keep an eye out."

He glanced at the hill, but Jessie's gaze hadn't left the booth. She stepped toward it, impatient with his reticence; but Bliss shook her head and gripped her mother's arm.

Chapter Five

It's okay," Jessie whispered to Bliss. She hurried to Burned Fingers, who was reaching down to open the telephone booth, disturbing dust from the folding door. One of the twins blinked away the grit. The other girl's eyes were closed. Both had dried blood on their foreheads.

They were crammed together, yet Jessie also noticed pretty round faces that could have defied any talk of famine. And the one who'd blinked revealed rich brown eyes with flecks of gold so radiant in the strong light that they might have been dancing in their delicate orbit.

What Jessie did not see was their most strikingly distinctive—and unsettling—feature.

She watched Burned Fingers offer his hand to the alert twin. When she struggled to stand, he asked if her sister could help.

The girl stroked her twin's face, saying, "We can get out now, but we have to get up." Though the silent girl's eyes did not open, she climbed to her feet with her twin—and astonished Jessie.

"See what I mean," Burned Fingers said softly.

The twins were joined along the length of their torso, which wasn't much wider than a typical adolescent girl's midsection, normalcy greatly underscored by their single pair of arms and legs. But the familiar features of their body made them appear that much more unnerving because they bore the unmistakable look of a two-headed human.

Conjoined twins, Jessie reminded herself. Siamese twins before the nomenclature changed.

She helped Burned Fingers guide them from the booth and trailer, realizing as they moved gingerly from their prison that in a land rampant with superstition and hardship, the twins' survival itself might be more stunning than their conjoinment—and a tribute to Augustus and his people.

Their clothes were burned off. Maybe torn off, too, she thought in a flood of revulsion. All that remained was a singed waistband holding a flap of cloth from a pair of pants or shorts, or possibly a skirt. Impossible to tell.

"Here, put this on," Burned Fingers said, handing over his shirt. Jessie draped it over their shoulders, fastening the two surviving buttons. It hung past their hips.

"I'm Jessie. And this is Burned Fingers." She tried to temper the uncommon with the ordinary before cringing over his nickname, which she knew must sound strange to any untuned ear—and quite possibly alarming to girls who looked like they'd survived a conflagration. But they didn't react and she didn't explain, instead introducing Bliss, who managed a smile, and Jaya, standing steps away. "What are your names?"

"Leisha," she said. "And Kaisha," she added with a nod at her quiet sister.

"Is she all right?" The girl's eyes were still closed.

"All right?" Leisha shook her head and rolled her eyes till they showed almost nothing but white. "They *burned* us! A tank burned up everyone. It was shooting fire at us. And we ended up in that." She twisted her head to glare at the booth, neck cords tight as winch lines. Then she gestured toward her legs. "They hurt so bad," an outcry that raised her hand to her charred hair. She clutched a fistful, drawing Jessie's attention to her scalp, burned pink in small patches and spotted with crimson dots, as if the sky had rained blood. Jessie spied splatters on their sides and thighs, and ash clinging to their arms and caked to the insides of their elbows. The girl's fist dropped from her head, opening to hair that had crumbled in her grip and looked like lint.

"I'm so thirsty," she pleaded.

"We have water but it's back at our caravan."

"How far?"

"Not too," Jessie fudged.

With help from Bliss and her, the twins started out of the ravine, Kaisha's eyes still closed.

"Is Augustus your father?" Jessie asked when they'd reached level ground. She thought the girls must be the twins whom he'd said so little about. Now she understood his secretiveness: his daughters could become fodder for cults, and targets of their savagery.

"You know him?" Leisha demanded. "Where is he?" She looked around as if she might find him among the boulders.

"He's with us back at the caravan," Jessie said. "He's okay. You'll see him soon."

Their father had a burn so prominent that she'd noticed it at first glance, the shape of a cross he'd branded on his chest where a gold or silver one might have hung from a chain before the collapse; afterward, precious metals and gemstones—and innocence itself—were readily surrendered for food and water.

That's what she needs as soon as possible. Jessie's eyes were on Leisha. *But not her sister, not if she's in shock.* Kaisha's head hung as limply as the hand by her hip, which hadn't moved. Jessie figured that each twin controlled the leg and arm on her side of their body. Biologically, that would make sense; but it made a quandary of providing aid if one girl could be in shock while the other was alert, if that was even possible.

As they started up the long gradual slope to the caravan, she automatically scanned the barren landscape and hillside for Pixie-bobs. Another reason to get back to those vehicles—*as soon as possible.*

Had they been white and not conjoined, the Alliance would have wanted the prepubescent twins for Wicca-free sex, once their menses began. But as Augustus had said, zealots didn't want African-American girls because they carried the "Curse of Cain," as the Alliance called it. But she also remembered him saying that the zealots never left you alone for long because "they're always seeing something you got." Even if it was lives they could end and a community they could slaughter. In the end, black skin hadn't saved his girls from abduction—and it singled out his people for murder.

The twins walked slowly with a rolling gait, Leisha wincing with every step.

Jessie wondered where she would place them on the caravan. Three blind girls and the babies whom they cared for already occupied the seats in the van that weren't piled high with crates of food, and the perches on the tanker truck could never accommodate burn victims comfortably.

Just get back as fast as you can. Their small group was an open, easy target that would never survive a Pixie-bob attack. Though no words were spoken, she saw Burned Fingers also surveying their surroundings from the scout position in front of them, his bare back glistening in the sun.

He'd borrowed her M–16, not that it would spare them if the feral cats attacked. He might kill a dozen, but even gunning down three times as many wouldn't slow a swarm of them.

He called Jaya to his side; the boy was lagging numbly behind Jessie, Bliss, and the twins. But he came to life with a big "Thanks" when Burned Fingers handed him his sawed-off.

"I can't shoot that and this," Burned Fingers said of the weapons. "And right now our job is to protect the women-folk," he added with a hick accent that he affected sometimes for a laugh.

Jessie smiled, but Bliss wasn't amused. She hefted her shotgun up to her hip as if to say that she didn't need *his* help. If Burned Fingers noticed, it might have reminded him that only three weeks ago the girl had almost killed him while trying to save her father.

"He touch you?" Jessie overheard him ask Jaya. "Because what he did was wrong," Burned Fingers went on. "Wouldn't matter whom he did it to—boy, girl, man, woman—it was wrong, but I've got to know something . . ."

Jessie leaned forward, openly eavesdropping and almost certain of the question he was about to ask—the only one that really mattered.

"Did he put it in you?"

Jaya shook his head.

"There's no shame in it for you," Burned Fingers said, "but you have to be completely honest for everyone's sake."

Jessie glanced at her daughter, who looked pained.

Jaya shook his head again. "He was going to, but you yelled at him and he ran away."

"He's going to be running from me all his life," Burned Fingers said. "If he ever comes anywhere near us, I'll hunt him down and kill him."

Jessie's spine prickled. A ruthless finality in Burned Fingers's icy tone promised death as much as his actual words, a fitting outcome, perhaps, of decades of earnest killing. But his message must have moved Jaya, who teared up and spat, "I hate him."

"And you've got the right. You hear me? You've got the right to hate him." He nodded at the boy's swollen eyes. "There's no shame in that, either. Go on. We've all had to at some point."

You? But she doubted her curiosity about Burned Fingers would ever be satisfied.

"That man's a rapist," he said to Jaya, "and you can bet he's raped others and that he'll keep on raping if he gets half a chance. I'm promising you, he's a dead man from this day forward."

Jessie was shocked to find herself choked up by his kind words and fierce vengeance against men who used children and draped their debauchery in the vestments of religion.

In the last few minutes he'd seethed with anger, offered compassion, and sworn the worst of violence, roiling contradictions that reflected what she'd gleaned of his complicated past: Oxford humanities scholar who could quote *The Waste Land* at length and recite ringing descriptions of the competition between gods and mortals from Ovid's *Metamorphoses*; renowned resistance fighter in the final days of the collapse who'd commandeered an army tank and turned it on rampaging soldiers until they burned him with white phosphorus; murderous marauder in the lawless years that followed; and now, late in life, a shrewd and intrepid fighter who helped lead the attack to free the girls from the Army of God and destroy the zealots' formidable outpost.

But his background was no more odd than the circumstances that led all of them to this point at this time with these girls.

"Leisha, has your sister spoken at all?" Jessie asked.

The twin shook her head. "Not since the tank came. It was crushing everyone, and it shot that fire at us. That's all I remember, and then he came."

"He?"

"The one with the box."

Telephone booth, but she wouldn't be likely to know about an antique supplanted by wireless technology in the early years of the century. All of it refuse now, electronic parts scattered by the trillions across the planet, dribs and drabs and vast waste dumps of chips and screens and candy-colored wires bleeding their toxic innards into the earth.

"Does Kaisha's skin that's hurt on her side feel like yours?"

"No, it's different in different places, but we're both burned."

"I know it's awful, but you'll feel better when we can get you a place to rest." Jessie peered past her. "Bliss, try talking to Kaisha." Her daughter held the girl's slack arm. "She might be in shock. See if you can get her to respond."

"I'm Bliss," she said to Kaisha right away. "It's kind of a funny name, I guess, everything considered."

No reaction.

"Kaisha's one of the prettiest names I've ever heard of," Bliss carried on. "How old are you? I turned fifteen today."

Still no response, but Jessie flinched; she'd forgotten about the birthday, and though she'd had ample distractions, she vowed to herself to make it up to her firstborn.

"How old are you?" she asked Leisha.

"Thirteen."

"You're teenagers."

Leisha nodded shyly. "So my dad's up there?" They'd just walked beyond the curve of the hill and spotted the far-off caravan.

"He sure is." Jessie could barely make out a black man darting from behind the tanker. He began running down the slope. "That's him. He sees us."

"Kaisha, it's Dad!"

The silent twin opened her eyes for the first time. "Daddy!" she cried out so loudly that Burned Fingers hushed her.

The girls tried to walk fast and stumbled, then Leisha reached for Kaisha and they held hands as they hurried.

Burned Fingers and Jaya stepped aside for Augustus.

"They've got burns," Jessie warned, but he must have seen this because he slowed and let them take the lead in drawing him close.

He kissed their round cheeks and held each of their faces in turn, shaking his head in open wonder. His hands hovered over their back, careful not to touch what he could not see; but it was clear that he wanted to hold them, to sweep them into his grasp and never let go. "You're alive," he said. "Alive."

"Daddy, Daddy," Kaisha whispered, as if to say *of course* in the midst of so much turmoil.

Burned Fingers broke in: "Sorry, Augustus, but we've seen Pixie-bobs."

The missionary looked at him with alarm, then drew his daughters' hands to his lips and kissed their fingers. Not letting go, he walked backward. Tears streaming, he closed his eyes, bowed his head, and gave thanks to his god. "Come-come, we'll take care of you," he told them. "It'll be okay now."

Jessie wished that were true. She returned to scanning the hillside and the slope behind them, hating those piranhas of the apocalypse.

Less than fifty feet from the caravan, her fear of the felines was crushed by a rumble. She knew what it meant before she turned, even before the twins shrieked in panic. They'd heard it at their camp, and she had endured it the night before and seen its menacing tread marks this morning.

The tank was a dark outline in the distance, but it grew larger and louder every instant, roaring up the slope. Worse—if that were even possible—the engine noise had alerted hundreds of Pixie-bobs, and they were swarming down the hillside that spilled onto the grade.

Tortured by his wounds, Hunt rode his aged Harley in near delirium up a winding, broken highway to Alliance headquarters in a former army base. It squatted on a bluff above a wide bend in a dead river riddled with rocks and military wreckage. Red sweat still blurred his vision from the blood streaking his face and head, forcing him to navigate the last several hundred yards of rubble-strewn road with unusual care.

He stopped at an imposing steel gate before slumping over the teardrop-shaped gas tank, much as he'd had to escape the ravine. Closing his eyes, he rested his shredded cheek against the tarnished metal, fully exposing the knife wound, wretched bites, and claw marks on his shoulder blade and both sides of his spine.

Countless dust storms had shaded the white brick entrance, and letters had fallen from a sign that once greeted soldiers and their families: WE C ME T FORT MC AU EY. Small, less heavily dusted ovals hinted at the insignia of the units that had been based there, leaving a gap-toothed grimace on a dead institution still hated by believers for permitting sodomites and mud people, Muslims and Sikhs, Catholics and Jews, and Pagans and apostates of all kinds to rise in the ranks, to actually *command* white followers of the True Faith. And then the fallen, wicked and wounded, wondered why a nation so cursed and abominable, a world so reviled by the righteous, had been harrowed by the Lord's sharpest plow.

Hunt had been present on the morning six years ago when His Piety swept his robed arm toward the dirty brick and said, "Let it crumble! Let it rot like the temples of antiquity, the heathen horrors of Thebes, Jerusalem, and Rome. No rag of religion was too filthy for them."

Now, briefly rested, he lifted up and saw that the gate hadn't opened. "Help," he yelled, sinking back to the gas tank without finishing his plea. He spotted the head of a Pixie-bob in the fuselage staring up at him, its body sheared off in his mad flight from the pack. Hunt kicked the face weakly and almost dumped the bike when his legs began to buckle.

He wheeled into a shadow before recognizing that it fell from the ninety foot cross that rose above the base, and could be seen and venerated for miles. The last of the oxyfuel had been used to weld it entirely from broken, burned, and otherwise useless weapons—rifles, handguns, cannon barrels, bayonets, bazookas, and tank parts. Even the face of Christ had been commanded from helmets, the body from the twisted tread of a blown up Abrams tank. The tortured looking figure appeared eerily real and full of wrath.

True Belief cannot be beat. Hunt repeated those words like a prayer, and they sustained him for another minute till a *creak* lured his eyes back to the gate. Five slaves, chained together, pressed their emaciated frames against the thick metal bars. Once, the gate had cooperated at the touch of a finger. Now it ran on the raw efforts of men too feeble-spirited for True Belief, who lived out the last weeks or months of their wastrel lives in servitude to the Alliance, each of their brows crudely and quickly tattooed upon arrival with an inky S—the black Curse of Cain for those whose white skin tried to hide their dark cause.

He stood, straddling his Harley to push it past the infidels, his back burning and red as flame. He found the kick stand and staggered off the bike. One of many guards patrolling the walls caught him and held him while another rushed forward.

They hurried him from the entrance, his body slipping from the weak foundation of his feet, fully weighting the arms of the men beside him. They passed the slave quarters, once a mesh run for the base's canine corps. He asked if Damocles had returned—or thought he had; the guards didn't answer, and he wasn't sure he'd heard his own voice.

He took air to try again when two more guards ran up with a stretcher and then scurried off with him. "My back!" he screamed from the sudden pressure of lying on the rock embedded inches above his buttocks. The guards rolled him on his side, giving him a view of two dozen slaves shackled to the spokes of a massive wheel whose hub was a turbine rescued from a dam. Their chests were chained to long steel girders that once held power lines for the Tennessee Valley Authority, and they trudged in circles in twelve hour shifts to draw water from a well. Teams of guards drove them with whips, truncheons, and the constant threat of machetes.

Concentric stone paths had been built around the hub after generations of slaves wore shin-deep ditches in the dirt. The hard surface added only more misery to their high mortality. Nearly every day a slave succumbed to heat, exhaustion, or hunger, hanging from his chains like a rag, bare feet bleeding on the long reddened rocks until hauled away for a proper beheading.

From what sounded like a great distance, an urgent voice said he might die and should be taken to the infirmary; but a commander insisted that His Piety wanted to see him in the Great Chapel.

Hunt closed his eyes, certain that God Almighty had saved

him for a hallowed death; and though filled with agony and pain, he glimpsed the white imminence of heaven, regretting only the loss of Damocles and the base in all its splendor—worship, water, food, slaves, and a bounty of girls who would bloom into wives. The most anointed beauties were culled every two months from stock at the fortresses pledged to the Alliance. He was to take a bride within a year. While most of the time the Lord's work would keep him far from her—and forced to confirm the depravity of soul dead men—he would vow a blessed fidelity to whatever female His Piety arranged for him. The need to procreate was paramount. It was in the Bible, and often on his lips as an unbidden reminder.

The guards carted him past rusting cyclone cages packed with old men in filthy white robes, survivors of the attack on Zekiel's compound. But they'd failed to protect their leader, an esteemed man of God and prophet. Neither did they protect their gas, girls, and the sacred trust the Alliance had placed in them. Each would be chained to a witch and burned slowly to death, their ashes falling together to force their souls into hell. Every burning at the base included a witch, and many were to be found, cunning creatures spreading Wicca, for no God of man would abide such a curse, such a dark seed of sex and deviltry. It was a lesson to the men of the Alliance that no price—surely not earthly life—was as painful as eternal death on the arms of a Pagan.

As the guards ferried him up the steps of the Great Chapel, he thought of the sodomite and could not help but wish the boy were dying, not he. Even more grievously, he worried that the Lord world banish him to hell for failing to bring His righteousness down on the naked sinner.

But I was going to, dear God, and You must know it's true. You know my heart. I cut him once and I had the knife in my hand.

He forced his eyes open and squinted at the marble steps, embedded mica glinting on a path as hard and bright and shiny as his faith.

"Water," he called. His Piety would want him to tell what he'd learned, and his throat had known only red sweat for hours.

A guard gave him a bota made of black hide. A trickle washed his hollow belly and gave him the strength, after a pause, to swallow three more times before resting the water by his side.

For the first time since the base entrance, a shadow fell across him, opening his eyes fully. Cooler air settled on his skin, and he saw another familiar cross—golden and gleaming—filling the broad space behind the chapel altar. Just below it, suffused by the glow, His Piety, round and bald and bearded, sat on an elaborately carved bishop's chair rescued long ago from a cathedral. The tall back rose above the prophet, whose wide bottom reclined on burgundy velvet padding, his arms on burled walnut rests. On both sides of him stood the Elders of True Belief, six men in white gowns as stained from use as their skin had been darkened by the sun. They formed a daunting V that received Hunt on the stretcher.

"Stand in the presence of the Lord," His Piety ordered.

The guards hoisted Hunt by his arms; he still could not find his footing.

His Piety nodded approval and spoke to him in a low voice. "Tell me what you found."

"Damocles? Did he come back?" Hunt gasped.

His Piety shook his head solemnly, working his jaw. A nut? Hunt wondered. He favored them, crushing a precious reserve with the three teeth that hadn't rotted from his braces, cemented into place a month before the collapse.

In the first days of the rebellion, the wires protected his mouth during a vicious beating by infidels who tried to raid his church—widely accused of hoarding. His Piety decided to keep his braces because he expected more battles with rebels, and added protection of any kind felt like a wise idea to Frank Louch, as he was known before the visions. Later, orthodontic tools weren't available; a lone attempt to remove the braces with pliers loosened a tooth, but not the wires. So they stayed on, a sign of privilege that he hid with silence until the sanctuary of the base was won.

But without proper care, most of his teeth shriveled to blackened nubs and cracked apart, leaving small decayed chunks to clutter the wires. His suffering continued for years, pain that he offered up to the Father so many times that he was forced to recognize his own sainthood.

His most prominent survivor was a dark tusk that protruded from his lips and attested to the original need. He tried to keep his few teeth and wires clean, causing the latter to flash strangely in the mote-stirred streams of sunlight that flowed into the chapel. His mouth looked like a cage from which vicious prisoners had escaped.

His Piety stopped chewing. "If you sent your dog, you found the gas."

"I did, His Piety."

"Tell me where you saw it."

He glanced at the black bota, asking permission with his eyes, which His Piety granted, pursing his lips. Hunt sipped, and with his throat refreshed, told His Piety the location of the tanker and van.

"Was Burned Fingers still with them?"

"I don't know a Burned Fingers."

"You must. The one with burned fingers? He's in his fifties, gray hair. Shaves."

Shaves? Now he was certain he didn't know him; he'd met only one man who shaved, a trader of iron scrap rumored to have died in his sleep last year, a fate bestowed by the Lord on so few.

"You're gone from the base too much if you don't know about Burned Fingers."

"His Piety, they stopped me before I could get close." His words came quickly, and he felt the strength that a challenge often gave him, especially when His Piety questioned his heavy travel.

"Stopped you? From what?" the prophet asked, as if he knew what had occupied him.

"From taking prisoners for you." He paused and looked into His Piety's blue eyes, mustering all his strength to speak clearly: "A demon."

His Piety rose from the cathedra. The loss of formality startled Hunt, and he expected to be struck or thrown to the marble for his failure to bring back the demon. But instead His Piety leaned so close that Hunt had to struggle not to turn from his breath.

"Demon?" His Piety asked.

"Yes, His Piety. It was just like you said. A demon. A beast. That's what I saw."

He began with the black skin and dark eyes, noses and lips, arms, legs—all the notices of normalcy—before he said, "And two heads."

His Piety's eyes widened. Hunt struggled to raise his right hand, bloodied by those savage cats, and extended his index and middle fingers, like the sinners who once professed their love of a false peace; but this shaky V formed a sacred oath: "From *one* body."

Silence. Barely a breath.

His Piety studied Hunt. "I have seen such a demon in my worship. I am not surprised." He lifted his gaze to the band of sunlight right above him, as if to the risen trove of Christ. "Dear God, I am so humbled to be honored, once again, by Your gift of prophecy. Please grant me strength for such a sacred burden, and the courage to remain a strong vessel for Your divine message."

He returned his eyes to Hunt. "The two-headed beast is a vile portent from the ashes of Hell."

"I found the demon covered in ash. *Crawling* in it."

"As I saw, as I saw." His Piety sounded pained, sickened. The Elders looked on him with concern. One took his arm as if he feared the prophet would falter.

In a reverential whisper, Hunt described the demon's nakedness, hard haunches, and long African legs, a wholly faithful rendering; yet his increasing breathlessness and awe—his repeated emphasis on finding the two-headed beast crawling from the hot ash "with cinders alive on that black skin"—drew a consuming stare from His Piety and frequent nods from the Elders. Hunt's own skin came alive as if startled by demon breath, or the cool quiet of hushed angels—who could tell amid such madness? But it was real, *real* as sin and blood and lust.

And the sensation that coursed through him, that imbued him with a lightness of being he'd never known, also lessened the weight on his feet. He could have stood unsupported by the guards, but they were so stunned by his affirmation of evil—by revelations rarely accorded such lowly servants of the faith—that they took no note of the miracle between them: his sudden strength from the provocation of an evil distillate, dauntless enough to violate God's earth in material guise.

His wounds felt like they were closing, the hacked bones in his back healing. The pain grew most assuredly soft and pliant, letting him stand straight and raise his eyes to the cross, to feel in its purity all that could save him. As much as the heathens bloodied his body, their wanton violence was necessary—maybe even ordained by God—to forge in him a greater will for the fight to come. He saw all this in a vision, though not so blessed as the heavenly language known to His Piety, but sharply etched and filled with the calling that had long claimed him.

He felt the chapel teeming with spirits, a gathering of good, a gathering of evil, a cavalcade of grace and hate and—always—godly wonder.

His Piety moved to the cross, bowed his head till his beard splayed on his chest, and prayed aloud. His importunate words filled the chapel. The Elders of True Belief flanked him, his entreaty now their own.

The prophet raised his hands, and the billowy sleeves of his gold-braided gown cascaded to his elbows. "A demon has arisen from the depths of hell. Of this we can be sure. But why does it have two heads. Why?" He turned to look at them, not for an answer because his eyes never beckoned, but to pause, perhaps to consider.

"To mock," he thundered. "That is why. To mock God the Father and God the Son as One. There can be no other reason." Searching *their* eyes now. Hunt dared not blink.

"The demon," His Piety intoned carefully, "must be enslaved and brought here. *This* is what the Lord commands of me." His voice widened, as if to embrace more than the chapel or base, or the earthly surrounds of sin and disgrace. "All True Believers must bear witness to the demon. The Lord has given us a test of faith that we must not fail, for this beast will destroy all God-given glories if Satan holds sway."

His Piety walked to the altar, drew a sword from a gold case, and raised it till the sunlight gleamed on the silvery surface. "We will look the two-headed monster in the eye, cleave it—with the mighty shield of God to protect us—and burn it to death. No lord of hell will crawl from a flame consecrated in the name of God before the assembled power of True Belief."

"His Piety, I fear we are too late," ventured a short Elder. "The tank might be attacking the fallen right now."

"The tank?" Hunt asked, surprised and deflated. "It found them?"

His Piety turned to him. "You confirmed what we knew about the truck. The tank's dog arrived before you. The collar was clear. But they knew nothing of the demon." Words that restored Hunt's sense of mission.

His Piety turned a curiously empty gaze on the short Elder. "We are in the Lord's hands. Do *you* forget that? Do *you* fear the Lord's righteousness? Do *you* not trust the Lord to do what is best?"

"His Piety," the Elder said, "I always trust the Lord to do what is best, and for you to divine His every intention."

"Then know that the tank's flames failed to kill the demon once, and here is our witness," he pointed to Hunt, "for he pulled the beast from blistering ash." His Piety's face came back to life, so flushed that Hunt saw it reddening through his beard. "Let the tank try to kill the demon again. Let them kill all the heathens and their children, too. Let them even burn the truck—if that is God's will. But I do not believe that is so. That is *not* what the Lord is telling me. The Lord," he looked at the Elders one by one, "is telling me that even if our tank kills all the fallen to get the fuel, which is their sacred duty, the demon will rise again because that is what a demon does until it meets the full force of the Lord Thy God on earth."

His Piety thrust the sword back into the band of sunlight and vowed to the Father and Son to burn the demon into hell forevermore.

"Amen," the Elders said.

"Amen," Hunt uttered, and then collapsed.

The armored tank raced at the caravan from less than a mile away, within easy striking distance with its long cannon. Jessie rushed Leisha and Kaisha to the gasoline tanker and gave them an open-air perch under the trailer, moving two more able-bodied girls to ladders up above. The twins cried out as their burns pressed against the metal grating.

Jessie forced herself to turn from them, searching wildly for Bliss and Jaya, recalling that the morning had started with the same task. She spotted the pair bolting to their respective posts: Bliss to the top of the tanker behind the cab, and Jaya to the van to ride shotgun.

Ananda?

In the van, she saw, when Jaya threw open the heavily plated door.

She wheeled around looking for Burned Fingers, and spotted the Pixie-bobs pouring down the bottom of the hill, a mass of fur as dark and wide as a mudslide. In seconds they swarmed the tank. Some were crushed but most leaped aboard, covering the camouflage paint with their writhing coats. Jessie saw in a glance there would be no protection from the cats for anyone riding on the outside of the tank or van. And there was no time to regroup.

A brief hope that the Pixie-bobs would cut off the tank crew's sightline—and stop the murderous vehicle—vanished when it churned on without changing course.

She raced toward Burned Fingers, who was studying the tank's approach, yelling, "They'll be on us next."

He raised his hand. "We'll never outrun them," he said evenly.

"We'll never outgun them, either," she shouted.

"Nope, we won't. It's a straight shot for them either way."

Still his words came calmly. And in the midst of her most convulsive fears—of ruthless firepower and voracious cats, whose howls now pierced the air—she remembered how relaxed and cheerful he'd been during the most terrifying moments at the Army of God.

He knows war, she told herself now as she had then. *"I don't care,"* she bellowed, as if he had spoken the words in her head. "I just want to go."

"Our timing is starting to look good," he said.

Good? "How can you—"

"Tell Maul to start driving. Brindle, too. I want both of them in motion."

"Of course." She turned to run, *finally.* He grabbed her arm.

"But tell Maul I don't want this truck moving any faster than you can walk. Then I need you back here, and when I say so, you've got to signal him—and *that's* when he's got to find a way to make this big fat fucker move."

Burned Fingers pounded the back of the tanker; but she was already racing to the cab, ears ringing with the howling, engine roar, and—rising above both—the deafening screams of terrified children.

Chapter Six

Jessie veered immediately from the girls on the gasoline tanker clamoring for help. Harsh as it felt, she had no comfort or hope to offer them, and definitely no weapons to make them feel safe—nothing to thwart the thunderous tank and squalling cats charging at them. She carried only her M-16 and Burned Fingers's mystifying instructions, and couldn't have explained them to herself, much less to the petrified girls reaching for her.

She leaped onto a rusty pipe that served as the cab's running board and smashed her fist on Maul's door so hard the pain startled her.

The big bald man peered out, eyes no more than slits, the whole of his face compressed by tension.

"Go-go-go!" she screamed. Then, before he could close the door, she shouted, "Walking speed. No faster." She'd almost forgot.

Maul nodded, sunlight catching his large dome, and before she could jump down the tanker truck lurched forward.

She weaved in front of it, wounded thigh begging for relief, and dodged the broken radiator grill bearing down on her like a shattered face. She looked up to see Maul mouth-

ing *What the fuck?* and waved him on with a "Don't worry"
he clearly couldn't comprehend.

Brindle opened the van's driver door seconds before she
ran up breathless and bent over. "Go, get out of here."

"Wh-What?" he asked.

"Go!"

Already she was pivoting toward the rolling trailer and
fixing her eyes on the armored tank, with its cannon, flame-
thrower, and machine gun pressing closer, now less than a
half mile away.

It better be good. Whatever Burned Fingers had in mind.

Lungs still heaving, she ran to the rear of the gasoline
tanker, but he had disappeared.

She swore loudly before spying him hanging by one hand
from the underside of the trailer. He clung to the frame like
a monkey, feet braced against the rear axle, free hand furiously turning a steel wheel with three stout spokes.

Fuel seeped from an L-shaped valve right below it. The
trickle quickly grew into a stream, forcing him to twist sideways as gallons spilled out, splattering the ground and mist-
ing his bare back till the pungent gas beaded like sweat; but
he didn't pause until he had it open fully, creating a powerful gusher. Then he pushed himself farther to the side and
dropped to the dusty ground, rolling away from the flood.

He jumped to his feet, chased by the spreading flow, which
formed a broad dark V as the tanker lumbered up the slope.
Jessie, grasping both his plan and its horrendous peril, tried
wiping the gas off his back with the hem of her shirt as they
backpedaled. Failing, she pulled off her ragged cotton tee,
casting aside modesty to dry his skin.

The armored tank, a dark, howling mass of Pixie-bobs
clinging to every available surface—hanging from the
cannon like a drooping sleeve—raced within a thousand
feet. But Burned Fingers never glanced away from the fuel
rippling down the slope, his body bobbing as he continued to
back up. To Jessie, his up and down movement looked like a

man counting down to a cataclysm, a possibility that chilled her to her core. She was frantically pulling on her damp shirt when he turned to her.

"Tell Maul to haul ass." Then he slipped back under the trailer with the ease of a gymnast.

Maul already had his door open. "Haul ass, haul ass!" she yelled, unconsciously echoing Burned Fingers in her escalating panic.

The cab heaved from the sudden acceleration, but not so fast that she couldn't spot the van now a half mile ahead of them.

She sprinted back to see Burned Fingers cut off the fuel, then drop to the dust once more; but this time he scrambled to the spill, pulling out a flint and steel before pausing to look up. The armored tank was tearing across the fuel drenched ground, so close that Jessie could see the wild eyes of the Pixie-bobs.

Burned Fingers kneeled and struck the flint till a fireball bloomed. It raced at the tank, engulfing it in flames twenty, thirty feet high, and spread all the way down the slope, growing hundreds of feet thick in seconds too quick to count.

She felt a surge of relief—and didn't see the flames rising up Burned Fingers's pants until he was rolling on the ground to snuff them. Pained, he jumped to his feet. Both of them backed away from the fire as smoke instantly enveloped them, a thick black shroud spawned by the chance mechanics of wind and warfare.

Jessie glimpsed him wheeling away, covering his eyes, but lost him when the acrid plume forced her own eyes shut. She staggered through the darkness, lungs burning fiercely, finding her way out, only to spot another dense black cloud churning toward her. She bolted from its path and watched it chase the truck.

The howls of the Pixie-bobs grew, and as the tank roared closer she saw a ghastly sight through the flames—screeching cats leaping from the turret and the tank's broad platform, dropping from the cannon like big drips of sizzling candle wax, all of them ablaze and feeding the fire.

Their screams never sounded more human—infants trapped in a boiling inferno—and their dark darting forms could not have looked more tortured. Blinded by the broiling heat, they scurried crazily in the flames, running into the tank and one another. Or they stopped suddenly, like they were frozen by fire, then arched their backs hideously, driving themselves to the tips of their melting toes, as if in water, not flames, stepping once, twice, even three times—a death dance, it seemed—before collapsing and twisting on the gas-soaked ground, spasms bathed in orange and red and blue.

The tank rolled on, a furious, impervious monster shedding a flaming coat, crushing an untold number of the beasts it had borne.

But even witnessing this annihilation didn't prepare her for the shock of seeing the long cannon poke from the receding fire and smoke. She'd thought the tank would burn up or explode, but it kept rolling until she could see all of the turret with its terrifying weapons, and then the entire length of desert camouflage paint that covered every square inch of steel, scorched and sooty but still visible, *still* rolling.

Why had she thought they could stop it? What pathetic hope had led her to believe that an armored tank engineered to roar through the burning oil fields of the Mideast to take Riyadh, Tehran, Baghdad, and Abu Dhabi could possibly have been foiled by a few thousand gallons of fuel splashed on the ground?

You stupid, stupid woman. She hated herself for having fallen victim to such simple-minded optimism. And she hated Burned Fingers for carrying on like he could work grisly miracles against a massive killing machine with nothing more in his goddamn quiver than gas—*gas!*—and his unchartable gumption.

Backing up, she turned to see the truck a hundred yards off, belching oily smoke from the twin stacks that rose like curved horns over the cab, more demonic looking than ever.

The ground shuddered, and she saw the armored tank slowing now that it had left behind the flames and its target was in full view. The truck and everyone on board could be blown into a bubbling cloud any moment. Yet she ran toward them, not wanting to die alone—or to be taken by the crew inside that monstrous weapon.

The armored tank finally halted. Its engine no longer bellowed, and the cries and shouts of the children might have softened. She heard only her harsh breaths and hard footfalls as she gained on the long trailer; the truck was old with a heavy load, the slope unrelenting.

Glancing over her shoulder, she spotted the cannon rising until it appeared to point at the truck. A ribbon of the blackest smoke swept over the turret and then her. Eyes tearing, she spied the trailer's rear ladder and climbed all the way to the top before she could breathe without the harsh tang of gas fumes.

When she looked for Bliss, she saw her daughter on the front of the tanker staring past her, shaking her head, forlorn as death itself.

Then she saw why: the turret was inching left to aim the cannon directly at them. A grim adjustment. In the same glimpse, which left her weakened and sure they'd all be killed, she spotted the flamethrower that Leisha said had been unleashed on Kaisha and her, and knew there were much worse deaths than the quick one promised by the tank.

BOOM. The shot left her ears ringing, and she heard a rocket rip over her head. A streak of heat fine as a hair comb settled on her scalp and made her wince, and a rumble of air came alive on her skin.

Pale gray pillows drifted from the cannon muzzle. A mile or two away an explosion rocked the air, more ravaged earth ripped apart by heat and flames.

The little towhead Cassie cried, but afterward an ominous silence ensued. The cannon dipped without violating this quiet accord, an unseen eye sharpening its aim. But it didn't fire, and Jessie thought they might have been given a warning shot: one over the bow, one over your head, one over just about anything was as much warning as you were likely to get in this life.

She shouted to Bliss, "Stop Maul. Stop him!" She knew she sounded hysterical and was succumbing to one more ruthless hope, but what was the point of pushing on? Suicide? Any plans for defeating the tank had shriveled.

The truck shook as its aged brakes clawed the wheels, but she kept her eyes on the tank. Then she noticed fire and smoke shifting in dying patches behind it, except for a declivity about fifty yards farther downslope where gas had pooled and flames still roasted the air. And everywhere on the blackened ground she saw the smoking ruin of dead cats, the stink of burned fur and flesh following them up the hill.

The rear hatch of the tank opened and a man in a thick vest and helmet rose, exposing no more than his head and shoulders. "Don't move," he yelled, "or we'll burn you to death!"

The same threat she and Burned Fingers had issued at the Army of God, before they burned and killed innumerable acolytes and guards. Odd to hope for compassion in the shadow of that memory; odder still the false equivalencies that insisted on themselves in a crisis.

The van never stopped. But why would the tank crew care? The gasoline tanker was the prize. Once the crew took control of it, they could hunt the van at their leisure. It would run out of fuel soon enough.

We're dead, she thought. She didn't even know where Burned Fingers was.

The last she'd seen of him, he was escaping the dense smoke with her.

She studied the charred ground for his remains, but for all the evidence of him that she found, he might have been vaporized by the fire.

Not quite, but blisters were rising on Burned Fingers's chest, back, legs, and hands, though none proved as painful as a nasty bite from a Pixie-bob. The cat had mauled his leg as he dashed through the spotty flames to the armored tank. P-bobs were dropping left and right but the one that ripped open his calf was on its feet reeling and jerking—all the fur on its back scorched off—when its stubby head banged his leg. Biting from reflex. The worst part was, he didn't dare shoot the half-baked bastard for fear of alerting the tank crew. He hated the cats, even their name: *Pixie-bobs?* Made them sound like fucking stuffies, a cute toy he might have given his kid before his kid was murdered—*by Army assholes with tanks.* And they didn't just kill him, which would have been kind by comparison.

He had hoped the old Abrams would have been compromised enough for the smoke and flames to asphyxiate or cook the crew—or blow up the whole jury-rigged beast. *Some* kind of malfunction. He had reason to hope: the electronics in these relics were long dead, and they rolled along mostly on the dark genius of Alliance mechanics and the verve of crews that varied in number from one to four, plus a messenger dog.

But when he'd seen the tank survive the wilting flames, he gave up any faith in a malfunction and made his dash, scaling the armor over the top of the treads by pulling himself up on the bars that enclosed the cargo area near the back of the turret. An approach from directly behind risked less exposure, but only the uninitiated attempted to mount a moving M1 from the rear—and they tried it only once: the broad stream of exhaust from the huge engine reached 1,700 degrees.

Now he hunkered down in the cargo area, finding little to crowd him. Little to hide him, either, but immensely pleased that in spite of his best efforts, the tank hadn't been destroyed; taking control of it would be an unexpected coup, though it wouldn't be the first one he'd hijacked: in the final days of the defeated rebellion, he seized that vintage World War II tank, drove it down Bay Street in Baltimore, and turned it on murderous soldiers who were trying to exterminate the last of the resistance.

But the Abrams was the finest combat beast in its time. *Still is,* he reminded himself, pulse thickening when the tank commander opened the hatch and threatened to burn to death everyone on the truck.

Burned Fingers rose up till he could see the back of the guy's head above the upper reach of the hatch door. He hoped the engine idle would cover his advance on the commander, and that the tank's armor—a foot of solid steel in places—would silence his movements to anyone inside. He also had to hope that some kid on the tanker truck wouldn't give him away by staring or pointing to him. A lot to hope for.

He had his sawed-off in hand but didn't want to take out the commander from back here because someone inside would drag the guy's body down below and seal the hatch—and any hope of taking over the Abrams would disappear faster than hooch at a card game.

Eyeing any potential source of noise, he advanced on his elbows in a classic combat crawl, lifting his arms deftly, then settling them down smoothly; the same with his legs, driving forward by applying even pressure on his knees, acutely aware of the friendly eyes on him. Those kids were a savvy lot, but it still made his *skin* crawl to depend on them.

He moved about halfway across the turret. Four more feet to go. But fear—and he valued it for keeping him alive—could turn even the shortest distance into a horror.

The commander was ordering everyone off the gasoline tanker.

Play along. Do like he says. Make him keep his goddamn eyes on you.

A couple feet more and he'd be ready to take him, but this was where it could get sketchy. He had to silently shift the sawed-off to his left hand, not his preferred mode, so he could use his right to unsheathe the knife that he borrowed to replace the one he'd planted in that bastard's back. He'd learned that using a knife in close quarters could get better results than a gun, which always offered the promise of a less gruesome exit from this life.

Slowly—*always* slowly—he climbed into a crouch, feeling every hard year of his life, and guessing the commander would have youth on him. Damn few didn't.

He looked past him to see Jessie and Bliss climbing down from the top of the trailer. Maul and Erik from the cab. None of them rushing or stalling. Just doing what they were told and keeping their eyes off him. But in a few seconds he'd need their help, and then he wanted them running as hard as they could.

After a full, deliberate intake of breath, he launched himself forward, wrapping his left arm with the sawed-off around the commander's head and slicing off his helmet with no regard for his neck or face.

As he'd figured, the guy tried to grab the sawed-off—a powerful lure. Burned Fingers used the momentary distraction to plunge the full length of the blade into his cheek, using a sidearm motion to drive the tip out the other side of his face. Then he pulled the knife into the thick muscle wrapped around the hinge joint in the back of his mouth, opening a three-inch gash in his cheeks, enough to glimpse the commander's filleted tongue, the top half of which hung by a mere quarter inch of hemorrhaging tissue.

Now the commander's hands flew to his face, and Burned Fingers flicked aside his sawed-off. It clattered on the deck of the turret close to them, but given the guy's circumstances and condition, it might as well have been a mile.

He sawed into the joint with a single forceful motion, sinking the blade deeply into bone before shouting into the tank, "Anyone comes near him, I'll kill him and you."

The commander struggled, squirmed, and groaned horrifically, forceful testimony for his crew—if he had one.

Burned Fingers saw Jessie and Bliss racing toward him, the girl with her shotgun. He spoke into the commander's ear. "You're alive 'cause I want you alive. I want you dead, you're dead. *How many men down there?* Show me fingers. Don't even try to talk, fucker."

Nothing but more moans and frantic struggle.

"Show me! Are you fucking crazy?"

The commander still offered no response. Burned Fingers guessed that meant more below. One more? Three? He sawed deeper into his mouth, trying to roust an answer, yet knowing the guy might raise any number of fingers at this point. But he tried one more time anyway, "Tell me or I'll cut your fucking head off. *How many?*"

When all the commander did was claw at his knife hand, Burned Fingers cranked the blade like he was coring an apple of old, gouging out gum and molars—a chunk of meaty jaw thick enough to make the guy gag.

Useless fuck. He had heard some of his old marauders say that they didn't feel anything when they killed. Even kids. "Not a fucking thing," in the blunt words of Anvil, who used to drive for him. But Burned Fingers felt plenty when he killed a man—an intractable desire for vengeance. What he didn't feel was another guy's pain. Why would he ever want to? He had plenty of his own.

Bliss scaled the front of the tank, her shotgun aimed at the hatch.

Good work.

"We're dropping a gas bomb down there if you don't shout out your number *now*," he yelled into the hole, catching sight of the swelling blood puddle below them.

He had no gas bombs—they were rolling away in the van—but even if the commander wriggled free somehow, he wouldn't be saying much.

"I'm dragging this asshole out," he said to Bliss. "Get your gun aimed right in there. Don't let up. That's it . . . Jessie," she was pulling herself onto the tank, Maul a few steps behind, "exterminate the bastards if they try to get out. Keep them in there; I want to burn them to death."

He looked down: dim shadows, no sign of life, save the blood still pooling. But Burned Fingers didn't believe the guy was alone. The Alliance wouldn't risk it. Even with a tank, something could always go wrong, and it had: him.

"This is your last chance," he shouted. "Push your goddamn guns out where we can see them or I swear I'll fry every last one of you to death."

Jessie aimed her M-16 into the tank, ready to fire. The commander's legs disappeared beside her as he dragged him out of the hatch. From the corner of her eye she saw him cut the man's throat and dump him on the deck of the turret.

Executing the wounded, she said to herself, which was what he'd done so reflexively at the Army of God when he'd put a bullet into each of their heads.

She forced herself to remember that the commander was a killer, a butcher, really, just like any other men who might be down below. They had only one purpose out here: to kill anyone trying to save prepubertal girls from abduction and systematic rape, which could lead to their deaths before many of them reached their mid-teens. And those actions were far more abominable than the pain exacted by Burned Fingers, inconceivable as that seemed when the commander's legs spasmed and his carotid artery poured the last of his life onto the turret.

Executing the wounded, not the innocent. Eden would have done it, too. So would I, she realized.

Burned Fingers grabbed her shirt. "Bear with me," he whispered, cutting off a length of her fumy tee and then sparking the fabric.

It caught quickly, and he yelled, "Here comes the bomb," and dropped the flaming swatch into the tank.

A powerful explosion followed almost instantly. It rocked the Abrams violently and sent Burned Fingers sprawling next to the dead commander. She and Bliss managed to back up and stay on their feet, but Maul stumbled, tripped, and fell off the front of the tank.

Smoke and flames shot from the open hatch, and Jessie yelled, "Get off, get off!" while she and Bliss scrambled and jumped.

Burned Fingers landed near them as smoke issued from around the turret, floating up in a dark circle; but her fear that the tank would blow up and shred them with steely fragments didn't materialize.

"Guess they overreacted." Burned Fingers, bare chest bathed in the commander's blood, watched the smoke ring drift apart.

Jessie caught her breath. "They?" she asked.

"Whoever set off the bomb or rocket or whatever they had rigged. I thought I could bluff them and that the second they saw fire they'd try to tear the hell out of there. I didn't figure on a suicide bomber taking out the tank and whatever ammo we might have found."

"Is there any chance someone could still be alive?" Bliss asked, raising her shotgun. "In some bomb-proof compartment or something?"

"You felt it. You heard it," Burned Fingers said. "Knocked me down and him right off the tank." He nodded at Maul. "I don't think I'm going to be seeing much more than a bunch of mangled metal when I get down in there."

It didn't take long for the air to clear, or for Burned Fingers, armed with his sawed-off, to find the remains of two bodies in the tank. "But no dog," he said, climbing out of the hatch, "and I looked real carefully through that mess. They must have released him before coming after us, so we've got to figure the Alliance knows we're here, or will soon enough."

"How can you be so sure they even had one?" Bliss asked, looking up at him on the tank.

He flipped a singed but well-chewed bone down to her. Human tibia, Jessie recognized at once.

"Because even the Alliance isn't eating their own—yet."

"Any ammo at all?" she asked him.

"Nope. They had one extra rocket, and I think that's what they used to blow themselves up." His eyes wandered the length of the tank. He shook his head. "Sure would have been a game-changer."

"Yeah," Bliss said wistfully. "How's our gas?"

"We've got plenty," he said, spurred from his reverie. "Tanker holds nine thousand gallons. I'm guessing we lost a couple thousand, that's all. But it worked out all right, didn't it?" He smiled, and his eyes appeared to land on exhausted flames licking the slope a few hundred yards away.

Jessie caught his self-congratulatory tone but didn't bedgudge him: he'd earned the right to take credit. "Nice job," she said.

Scavenging time. She grabbed the tank commander's helmet and Kevlar vest and handed them to Teresa. Burned Fingers had already claimed the man's bloody shirt.

The van was heading back; Brindle must have been checking behind him.

"Can they get the tank going again?" she asked Burned Fingers, who jumped down. "Maybe we should try to make sure they don't."

He dusted off his hands. "There's nothing we have that could match what went off in there. Nothing even close. Be a waste of gunpowder."

"What about the machine gun?" she asked.

"Ammo's all gone. Like I said, everything was set to blow. But we'll take the gun anyway. You never know. And don't worry about the tank. They'd need General Dynamics to get it moving again."

Now there was a name she hadn't heard in years. "What about tearing it down so they can't use it for parts?"

"Don't have those kind of tools, and we don't have the time. Best thing we can do is put some distance between them and us. This thing," he patted the massive tread, almost affectionately, she thought, "has a range close to three hundred miles, so I'm guessing we have a decent enough head start. There's just no telling what else they've got. I never could get close to the place, so I never figured them for anything like an Abrams. It makes you wonder."

I'd rather not. But she couldn't keep herself from the fear of another tank coming after them. She wouldn't say anything about it, though. Then she realized it wouldn't make a damn bit of difference if she did: no one on the caravan, not even little Cassie, on Ananda's shoulder for a round of chicken fights with the other kids, could possibly avoid it.

Esau watched Hunt awaken slowly. Light shined through a louvered window, casting sharp rectangular shadows on his master's bed. A stained blue blanket with frayed edges lay by Hunt's side, leaving his legs and bottom uncovered.

Above him hung a dusty white fan, base separating from the cracked ceiling. The lone remaining blade hadn't moved since the final blackout—long before Esau was born on the border of the Great American Desert, a land decimated by fire, drought, and death.

Scum crusted his master's lips and crowded the corners of his mouth, but most of his face was bandaged. So was his back, chest, one of his legs, and both of his hands. The cloth was gray and thin from many hand washings, and bore the dark memories of earlier wounds like a palimpsest.

Esau, wearing only a darkly stained skirt sewn from the worn-out gowns of True Believers, rose from his vigil by the window. "Do you want more water?" he asked softly. Hunt didn't make him say "sire" or "my lord" when he addressed him, unlike most of the men he served.

Hunt nodded, and Esau hurried to hold the heavy jug to his lips. He had seen his master push water away; once, Hunt shocked him by spitting it out, whispering to himself that it tasted terrible, "like chemicals."

Even more astounding, he had blamed the water for the tumors, which was a sacrilege because everybody knew that most tumors were the devil's deadly blight. Then Hunt stared at him, as if to command silence about his heresy. But he needn't have; Esau never would have breathed a word to anyone. A slave who betrayed his master always burned, regardless of the fate assigned to the one he served.

But today Hunt drank the water thirstily and said nothing

of the tumors that afflicted so many. They grew from torsos, some so large they looked like angry fists trying to punch their way out of a back or belly to pummel the world.

The rheumy-eyed doctor cut out a small number of them. Two of the Elders had endured such operations; one of them survived. And His Piety had braved the removal of a dark one from his chest only weeks ago. But the prophet himself exorcised the tumors in the chapel if they turned red as boils and oozed dark, odiferous liquid—true signs of demonic possession.

Only His Piety could tell if Satan had invaded a body, and it was a certain sign of the Devil's grip if the believer screamed when the sacred sword cut him. Or if he bled to death.

Everyone witnessed the exorcism, and everyone knew Satan's devious role, even the lowliest slaves in the fields. So his master *must* know. Why would he blame the water when Satan hid everywhere?

Esau checked himself every night for tumors, then gave thanks to God the Father and God the Son for another day without sickness.

"What happened to me?" Hunt asked.

Esau fell to his knees by the bed, alarmed at how lost his master sounded. *Don't die.* So great was his fear of losing him that he took Hunt's hand, moistening his bandage with his tears. Hunt was good to him, fed him well; sometimes he even slipped him meat so he wouldn't weaken and end up on the water wheel, like other slaves who were then beaten and whipped and had their heads chopped off.

He had suffered terrible masters. When Hunt left the base, he had served many men; most cared little for his happiness, though some were as kind as Hunt when it served their most intimate interests—when they reached under his skirt or signaled him to his knees.

But most demanded nothing of him in this regard, and used his lean strength for eighteen, twenty hours a day to drag supplies around the huge fortress, dig holes, or rebuild walls defeated by tornados, sudden windstorms, or drenching downpours. Or by the strange orange clouds that exploded and sent powerful gusts—and sometimes flames—across the land. Those clouds were always a sign of evil.

In a world so rife with sin and early death, he was lucky to have a master who honored his supple touch and willingness to please, scarcely believing that men such as he once paraded their iniquity for all to see. Sin, Hunt often told him, must be private and spoken of to no one. He compared it to a contagious disease that must be quarantined, lest it spread. Confession, his master also said, was a denial of God's complete knowledge of our every thought, a practice of Papists, of which few—thanks be to the Father and Son—survived.

His Piety, who would have been the one to hear such confessions, had offered Esau the same stern commandment: "Confess only to God. Speak of sin to no man, if you want forgiveness from the Almighty."

Esau was twenty-two, and could expect to live a long life—another fifteen, twenty years if he was fortunate and served his master faithfully. Hunt was much older, thirty at least, and his master's interest in his slave's body was already lessening.

Maybe he makes slaves wherever he goes. As long as they're not females. Wicca was the worst way to die. Hallucinations and fevers, murders and suicides. Worse even than the water wheel.

"I asked what happened to me," Hunt said.

"You fell in the chapel, right in front of His Piety. They took you to the doctor. He worked on you for three hours. How do you feel?"

Hunt ignored his query. "When was this?"

"Three days ago. You have been sleeping most of the time. I've given you water twice."

"Water," he repeated ruefully. Then he asked for his radio.

Esau hurried to a shelf below the window, carefully carrying an old solar powered Sony to Hunt's bed. It was his master's most prized possession, one of the few on the base. Maybe in the world.

"Keep it low," Hunt said.

Esau nodded, guessing his master's head hurt horribly from all the bites and scratches.

He pushed a button on the smooth metal surface, and a tiny green light brightened. A second later a man's voice reached them: " . . . House has been evacuated. The President is hunted. The White House has been evacuated. The President is hunted." The same words over and over, year after year.

But it soothed his master to listen to this man from another world. He turned on the radio whenever he returned. But how did the voice survive? *By a miracle?* Or was solar power also replaying the message from up in the sky, where satellites were said to circle round and round the globe in endless orbits for all of time?

Months ago he'd watched Hunt press a different button, "Scanning the spectrum," he called it.

"What are you looking for?" Esau had asked.

Hunt stared at him in a new way, and he felt a threat as real as swords and fire. But then his master said, "Radio Tierra."

Esau nodded, never asking what Radio Tierra was; and Hunt never told him or searched the spectrum again in his presence.

Now he asked him to shut it off, and Esau carried it back to the place on the shelf where the sun shined the longest.

When he tried to return to his master's side, Hunt waved him away. Esau retreated to his wooden stool by the window, sitting for only a moment before a hard knock rushed him to the door. Before he opened it, he looked at Hunt, who moved his hand weakly in approval.

His Piety swept past Esau without any acknowledgment, not even a secret one. His Piety often ignored him when others were about. An Elder waited in the hall holding something by his side. From the strain on his face, it must have been heavy; but Esau could see little of it at a glance, and didn't dare stare.

Turning, he saw His Piety standing over his master, studying him, not speaking.

Hunt nodded to show the prophet respect. His Piety remained silent, then waved to the Elder, who entered, shocking Esau with his burden.

"You have survived a great trial for a most sacred reason," His Piety announced to Hunt. "The most sacred reason of all for a man of this life. You must find the demon, and you must tear it from the arms of the heathens any way you can. There is no greater glory to God than to bring the two-headed beast back to us, for we are the ones endowed by heaven with the power to destroy it forevermore. But if you don't return with the beast of hell, this will be your last mission."

His Piety glanced at the Elder, who handed him an old and grossly chipped army ammo case. His Piety held it out, but turned his head away, as if the dented green box radiated evil, even in his most blessed hands.

Hunt, weak as he was, tried to pull away; and Esau had to restrain himself from rushing to his master's aid.

Without looking down, His Piety unbuckled a metal clamp, setting off a sharp metallic ring. He reached out his hand, and the Elder laid a knife from the sacristy across his palm. The blade was silvery like the chapel sword. Carefully, His Piety opened the lid, and Esau saw sunlight passing above the open case, dark dust whirling in the air. The sight made him feel as weak as his wounded master.

Hunt turned away. His Piety warned him not to. "*You* must see this." The prophet also lowered his eyes to the case, using the knife's shiny surface to scoop up a soft black mound. He executed this step precisely, then spilled the ash back into the case slowly. The sunlight stirred with dark motes, and Esau feared that the witch's remains were slinking into the room.

"There can be no other way, Soul Hunter. I will be forced

to have you covered with the ashes of witches, all of you by all of them, and then they will be burned again with you. There will be no salvation. There cannot be. I'm sure you understand that."

His Piety spoke with the weariness of a prophet who bore the responsibilities of this life and the next.

"But we are generous," he went on, "and we want you to succeed. *I* want you to succeed. I want you to have all the glories of heaven. We will make sure you have the tools you need to bring back the demon. We will even let you give them the gas, if they'll give us back the beast. They will have a choice, and so will you: heaven or hell."

"The gas?" Hunt asked in a husky voice. "You would give them the gas?" He spoke with his eyes still darting from the witches' ashes, as if to escape their evil claim. His Piety snapped the case closed.

"To get the demon, you will tell them the gas is theirs and that they are free to leave. The heathens are heading to the Bloodlands, that much is clear, though they cannot know what the desert holds for them, and there is nowhere to hide. We are alerting our allies. They will take the tanker after the demon is ours. We offer a great reward for the gas, but none so great as the one you will receive when you return with that beast of hell."

"Will I have the tank to help me?"

"The tank engaged them and failed," His Piety said matter-of-factly, as if he would not dwell on this. But Esau was astonished. *Failed? The tank?*

Then His Piety smiled and leaned closer to Hunt. "We will have the holiest of ceremonies planned for your return with the demon. Our prayers and hosannas will be heard in heaven, and the screams of the demon will shake the earth for days and days—and echo in hell for all eternity. The demon's agony will warn Satan's creatures of the fate they'll share if they should rise from the flames."

His Piety handed the ammo case back to the Elder, pausing before returning his attention to Hunt. "Please don't

make me condemn you to the flames. An eternity in hell."
He shook his head. "You would never know the infinite
glory the Lord bestows on all True Believers. But if you
bring back the demon," his words brightened, as if infused
with the Spirit, "all of paradise will be yours for all of time."

Esau lowered his gaze when His Piety and the Elder left.
He closed the door and took a steadying breath before turning back to Hunt.

His master looked past him numbly, seemingly battered
by what he'd heard. He swatted feebly at the dark motes still
stirring above him.

Then Esau saw his master's eyes lock on the radio, and
though Hunt made no sound when he moved his lips, Esau
read them easily because he'd heard the words so many
times: "The White House is evacuated. The President is
hunted."

Chapter Seven

Augustus stepped carefully around the charred remains and rubble, as if fearing to desecrate the dead. Leisha and Kaisha trailed a few feet behind, still clothed in Burned Fingers's shirt. Everyone else on the caravan waited back by the truck out of respect for the lone survivors of the religious settlement.

No one spoke. The younger girls looked especially haunted as they watched. Even the babies in the arms of the three blind girls were quiet. A quick count showed more than seventy African-Americans killed, including scores of women and children. Nothing moved but the hearts of the aggrieved.

Everyone had agreed that Augustus's actions at the Army of God earned him and his children the right to stay with the caravan and settle in the North, but not everyone agreed to stop and let them pray over the massacre. Burned Fingers had been outspoken in urging them all to keep going, but Jessie shook her head once and nothing more was said. They would grant Augustus and his girls time for their sorrow.

The missionary's wife—the girls' mother—lay among the murdered, flames having rendered her indistinguishable from the others. Jessie felt their loss. Less than a month ago

Burned Fingers and his marauders had massacred almost all the adults and most of the children at her camp. Seeing the slaughter now filled her with memories of Eden so sudden that her legs weakened. She lowered her eyes, though she found no relief in the armored tank tracks. The steel tread had chewed up the earth and spit up chunks of hard-packed dirt everywhere she looked. Pitifully easy to imagine the beast backing up, the two-man crew coolly repositioning the flamethrower and cannon, coldly impervious to those who must have pleaded or prayed or screamed, caring only for the blunt efficiency of industrial death.

Raising her gaze from the tracks of the killers to the butchery they'd left behind expunged the last tremors of revulsion that lingered from Burned Fingers's merciless slaying of the tank commander. Even this many years after the collapse, Jessie sometimes wished for a world simple enough to condemn violence, to appraise it rationally and from a cosseting distance; but the final opportunity for that had been squandered—along with the hope of survival for most of humanity—only a few generations ago. From a historical standpoint, the collapse came in a blink after a long slow buildup of toxic waste in the sky, land, and water. But once the breakdown began it proceeded at a ferocious pace, an insatiable animal rising from the filth with a maw colossal enough to eat the earth. With its arrival every pretense of peace vanished, and what remained of the world and humanity was plundered by the rapacious and profane.

Unlike her own camp, Augustus's had no wall to hide the horror, to offer even the illusion of resistance in the aftermath of murder. With agonizing ease, she saw that the smoke that had first signaled the slaughter was but a hazy reflection of the sharply defined terror below.

She expected the air to shift, to carry the acrid rot to her, as it had when she'd seen those black clouds boiling from a ridge only a few days ago. But it didn't. At this distance the air was as unmoving as death itself, though she guessed Augustus and the twins were drowning in the carnage, not only the odor and the shattering proximity of death, but the utter absence of sound where children had once played and adults might have broken the stillness with laughter or the ringing promise of prayer.

Every murmur they ever made to their god had perished. She could almost hear their pleas as she stared at their ruin, scarcely believing that even the missionary would say this massacre of innocents was according to His plan. But her belief in the Kingdom of God and all His saints—always *His, His, His*—had died in her early twenties, when evidence of heavenly indifference could not have been greater—or more brutal—for *His* stillness. She had found her faith—and no little comfort—in faith's weighty absence.

Augustus walked to the center of the devastation and dropped to his knees, openly bereaved.

His girls did not stray from the periphery, holding each other as they, too, lowered themselves to the scorched earth. A wail rose from the tear-streaked twins, enveloping all who watched, a keening so acute it twisted Jessie's gut, an ache so deep it could have been a volvulus.

Without Jessie noticing, Bliss and Ananda took her in their arms to form a tight huddle. This is what she believed in, the primal comfort and sanctity of family.

Augustus climbed to his feet, weary in the shoulders, yet he raised his hands to the sky, and though Jessie could not hear his words—or even if he spoke—she knew he was beseeching his god for the reason He had forsaken his kin. The man could have been a Canaanite, a revenant of the Old Testament imploring the Lord to end the land's lingering curse.

Jessie pulled her girls so close she could hear their breathing, and in this profound physical intimacy she knew that when children die, we murder god. We must. We become executioners—reluctant or otherwise—of our most tended delusions.

Augustus's hands dropped to his sides and he walked among the dead whom he'd loved so long. He appeared barely sentient, but bent over and picked up a metal cross.

A foot long at least. Maybe the cross for the steeple of the church he'd said they planned to build.

He shook his head, flipping the relic aside. She heard the weight strike the earth, and saw him turn from the crown of ashy dust that rose in his wake. After walking several steps he surprised her by retrieving it, brushing it off with his big hands. He looked at his daughters, and their eyes met his, climbing higher when he lifted the cross above his head and began to turn slowly in a circle, blessing the fallen with a prayer that strengthened with every step. His face glimmered with tears in the dusky light, and he didn't stop moving till he faced his girls again. They rushed to him, and he embraced them gently, their burns so recently dressed.

Behind their backs, which faced the caravaners, he held the cross like a shield.

The three of them walked back, holding one another closely.

"I wish we could give them a proper burial," Augustus said. Before Burned Fingers could object, he added, "But I know we can't. You don't sacrifice the living to honor the dead."

"Is that in the Bible?" Ananda asked him.

"Not that I know of," Augustus said. "But it's in here," he tapped right above his heart, "so I know it's true."

"You gave them a lot," Jessie told him gently. He looked at the cross he still carried but said nothing.

She cleared her throat. "You have a well, right?" she asked.

He led them to the far side of the settlement, where they found more dead crowding a hand pump that never could have saved them. She, Augustus, and Burned Fingers took turns on the long iron handle until every jug, jerrican, and stomach was full.

"It's just like when it rained," Ananda said quietly as they walked back, raising the specter of happier times when everyone in their camp had danced in the rare downpours and drank all they could, when clouds brought holidays from sun and grit and thirst.

Jaya and Erik formed a makeshift table from a long board they'd scavenged from the debris, setting it up so the truck blocked the view of the desolation. Jessie glanced at Augustus and his girls, and felt horrible about having to feed the caravan so close to the source of their grief. But if they didn't have dinner now, they'd have to eat in the dark—and risk luring all kinds of predators.

Brindle, Gilly, Bella, and Imagi loaded the table with two crates of food, one that had yet to be opened. Imagi drummed the board and clapped happily, and Jessie couldn't help wondering if her Down syndrome, in this world, was actually a blessing.

"I d-don't kn-know what th-this s-s-stuff is," Brindle announced after prying open the sealed crate. "Some k-kind of m-m-mystery m-meat. B-But it's b-b-been smoked, and it s-smells ok-ay."

Probably more lizard, Jessie thought. Or some kind of reptile.

The flavor came back to her slowly; more than twenty years had passed since she'd tasted it. "Chicken?" she exclaimed. She stared at the knife she used for eating. "I don't believe it."

"It's really *good*," Ananda said, putting aside a book of letters that she and Burned Fingers had found in an abandoned house not long after her abduction. A father had written them to his daughter on her birthday about the big events of her life in the past twelve months. But in the last letter—before all the blank pages—he said there were "problems" in the country.

Ananda loved to reread them, even though they bored holes in her heart with their portrayal of a world filled with orchards, movies, soccer games, dances on a real stage, summer concerts in a grassy park—so many wonders— horses, skiing, *snow!*—that she'd spent days daydreaming about them all.

But right now not even the sweetest heartache could compete with the taste of chicken. She'd never eaten fowl, though her mother had taught them about grouse so slow "you could hunt them with a rock," and pheasants so pretty that people spent lifetimes painting pictures of them. Where *are* those pictures? Ananda wondered. What happened to them all?

And once, there had been geese and wild turkeys and dozens of species of ducks. Solana, sitting a few feet away and still recovering from deep machete wounds inflicted by a marauder, had drawn all kinds of birds in the dust for one of the camp's history and science classes; after the collapse, Ananda's mother said the two subjects never should be taught separately again. Solana was her mom's closest friend, an auntie to Ananda and Bliss.

The pretty, oval-faced woman sat across from Burned Fingers, long black hair falling over her back and shoulders, hiding most of the fat red scars. She had never spoken to him. Neither had Maureen and Keffer Gibbs, whose three children also had survived. Ananda watched Solana chew slowly, savoring her food. So were many others.

Jessie also noticed the rare pleasure people took in eating, even Callabra, the strong sixteen-year-old whose tongue had been taken by the beastly men at the Army of God. Jessie suspected that for the adults, it wasn't simply because the meat was immensely flavorful, especially compared to lizard loins. It was knowing that chicken actually existed somewhere.

Hannah confirmed her suspicion by asking Burned Fingers where the Army of God had gotten the meat. At his insistence, they'd taken considerable risks to abscond with all the food they could find at the fortress.

"Not sure," he told the gray-haired nurse, who kept a six-inch steel spike hidden in her thick braid. "Those crazies were dealing with lots of traders, and I heard some of them came all the way down from New England and what use to be Canada. Look," he turned to the others, "I hate to break this up but we've *got* to get moving."

Gilly and Bella, best friends since early childhood, asked

if they could take their portions onto the truck so they could make the meat last even longer.

"Sure, fine, eat on the go," Burned Fingers said. "Used to be America's favorite pastime."

"It was?" Gilly asked, stunned.

Jessie watched him spring to his feet without answering the girl's question, though he was quick to nod approval at Brindle and Jaya for immediately packing up the food crates; and he offered Erik a "Good move!" when the young man loaded the scavenged board onto the roof of the van.

The trailer rumbled when Maul fired up the truck engine; Jessie felt it all the way through her body as she perched on the walkway atop the gasoline tanker, once more studying the land they were leaving.

They followed the van up the slope, using heavy ramps to negotiate sudden eruptions or erosions of the road. They reached the crest with just enough light to give them the expansive view promised by arduous days of climbing out of a deep Appalachian valley.

All around them the air looked smoky, like the namesake mountains themselves. To the east they spied sheered-off peaks, blown up and bulldozed apart for the last veins of coal in North America. Entire mountaintops were blasted open so more 300-million-year-old fuel could be torn from the earth and burned into the corrupted sky, adding gigatons of carbon to the greenhouse gases widely known to have been heating up the planet. The crimes against nature—against humankind's own best interests—were staggering to Jessie, inconceivable, and for what? To eke out a few more decades of extortionate profits for a self-immolating economic and industrial system?

She noticed most of the caravaners staring at the scarred mountains, criminal evidence that would last eons—and the dismal legacy of the most reviled generations in history. Little wonder mobs hunted down and viciously executed aging CEOs and political leaders, then targeted media sycophants and phony populists who'd played their fellow citizens for fools—and paid dearly for their duplicity. Or that the graveyards of the wealthy were defiled, bodies exhumed in spasms of hatred. Nothing remained sacred. Lavish mausoleums, gold-plated banks, and marble-halled trading houses were all defaced with the rebellion's loudest cry: KILL THE 1%$!, red-painted graffiti that spoke dozens of languages as it traveled the world wielding its vengeance.

Ananda took her mother's arm, asking, "Are those lakes?"

"Sludge ponds," Burned Fingers answered. "Must be solid poison by now. Let's hope it doesn't get windy."

"Ponds?" Jessie said. "They look like the Great Lakes of Death."

Below them, lost in the haze about twenty miles away, lay the border of the Great American Desert, endless and mostly flat, once home to tens of millions of bison, dozens of native grasses, an uncountable number of songbirds, and more than thirty Native American tribes.

After exterminating most of the flora, fauna, and First Nation's people, American settlers turned it into one of the most productive agricultural regions in the world—by the short measure of monoculture. But temperatures rose disproportionately higher in the country's interior, a jump long predicted by climate scientists, and roundly denounced by farm-belt politicians and the Ph.D.'s they persuaded with all the perks of wealth. Their collective refusal to acknowledge the region's decline continued even as the Great Plains turned to desert, a despoilment accelerated by a finding long reported by hydrologists: the twentieth century was anomalously moist in much of the Midwest and western U.S.

When climate chaos and higher temps were added to the volatile mix of a rejiggered environment and drier conditions, the Great Plains agricultural bubble burst.

The reign of wheat, corn, soybeans, and hogs proved predictably brief, from Jessie's perspective as a wildlife biologist. The yardstick of millennia no longer applied when the calculus included humanity's impact on the infinite interlocking of all life.

"I'm thinking we should pass on lighting a torch," Burned Fingers said to her. "What do you think?"

He wasn't really asking, just reaffirming their co-leadership after taking full command to stop the tank. She appreciated the impulse and nodded. Who knew what was lurking out there?

The Gibbses had guard duty tonight. Jessie handed Keffer her M–16. His wife, Maureen, an accomplished gunner in her own right, would work the second half of the shift. Jessie reminded him to watch for panther packs.

"I'm still worried about the Pixie-bobs." He brushed light hair out of his face, and she remembered finding the Gibbses and their three children playing possum under the dead bodies of their compatriots the morning after the camp had been attacked.

"We should be leaving the P-bobs behind," she told him. "They're more mountain animals. The panthers roam a lot farther."

"I'm so sick of cats," Keffer said.

"You and me both."

"You see where little Cassie found herself a Pixie-bob kitten?"

"What?" Jessie blurted.

"Yeah, and she's planning on keeping it."

Not going to happen. Jessie marched right over to the truck and found the towhead at the center of a group of girls gathering under the trailer.

"Hand over the cat," she ordered.

"Mom! It's so cute," Ananda protested. Teresa and M-girl glared at her.

Pick your battles carefully, Jessie warned herself. What was she going to do anyway? Wring its little neck in front of them?

Cassie bent over her kitten protectively.

"May I see it?" Jessie asked.

"Sure." Cassie smiled, lifting it up proudly.

Yes, a soft, furry kitten—and to Jessie's eyes, evil looking. "Where'd you find it?" she asked.

"Wandering around. I think you killed its mama," Cassie said darkly.

"Before its mama could kill us," Jessie could not refrain from saying.

"But we can show it a different way to be," the girl insisted.

"How are the dogs taking it?" Jessie asked the group. Now that she'd seen the kitten, she realized that Hansel and Razzo had been ornery of late. It galled her to find that the hounds had known about the Pixie-bob before she did. But how could they *not* be aware of a mortal enemy, in the most exact sense of the term?

"Not real well," Ananda said. "I think they want to kill it."

At least they've got their priorities straight. "So what are you planning to do with it?" Jessie asked Cassie in as calm a voice as she could manage.

"Protect it," the child said emphatically. "Just till it gets older. Then it can take care of itself."

"That's an understatement."

"And it'll still be nice to us," Cassie said. "You'll see."

You're never going to win this one, Jessie told herself. Everyone adored little Cassie. The girl's mother had been murdered during an attack on their camp down near the Gulf Coast, and her father was gunned down trying to take control of the gasoline tanker at the Army of God. She was everybody's favorite orphan, especially Maul's; the big truck driver's own daughter had been killed, and Cassie was the only child of his closest friend.

"Let's see how it goes," Jessie said, leaving herself a small opening. "I want everyone to bed down."

Cassie nodded, eager to snuggle with her kitty. Jessie reminded herself that not too long ago Pixie-bobs were house cats.

Till they got a taste for wild living—and people.

In the morning, Jessie found Maureen sleeping on her watch. She nudged her, and Keffer's wife flushed as red as her hair, apologizing profusely before adding quickly, "But there's no excuse. I know that. Did anything happen?"

Jessie shook her head and walked away with her automatic rifle, thinking that Maureen, with more kids than anyone else, might be too worn-out for guard duty; no matter how sharp her aim, she was useless if she was too tired to stay awake.

The caravan started winding down to the desert, brakes screeching murderously on both the tanker truck and van.

"If we can make it down without losing control of this thing," Maul said, climbing into the cab after a short break, "we should be set for a long way."

His words spooked Jessie, leaving her to imagine the truck barreling down the hill without brakes, children clinging desperately to the struts and ladders. But by mid-afternoon the worst of her immediate fears hadn't materialized, and she accepted that the truck's mechanics—whoever they were—had done a credible job of keeping the decrepit look-ing vehicle in reasonable operating condition.

Now they were heading down the last stretch of uninter-rupted roadway. Without question, they'd covered more dis-tance than on any other day.

When the slope gentled and Maul braked, Jessie grasped the enormity of the journey ahead. Except for rolling hills, the horizon looked unbroken for a thousand miles, and ev-erywhere she gazed she saw heat shimmers, so many it was as if she had a visual disorder.

Bella and Gilly, the first as light-haired as the second was dark, jumped from the tanker, scrambling to uncover a stub they saw sticking through the dust.

Burned Fingers ordered them to freeze, warning that the stub could be hiding a land mine.

But sometimes a stub is just a stub, Jessie said to herself after he found that it formed the top of a barbed wire fence post.

And who would want to waste mines out here?

All the girls began to uncover posts. It quickly became a game as they raced farther and farther afield.

Burned Fingers eyed the buried fencing and said, "I guess the oceans aren't the only things rising."

"This is the same thing that happened in the Dust Bowl." Jessie stooped to scoop away soil, unearthing the top of a tumbleweed. "These things would roll into a fence, and the more dust they caught, the more they'd block."

She slapped the sandy soil from her hands and stood. "And then, a century later, it started happening again. Miles of fencing would go under in a few years." She stared at the emptiness before them, girls running and laughing in her lateral vision, making her smile for a moment.

"They tried planting millions of salt cedar trees to try to block the wind, but they sucked huge amounts of moisture out of the soil." Bliss, Ananda, and M-girl started listening in, and Jessie found herself becoming more consciously tutorial. "Those trees were non-native, but back when it was still raining some, you could get away with using them. But when the rains just about disappeared, those trees sucked out every last drop, and the soil turned to dust. Then the pigs started getting loose from huge farms, or they were let go because nobody had any food to feed them anymore, and they foraged everywhere, which loosened up the dirt even more.

"That's when it really started blowing. It made the Dust Bowl look like a sneeze, and these fences weren't the only things disappearing." She glanced at the posts. "Entire towns got buried. It was one mistake compounding another. Stuff like this happened thousands of ways all over the world." She looked at the desert. "This is what *we* got in the end."

"Was it like this before they started farming?" M-girl asked. The fifteen year-old's name was Miriam, but her deceased parents always called her M-girl, and so did everybody else. "Originally, I mean."

Jessie quickly told her about the Great Plains before the settlers arrived.

"Do you think anything's living out there now?" M-girl sounded frightened, and Ananda pulled her close. The blisters on M-girl's hands and feet had healed nicely since her rescue of Ananda and Teresa from an Army of God attempt to burn them as witches.

"I doubt much of anything is living out there," Jessie said. "But we don't know for sure. The reason I doubt it is the more biomass you have, the more opportunities organisms have to adapt, in a Darwinian sense. Someone said that a long time ago, and looking out there, I don't see much biomass, so I don't see a whole lot of opportunity for life to adapt and survive."

"Biomass?" Ananda asked. Jessie felt certain it was on M-girl's behalf, because her daughter certainly knew the meaning.

"Everything that's alive out there, or in any place."

For Jessie, each explanation of a scientific concept was underlaid by the tragic sense that no matter how diligently she tried to pass on her knowledge, she'd never be able to share more than a fraction of what she'd learned in her many years of schooling. It pained her to know that this heartbreaking devolution of education and understanding was probably taking place wherever humans survived.

"It makes *me* doubtful about water," Burned Fingers said. "We're going to be rationing all the way across this stinking desert. It's hard to believe there's any out there at all."

Harder still to believe it two hours later when they came upon the first skeletons. A group of five had died, though the only evidence at first was a partially uncovered skull spotted by Zita Gibbs, Keffer and Maureen's flame-haired eleven year-old. The poor girl screamed when she saw it and ran to her mother as soon as the truck stopped.

Nearby, Jessie and Burned Fingers found four other skeletons under a thin layer of crumbly dirt. No sooner had they started rolling again than half a dozen girls spotted a pile of bleached bones and skulls sticking out of the whitest sand Jessie had ever seen. Hannah thought they'd found a small plague pit, but that didn't strike Jessie as likely. The pits were usually huge, well-organized mass graves for those killed by Wicca, or by the hallucinatory violence the virus unleashed in its victims.

Burned Fingers waved her over. "I did a quick count," he said. "There's at least forty of them."

She joined him poring over the bones, finding it odd that the skeletons hadn't been eaten. Then she realized dozens of them could have been dragged off already. *More bones than takers.*

The children and other adults stood back, perhaps out of fear, perhaps out of recognition that Jessie and Burned Fingers each possessed their own expertise when it came to the dead.

Without a word, she knew they were searching for a cause of death other than the harsh desert conditions. How likely was it that so many would have ventured out so unprepared? And where were their packs and tents—*any* of their possessions? Even a scrap or two.

Burned Fingers found the first evidence of mayhem, handing her a scapula with a round of lead lodged in a concavity. "Someone's been doing a lot of killing out here," he said softly, pointing to a skull with a bullet hole in the frontal bone.

Jessie nodded. Minutes later she found a small pelvic bone—a child's, most likely—that looked like it had been shattered.

"They were slaughtered," Burned Fingers said in the same careful voice. His eyes rose to the emptiness that surrounded them, as if he expected it to erupt.

"Look." She held up a fully intact ankle bone and metatarsal, explaining what they were. "We'd never be seeing this if they'd been hit by a land mine."

"That's good, but it doesn't mean they're not lying around out there."

There was little other comfort in the evidence they dug up, and she also took to glancing at the desert every few seconds. Not a trace of anyone, but with soil this light and sandy, a single breeze could obliterate tracks—or bury untold number of dead.

The realization forced her to accept that she could be crouching over scores of bodies, a veritable warren of bones that could extend for miles. Who knew what this century had done to 65 million midwesterners? Everything before her could be a massive unmarked grave. They'd already come upon almost fifty bodies—and ample proof of murder.

Who did this?

Burned Fingers stood slowly, his only obvious sign of age, eyes once more fixed on the all-encompassing emptiness. His hand fell to his sawed-off, a reflex she also knew well by now, though he didn't draw his weapon.

"Hic sunt dracones." He didn't translate his words. She didn't need him to. As a scientist, she had a working knowledge of Latin, and he'd uttered a familiar expression: "Here be dragons."

She rose beside him, noticing most of the caravaners staring into the void of the great desert, as silent and solemn as they'd been at Augustus's camp, and for much the same reason: bearing witness to the murdered—and what it could mean to them.

But why were these *people killed?* That question needled her. *And why here?*

Why not *here?* she countered herself. *People are killed everywhere.*

Her eyes drifted down to the bones, and she saw that the dead might have been heading north. *Like us.*

"Who do you think did this?" she asked Burned Fingers. Others drew closer.

"Someone who wanted what they had," he said simply.

"Or someone who didn't want them getting any closer to wherever they were going," Maul added. Cassie and her kitten pressed against his side. His hand rested on her shoulder.

"So where do you think they were going?' she asked Maul.

"Why would anyone go back there?" He lifted his hand from Cassie to shade his eyes and squint at the mountains they'd fled. "Especially if word's out about the North."

Burned Fingers shrugged. "We don't know, so we go," he said, repeating the very words he'd used weeks ago at the start of the journey.

Jessie switched her M–16 to "full auto," as Bliss picked up her shotgun. Even Hannah popped the cylinder to check the bullets in the revolver Jessie had loaned her.

"Drive slowly," she heard Burned Fingers warn Brindle. To Maul, he said, "You've got to keep back a hundred yards. And both of you keep your windshield armor down."

"No kids in the van," Jessie said, returning to the group. When the tallest blind girl, Angelina, stopped burping a baby to argue, Jessie added, "I'm sorry, but the van's going first. We don't know what we're facing, and we're not going to lose you to a land mine."

Angelina rolled her milky eyes in disgust. Jessie couldn't blame her. It was hard enough to care for a baby in the van, much less while perched blindly on the tanker.

Then she flashed on them marooned in the desert days from now, the van destroyed by a mine, Brindle dead, the truck unable to move forward without them acting as human mine sweepers—and unable to retreat for fear of the Alliance and whatever arsenal they'd sent after them.

Bury your goddamn fear, she scolded herself, knowing the admonition had the half-life of a smile at a time like this.

"She's right," Burned Fingers said. "Everybody's got to ride on the truck except for Brindle and a good pair of eyes up on the van to look for any signs of trouble."

"I'll do it," Bliss volunteered. So did Jaya a second later.

Jessie almost refused her daughter, but couldn't. It would have meant consigning the risk to someone else. Nobody's kid could be exempt, but two of them at a time? *No way.* Before she could speak up, Burned Fingers nixed the idea.

"In rotation only," he said, failing to hide his amusement over Jaya's eagerness to share any duty with Bliss, even the most dangerous. "And every hour we need a fresh pair of eyes to take over. They get tired and lazy in the sun. Jaya, we don't want you riding shotgun, either. The van's just for Brindle and whoever's pulling lookout duty."

Bliss patted her boyfriend on the back, then climbed onto the board that Erik had strapped to the roof. Her sandaled feet hung over the windshield armor, her eyes already studying the great unknown that stretched out before them.

Jessie ushered the younger girls to the tanker trailer knowing it would be a challenge to find perches for all of them and that few would prove comfortable. After seeing the bones, the children had ceased their exuberant talk of finding fences—or the real treasures they hoped lay buried in the sandy soil, like swing sets and bicycles. She considered their loss of enthusiasm a blessing: running fearlessly around a killing field would have been foolhardy. Yet as she looked at Bliss atop the van, her unease returned in full, and she had to forcibly remind herself there had been no evidence that mines or IEDs had been used in the massacre. But she found it unnerving and almost unconscionable to seek relief in bullet-riddled bones, especially those of children, and this made her desperate to get the caravan's girls on board—as if clinging to the tanker could save them.

The solace you seek reflects the world you see. She couldn't remember where she'd heard or read that—it had been many years ago—but those were her thoughts when she spotted the oldest girls, Teresa and Bessie, digging up a long sheet of metal.

Jessie was about to shout when they turned it upright, revealing a blue sign that said: OHIO WELCOMES YOU—TO THE HEART OF IT ALL! The large white lettering was superimposed over a smaller outline of the state, and was as poignant a remnant of the past as she could have imagined at that moment. As a child she had spent most summers at her grandparents' beach house at Cape Hatteras. Hardships already were a part of her life, but everytime she and her mother made it past the fading Welcome to North Carolina sign, she always brightened with the promise of playful waves and sand castles, beach tag and long summer evenings talking and laughing and watching the surf—and forgetting the world caving in all around them.

Now she walked toward the two girls, overhearing red-haired Bessie ask Teresa if Ohio had been one of the states, or a country.

"It was beautiful," Jessie said softly, more to herself than to Bessie, and more about the country as a whole than the state.

"Definitely a state," Teresa said, eyes quickly back on the sign. "What's this?" She brushed sand and dust from the word Ohio, baring a big X gouged into the name. A deeply etched CITY OF SHADE appeared right above it.

Burned Fingers hustled up beside Jessie. "The 'City of Shade welcomes you'?" she said to him. "Ever hear of—"

He cut her off with an explosive expletive. "That was the nickname of a huge hellhole that used to be a penal colony. It was a privately run place where all the psychos, sex criminals, and completely insane people were dumped, but what I heard happened . . ."

Here it comes, she thought. There's always a kicker with him.

" . . . was when the rebellion started, the army shipped thousands of political prisoners there, figuring they wouldn't last a week, and I'll bet they didn't. Then, when everything fell apart, the inmates supposedly took over the asylum."

"What about Wicca? It must have wiped them out by now."

"Maybe. Maybe not. Look out there. There's nothing. It's pretty damn isolated, just like you were in that dead reservoir."

"But we practiced strict abstinence, and got away before it got really bad in the cities."

He snorted. "They got away, too, even if they didn't want to. I'm not saying they didn't get hit with the virus. I'm just saying that the army might have done some of those crazies a favor, sending them out there. I haven't heard of that place in years, and all I really remember was to stay away from it, no matter what. I never even knew where it was exactly. Who would?" he added, shaking his head at the endless unmarked stretches of sand.

And here we are.

"But look at these bodies," she said. "Everybody's dying out here. They must have, too," once more finding perverse relief, rather than simply fear or anguish, in the bones they'd found. But she was driven to seek any kind of comfort from the horrific prospect of encountering men brutal and insane enough to have survived the Hobbesian world Burned Fingers had just described.

"I hope you're right, and this thing," he nudged the sign with his foot, "is some asshole's idea of a joke, but I wouldn't bet on it, and I wouldn't count on them being dead. They . . . had . . . water," he said, pronouncing the words slowly, like a death sentence. "Enough for a big prison colony. I heard it was the size of Rhode Island. And they didn't have kids." He nodded at the boneyard. "So I don't think they're the dead ones, at least not here. I'm figuring them for the pythons who pounced on whoever went past. Looking at this, I'd say they had a steady stream of meat." '

"People?" Jessie blurted. Teresa and Bessie dropped the sign and stared at him.

"Yeah, people, and whatever food they carried," Burned Fingers said. "Those bones were picked clean."

Like the toll tenders.

On the way to the Army of God, Jessie and her companions had to pay panther meat to pale, torchlit men who'd taken armed control of a long mountain tunnel. To have refused would have risked being slain and eaten themselves. The uneasy journey to daylight turned ghastly when they spied the tenders' ample collection of human skulls and curtains strung with the smaller bones of hands and feet.

She eyed everyone on the tanker truck—the younger girls, adults, Jaya and Erik, Augustus and his twins—and flinched at what this hoard of humans would mean to savages.

And then she looked past the caravaners to the tarnished gasoline tank itself, and knew that as long as they needed fuel, they would be hostages to guns and might and the unhinged desires of men. But without the gas, they were dead.

Almost everything had changed for the worse in the past hundred years, but as Jessie walked to the truck she knew they now faced the grim possibility that some of the most monstrous crimes of the century had taken place in the vast unmarked graveyard they had just entered.

Chapter Eight

Hunt struggled to sit up in bed, setting off a *crack* sharp as a broken tooth. Esau wasn't sure whether it issued from his master's tired, clawed body, or his rickety headboard.

The slave rose to help him, but Hunt waved him off, fumbling with the frayed blanket. A crusty bandage fell from his cheek and landed on his lap, exposing dark scabs tough as snake jerky. A tangle of them converged into a thick wound on his jaw, like the parched tributaries that once flowed to great rivers and reservoirs. He reached for the stained bandage, grimacing when he knocked it on the floor.

Esau caught his nod and rushed from his stool by the dusty window. The slave crouched by the bed, a sharp smell scouring his nose. He snatched up the dressing and dropped it into a wicker basket whose reeds had split and unwound in dozens of places, giving it the dazed look of a prickly desert plant.

When he turned back, his master's eyes, flat as sunlight, stared out the window. Or at a reflection of his exposed skin? Esau had overheard the doctor tell Hunt he'd have scars. "Bad ones."

Like my S. The slave's fingers rose to the big black tattoo branding his forehead. Much as he hated the inky symbol of enslavement, he found himself cringing more over Hunt's disfigurement. His master had been so handsome, so different from His Piety and the other old goats who demanded his attention. But as soon as he thought ill of the prophet, Elders, and acolytes, Esau flooded with guilt and turned his eyes inward to his festering soul, begging forgiveness from the Almighty.

He listened for the calm words of God, wanting to hear them. *Just this once.* Emptier than ever, he looked back at Hunt, who now faced him fully, and saw that the doctor hadn't lied. Scars blighted most of his master's features, absent only where another bandage covered his brow. Esau had been so shocked by those bone-deep claw marks that he couldn't help imagining a Pixie-bob wrapped around his own skull, trying to rip out his eyes. His master was lucky to have survived with his sight.

No, not luck, the slave scolded himself again. *Providence. The Lord's will be done.* Repeating to himself what the prophet had told them all.

"Water." Hunt's voice sounded phlegmy from sleep, but stronger than since he'd collapsed in the chapel. "Then food. Protein. Whatever looks good."

Good? Esau didn't think any of the provisions looked good. Fewer traders had arrived in the past month, and yesterday two of them showed up badly blistered from hauling hand carts with wooden wheels, not the small jeeps and trailers they'd used for years. Slaves had whispered of fuel shortages.

He had even heard fierce rumors of a breakdown in Alliance power. He feared any upset. His circumstances could be so much harder, and he saw this whenever he looked at slaves who were worked to death on the huge water wheel, or saw broken, wailing men waiting to be burned or beheaded for real or imagined offenses.

There were other signs of trouble. No new slaves had been delivered in weeks. At the same time, Esau had noticed a lessening in the hardships endured by some of them—and a rise in their boldness. These were mostly modest displays, like working slowly or murmuring to one another. But even these small acts of defiance normally would have warranted a whip or truncheon.

Only the shipment of girls continued apace.

His master slowly worked his legs out from under the blue blanket, fabric so thin the slave spied skin through the weave. Hunt's gown bunched-up around his hips as he hung his legs off the side of the bed, planting his feet on the floor. He moved his toes tentatively, then stood, leg muscles tightening as his hem fell.

He thought Hunt still looked stronger and more alluring than most of the naked younger men whom His Piety selected as models of chaste and healthy manhood. Their likenesses were carved into wooden statues that adorned the prophet's spacious home, which once housed the base commander. And a life-sized figure filled a corner of His Piety's chapel office. He'd used the statue when Esau was first brought to the base in chains to tell him about his body, starting with his thighs.

"Flex those muscles, like this," His Piety had pointed to the figure, "so I can see what you've got." The prophet touched each part of Esau's upper leg, touting them in turn. "This is *Rector femoris*, and over here," his thick fingers dug into Esau's flesh, "you have *Vastus medialis*. And this," he probed so painfully that Esau gasped, "is *Vastus lateralis*. And these are the adductors," spoken as he ran his hand up the inside of the slave's leg, pausing to fondle him. When Esau frowned from the man's clumsy touch and the stench of his panting, His Piety squeezed the slave's testes and calmly said, "Please don't ever do that when I am taking the time to minister to you." Then, more sternly—and with a hard tug—he added, "I *mean* it."

As Esau doubled over, the prophet shifted to the statue and caressed the figure's "gluteus maximus," pronouncing the words in a quavering voice before turning Esau away, lifting his soiled skirt, and forcing it into the slave's trembling hands. His Piety moved his fingers from what he called the "gluteal crease" all the way up to the "natal cleft."

"It's important for you to know the names of your parts," he said to Esau's back, "because as a strong young man, you are made in the very image of God."

What Esau heard next was the prophet's breath grow even quicker, and then it coated his buttocks, turning them moist. Seconds later His Piety licked him for the first time.

Now Esau watched Hunt check his footing before pulling his gown up over his head, seemingly indifferent to the slave's open appraisal.

"My clothes." Hunt pointed to pants that had been laundered and folded for him.

"Can you wear them with that?" Esau glanced at a thick bandage on his master's shin.

Hunt unfurled the stained wrap, revealing more hard scabs, and held it out to him. Esau dropped the dressing into the basket as his master eased his pants over his wound, spurning any hands-on help.

"Get my shirt and boots."

Esau gathered them up, excited by the feel of the soft fabric and the smell of old leather. He made no effort to hide his desire, which tented his skirt; but Hunt looked right through him, slipping on his sleeveless shirt.

"You may tie them," Hunt said, offering his booted foot and a sly smile, his only acknowledgment of his slave's readiness to please. But Hunt made no other suggestion of interest, and Esau hurried to his knees, finding his master's eyes focused not on him but on the window once more.

The slave contented himself with the combat boots, considering his chore an honor. The boots were so rare, taken from a vastly diminished stock on the base.

When he finished, his master stretched his arms above his head, then bent them at the elbows like wings. Still holding them aloft, he twisted his torso from side to side, eyeing the mostly unscathed skin from his shoulders to his wrists; only his badly bitten right hand was still bandaged.

"May I go for your food?" Esau asked.

Hunt stared at him. "What did you learn while I was sleeping?"

"Learn? Only to worry that you wouldn't be standing like this ever again. I'm so glad you're—"

Hunt abruptly waved him silent. "You know what I mean. Was I talking in my sleep again? I was delirious. I had a fever, sweats, nightmares."

"You said very little."

"What *did* I say?"

"You called out my name twice." *You said you loved me.* Only *me.* But Esau always imposed careful limits on his most outrageous lies.

"What else?" Hunt asked impatiently.

"You said something about the president being hunted, and the White House." Another lie, intended to bolster the first one. "Like on the—"

"That's all?" Hunt interrupted again.

"That was all you said."

"Because—"

A sharp knock cut Hunt short. One of His Piety's favorite messenger boys bowed until he saw that it was a slave opening the door. He peered past Esau, speaking directly to Hunt, who braced himself against a delaminated bureau.

"His Piety wants to see your slave."

Hunt appeared surprised, but told Esau to go. When he turned to leave, though, Hunt called him back and ordered the messenger boy to close the door and wait in the hallway.

"Tell him I'm ready," Hunt said quietly.

"Are you sure?" Esau did not want him to leave, and he had been back such a short time.

"Did you hear me?' Hunt glared at him. "I am ready."

Esau apologized profusely, bowed, and backed away. Hunt sat heavily on the bed.

The slave trailed the messenger boy down the hall, hoping

His Piety did not want to take his pleasure with him. The prophet's touch curdled his skin. But thankfully, the man was extremely old, fifty-four, and most of the time pleasure was only a memory for him, his attempts to achieve it brief and—for His Piety—disappointing.

Esau worried mostly about his master leaving him to more able-bodied men for weeks or months. While a few demanded sexual favors for themselves and friends, most expected him to work at hard labor on little sleep. The slave couldn't say which burden he loathed more, only that he'd known a great blessing when His Piety ordered him to stay by his master's bedside. The thought of returning to much harsher obligations made him frantic. And if Hunt were killed—or came back without the demon and was burned to death—his own prospects would darken precipitously.

The messenger boy, Abel, stayed two steps ahead of Esau until they left the building. Within minutes they passed bony men, burned black as Africans by the frightful sun, digging a new latrine with picks and shovels. The odor was nauseating. An unfortunate few pounded the fill with bare hands and rocks to try to stop the waste from bubbling up when the hard rains fell, a cruel trick of the murderous earth that none of the True Believers understood.

Bathrooms in private quarters, like Hunt's, had been looted lifetimes ago for plumbing that could be cut, pounded, and forged into valuable weapons—spears, knives, swords, axes, spiked balls on chains—anything that could stab, maim, cudgel, and kill.

Half a block away, Esau and Abel came upon more slaves carrying armfuls of rocks to patch a residential cul-de-sac. The blacktop had eroded so widely that most of the surface had been replaced. It appeared rough and painful to walk on.

"Do you know why His Piety wants to see me?" Esau asked Abel softly, so he would not be overheard. The messenger boy looked around warily and shook his head. Slaves were not permitted to speak to one another, but when they could, they often did. The punishment was not severe. Slaves might be lashed or forced to suffer a half day of labor without water, but they weren't burned or stoned to death for brief conversations.

Esau had heard that Abel was born of "high blood," as were a number of other slaves who were rarely rebuked for minor infractions. They were reputed to be the offspring of Elders or His Piety, but parentage was rarely bruited about because that was a grave transgression for any slave of any lineage.

The messenger boy glanced around again. "It's not to *help* His Piety," he told Esau. To "help" the prophet was slave code for servicing his flagging desire. "The Chief Elder is with him. They've been talking all morning."

Both slaves quieted when they spotted four hooded girls in long dark gowns ahead. Their bare feet were tied together with frayed rope, causing them to stagger as they tried to keep up with two old men in boots who were herding them into an alley paved with specially sharp stones.

"His Piety's Memorial Drive," Abel snickered. Esau didn't risk a response. The messenger boy didn't appear to notice and went on, "They're new ones. They got here yesterday. They're really beautiful. I got a good look at them on my way to get you."

Esau stared at the girls, trying to feign interest, but with Wicca infecting men who had sex with unclean females—and who could ever be sure of their history? An Elder had gone mad with the disease after having sex with his eleven-year-old bride—the slave considered his desire for boys an act of God's benevolence. Not that he'd ever admit so aloud because the Alliance forbade all same sex contact, which made seeking out men and boys both exciting and dangerous to him. Only True Believers—men of presumed virtue—acted with impunity. And only His Piety had pretended to teach Esau about his body when he raped him.

The slave saw Abel steal repeated looks at the girls, but why did he bother? Their shapes were hidden under the loose garments, their heads turned forward under floppy hoods. But Esau had never experienced the fervid way that lust for a girl could direct and dominate almost all of a young man's impulses. What he did feel certain of was that even as a high-born, Abel's desire was hopeless. These children were reserved exclusively for True Believers, the free men of God who had their choice of the youngest, purest females who passed through the front gate under the steely gaze of the towering, all-knowing crucified Christ.

The new crop, like the scores of girls who had come before them, had been shipped to the Alliance from fortresses aligned with it. Every girl marched or dragged onto the base was destined for the bed of a man two or three generations older—and just as fated to disappear from his withered arms after her first twelve periods, when sexual activity would make her a likely carrier of Wicca.

What happened to the girls afterward was a secret no one, to Esau's knowledge, had ever revealed.

As they neared the chapel, an Elder approached from their right. Abel's eyes widened, as if he'd been caught touching himself—another grievous sin for a slave—but the old man passed by mumbling to himself. A lot of them mumbled. Esau had heard them claim they were praying, but sometimes their words made no sense, or they were complaining to themselves about food or bedding or His Piety's choice of a wife for them. As if they had cause for complaint.

Abel led Esau to a kneeling platform on the far side of the chapel steps. Every slave had to lower himself to the sharp stones and broken glass, then bow before a steel cross anchored in the rocks. Only after clasping his hands in prayer for a full minute to beg God's forgiveness for his impure thoughts and depraved body did Esau dare relieve his throbbing knees. He had seen slaves thrashed for standing too soon, which was not a minor offense. A separate kneeling platform hidden behind the chapel received all females. He rose, pleased to see small cuts on his knees, proof of devotion that His Piety often checked.

After climbing the marble steps, Esau held the chapel door for Abel, another unspoken obeisance to the high-born. He followed Abel down a wide hallway that wrapped around most of the building. Decades earlier the carpet had been a deep, rich blue: "Like the cool sky of heaven that awaits all True Believers," His Piety had proclaimed from the pulpit last year. But when Hunt volunteered Esau for chapel cleaning, Esau discovered mice droppings in every square inch of the knap, though he'd glimpsed the creatures themselves only a few times. They bred prodigiously, but were hunted by snakes that nested in the chapel's foundation. On three occasions serpents slithered across the altar during services, and each time slaves were forced to hunt them down. Many were bitten when they attacked the nests. Some died. And the snakes always returned.

His Piety's office stood across from a wall separating the chapel from the work area. Esau and Abel were permitted to enter the anteroom without knocking. Opening the door set off a bell's pleasing tinkle. It was the sweetest sound Esau had ever heard, and always provided the visit's lone pleasure. He and Abel stood just inside the door, where they awaited the Chief Elder, who was His Piety's closest aide.

A pew long enough to sleep both slaves pressed against the wall to their left, but neither of them sat on it. That convenience was for True Believers. The unfairness gnawed at Esau, even though resentment and envy of the elect was a serious sin. But sometimes he couldn't help himself. True Believers violated his body at will, yet he dared not sit on the pew because it would somehow sully the sanctity of *wood*?

In silence he begged the Lord's forgiveness for his heresy, praying that God would understand that he was hot and tired and plenty scared, still worrying about Hunt leaving and the days of hard labor that would follow. He didn't know how many more he could survive.

The Chief Elder opened the inner door to His Piety's office. Esau glimpsed the prophet at his desk. A large cross hung from the wall behind him.

"Wait right where you are," the Elder said to him. He was a tall, gaunt man who peered at them through spectacles that contained only one lens, leaving his uncorrected eye watery and unfocused. "You," he pointed to Abel, "wait in the vestibule."

The Chief Elder swiftly closed the half-light door, though little sunlight spilled into the anteroom because the glass had broken long ago. It had been replaced by plywood that was bowed and pulling away from the side of the frame, yielding a vertical opening a quarter inch wide. His Piety and his Elders always appeared to forget this when they talked in his office, and they often kept slaves waiting in the anteroom. But in Esau's most resentful moods he considered it just as probable that church leaders found men like him invisible—wholly unworthy of heed—until they needed them. He'd also wondered whether His Piety and some of the Elders had trouble hearing. They often spoke in loud voices—or failed to hear themselves mumbling—and repeated their words even more boisterously if they believed they'd been misunderstood.

Not that Esau had learned much from behind the poorly repaired door. Lots of loud whispers about the Gospels, especially Revelation with awed references to the "mark of the beast, 666," and big man-eating mammals like leopards and lions and, most ominously, bears—"The symbol of Russia!"

They sounded like men amazed by their own wisdom. But the slave's musings about His Piety and the Elders seized him with panic, which he tried to purge with prayer, for he knew his thoughts would condemn him to hell. They were even more heretical than his master's bewildering words about tumors and the drinking water's chemical taste.

This morning he heard little behind the door, and this intrigued him more than most of what had reached his ears in the past. Were they reading, praying, or whispering something so mysterious they'd drawn themselves closely together?

He was sorely tempted to move forward, maybe just a step

or two—nothing that would be immediately noticeable to the Elder were he to step back out. But if he was caught eavesdropping, he knew they would kill him. Spying on His Piety was a "capital crime," and even a True Believer had been burned to ash two days before the last hard rain for listening in on the prophet.

"He did it for Satan. None other," His Piety had declared as he stood in the darkness, face flaring red and orange from the torch he wielded before them.

The Judas chained to the stake behind him had shaken his head wildly and grunted, but a gag held and the prophet swept the flame over mounds of knee-high kindling that crackled loudly. In minutes the blaze burned the cloth from the trespasser's mouth. It fell in a sudden incineration that shot out long tongues of fire, but the sinner could no longer deny his betrayal of God the Father and God the Son. He could only scream, a harrowing unearthly shriek from a hole in his melting face.

Now, Esau leaned forward to draw himself inches closer to the door. He heard His Piety say, "It's the Dominion. *The Dominion.*" The prophet sounded alarmed, and his voice lowered in an instant.

Twice before the slave had heard of the Dominion, both times in hurried remarks by Elders who spoke as if it held the power of life and death over the whole planet. But what was it? Not God. They didn't speak of it with reverence. They spoke of it with dread. And it was blasphemy to call thy God by any other name.

Esau wanted desperately to slip closer to the door. Information was a slave's only currency, tender that could buy favors of food, water, and work, that could ease hard labor, depending on the overseer.

But you're dead *if they catch you.*

He studied the floor. Only carpet and concrete—no floorboards to protest his stealth.

You can do it.

Two steps. That was all he allowed himself. He no longer

felt weak or hot, but alive enough for stealth. Actually hearing His Piety talk about the Dominion had made him move. Whatever it was, the Dominion scared the prophet, for surely, Esau thought, he had heard fear in his leader's voice. But that confused him. His Piety scared people. His Piety had them burned, beheaded, blinded, stoned to death. *His Piety* frightened?

Now he heard him say Hunt's name, no doubt about it, and Esau's feet eased forward, as if of their own accord. Then he thought of a ruse that might work. He'd creep to the door, and if it opened he'd fake fainting, like he'd fallen forward.

Across the room? Don't be stupid.

But he did move across the room, veering sideways so the opening along the frame wouldn't give him away. He stopped but a single step from the door, hearing their whispers clearly. His Piety spoke with such urgency that it shocked Esau, and it was all about the Dominion. Whatever they'd said about his master was lost to him.

"They'll never let us go north if we don't find a way to stop them," the prophet said in a hushed voice. "And that will cost us much more than a tanker of gas."

"*Their* gas. *Their* tanker," the Chief Elder responded as urgently.

A hand struck a desk, startling Esau. Or was it a head? Had His Piety collapsed like Hunt?

No, a hand. The sound issued again, a distinct pounding. It had to be His Piety. No one would defy him so.

"Control the border." The prophet spoke slowly, no longer whispering, as if he could brook no misunderstanding. "No one crosses the Bloodlands. That's all the Dominion really cares about. We can't let anyone get up there. There are no exceptions, not even for us. If we do our job, *then* we get to go. If we don't, we're not going anywhere." Neither man spoke, and nothing stirred but the haunting, God-riven interludes that tormented them all.

Esau put his hand to his lips, afraid to breathe, and felt the Elder's eyes boring through the door. Then he imagined the man stealing up, only inches away. The slave wanted to move but couldn't, not in such an unbroken silence.

"So you want me to hire them?" The Elder's voice rose from deep inside the office. Esau finally took air.

"Not just them," His Piety replied quickly. "Hire everyone you can. Promise them all the girls and gas they want. Give them gold, anything it takes."

"What gas? If we lose that tanker, nobody's going anywhere. We'll be promising gas we don't have—and might not get back—to criminals, absolute thugs. Do you really want to do that?" Esau heard the Elder shudder, as if a cold wind were sweeping the room. "Or haven't your visions shown what could happen if we make a deal we can't keep?" Esau could scarcely believe the Elder's impertinence. No, *sacrilege*: questioning His Piety's visions. "We're dealing with savages," the Elder went on. "And where are we going to get more gas if we don't get that tanker back? There's no more Reserve to count on."

What? Esau's head jerked up. The Strategic Petroleum Reserve held the continent's only inventory of gas, its very name revered by everyone on the base.

"Russians," His Piety said. "They're pirates. Fools."

What did Russians have to do with anything? Esau had heard that bands of them had taken over Europe, not that anyone cared. It was supposed to be a land of endless winter, even the southern climes of Spain and Portugal.

The slave got his answer when His Piety spoke again, this time much less dismissively. He might even have been shaking his head. "We always thought they'd sail right from Siberia. No one ever thought they'd come all the way across the Atlantic."

"That's why they did it," the Elder said insistently. "And they must have known they'd run into the Dominion up there. They sure didn't run into much of anything at the Reserve. They moved into the Gulf and took it in less than a week, so that tanker is about all the gas we've got. And everyone's going to want it."

"We'll get the Reserve back. You'll see." But Esau thought His Piety might still be shaking his head.

The slave leaned even closer to the door—and almost stumbled. *To your death.*

"When? When are we going to get it back?" the Elder asked loudly. "If we don't—and I have my doubts—our only hope for going north is driving away right now. The Russians are taking over the whole country just like they took over Europe, and now that they've got the Reserve, they've got all the fuel they'll need to head north. That's a nightmare. If they get up there and wipe out the Dominion, we'll be wiped out. But what it means to us right now," the Chief Elder's voice thundered, "*is we can't count on getting any more gas.* And if we don't get it, we can't share it. Then we'll see how much loyalty there is out there."

They said nothing for several seconds. Esau imagined them deliberating, then used the last of his nerve to backpedal slowly, quietly, an eternity before he stood safely again. He was pleased he could still hear the Elder say solemnly, "With the Reserve, the Russians have everything."

"Not everything," His Piety countered. "They don't have the North yet, and the Dominion has fought off every attempt to take it."

"Don't they need gas? They're not living on sunshine," the Elder said. "I've never figured out what they're doing up there."

"I don't think they're using gas," His Piety said, also sounding perplexed. "They just trade in it. There's been no word of it up there, and no shipments have gone north for as long as I can remember."

"Well, we need whatever they're using, because we sure don't have it. We're down to a grand total of eighteen hundred gallons underground."

"That's enough to go after the tanker," His Piety said.

Another lengthy pause followed, and just when Esau thought he'd have to creep back to the door, His Piety spoke up.

"That's why we must give Hunt everything he needs. But hire the others, too. Make sure they know that traitor, Burned Fingers, is still with the heathens. That should get their blood running." Esau heard a smile in His Piety's voice when he spoke of the marauder named Burned Fingers. "And make sure they also know the reward for killing all the heathens will be more than anything they've ever seen. But they must bring back the heads as proof. I want to see every last one of them—except for the demon's. I want that beast alive. *Only* the demon gets to come back. So first they'll have to negotiate for the beast. They can offer them safe passage—if they hand that creature over. Then, after they have the demon, they can go to work."

"What if they won't give it up?"

"They won't sacrifice everyone for the demon. Would you?"

"I wouldn't even countenance a demon, His Piety. But they've taken the demon with them."

"Because they worship demons. But I want that beast back here." Esau heard His Piety pound his desk again. "There can be no escape this time, or any excuse. The demon must be cleaved and burned. That's all our Lord asks of us. Nothing more. If we can't protect His kingdom on earth, what can we do? Now bring me the slave."

"What if the demon is killed?"

"That is unlikely," His Piety said with great precision. "It survived the tank and fire. But if God in His wisdom wants the demon to die out there, then both heads must be brought back—*still attached to the body.* That is critical. All True Believers must see the beast and know the evil is real."

Esau heard footsteps, then the Elder opened the inner door. He studied the slave, then lowered his gaze to the floor. Esau glanced down, too, worried that his filthy feet had tracked up the carpet.

"Go in. His Piety wishes to see you now."

The slave had been summoned to His Piety many times, but had been ushered into his office proper only to pleasure him. Otherwise, His Piety spoke to him through the open door. But after the urgency of all he'd heard, he could not fathom that he'd been beckoned to "help" the prophet.

He felt this more strongly when he stepped through the doorway and found His Piety's personal slave standing by the wooden statue of the naked boy. The lithe, girlish looking blond youth did not acknowledge him, and Esau figured he'd been there the whole time. He held the most trusted position for a slave, and Esau guessed the boy was also among the high-born.

His Piety had moved from his desk to an ornate, hand-carved chair. Not as grand as the cathedra in the chapel, and made of a much lighter colored wood, but as thickly padded.

"Come here." His Piety directed Esau to a spot in front of him.

The slave lowered himself and bowed his head. The prophet offered his hand, and Esau kissed his bulbous gold ring. He had kneeled before His Piety many times, but never to place his lips on anything so hard or tolerable as the ring.

"Look at me," the prophet said. Esau raised his eyes. "You will accompany your master when he is strong enough to chase the heathens. You will see to his welfare and help in any way you can." His Piety paused, as if to lend the fullest possible meaning to those last few words. "You have been loyal to him and to us, so if his mission succeeds—and it *must*—your loyalty will be rewarded: you will return a free man with all the rights and privileges of a True Believer."

Esau realized he must have looked as stunned as he felt because the prophet nodded and repeated his promise. Then he added, "Hunt will have his orders. Yours are simple: aid him, and make sure he survives, even if it costs you your own life. The Lord will grant you bliss forever if you perish protecting him. I have seen this in my visions, so you know it's true." But Esau could not help hearing the Chief Elder's mockery of the prophet's visions. His Piety smiled. It didn't look kind. It looked cunning, and that also made the slave uneasy.

"A free man," His Piety said once again, "but do not under-estimate the challenges you'll face, and know that Hunt will be told to kill you if you fail him in any way." The prophet leaned forward. "One more thing. You will not speak of this to anyone before you are freed, or I will kill you myself in the name of the Father and Son."

"Yes, His Piety. Thank you. May I fulfill a request of my master by passing along a message to you?" His Piety nodded. "He asked me to tell you that he is ready."

"Go. Leave." His Piety shooed him away as if it were be-neath him to hear such important information from a slave.

A free man, Esau said to himself as he left the office. He'd never heard of a slave being freed. Or of a man like him even offered such a reward. And that stopped him after he exited the anteroom because no matter the heresy, no matter how sinful it made him feel, he could not refrain from wonder-ing if the reward was a chimera. His first inklings in the office now loomed larger and darker. Maybe that's why he'd never heard of a slave becoming a free man. Maybe they were promised freedom, sworn to silence, and then sum-marily killed. That scared him more than chasing a demon and fighting heathens.

As he started toward the chapel entrance, he saw Hunt walking toward him. *You can tell him.* Esau desperately wanted reassurance the reward was real, then reminded himself that His Piety had vowed to personally kill him if he spoke of it to anyone.

His master brushed past him without a word, and while Esau assumed he was hurrying to a summons of his own, Hunt's aloofness heightened his anxiety.

Moments after he returned to Hunt's room with food, Abel knocked on the door again, telling him to go to the front gate. This time the messenger boy did not escort him, and Esau walked as fast as he could, heart beating loudly in his ears.

He spotted Hunt's motorcycle by the entrance. Attached to it was a sidecar rigged like an iron cage and provisioned for a long journey.

Esau realized they would be leaving right away. He hadn't been permitted off the base in years, and then only for a few hours of wall building. His elation soared when Hunt rose from the other side of the big bike, tossed a wrench into the sidecar, and pointed to a small pile of clothes on the motorcycle seat.

"Put them on. I don't want you looking like a slave. You'll start looking like a free man now."

A free man. Someone else had spoken the words. Someone else knew. It felt confirmed.

Esau picked up a pair of pants and shirt. Beneath them—astonishingly enough—he found a pair of boots. He'd never even owned a pair of tire-tread sandals.

But what about the S? Before he noticed what he was doing, he rubbed his brow, as he had two hours ago.

"No one can see that until they're close," Hunt said. "And no one's getting close unless I want them to. Grow your hair. It'll disappear."

Grow my hair. Slaves had to chop it off with knives. Maybe he *would* be freed.

He rushed to a latrine and changed. The pants felt odd, but he loved them. The shirt, too. He stepped from the privy to put on his boots. Then he carried his filthy skirt to Hunt, who was watching slaves in chains trudge out of the gate, as he himself once had.

Hunt threw the skirt at the slave master, shouting, "Give it to one of them, or keep it for yourself. You never know."

The man's face reddened but he merely nodded at Hunt, whose easy authority could not be questioned by a guard. Had he known Soul Hunter's meek origins, his envy might have flared into open resentment of the blond man's prerogatives.

More than two decades ago marauders had taken Hunt slave in a murderous raid. The five-year-old arrived at the base roped at the neck to other boys. Hunt had no memory of his parents and never would. His Piety claimed him at the gate below the giant Jesus on the cross, drawn to Hunt as a serpent is to the eggs of its own kind, gleaming in the dark deracinated barrens of childhood.

Hunt was a handsome boy with a wedge-shaped torso that grew more sculpted and appealing with the passage of every year. His Piety took him as a lover at once, a secret stain on the prophet's soul, already blotted with the blood and semen of other boys.

Hunt loathed the old man's incessant urges, ending his sexual enslavement in his mid-teens when he could claim the imperatives of his own body by forcibly forestalling those of his putative master. The abrupt rejection left His Piety standing in silence, quivering with anger, desire, and the most powerful longing of all—for the youth of another, and the youth of his own so long passed, conflating the two, as they often are, in the abject blur of aging.

No threats were ever spoken, no words arose from the secrets His Piety and Hunt had shared. The young man quickly claimed the mantle of Soul Hunter by tracking down escapees, violating the youngest and weakest—often for sex, sometimes for the unencumbered pleasure of their pain. He returned all of them to the base bound by the neck, as he had been. Boys, girls, men and women—bony, starved, and broken from the their encounters with him—were then slowly incinerated in the unshakable grasp of posts and chains, wood chips and coal.

Hunt watched them scream and writhe and die, ruing not their grim demise but his own lingering iniquity, a sinuous haunting from high above where the sky came alive with heavenly claws. For days after the burnings he whispered hurried prayers of contrition, not for his violence or their gruesome deaths, but for the pleasure he'd taken with the young: memory sharp, selective, unforgiving.

But when his latest boy had lain naked and savaged in the dusty ravine, blood pooling above his pale buttocks—and Hunt had realized that the Lord alone, not his parents or His Piety, had placed him on earth to confirm the final depravity of others—he'd gleaned a blink of eternity's most consoling gaze, the sacred sanctions and godly injunctions that left him purer, stronger, and more empowered than ever.

He kick-started the old Harley and slapped the seat for Esau to get on. The slave straddled the cracked leather, found the foot pegs, and wrapped his arms gently around his master's scabbed and bandaged body, hand brushing a pistol in Hunt's belt.

Two guards waved them through the gate. Hunt gunned the engine. A cool wind soothed Esau's skin, stealing up his pants and shirt. He felt christened by the righteous spirit of God, as if the Lord had answered his prayers and most fervent pleas in an infinitely resonant voice, filling his inner emptiness at last. In these suddenly pristine moments he felt unbeholden to men or boys or the desires of the flesh, and thought to ease his light hold on his master and lift his cheek from Hunt's warm back, but couldn't.

He blamed his failure on the motorcycle's speed, faster than memory itself—or so it seemed to Esau as he gazed upon a world unshaken by walls, gates, or gun towers. But it wasn't speed that kept his arms and hands on Hunt, or the impediments of a rough road. It was the mystifying force he felt only for the man he held.

The sidecar rattled next to him, heavy with the implements of carnage. He'd thought of escape often, but never anticipated the maelstrom sweeping him from the life he loathed.

To hunt heathens in the name of God. To kill them all. To fill a cage with the dangerous fury of a two-headed demon from hell.

To know the sacred blessings of a True Believer.

Chapter Nine

The caravan trundled deeper into the Great American Desert, past mounds of large human bones—femurs, ribs, mandibles—and smaller ones that looked like the cracked, bleached joints of a vast bloodless body. But from Jessie's seat up on the back of the tanker trailer, the desert they claimed hour by hour looked no different from the wasteland they left behind. The caravaners were in the graveyard of the Midwest, "the heart of it all," as the old Ohio welcome sign said, now littered with the debris of bludgeoning, crushing, shooting, chopping. The sands offered few burials, save what the earth itself spared when driving winds and torrential rains swept the bones to new places of rest. Migratory in death as they had been in life, they appeared from the depths blanched and ghostly, as haunting as the vanished territory they claimed.

Jessie and Burned Fingers no longer stopped to examine the remains. The children didn't need to see any more cruel evidence. Their nightmares were a contagion that gripped the youngest girls before waking others with the same feverish sweats and chills.

But no matter what the caravaners did, they were never far from the bones. Last night, after stopping to bed down,

Jessie idly scooped up the smooth surface only to find more of the dead—the clustered skulls of infants and toddlers under a thin layer of sand.

The bones' ubiquity followed from all she knew of the collapse. With the disappearance of 65 million midwesterners, the remains she spotted, for all their rigid horror, provided but the tiniest glimpse of everyone who perished. And the bones could never account, in the most precise sense of that measured word, for the untold millions of refugees who died crossing the broiling vestiges of the Midwest for the East and West coasts, the Gulf or Great Lakes, seeking the cool fiction of water in a rapidly heating world.

Why are we *alive?* That question gnawed at Jesse as they rolled over a gentle dune and saw another outreach of emptiness. *And for how long?* Her eyes roved the dead, and she knew that these people, whose bones they now trampled, must also have wondered about their survival—before they succumbed, if not to murder and cannibalism, then to starvation or thirst, accident or disease.

Five days ago the girls had found the welcome sign with City of Shade scratched over the word Ohio. Five days without a single cloud, and five brief nights to absorb cooling sand and tumultuous dreams—and consider the threat of an old penal colony overblown, the idea that inmates had literally taken over the asylum absurd. "They died, too. Everything died," Jessie murmured as she looked up from yet another tangle of bones, shattered points sharp enough to have clawed away the absent flesh.

"Hold on," Burned Fingers shouted from atop the truck cab, a grueling roost every bit as hot and exposed as the one she claimed about fifty feet behind him. Jessie winced when he jumped from the lumbering vehicle, as if she felt the impact in her own creaky knees. But he was already scurrying away, studying the sand.

Maul stopped the truck seconds later, and Jaya, up on the van ahead of them, reached down and pounded the door to signal Brindle.

Ananda and M-girl spilled from the side of the trailer, hand in hand, as they had been since surviving the Army of God. Ananda nuzzled her girlfriend, a sign of romance that made Jessie smile. The two had been inseparable growing up in the camp, though the gentle tones of intimacy didn't sound until Ananda, three years younger than M-girl, approached adolescence. Jessie had also heard each of them use heroic terms to describe how the other saved her life after the abduction, admiration almost as necessary for love as physical attraction. M-girl still bore scars from pulling Ananda from flames when the zealots tried to burn her as a witch.

"That's how I knew how I felt about her," M-girl had told Jessie shortly after the start of the journey. "I would have died for her."

You couldn't ask for a greater love for your daughter. And while the joy the girls shared made Jessie happy, as a biologist she recognized the early onset of physical affection reflected severely shortened life spans, no longer now than in the Middle Ages when young brides were common—and may have been necessary for the propagation of the species.

She watched M-girl share her water ration with Ananda, as she herself did every day. Her daughter had shown the first signs of an unquenchable thirst about a year ago. But their generosity was leaving Jessie and M-girl parched—and Ananda was still weak.

Recently she also complained of dizziness. Jessie tried hard not to think about the most likely threat to Ananda's life. Her girl had survived so many horrific dangers it seemed insufferably unfair that a disease conquered a century and a half ago might slowly kill her. But its simple remedy hadn't been available for decades. And to think she had worried for so long about Ananda becoming involved with Erik, or some other boy, and possibly contracting Wicca.

Her daughter laughed with M-girl, and spilled water from her cup. Be careful, Jessie wanted to yell, but Ananda looked so stunned by the sand's dark bloom—and offered such an anguished apology to her partner—that her mother said nothing.

We'll find more water, Jessie thought as she climbed off the trailer and started after Burned Fingers. *We have to.* Food stocks would last another six weeks, but none of the caravaners would live long enough to eat them if they didn't find water.

The sand felt noticeably fine. Jessie sank into it with each step, worried that a bone shard would pierce her sandals. Hansel struggled on his three legs, and Razzo sniffed in fits and starts. Watching him, she wondered if along with so many other remains, they'd already driven by—or over—the City of Shade.

Burned Fingers looked up as they headed toward him. He stood well off to the side of the truck, pointing to large paw prints in the sand. "I couldn't believe the size. That's the only reason I saw them."

Much larger than a man's foot. That's what Jessie noticed first. And there were four of them, front and hind, with claws apparently several inches long; the fine grains blurred the most telling details. Some of the tracks appeared to have been brushed over, leaving foot-high berms on each edge of a serpentine shape, which narrowed at the end.

"That's a tail," she said to Burned Fingers. The realization registered with empirical clarity, as if she were looking at casts of dinosaur bones in a long ago laboratory.

"A big one," he said.

What didn't register with such professional equanimity was the sum of all these clues. The dogs were also plenty agitated. The fur on Hansel's neck stuck out like quills, and Razzo buried his snout in the sand, sniffing furiously. She ordered them back to the truck. She and Burned Fingers didn't need hounds to track a beast this huge, and she didn't want them near any creature that might be able to eat a big dog in a single bite.

"Ever hear of *Varanus komodoensis*?" she asked as they followed the tracks up a long rolling hill.

"Jess, it's been forty years since I studied Latin, but I'm guessing—"

"You used it yourself when we saw the first bones: *hic sunt dracones*."

"Oh, Christ," he said, shaking his head and swearing with noticeable restraint. "The last thing we need are those goddamn things."

Komodo dragons had escaped zoos decades ago, along with other ferociously carnivorous creatures. But lions and tigers and polar bears were ill-equipped to survive the rapidly deteriorating environment, while the giant lizards might have been uniquely suited to prosper in the heat.

What Jessie was certain of was the immense danger of letting a dragon take them by surprise.

The beasts could eat eighty percent of their body weight—four children or two adults—and ran as fast as dogs. They were no more native to North America than puff adders or elephantiasis or a host of other horrors that had arisen in the tropics, then spread widely with the warming.

Her eyes shifted back to the tracks. The morning light, soft as it would get all day, cast a deceptively harmless looking orange glow that made the sands look like the enticing photos of the Sahara Desert she'd seen as a child. But she found nothing inviting about the Komodo's paw prints disappearing over the short crest. She checked her M–16 to make sure it was on full auto.

"I can't say I'm real fond of anything with the word 'dragon' in its name," Burned Fingers said. "You think we're safe up on the truck?"

She shook her head. "They can stand on their hind legs. They could tear a kid right off the side, or us on top."

Burned Fingers raked his gray hair with his good hand. "They run in packs?" he asked.

"They didn't use to."

"We used to say the same thing about panthers and P-bobs." He and Jessie were still moving, but they lifted their eyes to the crest, as if fearing the beasts would come storming over it any second.

"But Komodos are lizards," she said. "The world's biggest, and they've always been at the top of their food chain."

"*How* big?" Despite his emphasis, he was still keeping his voice low. "I only saw one in a zoo, and that was a *long* time ago."

"They can get to be ten feet," she whispered. "Three hundred pounds."

"So I'm not going to be killing it with this," he whispered back, lifting his shotgun.

"Nope, not likely." She nodded once at her rifle to indicate the weapon of choice.

With sand burying their ankles, every step proved strenuous. At least once a day they'd had to dig out the wheels of the truck or van to keep moving. *Where did it all come from?* Sand took millions of years to form. It didn't just appear in a matter of decades. *It does now,* she corrected herself. Sandstorms were moving entire deserts around.

They slowed as they approached the rise. Silence enveloped them. The sand absorbed even the sound of their feet. Moments later they spotted the Komodo's characteristic white waste—from its inability to digest calcium in the bones of animals it ate. Jessie would have paused to study the excrement for signs of distinctly human remains, but they heard an agonized, indecipherable whisper.

She looked at the top of the rise, leaned forward and cupped her ear. "That's a woman," she said softly.

A few more steps revealed a grisly scene. As unscientific as it sounded, *monster* was how Jessie thought of the Komodo in those first seconds. The dragon crouched in a depression about fifty feet away. Even from this distance they could smell the animal's vile odor. Its loose, thickly pebbled skin formed a ridge along the sides of its long neck and folded into a thick flap across its broad brow, giving it the appearance of a dense, stupid beast. A woman in her late teens or early twenties, with an extraordinarily pretty face, lay on her back near the Komodo's gaping mouth, her long blond braid splayed on the sand, the skin of her chest and stomach torn apart. Her eyes open, blinking.

The lizard was twice her length and easily three times her mass. Huge. Well fed, not emaciated like so many creatures these days. But it was no more animated than the woman, who was now so quiet Jessie heard her own startled breath.

Communicating with only gestures, she and Burned Fingers circled wide as they approached the dragon slowly. She wanted an easier kill shot, but kept her weapon aimed at its head the whole time she moved. She assumed a Komodo was as dangerous as any other large carnivore feeding on prey. If the beast tried to take another bite of the woman, or moved so much as one inch toward them, she'd do her best to empty the clip into its brain. At this distance, it could be on them in two seconds.

But the dragon didn't move. It didn't appear to notice them at all. She watched its body expand and contract with every breath, like a big bellows, and figured if it did stand on its hind legs it would tower over them T-rex style, though at "only" about half to two-thirds the height of the most feared beast of the late Cretaceous Period. *Of any period,* she added quickly to herself. Then she studied the Komodo, reminded that she'd felt plenty of fear in the late—and greatly diminished—Anthropocene.

As they angled closer—and the beast's stench grew stronger—the woman made eye contact with Jessie and said, "Help. Help me," with unmasked terror.

"Can you hear me?" Jessie asked across the divide, daring to move no closer or raise her voice, even though she knew that Komodos had terrible hearing.

The young woman only repeated her plea. The dragon's gaze never shifted from a point right in front of its dull, reddish brown eyes.

"If we could get her to crawl away," Burned Fingers whispered, "even a little, we might get her—"

Jessie cut him off with a head shake. "She can't move. They have venom that makes you go into shock and bleed." She eyed the Komodo down her barrel. "But if I shoot that goddamn thing, it could fall on her."

"You will not shoot that animal," said a man with a strong Caribbean accent.

She and Burned Fingers spun around. A powerful looking African-American, appearing every bit as well fed as the Komodo, had crept up directly behind them. Wearing a clean white robe and hood, he stared at them through dark aviator glasses. Bandoliers crossed his chest, and he had a classic bolt action rifle aimed at them.

"That dragon is more valuable than you will ever be," the man said without lifting his eyes from the barrel. "So put your guns down or die."

Burned Fingers glanced at his sawed-off, and Jessie wished she'd spun around shooting; she might have killed the gunman before he could pull his trigger. But the last time she'd tried that, a marauder almost severed her femoral artery.

"Drop your weapons." The man held his aim while a smile broadened his face, as if he relished the prospect of murdering them. His straight teeth looked especially white against his black skin.

When neither she nor Burned Fingers obeyed his command, he drew his cheek from the burnished wooden stock and shook his head without once breaking eye contact with them. Nothing about his speech or gestures appeared hurried. "Trying to shoot me would be even more stupid than shooting the dragon."

"You might get one of us with that relic," Burned Fingers said, nodding at the vintage rifle, "but then you're dead."

He shook his head again, and in the next instant they saw why: armed guards marched over the rise with slaves chained to an old, empty circus wagon. The red paint had faded, gold filigree on the trim boards was peeling, and a painted American flag, emblazoned on the baseboard, had snapped off. But the iron bars looked strong.

"Who are you?" Jessie demanded. She turned back to make sure the Komodo wasn't moving.

"I am the Mayor for Life," he said in the same easy voice, but there was nothing casual about the way he held the bolt action on them. "And I will tell you only one more time to drop your guns." His tone hardened as metallic clicks forced Jessie and Burned Fingers to freeze. The Mayor's smile returned as half a dozen gunmen closed in on them from behind.

Jessie laid down her weapon, straightening as screams and cries came from the direction of the caravan. She tried to race across the sand, but a man tackled her. A second gunman jammed his fat black revolver into the back of Burned Fingers's head. The marauder dropped his sawed-off. Jessie was dragged by her hair to her feet as the slaves rolled the wagon past them toward the Komodo.

"This is actually your lucky day," the Mayor said. "If you had not gone looking for our beast, you would have been destroyed by mines. Do you know *where* you are?" He spoke with notable emphasis for the first time.

"The Great American Desert," Burned Fingers said, looking directly into the dark glasses.

"We call it the Bloodlands. It could get very messy for you, too, if you cause any trouble while we try to get the dragon in the cage."

A gunman signaled the slaves to turn the wagon around after they'd towed it within twenty feet of the Komodo and woman. The lizard's eyes moved, but the rest of it remained still. Four slaves eased a ramp from the rear of the cage, resting it carefully on the sand. They kept glancing toward the Komodo. If the creature attacked, they'd be trapped by their chains.

The gunman who directed the slaves unlocked a metal cuff on a short, muscled man and pointed to the woman. The slave crept forward on his hands and knees. When he neared the Komodo, the dragon's yellow forked tongue flicked at him, triggering the slave's panicky retreat. He backed into the barrel of a handgun.

Jessie noticed the Mayor's bolt action now slung over his shoulder, her M–16 pointing toward his newest prisoners. His smile beamed brighter than ever.

The slave moved back to the woman, taking her arm and dragging her away quickly, leaving a trail of blood on the sand.

"She tried to escape," the Mayor said to Jessie and Burned Fingers. "But he tracked her down because he was even hungrier than her."

Now Jessie could see the extent of the woman's savage mauling and knew her survival was doubtful. A gunshot sounded from behind the dune that she and Burned Fingers had come over minutes ago. Jessie spun around. A burly man grabbed her arm so hard she felt bruised. Looking back, she saw the Mayor nodding at the gunman with the slave. He seized the wretch's shoulder and pointed a pistol at the cage.

The slave hesitated only briefly before wrestling the woman's arms from her sides and dragging her up the ramp. Her eyes widened and she started screaming as the Komodo trudged toward her, drooling pink saliva. The creature flicked its long, strangely bright tongue at the bloody sand, then hurried after her feet.

"No, no," the woman shrieked, trying to pull her legs up to her body. Each touch, taste, and smell of her made the beast move faster.

The Mayor nodded when the slave hauled the woman to the front of the cage. A guard opened a narrow door for him, and the slave jumped out of the wagon. The guard locked the door right away as gunmen secured the rear of the cage. The Komodo stood over the woman, its huge head unmoving as its tail snaked through the bars and hung to the ground.

A child's cry drew Jessie's gaze back to the dune. Another group of gunmen were gathering the caravaners. Leisha and Kaisha, the conjoined twins, were roped to their father. None of the others were tied up, except for Hansel and Razzo, leashed to a gunman with a truncheon.

The Mayor stared at the twins and yelled loudly, "Bring me those two," enunciating each word precisely before glancing at the cage. The Komodo still stood over the woman, neither of them moving.

A gunman forced Augustus and his girls forward, and warned the other caravaners not to move.

The Mayor stepped close to Leisha and Kaisha, peering at the peculiar V formed by their short necks. When he reached to touch them there, Augustus said, "Don't, brother. Don't do that."

The Mayor turned to the missionary. "Do you know what you have here?"

"My daughters," Augustus said fiercely.

The Mayor shrugged. "You have something the Alliance wants very badly. Something they will pay enormous sums for. In fact," he gazed at all the caravaners, "they will want all of you because nobody gets to cross the Bloodlands. No . . . *body.*" The poor play on words appeared to amuse him. "But you two," he returned his attention to Leisha and Kaisha, "they will want you most of all." He leaned closer to the girls. "And do you know why?"

They didn't respond. Jessie kept an eye on the wagon. The dragon's head hung over the savaged torso of the young woman, its dark rubbery lips spilling long strands of saliva onto her exposed intestines.

"I will tell you why," the Mayor continued, still inches from the girls. "Because they are insane. Did you know that? They are a great power, and they are insane. They think you are a demon from hell, and nothing you say will ever change their minds."

"You can't give them to the Alliance," Augustus pleaded. "They'll kill them."

"Yes, they will," the Mayor said calmly. "And the way your daughters will die will be terrible." He took off his glasses, the whites of his eyes as starkly prominent as his bright teeth. "But we made our peace with them long ago. We keep the Bloodlands clear of all travelers, and they bring us girls like her." He put on his dark glasses and looked back at the wagon. "After they have a baby, they are shipped to us. It is a profitable arrangement, and we will do nothing to interfere with it.

"You," he pointed to the gunman by the twins and their father, "do not leave them, no matter what. And you two," he stared at the girls once more; Leisha was crying, "accept your fate, and count yourself—"

"Please, no. *No,*" the young woman in the circus wagon screamed.

The Mayor and everyone else stared at her. The woman was swiping feebly at the forked yellow tongue probing her ripped torso.

Jessie caught Ananda's eye. *Don't look,* she mouthed, but needn't have. Ananda and M-girl were already holding each other close and lowering their gazes to the ground. But Bliss stared at the cage. Most of the others did, too.

"As long as we use bait—and they are hungry—they will climb into the wagon, so we keep them hungry," the Mayor said. "And wait till you fight him. There is nothing like a Komodo in the fight pit. He is a monster. You will see," he said to Burned Fingers. "Maybe you, too," he said to Jessie. "I like what I see in you."

She looked at Burned Fingers, who glared at the Mayor. The man's teeth were on full display, his pleasure unmistakable. Jessie wondered if he was insane, too, if this desert he called the Bloodlands eventually turned everyone into a crazed shell of what they had once been. If its most brutal survivors formed a massive black hole that forced the unwary into the final gravity of its inescapable grip.

A slave lifted a large canister with a long hose, feeding water into a trough that stood to the woman's side. The lizard stepped toward it, crushing her foot. She screamed. The beast drank, lifting its head to drain the water down its long throat while the woman clawed the air as if she might pull herself into the open sky beyond the bars.

The Komodo looked at her dumbly, then clamped its massive mouth around her bloody chest and back and lifted her off the floor. Its movable jaw opened wide, like a python with a pig, and in a series of bites the giant lizard worked the flailing, shrieking woman around its maw until her head disappeared into its throat, leaving most of her torso hanging out of its mouth, legs kicking wildly. The Komodo gulped three more times, inhaling all but her feet, which no longer moved. Then they vanished, too.

"Do not try to escape," the Mayor said.

Gunmen pushed Jessie and Burned Fingers forward, and slaves dragged the wagon away.

Jessie's legs felt wobbly. *Who are these people?* She eyed the guards and gunmen closely for the first time. Many were covered in burn tattoos of spears and swords and viciously coiled serpents—crude welts carved by fire—up and down their bare backs and chests. Their *faces*. Most were African-American, but not all. Standing only feet away were three brutal looking white men with thick beards and identical fleur-de-lis tattoos on their arms; two Latinos, also heavily inked and burned; a broad-shouldered albino with thick Slavic features, cloaked in fabric pale as his skin; and two Asians.

The slaves were of a similar ethnic mix, but with far fewer burn tattoos. Otherwise, little but chains and lack of weapons distinguished them from their captors, until she noticed two men, shackled together, who were each missing an eye. Then she looked at the other slaves closely and saw an empty red socket peering out from every one of them.

Once the procession settled into what felt like a shocked rhythm to Jessie, she tried to account for everyone on the tanker truck and van. The gunshot she'd heard earlier still plagued her.

"Turn *back*," one of the white gunmen ordered her.

She couldn't. Not yet. She was still trying to find little Cassie among all those larger bodies. The girl might have slipped away, or run off. That's what she'd done at the Army of God. Jessie doubted the Mayor's gunmen would have shot

Cassie, given any girl's value. *But they might be crazy as him.*

The gunmen backhanded her without another warning, snapping her head to the side. She yelped from the impact of his stiff leather wrist guard, which scraped her cheek raw and left it burning.

She was so stunned she had to force her breaths, and warned herself not to falter because it felt like that could be fatal. She tried focusing on her thirst, trading one pain for another, which helped until the air filled with the Komodo's flatulence. She thought she'd vomit. Several guards and the Mayor laughed.

They labored across the sand, stopping when the slaves were ordered to dig out the wagon's wood and iron wheels. The Mayor demanded Brindle, Jaya, and Erik help them, conspicuously overlooking Augustus, still tied to his girls. That's when Jessie realized that Maul, the tanker truck driver, was missing. With another scan of the caravaners, she confirmed Cassie's disappearance. Maul was devoted to her. She was his dead friend's daughter, and Jessie had no doubt the big bald driver would have done everything he could to save Cassie, even if it meant getting shot.

The Mayor watched the men work, smiling wider than ever. He might have been on a beach outing, for all the pleasure he took in the sand.

They climbed a large dune that opened onto a twenty-mile view of the desert. Through the harsh eastern glare, she spotted what must have been an old wrecking yard with cars stacked eight high in long rows. Sand had drifted over them randomly, burying up to three levels of the smashed and burned vehicles, while leaving the first row visible only feet away.

But the wrecking yard wasn't as lifeless as it first appeared. Shirtless, nearly naked men wormed their way out of the narrow openings, climbing down from even the highest levels with the ease of apes before jumping the last ten or twenty feet to the soft sand. The hundreds of windowless, doorless cars looked like a massive beehive coming to life, and the men who emerged shielded their eyes and stared at the wagon and long line of slaves, captives, gunmen, and guards.

The Mayor gestured dismissively at the ragged men of the wrecking yard. "They are a defeated people but they trade with us. They bring us dried vegetables and fruit, and we do not kill so many. Fair is fair," he laughed. "Otherwise, we don't need them. We have many slaves." Jessie heard another layer of accent under his Caribbean inflections but couldn't place it. "And now we have more slaves—and pretty girls to sell to the Alliance."

Dutch, she thought, trying to ignore his continued threats against them. From one of their old colonies. Aruba or Curacao. But nothing in her estimation could explain the madness with the Komodo, except for the world they'd all inherited equally.

"Is that where we're going?" Burned Fingers asked more gently than Jessie would have thought possible for him.

The white gunman who'd backhanded her cracked Burned Fingers on the head with his rifle butt. The marauder dropped to his knees, swaying under the unblinking gaze of the man. His back was riddled with fat red welts so mean-looking it took Jessie several seconds to notice that the burn tattoos formed a constellation of crosses. The gunman pressed his rifle to Burned Fingers's ear and ordered him to stand.

Burned Fingers staggered to his feet, the first signs of physical weakness that Jessie had ever seen in him. She would have taken his arm, but feared it would get them both killed.

No one spoke till they descended the dune. Then the Mayor turned to Burned Fingers, and all of them stopped. "This is where you are going, burned man. This is where all of you are going. The City of Shade. I want you to take a good look at this magnificent palace."

Jessie risked lifting her hand to block the sun from her eyes. Apparently, this was permissible because some of the slaves did it, too, and no one was struck. A few miles straight ahead she made out an enormous shelter the color of sand. It blended so smoothly with the surrounding desert that she hadn't spied it from afar. But a palace?

The flat roof looked six or seven acres large, big as the ones that enclosed stadia early in the century, and rested on scores of pillars. The area below the roof was open, but so densely shadowed she could not see into its blanketing darkness, certainly not from that distance.

On the west side of the structure, farthest from where they stood, scaffolding had been erected along a thick corner column. As they walked closer, she saw more dark-skinned men scurrying up the sides bearing heavy-looking sacks on their backs. When they reached the roof, they unloaded bricks.

So they've got water, she concluded quickly. A lot if they can spare it for this.

The procession plodded on in silence until they came within a hundred yards of the shelter.

"We have the biggest shadow in the world." The Mayor put up his hand to stop them, then pointed to the darkness. "Every day we build the shadow bigger, blacker. It is black as coal, as you can plainly see. Someday it will be as big as the desert, bigger than the dreams of the pharaohs. But only America has such greatness now. Already people come from faraway lands to see our shadow and fighting pits."

What people? Jessie asked herself.

"We host the world," the Mayor said. Then he repeated himself, as if it were a marketing slogan. "We have clay and water that never stops. We have all we need to build such magnificence."

In the foreground, the tip of a guard tower poked a couple of feet from the sand, confirmation that the looming edifice—this bizarre effort to manufacture shade, as if it were a real commodity—was built on the foundation of a huge prison. The wiles of madness, she thought as her eyes turned back to the Mayor.

He ordered the guards to take the children to a nursery, and all the adolescent girls to his chamber. "Prepare them as I like."

"Don't you *dare* touch them," she screamed. She tried to bull her way to the Mayor, knowing how futile her words sounded and how easily she could be crushed. But she could not stand by in silence while the children were taken away.

Four guards grabbed her almost immediately.

"You are a fighter, woman," the Mayor said. "That is what I thought. Take her to the most special pit. And the burned man, too."

Guards dragged them both away. Jessie glimpsed the edge of the brittle-looking roof before they forced her into the shadow. She whipped her head around frantically, trying to assess as much as she could as fast as possible. Were there interior walls? Support beams? Dormitories? An armory? Lockups? An obvious bedroom? But her sun-strained aging eyes couldn't adjust to the darkness quickly enough. She might as well have been blind.

"Jump!" a guard shouted in her ear, startling her.

"What?" She couldn't see the ground. She was so frightened she could barely feel her feet.

Guards grabbed her arms and twisted them painfully behind her back.

"Don't do this!" she screamed.

They hurled her forward. All she could grab was air as she plunged into a steamy rank emptiness that could have been as deep as inner earth, for all she could see or feel. But even in that horrific instant of falling—with her heart thundering in her ears—she heard furious claws rising from the blackness below.

Chapter Ten

Harrowing screams erupted in the heat. Little Cassie gripped a truck ladder so hard her hands felt soldered to the steel. Slowly, she raised up on her toes, peeped over the top of the tanker trailer and saw her friends running wildly from a horde of armed men swarming down the dune, most with burn tattoos of horrible swords and snakes on their backs and chests. Their *faces*. They looked scarier than the marauders who attacked her camp, killed her mom, and crushed to death her only sibling, Jenny, with a jeep.

Cassie leaped to the sand, landing on all fours, and bolted. Just seconds ago they were petting her Pixie-bob kitten in the shade of the truck, or playing monkey bars on the trailer, waiting for Jessie and Burned Fingers to come back. Now the kitten was lost, and all of them were screaming, "Run, run," and dragging one another away.

But they were caught in the open, and Cassie worried that the crazy-looking men would start shooting any second. Then she remembered Burned Fingers saying nobody with half a brain killed a girl these days. And Maul and Brindle and the other grown-ups would never use their guns in the middle of a mess like that. From what she glimpsed through the opening under the trailer, the raiders were plenty brutal without bullets. A big one threw Ananda and M-girl to the ground, then kicked and stomped them.

The vicious attack made Cassie run even faster. Her tiny chest heaved so hard she thought it would tear open. But she wouldn't give up. Although everyone called her "little" Cassie, the nine-year-old towhead was fast and wily enough to have wiggled away from horrid people at the Army of God. But the sand made every step a struggle.

Hard for them, too, she could see with another glance back at the raiders, still chasing down the caravaners. Augustus and his daughters were getting clubbed to the sand. So were the Gibbs kids; their red hair looked like three fireballs blazing in the sun. And Solana was huddling with Imagi. The Down syndrome girl had bundled herself into a ball and was screaming.

Where are you *going?* Cassie demanded of herself. If she hadn't been so frightened, the question might have slowed her. She couldn't spy a single rock or dead tree to hide behind. Nothing but an endless empty sheet of desert. Then she saw it.

Scrambling another fifty feet, she jumped over a ripple of sand no more than a foot high, landing in the lee of a form sculpted by wind.

She began digging like a dog, though for every handful she scooped between her legs, half a handful spilled back in. And she kept looking up, sure the gunmen would wheel around the truck any second and spot her. Each glance showed more of her friends thrown to the ground and beaten. Two gunmen whipped Brindle and the boys with chains.

Cassie pawed feverishly at the sand until she spotted the heavily booted foot of a man sprinting toward the rear of the trailer. A blink later Teresa burst from behind it, and then Cassie knew the man was chasing her.

But what could she do for Teresa? For any of them? As Teresa screamed, Cassie hurled herself into the shallow trench she'd dug.

Escape. Get help, she told herself. *But where?*

She brushed sand on top of her until she was almost covered. The ripple rose inches above the left side of her face. It looked like the smooth shapes she'd seen on the shore of the dead Gulf, and might hide her from anyone distant. But if they got close, she knew they would see her.

My footprints! She moaned, feeling so stupid. Then, as if in terrifying confirmation, she heard someone racing toward her. She had to make a decision fast: stay or run?

The footfalls grew louder. *Two* someones. Her legs shook, so jellied she didn't think she could stand. She pleaded silently for the world to go away. All of it forever and ever. *Amen.* That last was all she knew of prayer.

Without shifting so much as a spoonful of sand, she rolled her eyes toward the ripple. All she could see was sand and the "damnable sky." That's what nurse Hannah called it. The loudest footfalls sounded like they were on top of her, just feet away. A few more steps and—

BOOM. The gunshot sounded like an explosion, and left her shaking hard enough to spill sand from her belly and legs. Someone fell, the impact so close it shook more sand from her skin. And the other footfalls were *still* coming.

She squeezed her eyes shut so hard she blocked the burning light and entered a dark place with sparkling pinpoints of color. Sometimes she did this for fun, to see the reds and yellows and violets of flowers she had never seen in the real world. She did it now to try to shut out the murderous threat drawing nearer.

"Get your ass back here, Jester," a man yelled from afar. "You nailed him and we need you, or we're going to have to start shooting these bitches."

The footfalls stopped so close Cassie was sure the man called Jester would see her or the dug up sand.

I'm a girl, I'm a girl. Please don't shoot. Already rehearsing what she'd say.

"Give me a goddamn second," Jester yelled back.

"No, *now.*"

"I'm checking him for guns."

Jester sounded close enough to grab her. This time when she looked toward the ripple, she saw a man with tan, leathery skin trying to roll someone over. He was struggling with the body, swearing, one grab away from her.

Cassie closed her eyes again, unable to bear the look on his face. *A killer.* She heard him grunting hard and held her breath, fearful that any movement would disturb the stillness. He swore and his footfalls receded, like the oily black tide of the Gulf.

She listened intently, still burrowed under a thin layer of sand. *Like the egg.* She and her sister Jenny had seen one on the shore, miraculous and white. They knelt and stared at it. Jenny wouldn't let her touch it. "It might be alive," she'd said. "Let's leave it alone." But even then the black tide was coming.

Now, Cassie thought that if the sand on her skin were a shell, no one would see her, no one would touch her—at least for a while—and she would have everything she'd need right by her side. Being an egg would be better than being a girl. Everyone wanted to touch a girl. But even that didn't worry her as bad as the one question that loomed above all others: *Who got shot?*

Fewer screams reached her, and she finally dared to lift her head, but only a little, and so slowly that she felt individual grains of sand roll off her cheeks and chin and narrow chest.

She peered over the ripple. A man with a broad back and ammo belt stood by the rear of the tanker trailer, shading his eyes. He turned toward her and she dropped back down, feeling the hot sand scald the back of her neck. She didn't move, frightfully uncertain whether he'd seen her. The pain pulsed away.

No footsteps followed, and she was glad her hair was as light-colored as the desert.

"You two stay behind," a man bellowed. He sounded like the guy who'd yelled at Jester.

No, don't stay. Go!

For ten minutes she didn't move, doing her best to ignore the itching that jumped around her body like sand fleas. But they didn't itch, she reminded herself. Not at first. They bit, especially fair-skinned people. "Because yours is thinner," Hannah had explained. But no one ever told Cassie why sand fleas got to live, but not flowers.

When she could no longer endure the sun and itching, she raised her head again. This time little sand fell from her, and she saw that she'd lain almost fully exposed. No "camo." That's what Brindle called using nature's colors to cover up. Except he stuttered so badly you had to listen forever when he tried to talk. "And don't finish his sentences for him," Hannah had said. "Unless it's an emergency," Jessie added quietly.

This sure is an emergency. Cassie knew you could do anything you had to at a time like this.

The truck started, startling her. It sounded so close. Close enough to crush her like that jeep killed Jenny. Now it was rolling. She could hear the trailer rattling and smell the exhaust. *You* have *to look.* A deep breath later she did rise up all the way and saw the van moving behind the truck, heading off around the dune. She also realized why two of the men had been ordered to stay: to drive the vehicles, not to search for her.

She didn't see anyone on the roof of the van or hanging off the trailer, but she ducked anyway. You never knew. When she could hardly hear them anymore, she sat up. They were gone. She stood, eyeing the emptiness. It was like the caravan had never been there.

"Not everybody's gone," she whispered, too reluctant till now to lower her eyes to the sand and follow the tracks that came toward her. In an instant that wrenched her heart, she recognized the man lying facedown with blood on his back. Cassie shook her head violently.

Disbelief gave way to grief, and she lunged over the ripple to his side. Already weeping, she lowered her face to Maul's.

"It's me, Cassie. Are you okay?" Throwing questions—
hope—against the great weight of evidence. She'd known
Maul all her life. He was like a trusted and deeply loved
uncle. His daughter was slaughtered alongside Jenny in the
attack on their camp, and after her own father was gunned
down at the Army of God, Maul had cared for her like she
was his own child.

He didn't answer her. She hugged him hard, as if she could
squeeze life into his quiet body. She bawled loudly and sat
on her heels, unforgiving of the world, even of her place in
it, and so filled with loss she didn't care anymore who heard
her: "Mom, Dad, Jenny, Maul." Her own list of the dead,
screamed to the sky.

She leaned back over him, coughing convulsively from
crying. "Say something. "

But only Cassie's agony rose from the desert floor: "Mom,
Dad, Jenny, Maul. Mom, Dad . . ."

She pounded her chest with every name, bludgeoning the
love that left her so bereaved.

Jessie fell at least fifteen feet in the darkness. Her arms and
chest took the brunt of the impact. If the sand hadn't been
deep and soft, she was certain she would have shattered ribs
and possibly her pelvis. But the fall did knock the air out of
her, and she clutched herself, unable to move at precisely
the moment when the sound of those claws made her want
to spring out of the pit and fly away. It wasn't the first time
she'd wished for a different world.

She smelled the Komodo dragon's unmistakable stench,
and knew it had to be near. She tried to roll over to reach
into her pants for the flint knife she kept strapped to her
thigh. After the guards grabbed her M–16, they did a poor
job of searching her—and she would take any protection
at this point, however risible. But when she attempted to
move, she croaked loudly from the crippling pain, then

cursed herself for marking her location so clearly in the blackness.

A *thump* sounded beside her, and despite the throbbing, she pushed herself away. But it wasn't the Komodo, it was Burned Fingers. He jumped to his feet, already recovered.

"Jessie?" he whispered.

"I'm here," she managed softly. Her eyes were adjusting to the pitch, and she could make out Burned Fingers's silhouette once she knew where to look.

He kneeled beside her. "How bad are you hurt?"

"Not too. Where is that thing?"

"I'm not sure."

The clawing had stopped when Burned Fingers hit the sand, as if the beast were waiting, too. Jessie dragged herself to her hands and knees, finally able to breathe. He helped her stand.

"I've got a small blade," she said.

"Me, too." He held his up, but she could barely see it.

She retrieved her knife, thumbing the edge without thinking. Sharp enough for surgery, according to Hannah. But Jessie knew nothing short of her rifle could stop a Komodo.

Burned Fingers walked the pit's perimeter, running his hands over the hard wall. His shadowy form looked like a hunter circling in the night. He stopped once to tap a surface. It sounded wooden. When he'd circled back around and stood only feet from her, his hands moved over what looked like a gate about eight feet wide and six feet high. Big enough for that monster, she thought.

Burned Fingers knocked again, and she saw he was trying to gauge the gate's thickness and strength. But the noise roused the saurian and it thundered immediately to life when the creature charged the barrier. The wood shuddered and metal hinges screeched like they'd shear off. Burned Fingers forced his shoulder against the gate and dug his feet into the sand. Jessie joined him.

With every thrash she felt the dragon's crushing weight

and strength. When the lizard settled, they backed away and Burned Fingers pointed to a wooden bar on the door.

"That's the only thing keeping him in," he said in a markedly soft voice.

"That was another gate over there?" she asked, nodding at the other side of the pit.

"Yeah, about the same size, but the smell wasn't so bad so I think it's empty. It's probably for the one in the wagon."

Two *Komodos?* Jessie returned to thumbing her blade. *What good is that thing going to do you?* Then she thought of her carotid artery, and how she'd slit her neck before letting some giant goddamn lizard swallow her whole. She'd rather bleed to death from her own hand than die like that young woman.

The clawing resumed, rhythmic, relentless. It was as if the Komodo, as prehistoric as any creature that stalked the modern era, sensed that nothing—not wood or steel or even the hardest stone—could thwart its unshakable appetite for long.

"I think they're keeping that one hungry," Jessie said, eyes back on the gate. A warm sticky weight slid over her foot. She jumped aside, stifling a scream.

"What?" Burned Fingers whispered.

"A snake!"

But when they looked down, they saw the Komodo's forked tongue protruding from under the bottom of the gate. Burned Fingers waited for the slimy length to discover his foot. When the tongue was fully extended, he pounced on it and stabbed the thick mass, then raked the blade down to the fork, opening a deep, two-foot gash. The dragon snapped back its bloody organ and smashed the gate, this time with such fury that Jessie feared it would shatter. She and Burned Fingers pressed against the wood once more.

"You think cutting him is actually going to slow him down?" she asked above the din.

"He smells and tastes with that goddamn thing, right?"

She nodded, and the beast did sound pained, banging its huge head against the gate.

A dull light appeared on a wall to their right. Burned Fingers pocketed his knife, and Jessie stashed hers in her waistband. They looked up to see the Mayor step to the edge of the pit. His boot tips cast small, crescent-shaped shadows on the wall. An older bald white man held a lantern. He and two Latino guards flanked the Mayor but stayed a foot or two back.

Jessie glanced around the pit while they had light. About forty feet in diameter. Not a lot of space to share with a fast, ten-foot predator. The walls were smooth, made from hardened clay, and bore dark stains that looked like blood splatters. Tall, too, about fifteen feet high, as she had guessed. She saw no way to climb out; even if they found hand- or footholds on top of the gates, neither of them could reach up to ground level. The pit reminded her of a small Roman coliseum, replete with man-eating animals.

The Mayor looked down into the pit. "What did you do to Chunga?" he asked. The beast quieted as the walls brightened.

Chunga? They've got names?

"I stomped his tongue when he slid it under that thing," Burned Fingers said defiantly, gesturing at the gate.

The Mayor shook his head. "You are lucky he did not tear it down. He has done that before."

Jessie noticed the bald white man studying Burned Fingers with such intensity that *she* found it unnerving. She figured there must be a huge bounty on his head. Burned Fingers ignored the man.

"That would spoil all the fun, wouldn't it?" he replied. "If he eats us when no one's watching."

The Mayor glanced at his aide, who took the Mayor's attention as permission to speak.

"We would prefer to have an audience," the man said

dryly, raising the lantern to bleachers that looked like they'd been looted from a school gymnasium.

"Our grandstand," the Mayor said, "will be filled on Friday night."

Friday night? They still follow the days of the week? Not everyone did. "What day is it?" She didn't assume that they used the same calendar, and wanted to know how long they had to live.

"Wednesday," the Mayor said. *Same as ours.* "Woden's day," he added.

That meant nothing to her, but Burned Fingers snorted. "So you think you're guiding the souls of the dead to the underworld?"

The Mayor's smile returned for the first time since he'd arrived at the pit. "You will be given swords. It will be a fair fight," he announced. Jessie found his lordly swagger almost as repulsive as the prospect of taking on a Komodo. Or two.

"Fair!" Burned Fingers shouted. "Has anyone ever beaten one of your beasts?" The Mayor didn't reply, but continued smiling. "I didn't think so," Burned Fingers yelled. "But you'll be placing bets on how long we last, won't you? You and whoever's filling up those seats."

"You are a mouthy man. It will be good to watch you fight. Now I will visit your daughter. What do you think of that?"

"Hey, son of Chunga, they're not mine."

The Mayor's smile vanished, but only briefly. He turned and left with his entourage. The pit darkened.

"What do you think you're doing, setting him off like that?" Jessie demanded.

"Leading with my nose," Burned Fingers said. "If you've got any better ideas, let me know. I don't know where this thing is going, but wherever it is, I want him off his game. I don't want one of those goddamn beasts eating me alive."

Jessie closed her eyes, consumed with a different, no less

horrifying fear: the fate of those girls in the hands of that man.

Cassie curled up next to Maul's body. Night was falling, but nothing frightened her as much as Maul's cooling skin. She felt his life drifting away from her, and no matter what she did she couldn't pull it back. Maybe that's why *she* felt so cold. She couldn't remember ever feeling this way. Her shivers lasted for a minute, sometimes longer, and made her teeth chatter so loudly she was afraid someone, or some *thing,* would hear her. Then the shivers would go away, but they kept coming back. And the bumps on her skin never disappeared.

Everything was getting colder—Maul, her, the sand, air, even her tears. They soaked the front of her shirt so much she had to pull the chill away from her skin. Most days she couldn't wait for the darkness, but tonight the twilight was terrifying. Nothing but emptiness surrounded her, and emptiness was death. It went on forever, and soon—when only the stars lit the sky—the beasts of the night would come looking for anything to eat. *Anything.*

She stared at Maul's belt, where the blood had stopped running down his back. He always carried a small axe, and a gun that he stuck in his pants. He was so brave, she figured it must have taken a ton of those crazy-looking men to make him run away. *No.* She shook her head, and more tears spilled from her cheeks. *He wasn't running away. He was coming after me.* She stared at him. *He got shot because of* me.

She pulled away from his body, scared of him, too. She'd heard plenty about ghosts. The older kids, especially the boys, Jaya and Erik, told all kinds of creepy stories, and though she loved Maul, missed him like she missed her mom, dad, and Jenny, he might be angry at her. He might blame her for his death. Of course he would, she realized. *You caused it.*

Her eyes lifted to where the truck and van had been. She wondered if other ghosts were stirring. But the dusky light still showed nothing but the emptiness. And only one bullet had been fired. "I'm sorry, Maul. I'm so sorry."

She fought her fears and huddled beside him, closed her eyes and clutched his shirt and hers together. "I'm really sorry," she whispered again. "Don't haunt me, please. Let me stay."

Moments passed. She didn't know how long she lay by his body before the bumps on her skin vanished and the shivering ended. She thanked him for the comfort. He'd always protected her. *He still is.* She opened her eyes on his slack face. *Someone should have protected you.* There had been so much gunfire in the past few weeks, and none of those shots so much as scratched him. Then one tiny bullet, all by itself, killed him. It was so unfair. Maul was a thousand million times bigger than a bullet, and it killed him.

His murderer, Jester, probably took his gun. He'd yelled that he was looking for it. But then he swore and ran off. Cassie knew she should check. It was getting dark, and the hungry beasts would find her. She reached down and tried to slide her hand under Maul's stomach but couldn't.

She started digging like a dog again, scooping sand until she could wriggle her fingers to where she thought the gun would be, right by his belly button. But it wasn't.

Then she looked around, listening for animals, and tunneled in from the other side, finding the revolver quickly. But it took another ten minutes before she hollowed a space big enough to pull it out. By then only stars lit the desert. They looked so close to earth they might have been beckoning her.

Sirius was the brightest of them all, and other than the sun, it was the only star whose name she knew. When she picked it out, she heard welcoming words. *Come here, Cassie. Come here.* But not like a voice in her head. It was like the heavens were reaching all the way down to her. The stars could have been the eyes of her mom and dad and sister, and the words she'd heard could have been theirs, too, a chorus come to claim her. She opened her arms to hear it again, but now only silence settled over the land.

When she was little and everything still seemed like so much fun, her mother told her the most amazing stories about the stars. Her mom cuddled with her and gave them all names, and some were mothers, some fathers, some grannies and granddads and uncles and aunts and cousins and friends. A whole world up in the heavens.

The brilliant night sky was always so much friendlier than the sickly blue of daytime. After the Army of God, Cassie had lain with the other girls while they counted constellations or gloried in the full moon. And in a brightness you could know only in the deepest blackness of space, she listened to Teresa or Bessie, or sometimes Ananda, snuggling with M-girl, tell stories of their own about how good life would be in the North. They described fruit trees heavy with peaches and apricots and plums and maybe even apples, and rows and rows of strawberries blinking red in all that leafy green. So many strawberries they'd get tired of eating them, but they would because each one would taste so good. And there would be feasts with juices and cakes and swimming parties by the sea, and never a gun. Not *ever*.

But she was so glad she had a gun now, even though she didn't know much about them. Ananda, just three years older, had actually trained with them, but not the girls in Cassie's camp.

She caught starlight on the barrel, maybe all the way from Sirius, and looked into the muzzle. She couldn't see a bullet, hard as she tried. Maybe you had to crank back the hammer. You couldn't shoot until you did that, so maybe you couldn't see a bullet till it was ready to fire, like it would say, "Okay, guys, I'm good to go," the way Maul always said when he started the truck.

She liked the idea of a friendly bullet.

Slowly, she tried to pull back the hammer. It was much harder than it looked when Maul used his thumb. She finally held the gun on her lap and pressed the heel of her other hand down on the hammer. When she got it cocked, she stared into the barrel again. It couldn't go off unless she pulled the trigger, so she wasn't about to make that dumb mistake. This one had a "hair trigger," whatever that meant. She guessed the trigger was thin as hair, but it didn't feel that way. Right now it felt hard as the barrel or the bullet that made her smile. *Okay, guys, I'm good to go.*

But even when she put the muzzle back up to her eye, she still couldn't see the bullet. *Why?* She saw all the other ones in the cylinder. Sirius gleamed off every tip.

Only one way to find out. She stood, moved the gun from her face, and pointed it toward the stars. She wanted to pull the trigger, and have the bullet pull her all the way to her mom and dad and sister in the sky. Now Maul, too.

She wished so hard, she did pull the trigger. Hardly at all, but the report made the ground shake and her ears ring painfully. But she hadn't moved an inch. Then she knew only one way a bullet could pull her to the heavens. It was sure as her finger, as bright as the memory of her loved ones.

They're waiting for me.

So was the bullet, stealthy as a shadow. She found the hammer and pressed the barrel against her heart.

Good to go . . .

Her heart beat harder, quickly drowning out any other sound, any other thought, save the names she screamed to the sky one more time: "Mom, Dad, Jenny, Maul."

I'm coming.

Guards marched the girls into the Mayor's large bedroom, unlike anything Bliss had ever seen. Yellowed canvas hung from the ceiling like sails, and she wondered if they'd been salvaged from boats. The heavy cloth walled off a square space that overlapped in places, but also left small gaps every few feet. Brick pillars rose to the roof in each corner.

The tips of what appeared to be long human bones—femurs or tibias—were mortared between the bricks or protruded from the columns, reaching like calcified antlers to the ceiling. The bones bore a grotesque resemblance to the rebar she once saw at a destroyed dam.

Six torches blazed on tall stone stands. The air was smoky, and the movement of the girls to the foot of the bed stirred the flames and shadows and smells, casting a strange play of light and dark on the canvas.

Jaya and Erik, and the adults captured in the raid, were forced at gunpoint toward the other end of the City of Shade. Beaten and bloody, they complied quietly. So had the girls now gathering on both sides of Bliss, as if seeking protection from the only one among them who had proved herself in battle.

The largest bed Bliss had ever seen squatted in the center of the room, not flush against one of the canvas walls. Its placement appeared odd, the mattress amazingly real. A lush-looking turquoise quilt with an elaborately embroidered black-skinned knight on horseback covered the expanse. He was armed with a silver lance that shimmered in the torchlight from thin metal strands woven into the fabric. She noticed still more of the metal in the armor protecting the knight and his horse. A green plume rose whimsically from his helmet. Another glance showed the feathers to be real. Then she saw that shorter ones formed the red lion on the knight's yellow shield.

Bliss longed for the quilt more than any comfort in memory. She could already hear her mother saying, "In this heat?" But the fifteen-year-old wanted to lose herself in a fantasy world filled with forests and cool shade and icy streams, and tournaments where knights jousted for the amusement of maidens in long, pretty dresses. She looked up from the bed wondering what it would feel like to be protected instead of trying to save everyone else, this time in a room made from bricks and bones and—no doubt—blood.

Long fat pillows extended the full width of the bed, which could have slept five or six girls easily. Bliss noticed a quill poking out of the one in the middle. It might not have caught her eye but for the dark down puffing out below the pale tip. She'd heard of goose down and thought it possible that geese had survived in the North, but how did their feathers get all the way to the desert?

She wished she could spread out on the quilt, rest her head on one of those fluffy pillows and close her tired eyes—but not with the Mayor pushing aside the canvas only feet away.

He strode into the room like royalty, four subalterns by his side. One of them carried the M–16. Since the attack on their camp, Bliss had rarely seen the rifle out of her mom's hands. She had little idea where they'd taken her mother, only that she and the girls were pushed into the City of Shade far from where Jessie and Burned Fingers had disappeared into the shadows.

She flinched when the Mayor took the weapon and, beaming oddly, swept the muzzle past each of them. Having fired the M–16 on full auto, she knew how easily you could work the trigger. She was considering the potential mayhem when the Mayor lowered the rifle, still smiling "like a bounty hunter." That's how her father once described a man who loved to ensnare people. The Mayor sure did.

He waved away all but two of the guards, leaving one on each end of the line of girls. Everyone but Imagi was quiet. The round-faced girl sniffled noisily.

Bliss glanced at the M–16 as discreetly as she could. It was the single weapon that could allow her to blast their way out of the City of Shade. Whatever the Mayor wanted to do with them, short of murder, it wouldn't be with the rifle in his hands. She might get a chance to grab it. "You makes your own breaks" was another line her dad had favored. But he'd never caught a break with Burned Fingers, whose marauders bashed in her father's head and put him in a coma.

Killed him. If anyone from the caravan had to die in this cesspool, she hoped it would be that son of a bitch.

She looked left, sizing up the guard, who couldn't have been older than twenty.

The Mayor caught her glance. "You like the young man?"

Bliss shook her head, but let a smile crease her face. Better to have the Mayor think she found the guard appealing than to divine her deepest impulse: murder.

She wasn't squeamish about shooting anyone who threatened them, and when the other girls, or Jaya and Erik, passed the time arguing about the morality of killing, she remained quiet. Debates did not interest her. She had already slain Zekiel, the man who called for the massacre of her camp, saving her mother from him in the end. Survival trumped all. She would do it again—*now,* if she had even a small chance of succeeding. Everything she had witnessed in the last few hours convinced her the horrors begun in the desert would only worsen in the shadows.

The Mayor laid the M–16 on the bed with the muzzle resting on the pillow. The weapon looked strangely human. He sat beside it. "You come to me," he said to Bliss in his silkiest voice. "I want you to take your eyes off that young man. A girl so beautiful, she can distract young men and make them wish they kept their eyes where they belonged."

From what Bliss had observed, just about any girl could turn the eye of an older man. The Mayor's gaze traveled the length of her.

"I am a man of vast wisdom," he added. "Not like your mother or father. I am an elder of an ancient tribe, so old you cannot imagine. You listen to me, and I will tell you things you never knew. Come over here. Your world will grow. So will you."

Bliss feigned interest as she stepped past the younger girls, including her sister. She offered Imagi a comforting pat and wished she hadn't. The child grabbed her arm tightly. Bliss worked herself loose, to the amusement of the Mayor, and moved on, looking for a weakness as she approached him.

She needed to stun him long enough to hurl herself past his sizable body, grab the rifle and kill him.

As for the girls, she would yell for them to get down and hope for the best. She didn't see all of them getting out alive, not after their raw panic during the raid. If the M–16's magazine was full—and her mother was meticulous about such life-and-death details—she could mow down the Mayor and his guards and grab the kids. Some of them were a year or two older than Bliss, but seemed like children to her.

Broadening her smile as she moved toward the Mayor, she calculated that as long as she stayed close to him—even clawing his eyes out—the guards wouldn't dare shoot. They would have to drag her off, giving her precious seconds. And she knew how to use them.

Bliss weighted her last step, then launched herself at him, stabbing her fingers at his face.

"Stop!" a guard screamed.

The Mayor reared back, drawing away from her—and the M–16. *Good-good.* But he covered his face before she could rake his eyeballs. She reached quickly for his crotch and squeezed his testicles, twisting them fiercely and yanking hard enough to uproot a bush potato. He yelped and sucked air loudly.

She rolled over him, pulling her limbs tightly inward to give him less to grab, then seized the weapon, surprised at the ease of recovery. But even in his agony the Mayor's hand was fast as a wasp, forcing the barrel deep into the pillow.

"Down," Bliss screamed at the girls, and pulled the trigger, hoping the gunshots would shock him into letting go. White, brown, and gray goose down exploded into the air, showering the two of them. The canvas wall ten feet behind the bed jittered from the fusillade, but the rifle claimed only feathers and canvas. Though gasping, the Mayor's other hand gripped her neck. His thumb, brute as a club, dug deeply into her throat, disabling her instantly.

She released the weapon and stabbed at his eyes again, this time feebly.

"You should not do that," he said, voice husky with pain.

A guard dragged her off the bed and forced her facedown on the floor. For the first time since the attack on the camp, she had failed to work her will. She thought they would kill her right in front of the girls—give them a good lesson. *She* would have.

But the Mayor, breathing more evenly, prodded her with his big toe, his manner jokey, though his voice still sounded strained. "You look like the woman in the special pit, the one who tried to attack me. But she did not get so close." His eyes drifted to the M–16,. "I thought you would do that. That is why I say to you, 'Come to me.'" Bliss didn't believe him.

He glanced at the other girls. "They are not killers, but you," he squinted at her, "you are so young and you are a killer. Why is that so? What makes you want to kill a man so fine as me? Like mother like daughter?"

Bliss didn't answer. Guards rushed in and pushed aside the girls.

"It is okay," the Mayor said to the reinforcements. "They are good girls. Only this one, she is a problem." He nudged Bliss's back with the whole of his foot, and waved over a guard, whispering in the man's ear. The guard pulled a length of rope from his belt and tied Bliss's hands behind her back. Then he grabbed her hair and dragged her away.

"You two stay." The Mayor pointed to the guards he wanted. "The rest, go."

After they filed out, the Mayor studied the girls. "You are so sad. Are you worried about your friend? Do not worry about her. She could get you killed. You do not need her. Or maybe you are worried the big black man will pull down your pants and hurt you? Oh, yes, that is what you are thinking. I can tell. But this is not so. We are not like those crazy believers. We do not touch girls like you. We like you so much it makes us sad to sell you to those crazy white men because we know they will hurt you. It is a pity, but do not worry because we will see you again. Some of you, it is true, will die giving birth, but most of you will come back to us. That is right. We sell you, you have a baby, and then we take you back, like the girl with the dragon. She had a baby with the crazy men. But it did not live. So many babies die, too."

He paused, suddenly cheery: "Yes, you will come back. But that is a year or two from now and you will be so much older and all used up, and we do not like you so much then. And to be the honest man I am, I have to tell you that you do not like us so much, either, because you blame us for sending you away. It is not a nice world for you then. But I will not tell you bad news now. Now is the time for joy." He nodded at the guards. "Have them bring food and water for these fine girls. Something tasty. And bedding."

He smiled at his prisoners again. "After you eat such good food, we will have to tie you up, but this is not so bad, and you can sleep by my side. I like such company, to hear you breathe and smell your sweet breath. Girls are so wonderful. You make me so happy."

With alarming quickness, he turned to Ananda. "You are the sister and daughter of the ones who attacked me. You look just like them. Would *you* hurt me?"

Ananda stared without speaking. I'd kill you, she thought.

"Of course you would hurt me," he said. "You would do whatever you could to save your sister and mother. That is only natural. I understand. So I am going to have to watch you most carefully. I will keep you and your special friend close by me tonight."

Only then did Ananda realize she was holding M-girl's hand—and remembered her mother's warning that some men became agitated by seeing affection between women.

"No, I want you to come to me right now," the Mayor said, as if admonishing Ananda. "Here." He nodded regally to a spot in front of him.

"Don't do it," M-girl whispered.

"I won't hurt you. Come here."

"Don't." M-girl pulled Ananda closer.

"You defy me?" the Mayor asked M-girl. "Then you come here. Bow to the Mayor."

"They kiss," Imagi shouted, glaring at Ananda and M-girl. "Kiss, kiss, kiss."

"No!" Ananda snapped, staring back at Imagi.

M-girl wrenched herself away from Ananda and walked up to the Mayor, bowing.

"Why do you do this for your special friend? Why do you take her place? Because you love her?"

Don't say, Ananda implored silently.

"Because you are the leader," M-girl said.

"No, that is not why you do this," the Mayor said. "You do this because you love her. I do not understand this. Why do you love a girl but not a boy?"

Imagi stirred. Ananda threw her a furious look.

"Boys do terrible things," M-girl said evenly with her head still bowed.

The Mayor laughed. "This is so true, but girls kill with Wicca. Is this not so?"

"The girls get Wicca from men."

Back off, Ananda thought. Or he'll kill you.

"The crazy believers give you Wicca," the Mayor said. "We do not."

"What do you do to us when we come back after having babies?" M-girl asked in the same neutral voice.

Ananda caught herself leaning forward for the Mayor's answer, but he clapped his hands and offered his biggest smile yet.

"Now is the time only for joy."

Cassie heard the desert stir, a frightening rustle that rode the sand and drew closer every second.

Her instincts, honed by all the threats and terrors of her young life, turned the muzzle away from her chest and out into the darkness. She held the revolver with arms outstretched, just as Ananda had shown her when they used their hands for pistols and fired their fingers at imaginary killers.

What she feared now looked no more real than the savages she'd conjured with her friends. Only starlit-speckled darkness stared back at her. But the rustle grew louder and began to lose its softness. It sounded like metal. It sounded like machines. It sounded like man.

"Who are you?" she cried. "I've got a gun."

She stabbed the darkness with the revolver, pointing left, right, center, but saw nothing. She turned around. Nothing. She wanted the moon, the pale glow that robbed the land of secrets, but the moon had disappeared days ago. With enormous dread—the dead weight of final fears—she accepted what was drawing nearer: *Ghosts!* She spoke only to herself, frightened of giving the phantoms even greater power if she were to say the word aloud. But the fear infected her panic till it was shouting inside her head: *Ghosts! Ghosts! Ghosts! Coming to get* me.

She stared as hard as she could, trying to see them because if you looked really hard, you *could* see them. You could even feel them—if they passed through you. She shivered for the first time in many minutes, and her skin felt as clammy as it had since she pressed the gun to her chest. *Do it. Don't wait. Kill yourself.* For the first time acknowledging in the harshest terms what she had to do.

"Mom, Dad, Jenny, Maul," she repeated softly. Gaining strength from the sound of their names, the memories of each. *They're waiting for me.*

But before she could turn the gun back on herself, she worried the ghosts were waiting, too. What if they'd come whispering across the land to snare her at the moment of death, long before she could reach the stars? That's what ghosts did. They gathered their own and kept them. Forever.

The eerie noise grew louder. But ghosts didn't sound like machines or metal or anything made by man. She stared at the darkness so hard her eyes teared, as blinded by the night as they were by the glare of day. But movement snagged her attention, and she saw hunched figures darker than the desert spread out on the sand. They looked much larger than her. Maybe six of them.

Monsters?

She backed up, tripped, and fell on her bum. She struggled to stand and lost sight of them. She blinked hard and wiped her eyes.

"Don't come any closer." But she was murmuring to herself, too scared to shout. She looked at the gun. Even after Maul's death, she could scarcely believe little bullets could kill such big beasts.

Where are they? She'd lost sight of them. *Did they move?*

"I'll shoot. I will." Pleading mostly with herself. She thought about running—*You're fast*—then spotted the dark outline of one of them rising. The others stayed down. Cassie aimed and tried hard to yell, but her words were swallowed by the noise behind her. She spun around, still saw nothing, but the sound was so loud it shocked her ears. So loud the dark figure now standing had to shout, horrifying Cassie with the realization that a human—the most dangerous animal of all—was approaching.

"Don't shoot, don't shoot," a woman kept yelling. "Listen to me. That's a motorcycle. You don't want the man on that motorcycle to catch you. He's with the Alliance. Does that mean anything to you? The Dominion?"

What man? It was all Cassie could think. She turned back toward the screaming engine noise. She didn't see a man or motorcycle, but the sound was like a wounded, screaming animal. She pointed the gun at the woman, shouting, "Who are you?"

"We heard a shot," the woman yelled back. "We've come to help. We're not with them." She stepped forward. She wore a dark hooded cloak.

"No!" Cassie screamed. "Don't move." She shifted sideways to try to look both ways at once.

"Don't shoot," the woman repeated when Cassie pointed

the gun toward her again. "He'll hear it." She inched closer.

"Go away," Cassie cried. She looked over to see the silhouette of a bizarre vehicle racing toward her. Not just a motorcycle: A cruel looking cage was attached to it—and she saw the heads of *two* men, one behind the other. The man in back pointed to her, and the motorcycle slowed.

The woman leaped at Cassie, pried the gun from her hand and then fired twice at the men. Her hood fell back, and the second muzzle flash lit tight curls of white hair that spilled past her shoulders, and sharp features gaunt with terror. She pulled Cassie toward the other dark figures, all of them rising, running.

Cassie stumbled in the sand. The woman caught her and yelled, "Come on. Go!"

Cassie raced past her into the darkness.

Chapter Eleven

A bullet plunked sand inches from where Cassie staggered up the dune. She pumped her short skinny legs over the same stretch those terrifying men had swarmed down to attack the caravan and kill Maul, the desert swallowing her every step. She looked back and saw a muzzle flash blaze in the darkness. In an instant almost too quick for time, sand sprayed against her bare calves, stinging like jellyfish, the only sea life she'd ever seen. The white-haired woman hunkered behind her, firing back at a big guy by the motorcycle.

Another shot ripped into the sand. Cassie hurled herself left, lost her balance, fell.

She thrust out her hands to stand, burying her arms halfway to her elbows, then fought frantically to climb back to her feet.

She forced herself forward, hoping she was as hard to see as the woman and the others who'd crept toward her. *But they've got dark stuff on.* Cloaks. Hoods. Cassie's white-blond hair caught the starlight and flashed like a beacon. Features that had blended into the desert when Maul's killer crouched only feet away now turned her into the most visible target. She felt a second, even more powerful urge to surrender—"I'm a girl. Don't shoot!"—and claim the perversely founded immunity of her sex. But the darkly clad figures started disappearing over the top of the dune, spurring her on. She lunged forward, scrambling feverishly on her hands and feet like a bear cub.

More gunshots raised the fine hairs on Cassie's skin. She worried it was the first savage hint of a bullet's pain, but a glance over her shoulder showed her that she was slowly gaining ground. So was the woman, firing as she backed up the dune.

Cassie pawed her way higher. She was still bent over, zig-zagging the way Ananda had shown her and the other girls. It had turned into a game when they played it a few days ago, all of them pretending to shoot marauders and crazy Christians, then running away.

Now Cassie was reliving hers for real, barreling right to left before clambering straight for the top—still about thirty feet away. A bullet left a spoon-sized divot so close to her hand she might have scooped the lead from the sand. "Don't hurt me," she wept, "I'm a girl." But her voice was faint, more desperate than defeated.

The dune steepened. She lost a half step for every one she gained. Like digging the trench all over again. But she clawed her way to the top, frustration and fear so overwhelming she threw herself over the summit, heedlessly spilling down the other side till she heard men shouting and more gunshots—in *front* of her. She jammed her knees and elbows into the soft slope to stop her tumble.

Confused, gasping for air, frightened, Cassie curled up and stared into the blackness, searching for muzzle flashes—some hint of the destruction to come—then looked back up the trammeled dune for the murderous threat chasing her. Another shot issued from beyond the crest. She hugged sand and tried to stop shaking.

A gravelly voice shouted from below, "Stop, or we'll kill you."

Me?

Who was yelling? Not a cloaked one. She could just now

make out their silhouettes as they threw themselves to the sand at the bottom of the dune. Cringing on the slope, she felt like a target pinned to a wall.

A hammer cocked on a revolver—she'd never forget that sound—breaching a short-lived silence. More gunfire exploded. Six or seven muzzle flashes in rapid, almost uncountable succession lit the fearsome faces of the rabble who'd attacked the caravan. They were shooting from less than a hundred feet away.

Sand kicked up near Cassie. Her heart quailed. She couldn't go forward. She couldn't go back. Stunned, unmoving, she watched two of the cloaked men chewed up by another burst of firepower. One screamed, drawing more shots that stilled him.

A strong hand seized Cassie's arm and dragged her to her feet. She filled her churning lungs to scream but it was the woman, pulling Cassie to her side to shield her from the shooting below.

"Hold this." The woman shoved the hem of her cloak into Cassie's hand, "and *stay with me*."

They raced down the dune, angling away from the firefight.

"Cover us," she ordered her cohorts in a muted voice, but it might have set off shots that erupted volcanically. Bullets buzzed so close to Cassie they could have been wasps hazing her head. She squeezed the hem, still protected by the woman's body, but found it hard to keep up with her long legs.

They fled to the desert floor a couple hundred feet from the gun battle. The sand was firmer there and they moved faster. Bullets no longer buzzed so loudly. Cassie wanted to know who the woman was. Where did she come from? Where was she taking her? And most of all, what did she want from her? Because she knew that somebody always wanted something from a girl—and it was never good.

Still, the woman was protecting her, so for now she would stick by her side. To be lost in the black emptiness of the desert—or captured by those killers—frightened her far worse. Judge people by what they do, her mom always said. The hem in Cassie's hand felt more like a lifeline than even the stars that beckoned her so sweetly minutes ago.

But she still struggled to keep up, looking back every few steps to make sure they were okay. The darkness, thickened by distance, turned the gun battle into a series of echoing shots and tiny flashes of light.

"Stop staring," the woman urged. "It's only slowing you down. Faster!"

They started up another dune. Even though climbing over it would put them out of sight of the raiders, the slope rose so sharply Cassie wanted to give up, or at least rest. Her pace did slow. She didn't have a choice: Sand sucked at her feet, and once again they seemed to sink deeper with every effort.

"Take big breaths." The woman knelt beside Cassie. Only then did the child notice she'd stopped moving.

"I'm sorry." Cassie's breath heaved so hard she thought of powerful storms over the Gulf, lightning clawing jagged lines in the gray air, as if behind those dark dead clouds lived a brighter, happier world—if only those crooked fiery fingers could scrape the filth from the sky so the earth could start over again. *A second chance. That's all we need.*

"You sound wheezy," the woman said. "Do you have asthma?"

"What's that?"

"Probably not, then. Your folks would have mentioned it. I'm sorry I have to push you so hard. It's not much farther. This is the worst part." She smiled at Cassie for the first time. Her cheeks were full and dimpled, and her skin looked white in the starlight, not darkened and sapped by the sun. "Trust me."

Cassie did trust her. Then she remembered her mom. Not advice from her, or stories about the stars, but her mom's smile. It made her want her mom more than ever, and though she tried not to cry, her cheeks dampened.

"What's your name?" the woman asked.

Cassie told her. "What's yours?"

"Sam."

"Like the boy's?"

"That's right." Sam gently stroked Cassie's fine hair. "Cassie can be a boy's name, too."

"I know. I like that." Cassie also liked sharing the distinction with her. It made her feel safer somehow.

The motorcycle men must have caught up to the cloaked band at the bottom of the dune because Sam's friends were caught in a crossfire. Gunmen on both sides unloaded for a full sixty seconds. It sounded like forever to Cassie. There was no return fire when the shooting stopped, only shouts.

Sam buried her face in her hands and started shaking. Her white curls fell forward, covering her grief. Cassie put her arm around the woman's shoulder, like her mom had hugged her. Sam quickly wiped her eyes.

"We better go," she said stiffly.

"I'm sorry." Cassie looked down. "I'm getting lots of people killed tonight."

"No you're not. Those men out there are the ones doing the killing." Sam's face tightened when she looked toward them. "Not you. Don't ever think that. We've got to go. Can you run now?"

"Sure," Cassie said. "How far?"

"Not much."

The woman helped Cassie up, and they hurried to the top of the dune, where they spotted a small fire several hundreds yards away. Nothing else. It made Cassie worry about ghosts again, and Maul lying in the desert all by himself with no one to bury him. She couldn't stop herself from thinking of beasts that would eat him.

At least he's dead.

They descended the steep side of the dune. Despite her fears, Cassie liked the sand spilling from around her legs until they reached the firmer desert. Then they ran, her strength returning.

When they neared the fire, she noticed a blank gap in the

heavens where the stars had been, their light blocked by a towering structure. It was taller than anything she'd ever seen, except mountains, and had the shape of a huge building. She'd heard of buildings once so tall their tips could disappear into thick clouds. *The Empire State Building.* People would look through the railings on top and get dizzy. That's what her mom said. Some even fainted. Maybe that's what this was, a big building. The possibility excited her. Maybe they were in a city, or what was left of one. Those buildings supposedly survived, sometimes with sand burying the first few floors. But she'd heard they were as empty as the crab shells she and Jenny had found at the Gulf. Their mom had looked at one of the shells and said it was like a little coffin. She was always saying stuff like that. Except the shell had crumbled in Cassie's hand, and there was nothing inside. She wondered if buildings had become big coffins. Was this one?

A man rushed toward them with a torch. Cassie reared back, but didn't let go of Sam's hand. The woman leaned close to her. "It's okay. He's with us."

Us? Who's us? She wasn't ready for a new "us." There had been "us" at her camp, "us" at the Army of God with the other captive girls, and "us" on the caravan. What was this new "us?"

"Did they see her?" the man asked.

"Maybe," was all Sam said.

They hurried closer to the edifice. Cassie looked for an entrance like the ones she'd heard about in cities, with doors that spun around like merry-go-rounds. She'd never seen a merry-go-round, either, but they sounded like so much fun she hoped the desert hadn't buried the bottom of this building.

She was terribly disappointed to discover that the tall building was actually stacks of crappy old cars lined up in rows that seemed to go on forever. It was hard to imagine any of them moving on roads, but it was hard to imagine roads, too. She spotted the glow of small fires rising high into the darkness as they rushed along. The hidden flames reddened the faces of the people staring at them. Their eyes looked evil.

Minutes later the man darted down a row and led Sam and her to the rear of an old truck trailer. It was at the bottom of a tall stack of cars, its doors flush with the vehicles lined up next to it. She wouldn't have noticed the trailer if the man hadn't lifted a large metal lever to open it. The doors creaked loudly. As soon as she and Sam stepped inside, he closed them. The trailer was sweltering, and dark as a dead furnace. She heard the lever wedged back into place.

"We're locked in," she whispered to Sam.

"We don't want to get out. Not right now."

"Where are—"

A torch flared on the ground directly in front of them, interrupting Cassie's panicky question and adding to the heat. The flame came to life in such an odd place that she clung to Sam's leg, as a much younger child might have. After such intense darkness, she had to turn her face away, too. She saw four old jacks supporting the roof against the weight of the cars above it. Otherwise, the trailer was as empty as the crab shells. Another keen disappointment. Against all reason, she hoped to find herself in a building with marble and brass and burnished wood, the beautiful surfaces of a world her mother had described so longingly. With the most dreadful conviction, she knew she would never see that wonderful creation. Instead, the trailer made her feel empty, as if everything inside everything else would soon be eaten by all the other emptiness.

The torch rose from a wooden hatch set into the sand. The trailer had no floor but desert. A man's head appeared in the open hatch. His hair had been cut carefully. She had never seen such a thing. He held out the torch, staring at her.

"Her?" the man said. "That's who was shooting out there?"

"Earlier, yes," Sam said. She tugged gently on Cassie's shirt. "Let's go," leading her to the hatch.

"I'm Yurgen," the man said, climbing out. His beard was cropped as closely as his hair, and he wore glasses. Cassie had never seen anyone with clear lenses. "And you're?"

"Cassie," she said, frightened. She wanted to bury her face in Sam's cloak.

"Okay, Cassie girl, take a good look down. This is the ladder. It's all rope and branch. You won't have any light going down. I've got to put the torch out for the climb. You see that?" He reached down, shifting the ladder from side to side. She peered at it, and saw the rope disappear into darkness. "It sways. There's no wall to steady it, so watch your step. And we're missing a rung. You know what that is?"

Cassie shook her head. Sam explained: "It means you'll step down and there won't be anything for your foot. But if you keep reaching down, you'll find the next rung. We'll warn you."

The man stared at Cassie's legs. It made her uncomfortable. All her life she'd been taught the warning signs of male interest.

"She'll be able to reach it okay," he said to Sam. "But maybe you should go first, just in case. You can help guide her."

Cassie worried about him less now, and more about the missing rung. He might have sensed this because he said, "Really, you'll be fine. The minute you didn't get all scared when you looked down, I knew you'd be all right."

The girl forced a smile. Yurgen waited for Sam and her to climb on before he snuffed the torch. Much as Cassie liked ladders, this one did indeed sway a lot, and in the sudden blackness it seemed to sway even more. She felt like she was hanging in a vast open space where nothing was real but the rope, branch, and the darkness pressing in from all sides. Like emptiness would eat her, too. Leave her hollow as a husk. Her palms turned greasy, and she death-gripped the ladder, squeezing even harder when Yurgen stepped down.

His weight jerked them forward. Not much, but it lifted Cassie's feet higher than her head, and for a moment left her feeling like she was clinging to a ceiling. Her heart hammered mercilessly. The ladder straightened.

"Ready?" Sam asked just below her.

"Yes," she said, voice shaking.

"You'll be okay," Yurgen said from above. "I can pick the winners at the starting gate. You'll do great." He closed the hatch.

Cassie's stomach lurched. She gulped air and followed Sam, sliding her hands an inch or two at a time, never losing contact with the rope. The ladder swayed with each step they took.

She could not imagine a blacker or more forbidding place in the world. Seconds later her eyes squeezed shut in anguish. When Sam reached up and touched her foot, Cassie realized she'd stopped moving again.

"Do you hear that?" Sam asked.

"Hear what?" Cassie cried softly.

"Just listen."

She held her breath, and the whisper of flowing water rose from the void. Cool, moist air swept over her, lifting the heat from her skin and opening her eyes to the densest darkness she'd ever known.

Outside the Mayor's chamber the guard cinched Bliss's hair tighter around his hand and wrist till it looked snug as a glove. Then the bullishly built man jerked her head so hard roots exploded from her scalp. Her eyes spilled, but she did nothing to try to stop him. He'd almost snapped bones in both her arms when he pinned them behind her back, tying her hands so tight her fingers tingled painfully. Only her feet were free so he could drag her along. Though filled with a furious urge to kick and stomp him to death, she didn't dare try anything so futile.

Another guard rushed from the gloom and grabbed her right arm, defeating her last feeble fantasies of escape.

"She's going to Section R," explained the first guard with a smile. "That's where he wants her."

"Hey, he's got plans for her." The new guard, tall and lean and blacker than night, hurried ahead, then backpedaled to look her over. "I *like* you." He sounded surprised. "I like you a *lot*. You're a lucky girl." Still backing up, he switched his attention to the other warder. "We get first crack?"

"First 'crack'? Is that a joke?" He was white, but dark, too, from the sun. "I don't think we would be her first, would we?" He shook Bliss's head. More roots ripped out. She wept, unable to stop herself.

"What was that?" He shook her viciously. She cried out. "I missed that, too," he yelled. "You say something? You better say something when I ask."

"Not my first," she managed. "Others."

The black guard laughed. "They all say that. They don't know, do they? You're stupid," he yelled, still facing her as they moved. "It's much better if *he's* first."

He looked past her and she knew he meant the Mayor. Sick with pain, she still worried about Ananda, even more than the other girls stuck with that insane bastard. He might figure out that Ananda was her sister and take vengeance on her. Or he might realize Ananda was the daughter of the woman who defied him outside when the girls were taken away. Then there was Ananda's health. Would she get enough water? *Why does she need all that water? What's she got?*

"I'm not sure the Mayor's really going to want this bitch," the white guard said, hauling Bliss forward. "She tried to kill him."

"You did what?" The black guard stopped backpedaling, waited, and walloped her in the stomach with a fist as hard as a stone-headed club. Bliss's legs folded.

"Uh-uh." The white one yanked her upright. Her scalp screamed. "Don't make *me* work harder." Then he pushed the black man away. "And don't *you* go damaging the goods. She shows up hurt and you're fucked. Those guys'll be eating *you* alive. I'm not taking the blame."

"Look at her face, man. You fucked her over good." Blood trickled down Bliss's brow, and she thought she'd vomit from the pain in her belly. "Least you can't see my shit."

"I can wipe that off," the white guard said. "You go busting up her guts and there's nothing we can do."

But the black guard wasn't through with her. He shouted at Bliss from inches away, "You try to hurt my man again and I will bite your fucking face off. See how you like that."

Spittle landed on her cheeks and eyes. She tried to blink it away. He was still so close his teeth brushed her lips, smearing the top one. She tried to pull her face away, fearing he'd bite them off. The grip on her scalp tightened.

They turned, hauling her down a corridor formed by more stone torch stands. Night might have fallen. Bliss saw no daylight, but didn't know whether distant walls blocked a view of the desert.

She did see a large cage coming up on her right, crowded with women about her age and a few years older. She hoped the guards would leave her there—anything to relieve the agony of her hands and scalp and stomach.

Bliss looked for a door but all she saw was one large wall made from the same pale bricks she'd seen elsewhere in the City of Shade, with more bones for rebar.

Bones were also used as bars in the cage, like in prisons. The whole country was packed with prisons near the end, her father had told her a few years ago. They were sitting in their camp on a dry reservoir bed when he said he'd been put in a large federal facility in eastern Oklahoma on terrorism charges, but escaped in an uprising that freed five thousand political prisoners.

"The U.S. had more prisons than anywhere on earth," he explained. "Huge ones."

But even all those prisons couldn't keep the richest of the rich safe, he added, because the lone renegade the government and bankers and energy corporations couldn't control was the earth itself. When they tried—and he said they tried mightily for many years—the entire planet turned into a prison.

"There's no escape now, not for anyone." He had nodded at the reservoir walls surrounding them, and she sensed the torment of his last few words.

She felt a similar anguish now in the eyes of the young women staring at her through the bars. Bliss had never seen such ruined gazes. What made them like that? They looked starved, like they might tear off her limbs. Not just bony—everybody was scrawny—but gaunt, the sapped look of severe deprivation, of people denied so much for so long their skin seemed ready to turn inside out, to let blood—and blood alone—have its final sway.

Two of the prisoners reached for her. She saw scabs and gashes on both their arms. The black guard whipped out his truncheon, and Bliss heard a bone break, a *crack* so loud she was unsure whether it belonged to a living woman or skeletal remains. An unbearable scream blasted from feet away, and she knew the answer. Other howls followed, along with painful babbling she couldn't understand.

"Wicca," the white guard said to her, though in a tight voice. "And first chance they get, they'll give it to you."

"Or you," Bliss spat back. He jerked her arms up till she thought her shoulders would explode. But all he said was "Section *R*," like it was much worse than the cage, a simple letter that was more ominous than any taunt.

They dragged her faster, and she felt their unnerving excitement in the quickening pace. The horrors of the cage faded as a plume of torch smoke scorched her lungs. She coughed so hard her chin banged against her chest. She couldn't look up until they slowed down.

The smoky corridor ended at a walled room. Two guards with Asian facial features stepped from the sides of the entrance and opened a set of double doors. One of them grabbed a torch from a stand as Bliss was pushed into a fully enclosed amphitheatre with tiered earthen benches. Manacles hung from varying heights on a brick wall at the rear of the stage.

She made a frantic effort to back away, already sensing the worst. But the black guard who'd punched her now jammed his elbow into her jaw and smashed her shin with his club. Sharp pain shot up her leg so fast she shrieked and lost her balance. The white guard seized her throat to keep her upright. She found her footing, dimly aware that her leg wasn't shattered, and tried to move her mouth. She couldn't. The white guard yelled at the black one.

"Better hope you didn't break *that*."

One of the Asian guards untied her hands. Manacles were clamped around her wrists and ankles. Pain receded from her shoulders and scalp, and her fingers came to life slowly. Her jaw was still numb.

The four guards stared at her. The white guy shook bloody clumps of hair from his hand and said, "Yeah, she's a keeper all right."

He stepped closer and grabbed the neck of her shirt. She knew what he'd do before he did it, and that he wouldn't stop there.

Gunmen from the City of Shade lit a torch and started stripping cloaks and weapons from the bodies. Hunt stared at the dead for a full minute, appearing to savor the kill. *Or is he praying?* Esau asked himself.

His master reloaded calmly while the gunmen rushed to gather a sorry plunder: ragged clothes, two small, chipped pistols, a spear, a slingshot. A few flint knives. Esau wondered how the dead ever figured they'd survive, much less prevail.

The slave trailed Hunt down the dune. His master stood on the periphery before using his fingers to rake through sand around a bullet-riddled man. Then he rolled him over and checked underneath. He repeated his careful search with each of the fallen before unearthing a revolver near the fifth and last body. He turned to Esau.

"They were all dying. This one knew it, so he buried his weapon." The slave noticed the gunmen listening in from the shadows. "For a lot of them, saving something like this," Hunt held up the pistol, "is the most important thing they'll do in their whole lives. If their people had got here first, that's what they would have been looking for."

Hunt stood and wiped down the revolver with the tail of his shirt, eyeing the blue steel appreciatively. Even in the flickering torchlight the gun looked like a prize to Esau. His master squinted to check the cylinder, then cranked the hammer. It sounded well-oiled, ready to fire. He eased back the hammer and slid the gun into his belt.

None of the gunmen challenged his claim. None dared, in Esau's estimation, because his master had somehow assumed command without a threatening word to any of them. The slave knew it was more than Hunt's considerable size at play. It was his master's fearlessness, as if it would never occur to the fair-haired man that others would ever object to his taking the lead, or find themselves as capable as he.

Until tonight, Esau had not seen Hunt shoot or kill. Slaughter, really. His master had systematically gunned down three of the men from behind. Each had mortal wounds in his back and his face in the sand. Their assailant was no mystery.

The slave wasn't shocked by his master's pitilessness. He had long sensed a final unforgiveness in Hunt's eyes, an unblinking willingness to claim lives for the riven Christ of the cross, God the Father's most holy creation crucified by bent men of bent means. By filth, craven and cursed. To know Hunt was to know a man driven by the scourge of divinely endorsed fury.

Driven by more earthly needs, too, as Esau saw night

after night, though only God Himself knew what Hunt had claimed of the living all those times he rode from the base alone. *Boys?* The slave shook his head, but no mere gesture could cool the jealous burn in his belly. Y*ou're with him now,* he tried instead. But memories of their sex, vigorous and wild, immediately stirred Esau's body, and he said a quick prayer, not in penance but to drive away thoughts of pleasure that could point to his foul desire. Hunt wouldn't be the only unforgiving man in their midst.

What about you? he asked himself. *Do you forgive?* He raised his eyes to the night sky. *Do you?*

His master picked through the bounty grabbed by the gunmen. They made no attempt to stop him. "I want these." He held up two of the dark cloaks.

The slave hurried to take the clothing, seeing the men closely for the first time. They had burn tattoos, even on their faces. Esau thought the scarring cruel. He rued his own black S and could not understand why men would mutilate themselves so readily.

"Did anybody get away before we showed up?" Hunt asked.

"One guy," said a gunman with a peculiar shock of dark hair sprouting from the side of his otherwise bald head. The length was about an inch thick and hung past his ear. "We saw him take off for over there." He pointed to a distant dune barely visible in the starlight. "But we didn't see him for long, and these assholes had us pinned down."

Till we came along.

"Just one?" his master asked.

The gunmen nodded, though less assuredly, Esau thought.

"Because I saw two," Hunt said.

The gunman shook his head. His odd hair brushed his shoulder. "One, that's all."

"I saw one of these." Hunt gestured toward the cloaks. "But I saw something that was blond, too."

"No, I'm telling you, it was one guy." The gunman crossed his arms. His pistol pointed casually to the side.

Hunt studied him openly. "Was he from the caravan?"

"No way," the gunman said with equal insistence. His cohorts still held their guns by their sides, but Esau had already seen how easily five men could die. And his master had reloaded while these men rushed to pillage. "We took the caravan before it got dark. None of them got away."

"None?" Hunt still sounded skeptical.

"We got them all, I'm telling you. And they're not going anywhere. We even got a two-headed freak show. One of your 'demons.'" The gunman looked like he might laugh at Hunt's expense, but glanced a second time at the man looming over him and didn't.

Esau was shocked by the blasphemy. The gunmen had taken the demon from hell—the beast His Piety wanted more than any other—and could *joke* of such spawn?

"The only one we left behind was a big guy," the gunman went on. "He tried to run off and I killed him." He stuck out his hand, adding, "I'm Jester," as if his news and name should have dispelled all of Hunt's reservations.

Hunt ignored the offer. "Where?" he asked sharply, as if rebuking more than a handshake.

"Back over the dune," the gunman said sullenly.

They trudged to where the truck and van had stopped. Hunt took the torch and studied the ground.

"Lots of running around," he said, his tone calmer.

"Oh, it was fucking crazy," Jester said. "Bunch of bitches. We couldn't shoot, except for the asshole who ran off and gave me a nice clean shot. We figured you didn't want a bunch of holes in those girls. Not that kind anyway." He laughed.

Hunt did not. Esau suspected his master found the gunmen wanting in the most critical regards—faith in God, and a belief in the sacred role of females. The Alliance never made light of them.

"I want to see the man you killed."

"Sure." Jester shrugged and smiled, showing black and missing teeth.

They walked another fifty feet or so to the body of a large bald man. Hunt waved the torch over the length of it, lighting what appeared to be evidence of digging near the abdomen. He turned to Jester. "Did one of your men do this?"

The gunman shook his head.

"Roll him over," Hunt ordered.

"You roll him over," Jester snapped.

Hunt stared him down. When the gunman bent to move the body, Esau stepped forward. Hunt put out his hand. "You're not his slave."

After a struggle, Jester pushed the body over. They found a hand axe, but no gun.

"He didn't have one," the gunman said.

"He did," Hunt replied. "A good one. Someone fired three shots at us. High caliber, nothing like the popguns you found."

"It's that one." Jester pointed to Hunt's belt.

Hunt shook his head, and a smile crept across his face. It didn't look pleasant. "There were two of them that I saw, and only one was shooting. The others were already gone by then. And those were the *two* who got away."

He brushed past Jester, stepping around the dead man. Hunt held the torch out, then followed a short trail over a wind-sculpted ripple. He turned back to the gunman.

"Who searched here?"

"Me. That's why I know there was no goddamn gun."

"Don't ever take the Lord's name in vain around me."

Jester shrugged again.

In the space of a breath, Hunt drew a pistol and raised the barrel to the gunman's face. "Do you hear me?" Jester nodded. "Now put your gun away. Do not tempt me."

The man slipped his gun into his belt. Hunt did the same. Esau stared at Jester's weapon while his master turned boldly away and raised the torch over a short, shallow trench.

"So where's the kid?" Hunt asked.

"What fucking kid?"

Hunt grabbed the gunman by the back of his neck and

forced him forward. "The kid who was hiding right here, probably while you were wasting your time over there." He spun Jester around to the man's body. "It all makes sense now. The kid with blond hair. The kid who got the gun you missed. The gun that almost got us killed."

"No kid got a gun."

"No man leaves a good axe," Hunt said. "That's something a kid does. Or you."

He pushed the gunman away. When the man tried to draw his weapon, Hunt smashed it from his hand with the torch, then jammed the flame into his face. Jester staggered sideways, moaning and covering his eyes. Hunt glared at the other gunmen, shaking his head in warning. None moved.

"Kneel," Hunt ordered Jester. "Tie his hands behind his back," he said to his slave.

"Fuck you," Jester yelled.

Hunt clubbed him again, driving him to the sand before plowing the flame into his neck. The gunman screamed and rolled onto his side. Hunt pressed his gun into Jester's strange patch of hair. "Hands behind your back."

After pulling a leather strap from the man's belt, Hunt handed it to Esau, saying, "Tie them tight."

His master placed his boot on the small of Jester's back. "You're a fool. You missed a girl and a gun. I'll let your Mayor deal with you."

Esau straightened, satisfied with his knots. Hunt ordered Jester to stand. With his hands tied—and his face and neck burned, bleeding, and crusted with sand—he struggled to his feet. None of his compatriots moved to help him.

Hunt grabbed Jester's arm. "Now search him carefully," he ordered Esau.

The slave found a sheathed knife inside the man's waistband, but nothing else. He gave the blade to his master.

"You're good at that," Hunt said. "Now check this one." He pointed to the dead body. "Let's see what else this fool missed."

Esau pulled a six-inch steel knife from a pocket inside the right boot. He tugged them both off, along with the dead man's belt, but left the clothes. The shirt was stiff with blood, the pants fouled.

Hunt told the four other gunmen to drop their weapons. "You'll get them back when we get to the City of Shade. That's a promise. I don't want any of you trying to save his worthless life." He waved the torch at Jester, who cowered and fell. "I'd just have to kill all of you." Hunt sounded weary to Esau.

The men stared at his master until a short black man flipped his sawed-off single barrel shotgun on the sand. The others followed suit. Hunt had him gather the weapons, including the ones taken from the battle, then waved the men forward with his pistol.

"I want you about ten feet ahead of me. No farther. And you," he pressed his gun to the back of Jester's head, "stay right where I can see you." Hunt shoved him. *"Move!"*

The beaten gunman staggered along, his right eye closed. He made helpless attempts to rub it against his shoulder before squeezing it shut even harder, as if to relieve the pain. Esau watched him closely. The slave knew humiliation well—and the murderous impulses it provoked.

When they made their way back to the motorcycle, not far from where the caravan had stopped, his master told him to load the cloaks, boots, and weapons into the sidecar. But Hunt stopped him when he tried to add the steel knife to the pile. "You may keep that," Hunt said, stunning Esau, who had never been permitted a weapon of any type. To carry one on the base was tantamount to suicide. He slipped the knife into his belt, feeling a surge of power that almost unnerved him.

Hunt waved his revolver at the four gunmen. "Keep doing what you've been doing, and stay on firm ground. Don't go on the dune. We'll be following on the bike." He handed the torch to the short black man. "Keep it where I can see it. And you," he turned to Jester, "don't stop moving. If you slow down, I'll drag you from the back of this thing." Jester stumbled forward, still favoring his shut eye, which leaked a steady stream of pink tears.

Hunt straddled the bike and patted the seat behind him, as he had at the start of the journey. Esau settled on the torn leather, relaxing for the first time since somebody in a cloak fired on them and came close to killing his master.

The slave reached around Hunt and felt two pistols now protruding from his pants. He rested his hands on both of them, letting his fingertips linger on his master's warmth.

Hunt started the old Harley, and squeezed Esau's hand to him. The slave smiled and grasped his master's thick length, the bike vibrating powerfully beneath them. Then he gently kissed the back of Hunt's shirt, careful with his scabs, and tried to stop worrying about boys.

You're with him now, he told himself again.

The cool moist air thrilled Cassie, and she found the sound of flowing water so inviting that Sam had to urge her to slow down.

"You've *got* to be careful. It's a huge drop, Cassie."

But it was as difficult for the girl to ease up now as it had been to move only moments ago. Just as she managed to settle into a safe, steady pace, Sam warned that they'd come to the missing rung. She reached up and placed her hand on Cassie's ankle, offering a reassuring "There you go" after guiding her foot past the open space.

They climbed down for about five more minutes before the girl heard Sam step off the ladder. Cassie released her grip gratefully when the woman helped her down.

"Can I drink it?" the girl asked. A foreboding as dark as the air overcame her because she worried the water was poisoned with chemicals like plutonium, or the many other invisible killers that wiped out millions who had been spared Wicca and the most crazed human hands.

"Yes, it's totally safe," Sam said. "It's been thousands of

years since this water's been anywhere near the surface. But wait for Yurgen." He was climbing off the ladder. "He'll get the torch going so we don't trip."

Cassie stepped rapidly in place, barely containing her excitement, but even her escalating anticipation couldn't compete with what she saw when Yurgen sparked the torch and raised it high.

Despite her thieving thirst, Cassie's eyes were drawn immediately to a nearby wall that rose in sedimentary layers a foot high, an inch high, sometimes ten feet high—widely varying bands of radiant yellows, purple, rose, and buff.

Yurgen grinned at her amazement and stood on his toes to lift the light higher. As far as the glow extended, the girl saw a wall painted with the pristine colors of creation itself.

"Over here, Cassie. Yurgen, show her."

Sam turned her around as Yurgen cast the light on a turquoise-colored stalactite spilling from an arched ceiling so high the girl could glimpse but a fraction of its vastness. The inverted cone dripped water, as alive as stone can be.

Cassie almost slipped when she ran toward it, but righted herself in an instant, hugging the formation to feel the breadth of coolness, the wash of freshwater on her parched chest and belly and legs.

She saw Sam's eyes alive in the firelight, and asked for the water. She could no longer deny her deprivation, not even for beauty as immense as this.

They followed Yurgen through a forest of stalagmites and stalactites. Cassie thought of hide-and-seek, and the wonders that could come from playing with the girls down there.

They quickly crossed rock so smooth and seamless it felt soft, before weaving past clunky-looking boulders to a stony bank. *Is it really a river?* She had only heard of them, and could scarcely believe one flowed only feet away in the absolute darkness of inner earth. "A river?" she now asked aloud.

Sam nodded, tears spilling down her cheeks.

"Why are you crying?" asked Cassie.

"I'm just happy for you. Go on," she waved toward the water. "You must be very thirsty."

Cassie knelt, and Yurgen held the torch over the water. The girl scooped it up, startling the brilliant reflection of flame. She sipped carefully, and that made her cry, too, because the water tasted fresh and pure, as untouched as the sun or moon or girls unborn.

Plunging both hands back into the flow, she splashed her face, drinking lustily for the first time in her young life. Water snaked all the way down to her belly, and she felt the rich firmness of its chilly presence in her stomach, empty for many hours. Only after she drank her fill did she notice Sam's hand on her back. The woman was kneeling next to her, wiping drips from her own face.

"What is this place?" Cassie asked, marveling at the water and all she had seen in the past few minutes.

"We call it the Caverns," Sam said.

Yurgen gently squeezed Sam's shoulder. She rose, taking Cassie's hand. The three of them walked back across the smooth stone, but instead of weaving through the majestic turquoise formations, they bore right, following the floor of the cavern as it widened like a delta, as perhaps it had been millions of years ago. They moved by torchlight for another ten minutes, unencumbered by climbs or unwieldy descents.

When they stopped, Cassie looked up, spying at least a dozen people in the near distance huddling and talking around a smattering of candles. They stared at her for several seconds, but turned back to their discussion.

"Who are they?" she asked.

"Good people," Sam said. "Are you hungry? You must be."

Cassie took a deep breath as she tried to figure out what she needed most, food or sleep. "I'm too tired," she said. "Can I eat in the morning?"

"Of course." Sam took the torch from Yurgen and showed

her a gray blanket lying on a bed of white sand. "Do you think you could sleep here?" she asked. "We'll be right over there, if you need anything."

Sam held out the light, and the girl glimpsed more bedding about fifteen feet away. She nodded.

"You won't wander, will you?" Sam asked softly. "There are places you could fall and hurt yourself in the dark."

"No, I won't." Cassie wanted nothing more of wandering, much less in the dark. She wanted only sleep, and what she couldn't have: Mom, Dad, Jenny, Maul.

"In the morning, you'll be able to see everything," Yurgen said.

"You'll like it," Sam added. "It's fun. You can play in the water, and you'll meet some nice kids."

"Really?" Tired as Cassie was, the prospect of meeting other children roused her. But playing in water? She'd never heard of such a thing. "What about *my* friends?" She watched Sam and Yurgen exchange a worried look.

"We'll see what we can find out," he said.

Cassie lay on the blanket, her bones nesting comfortably in the sand. Sam tucked the soft fabric around her shoulders.

"You'll need this," the woman said. "It does get a little chilly down here."

"Sounds good to me," Cassie replied. Sam laughed.

She closed her eyes, and the two adults hurried off. When their footfalls faded, Cassie heard voices. Mostly men. She could make out little of what they said, and she was scared of the words they spoke most loudly: "attack," "kill," and "gun them down."

But then a woman talked. Maybe Sam. She sounded even more urgent than the men, and Cassie heard her clearly. "I'm telling you, we have to move fast. Come tomorrow, somebody might see our tracks and wonder why those land mines didn't go off near the dune. We ran right over where we took them from."

"Wait a second!" another woman said. "What about all the people they just took prisoner? They got about twenty of them, we saw them, and a lot of them were girls. Just like the kid you brought down here. They'll all get crushed, too. We can't go blowing that place up now."

The talk grew heated, but Cassie had drifted off after the first mention of land mines. She'd heard the word so rarely, it hardly frightened her at all.

Chapter Twelve

A lone torch burned in the Mayor's chamber. The sparse light faltered by his bed, leaving him in shadows dark as his skin.

"I want you to come here," he said to Ananda in his mellifluous Caribbean accent. "Lay yourself down next to a fine man such as me." He patted the quilt of the black knight in shining armor, reclining like royalty himself on two fat pillows. Then he smiled, and she saw his bright teeth in the gloom.

They had just eaten. True to his word—and his queer pronouncement that it was a time "only for joy"—the Mayor ordered slaves to bring them jugs of water and platters of food, more than Ananda had ever known in a single serving. It included smoked chicken that she figured might have been plundered from the van. But the one-eyed slaves—their empty red sockets more frightfully prominent than their other beaten features—also brought bowls brimming with greens in a peppery sauce, and a runty, tough-skinned, almost tasteless vegetable he called a potato.

"Not like the fine spuds in the days of old," the Mayor said with gusto, "but they will keep you regular."

Ananda had no idea what he was talking about, but the

provisions slaked her deep hunger and thirst—if not her fear, sharpened by his command to join him on the bed.

"Don't do it," M-girl hissed in her ear.

"I hear you," the Mayor said to M-girl. "You are the 'don't' girl. Always you say 'don't' to your little friend. Do not say that. You lay yourself down next to her. I want you both close to me."

A bony African guard, with a pistol and unsheathed knife in his belt, pressed his steely fingertips into Ananda's and M-girl's backs.

"But first," the Mayor raised his own index finger, "tie all their hands. No monkeyshines from girls." He laughed. "And take this beautiful quilt away." He eyed their dishevelment. "I do not want our knight to get dirty."

A squat Latino guard summoned a slave, who rushed to fold up the bedding and place it in a handsome, carved wooden chest. Other guards entered to bind all the girls' hands behind their backs.

"You two," the Mayor pointed to Ananda and M-girl, "come settle your pretty selves down." He patted the bed again. "The rest of you," he appraised them openly, "go lay your bodies down next to them. Except you old ones," he shook his head at Teresa and Bessie. "You get on the floor."

Ananda struggled on her knees to the Mayor's side, trying to keep her balance on the soft mattress. Dizziness and dread made work of every step. As she settled on a patched sheet, gray as shale, she turned toward M-girl.

"No-no-no," the Mayor said. "That will never do." He rolled her over. With her hands behind her back, she was forced to lie on her side facing him.

Imagi took the opportunity to try to burrow between Ananda and M-girl. The Mayor sat up, shaking his head.

"You are a pest, a big pest, and you try the patience of a fine man." He reached over Ananda and hauled Imagi to the edge of the bed. "You stay there." When Imagi wailed, he clamped his hand over her mouth. "You do not make a sound or I will scare you," he said bluntly to her.

"She has Down syndrome," Ananda said.

"Do not make excuses for such a girl. How can she learn?"

Imagi quieted, though Ananda wondered for how long. But mostly she worried whom the Mayor would put his hands on next. If he didn't touch girls for sex, like he'd claimed, why were they squeezed together all the way to Leisha and Kaisha on the far side? Bella and Gilly, and the two redheaded Gibbs girls, curled at their feet like frightened kittens. Plenty of choices for the Mayor. *Maybe he wants all of us.*

But he wants me *right here.* She watched his chest rise and fall from an inch away. To gain even this sliver of leeway, she had to press tightly into M-girl. The two shared a pillow.

The African and Latino guards kept a close vigil. The torch looked ready to die; a single tongue of flame lapped lazily at the dark. The Mayor, still on his back, turned his head toward Ananda.

"I like you girls in bed with me," he said softly, an intimate tone that unnerved her more than his actual words. She thought the others also might have heard him, certainly M-girl, who stiffened noticeably. "It is a great comfort," he went on, "but I must have my men here in case you get any dangerous ideas. I am a man of great fairness, so I should tell you," he tapped the tip of Ananda's nose with his pointer, sending her into a near panic, "that dangerous ideas can be most painful at night, especially to a girl so young and small as you."

What do you mean? But her stomach lurched as she realized exactly what he meant, no matter what he'd said about being a "fine man."

His big brown eyes opened wide, alarming her even more. "I know you understand the meaning of such things because you are not a stupid girl." He pulled her close, forcing her belly to his hip and engulfing her face with his hot breath. It didn't stink, but the raw heat of his innards scared her senseless. "You may keep your girlfriend with you. I do not mind the 'don't' girl. Not really. I think it is *sweet,* the two of you. Like candy. Do you like candy? All girls like candy."

She shook her head, neck so stiff it felt like a twig snapping. She worried that the worst kind of touching would now begin, but feared even more that M-girl would try to stop him—and get them both killed. M-girl had saved her life once before, and she knew her girlfriend would do anything for her.

Ananda reached back, pressing her bound hands against M-girl's stomach, thinking, *Don't. Don't. No matter what.*

Imagi started up again, no longer wailing but whimpering loudly. The Mayor groaned and rolled toward her, releasing Ananda.

"I want you to be *quiet*," he said angrily to her. "Or I will show you what I do with pests."

"May I hold her hand?" Ananda asked without thinking, afraid he'd do something grievous to the girl. "Just till she goes to sleep. It's what I do to help her feel safe."

The Mayor rumbled, and she thought he might explode in anger before realizing he was chuckling. "Safe?" he said. After containing himself, he added, "Tell her to behave or I will have to get rid of her."

"Telling her won't help." Ananda took a breath. "I have to hold her hand."

"Is this a plan, little one? Do you think, 'I will get my hands free and be brave like my big sister and mother?' Because you do not want to end up like them. Remember—"

"What do you mean?" Ananda's voice broke. *What did you do to them?*

He stared at her and shook his head. *Don't ask.* An unspoken command had never been clearer to her—or harder to obey.

"Remember what I said about dangerous ideas in the night and such a small girl?" She nodded. He untied her. "But she does not get free." He poked Imagi, which made her cry out. "You may hold her arm but that is all."

Ananda dared to prop herself on her elbow to reach over the Mayor. But she was tired and weak, and her arm shook visibly.

"May I sit up?" she asked.

"Yes, you may sit up, little one. I like to look at you, but first, I want to do this." He seized her arm—making the whole of her tighten—and drew it up alongside his body, farther from his pubis. Then he rested it on his chest. With his other hand, he pulled Imagi higher on the bed, too, so Ananda could still reach her. The girl cried.

"The game, Imagi. The game," Ananda said anxiously, using their peculiar code for "quiet." After a moment, Imagi settled.

"I know you do not want to touch me down there," the Mayor said, "and I do not want you to. We do not want to punish you in the night, do we?" He stared at her. She shook her head—*No, we don't*—and felt so grateful she almost forgot that he planned to sell them to the Alliance, where men had no such scruples. "But sometimes girls have the wrong idea about a man," the Mayor went on, "or the wrong idea about the wrong man. They think he cannot control himself, that every man is a beast, like my dragons. Or they look for special favors. They think, 'Maybe he will let me touch him down there, and then I can hurt him.' But this is never so with me. I am a fair man, I tell you this is true, so there are no favors, even for one so fine as you."

After Imagi fell asleep, he turned Ananda away so he could retie her hands. She smiled at M-girl, who quickly mouthed *I love you*.

Then he rolled Ananda back toward him and waved over the African guard, pointing to the foot of the bed. "The one with dark hair."

The guard rousted Teresa and brought her to the Mayor. Ananda had hoped he would tire, but he sounded ready to hold court. Only Imagi, snoring, separated the Mayor from the older girl.

"You and the one with red hair, what is your age?"

"Seventeen," Teresa answered with a tremor in her voice.

"But you do not have Wicca. How do you do that?"

"We worked in the bath house . . . at the Army of God.

The men were afraid . . ." Teresa paused, pursed her lips so hard they whitened and looked painful, before opening her mouth for a big breath. Then her words spilled out in a rush: "They were afraid because we touched all the girls when they were—" She stopped as suddenly, and Ananda sensed that Teresa was too terrified to say "naked," as if the word possessed a hidden incendiary power in a shadowy room with a bed, a man, and armed guards to work his will—as if the assurance he'd just given her, the "little one," could never apply to a mature young woman. "The men stayed away," Teresa managed. "From us, I mean. Not the young ones." Her eyes fell to the other girls.

He reached out and took Teresa's hand, separating her fingers. He studied them and looked at her palm. "And now you are too old for sex, even with a fine man such as me." He flipped her hand aside. "We are not sure what we will do with you. You do not have so much value. We could make you sick with Wicca. Then we could use you. Then we could have fun. We will see. So will you," he added to Ananda with inexplicable cheer. "Take her back," he said to the African, who jerked Teresa to the foot of the bed and forced her to the floor.

"You do not need to be so hard with her," the Mayor admonished the younger man. "She is a sad one in this world."

The Mayor turned his big eyes back on Ananda. She wished he'd go to sleep. How long would this go on? *All night?*

"Do you want more water?"

She nodded, wondering if she wore her thirst like some people wore their anger.

He sat up and the white guard handed him a jug the color of sand. It looked marred from use, like it might have been made by native people hundreds of years ago. She wondered how it survived, when they hadn't.

He placed the smooth opening by her lips, letting Ananda drink her fill again.

"Tell me, little one, do you get dizzy?" The Mayor handed the jug back to the guard.

"Sometimes."

"Sometimes? What does this mean, 'sometimes'? I saw you almost fall over when you got on the bed."

"It doesn't happen much." She didn't like his questions or attention. She just wished he'd go to sleep so she could, too.

"For how long do you get this dizzy feeling? And I do not mean when you look at a fine man such as me." He pointed to himself and chuckled again.

"Not long. Seconds. Maybe a minute. That's all."

"No, I mean how long do you feel this way? Do you feel this for two months? Two years?"

Ananda felt girls stirring on the bed, as if they were listening in. Imagi, thankfully, was still snoring. "A few weeks. I think it's from traveling, moving around all the time. That's all."

"I do not think this is so. Are you always hungry?"

"Everybody is."

"Yes, this must be true for you. Your parents, they do not do such a good job keeping you fed." Ananda could have screamed. "But how long do you have this thirst?"

She wanted to say, *None of your business*. But now he seemed to know something about her that she also wanted to know. Or thought she did. "I'm pretty sure I've always been thirsty," she answered carefully.

"I do not think this is so," he repeated. "How are your eyes? Do you see like always?"

That was the first question that actually scared Ananda. Her eyesight was getting worse, sometimes by the day. She hadn't told anyone, not even M-girl; but she understood, with the most awful feeling, that he might know a terrible secret about her. She didn't want to hear it anymore. *But he keeps asking me stuff.*

"I see fine," she said.

He called over the African. "Stand by the torch and put up some fingers. Do not say how many." The guard did as he was ordered.

"What do you see?" the Mayor asked Ananda.

"It's too dark."

"It is not too dark. I think you have—"

"Three! Three fingers," she interrupted. She did not want to hear him say what he thought she had. Ever.

"Two fingers. And this is new? Not seeing so well?"

Ananda shook her head no. Then he did the same, and she knew he didn't believe her.

"Do not lie to me again, and I will not lie to you. What about the burns on your legs? Do they heal as fast as your friend's?" He peered past her at M-girl, who whispered "No," like she was worried. Ananda threw her a furious look.

"Do not be angry at her. She is your friend," the Mayor said. "This is why she says this to me. I think you have diabetes. This is such a sad thing. The worst kind. The kind that will kill you soon. I have seen it before. My own mother, she had diabetes and took insulin. But then the insulin," he looked away briefly, "it disappeared and no one could find it anymore, not even me. She died. So many died from sicknesses that did not kill, but now they do. Diabetes, Ebola, polio. Even the flu. Your life will be short. I am so sorry to tell you this, but people who are dying, they need to know such things."

"No, you're *wrong*. I'm just thirsty. I don't *need* extra water. I took it because you said I could have it. I don't even want it anymore. Keep your water."

"You are angry. That is understandable. I could be wrong, little one, but I do not think so. You have so many symptoms of diabetes."

He brushed hair out of her face, then did it again. She wished she could stop him. She'd stopped Zekiel with words. The leader of the Army of God also touched her hair in bed. The zealot rubbed it between his fingers and told her that soon it would cover the most sacred part of her body. He kept toying with it, tugging hard enough to pull her face close to his. Terrified, she had asked him, "What is sin?" Zekiel had stopped and stared at the ceiling then. The Mayor stopped on his own now, but *his* words already doomed her: diabetes would go on and on and get worse until she died.

Ananda had thought she would die at the Army of God. She fought like an animal to survive. And she was brave. Everyone said so, and she knew she had been. She couldn't believe she survived the massacre and all those horrible men and the burning at the stake and a bloody battle, only to be killed by a stupid disease that wasn't nearly as bad as Wicca. Wicca was the only disease that mattered, right? *Right,* she answered herself fiercely.

Bastard.

She moved her eyes from the Mayor and looked around the room. The torch flickered. Only a tiny, blurry flame now. *It's going to die like me.* Tears spilled down her cheeks. *No, you're not dying,* she scolded herself immediately. *You're not a stupid torch.* But every time her eyes strayed to the blurry flame, she thought of what the Mayor said. She couldn't stop herself.

He shifted toward her. "Go to sleep, little one. Do not worry. This world, it is not so kind to ones like you. It is not a good place to stay." He rolled her toward M-girl.

When his breathing deepened, she buried her face in her girlfriend's shoulder. After several seconds, and without a word, they separated and peeked around. The torch had gone out but still glowed red, casting a blush on the African who stood by it. He looked sleepy, too tired to stare. Ananda wanted to make out with M-girl and forget everything she'd just heard, push as hard as she could against her girlfriend's chest and hips and mouth so maybe for a second or two they'd become one. Twice before they'd flooded with pleasure together, lifting so far from all they'd ever known of life they might never have returned. But now only their lips and tongues touched, and only for a glorious, bewitching instant before M-girl's eyes flew open. Ananda looked over her shoulder and saw the African guard watching them.

They lay in silence for several seconds before M-girl whispered, "What's diabetes?"

"Don't believe him." Lowering her voice even more, Ananda said, "He's just another killer. What does he know? He fed that girl to a monster." She wanted to spare M-girl her own fears.

"But something's wrong with you. You're weak. You know you are. You shake a lot, and those burns aren't healing. My scabs are almost gone."

"He's . . . a . . . *liar*. Have you ever heard of diabetes?" M-girl shook her head. "Me, neither. He's *crazy*. You know he is. So don't listen to him."

She wasn't trying to spare just M-girl's feelings anymore, she was trying to ease her own anguish. And she did feel better. Much better. Diabetes sounded like one of those silly things people worried about in the long ago, like zits or fat or catching a sniffle. That's what it was, a *little* problem. *And you've got* big *problems, like getting out of here.*

She couldn't fathom how. The glow of the torch vanished, throwing a blanket of darkness over the room.

"I love you," whispered M-girl. "I'll always love you."

"Don't say it like that."

"Like what?"

"Like 'I'll always love you' because I'll be gone. I *won't* be gone."

"I didn't mean it like that."

Yes, you did. But then Ananda realized that M-girl might have been trying to convince herself that she hadn't meant what she'd really said. "Listen to me, girlfriend: I'm not going anywhere. And I love you, too. I'll always love you," she added impishly, tapping her forehead gently against M-girl's.

They kissed deeply till weariness made them stop. Ananda wanted so much to wrap her arms around M-girl and hold her close, but all she could do was rest her forehead back against her girlfriend's, sharing the air they breathed as exhaustion finally stilled them both.

And the bed started spinning.

Bliss hung from the manacles, awakening in starts throughout the evening. The rusty metal cut her skin, and the pressure on her arms sent sharp pains through her shoulders. Tired, she tried to stand, but her shin throbbed where the black guard had struck her with his truncheon. She worried he might have done more damage to her leg than she'd thought, and her mouth still ached from his vicious elbow jab. But at least she could move it. A broken jaw could have been fatal without straws or blended food. She hadn't known any relief from the burning pain of her scalp; and from the excited remarks of men staring at her nakedness, she knew more blood had trickled onto her face.

Dozens of guards and gunmen had passed through the modestly sized amphitheater. To avoid their stares, she closed her eyes long before she tried to sleep. Even now they gathered near the small stage, only feet away, lathered with lust, mouths agape, fevered hands on themselves and one another.

The morbid sexual spectacle made Bliss dread what would happen if the guards left her alone. Two of them collected weapons at the door, and three more kept the gapers from climbing on the stage. Without the guards, she thought she would have been raped to death hours ago. But she knew the real reason for the armed presence wasn't to shield her—it was to protect the men from acting on impulses likely fatal to *them*.

A wiry Asian did make it partway onto the stage, just long enough to grab her pile of torn clothes. The guards laughed and let him keep them. They might have grabbed them back—if they'd known his plans. The Asian ripped apart her pants and shirt, sharing his bounty until the last shred was taken. A dozen or so men sniffed the rags like animals, violated them freely, and became the first group to actually storm the stage. The guards bellowed warnings and threats, and pushed them back. But no one was struck, and she closed her eyes on spasms and groans and the twisted, contorted faces that held no feeling for the object of their desire.

When the melee ended, Bliss heard someone in heavy boots walking toward her. "Look at me," he growled. His familiar, demanding voice reached only dimly through her fatigue and simmering fear. He repeated himself even more harshly.

With her head hanging down, she opened her eyes on the stage floor, a patchwork of peeling plywood and grayed planking. His shadow fell across thin vomit, and she recalled pain building convulsively in her gut from the black guard's punch. She thought she'd passed out—and maybe she had—but not before she sickened.

She also spotted the shadow of a knife coming closer. A second later, alert at last to the threat, she raised her head. The white guard who'd ripped out clumps of her hair—and stripped her naked—stood only feet away.

"Don't ever make me tell you something twice. I say, 'Look at me,' you *look* at me," he shouted. He crossed his arms, as if to hold himself back, and stared at her body. "You're putting on a helluva show. You think you're pretty fucking hot, don't you? Got all the guys dying for you." He glanced at the men behind him. She avoided their jumpy eyes. "Sure you do," he went on, arms still crossed, only now he was also appreciating his knife in the torchlight, angling the blade from side to side. He caught her staring at it and smiled. "You think nothing can touch you, not even this." He waved the blade in her face. Bliss forced the back of her head against the brick wall. She would have smashed her skull through it, if she could have.

He went on: "You're wrong. We *can* touch you. It's all in how and when we do it. You know why? 'Cause you're a porn queen. We've seen tons of them. You're just another skuzzy one. You'd give us the disease, if we gave us half a chance. You'd torture us to death with it." He waved the knife in her face again. "Wouldn't you?"

"No," she gasped. Her throat was so dry she could hardly speak.

"Uh-uh." He grabbed her jaw where his partner smashed

her. She screeched from the pain. "Wrong answer," he laughed, pressing the flat of the blade against her cheek. "Say, 'Yes, I'm a porn queen,' and make me believe you or I'm going to start cutting."

Despite his grip and the blade, she managed to parrot him. He let go of her face.

"Glad to see your mouth is still working. That's important. Now I'll tell you what I'm going to do 'cause I'm a good guy. I'm going to get you some water. But you pee it out and you're going to clean it up." He glanced down. "Looks like you've got lots of scrubbing to do."

He walked to the edge of the stage, returning with a dented metal cup. He let her empty it.

"Just remember, we don't ever clean up after porn queens, and you're not getting out of these things," he shook a wrist manacle, "till Friday night."

"When's Friday?" She had to know. The manacles were unbearable.

"You should have asked that before you drank all the water. That's two whole days from now. Then guess what?"

She shook her head. She was too frightened to offer the guesses that came immediately to mind.

"Uh-uh. You did it again. Stupid porn queen." He jerked her arm down so hard Bliss's shoulder felt sundered. She screamed, and more blood ran from her wrist. "What do you do when I ask a question?" he said with exaggerated patience.

"Answer," she cried.

"You got it," he said cheerfully. He released her arm. Pain grilled the length of her limb. "We'll let you go Friday night. That's Fight Night. After it's over, when we're all warmed up," he moved his fists like a boxer, "we'll be playing a game we all really like. Want to know what it is?"

"Yes." She spoke mechanically now, without feeling or regard for meaning.

"'Catch the Queen.' Isn't that cool? I'll be in charge, so don't you worry, I'll make sure to give you a head start. I always give the pretty ones a head start. Makes it more fun. And the rules are real simple: we catch you, and then we *kill* you, starting with all the porn parts. What's the porn queen then?"

She'd figured that out hours ago, and almost nodded before catching herself. "The reward."

"That's right." He flipped the knife, caught it smartly, and pointed the gleaming tip at her face. "Section R."

Chunga roared through much of the night. An hour might pass in silence, and then the dragon would wake Jessie again. His bellow, so sudden and sharp, brought back the ships' foghorns from her childhood, when she played on the sandy shores of Cape Hatteras and saw freighters and warships and oil tankers—and the bejeweled yachts they bought—fighting wind and chop and the treacherous currents that surged from the north and south and collided beneath their barnacled hulls. Mariners had called Hatteras the "Graveyard of the Atlantic," and standing knee-deep in its Gulf-warmed waters, undertow tugging at her feet, it had been easy for a scared but astute twelve-year-old to imagine the whitecaps as the burgeoning tombstones of an imploding planet, the endless mournful waves the aggrieved survivors trying to hurl themselves back to land, to the ever-eroding promise of life.

Jessie nodded off, only to be startled awake when the Komodo smashed the wooden gate, rousing her from a vivid dream. Again he roared, as if tortured by Burned Fingers's knife attack on its tongue. Or because he's starving, she thought. Clamoring to eat them.

She'd been dreaming of Eden and their long trek to the dry reservoir bed, when Bliss was a toddler and she was pregnant with Ananda. The dream was strangely silent, like a film in the old days with the sound turned off. Her husband was the focus, armed as he always had been with his rifle and bandoliers. She watched him cast them aside, as he never had in real life. They fell to a fully muffled earth, raising a squall of dust. He walked away in the eerie hush, never turning back.

Jessie sat in the darkness believing the dream meant she'd broken a promise to him, and so he was done with her, now and forever. But what promise? They'd never had time for promises on that grueling trip south, only survival.

Burned Fingers stirred a few feet away. They had settled about halfway between the two gates, trying to get as far as possible from the stench of those dragon dens.

"You awake?" she asked quietly, though they'd detected no guards or anyone else the night long.

"Most of the time."

"It sounds like that beast is trying to break out. Remember him saying he did that once before?"

"Nothing's broken yet. I've been listening. A couple of hours ago the one that ate the girl got back. I heard them getting it out of the wagon. There must be a tunnel they back that thing into. His name's Tonga."

"Tonga? Tonga and Chunga?" She rolled her eyes in the darkness. "The Friday night fight?"

"'Tonga the Terrible,' to be precise. That's what some joker called it, and it wasn't our smooth-talking Carib."

She shuddered thinking of the woman, and the man who'd put her to death. *We're dead, too.* To have brought their daughters on such a harrowing journey now seemed unforgivably wrong.

That's the promise you broke. She was thinking of her dream again. *The one to* keep *surviving.* She'd violated the heart of every decision she and Eden ever made: to protect their daughters. Though Jessie didn't know where the girls were or what was happening to them at this moment, she knew all the younger ones like Ananda were now imperiled by the most depraved men she'd ever met—those who had taken them to the City of Shade, and those who would turn them into child brides at the Alliance. Even if the girls were not harmed tonight or tomorrow or the next day, it was only because they were seen as the most valuable commodity on earth.

And what of Bliss and Teresa and Bessie, unprotected by the spare immunity of age and innocence? And the boys? A man had already tried to rape Jaya.

She'd failed all the children. And the loss of their exclamations and awe—even their soft breaths and sudden stillness—left only echoes of silence, in dreams as in life.

Even after reviewing the pressing reasons they'd fled the drought-whipped reservoir, she came up with nothing that could justify dying in the mouth of a beast, or leaving children to the horrors hiding in the City of Shade. The caravaners wanted more from life, but that had always been the fatal fallacy of humans. She blamed herself because she, of all people, should have known better. She'd seen millions of species fall prey to the planet's most ruthless horde. To think that more of anything but agony could ever be claimed without a staggering price was the most murderous conceit ever embraced by—

"Tonga's a little more laid back than Chunga," Burned Fingers said.

Tonga? Jessie was so consumed by worry and guilt and regret that it took her a moment to remember the second dragon. "He's digesting," she replied at last, the image so ghastly she despaired of saying so.

"That makes sense. I wonder how long he'll stay satisfied. Be nice to think we'd have only the one to deal with."

"It's still two. They'll kill anything that looks edible, including each other, and eat it later." She could scarcely believe he'd found encouragement of any kind in going up against a Komodo dragon so hungry or wounded that it was still hurtling itself against the gate that kept it from a meal, or revenge, or whatever drove its instincts.

"They can get by on a dozen meals a year," she said, recalling the detail from a graduate level herpetology course, "although judging by the one we saw, they've been eating a lot more than that for a long time." More facts came back to her: "And they digest something like ninety percent of what they eat. The rest—the hair, horns, claws—they cough up in a disgusting ball. It's supposed to really stink."

"That's just what this fragrance counter needs," Burned Fingers said, spurring faint memories of wondrous scents she hadn't actually smelled in decades, and which otherwise would have been unimaginable to her. He said something else she didn't catch, lost as she was in the pleasant realm of the distant past.

"I'm sorry, can your repeat that?"

"I was just wondering if there's any way we can kill *them*?"

"With a rocket launcher." She wasn't entirely kidding.

"How about with a damn sword?" he asked. The weapon the Mayor had promised them.

"Let me think." It was hard to reconcile fighting a pair of Komodo dragons with an ancient weapon. *Like St. Michael and the dragon.* Except that was myth, no matter what some people believed. Even thinking of taking on those beasts felt like nine parts resignation and one part resistance. But she was impressed that Burned Fingers could even strategize, and it sparked a dim hope in her.

"If they let both of them in the pit at the same time, it's possible—not likely but *possible*—they'll rip into each other for the right to eat us. That could buy us a little time. And if one of them gets torn up so bad it can't come after us, we might have a chance to fight the other one. But I just don't see the Mayor letting his two big attractions tear the crap out of each other. Which is why I think he's going to be really pissed when he sees what you did to his pet."

"What's the worst he can do to me, Jess? Throw me in a pit with a disgusting beast from the back of the evolutionary bus? He's already done *that*. I may lose some sleep down here, but it won't be over slicing and dicing some goddamn Komodo's tongue."

She couldn't argue with that. "Our only hope is stabbing them in the heart with a sword or spear, something sharp enough to cut through their hide and sturdy enough that we can really drive it deep into their chests. But that's got to happen fast because if we get bitten, it won't be long before that venom basically paralyzes us."

Chunga roared and smashed the gate again. It creaked loudly, like it might shatter. The ground shook.

"This could be over awfully fast," Burned Fingers said.

"If we're lucky."

"But if we're still here come Friday, the Mayor's going to make us wait before he brings the dragons out. I'll bet you anything he's planning on us being the big finale. He'll have us up there in chains watching all the hors d'oeuvres getting snapped up by God knows what."

Now Chunga roared, like he was in pain, and they heard a ghastly, guttural noise. Within seconds the worst odor yet wafted over them.

"Tonga just coughed it up," Jessie said, hand over her mouth and nose.

"The fur ball?" Burned Fingers sounded like he was also covering his face. "Makes me want to scream, too."

"It's called a gastric pellet, but 'fur ball' will do." It was so malodorous the frickin' beasts were known to rub their faces in dirt to try to get rid of the stink. Tonga was already banging around back there.

"That's the single worst thing I've ever smelled," Burned Fingers said, "and that's saying a lot."

Jessie agreed, but at least she could catch a full breath now. "What did you mean about him making us wait on Friday night?"

"I just think he'll have all sorts of fights lined up with all kinds of creatures. They'll be the undercard; we'll be the main event. Just like in the old days."

"You mean boxing?" she asked. "Hardly."

"No," he said, "I mean the fights to the death."

"Organized ones?"

He grunted.

"I never heard of them."

"I guess not, because you sure wouldn't have forgotten," he said.

"By the time I was old enough to notice anything, there wasn't even Internet. But you do have a few years on me."

"Yeah, I guess I do. Well, they'd get poor fuckers from Africa or Asia, South America, sometimes from the developed world, including this country when people got desperate enough, and you could vote from home on the kind of weapons they'd use—chains, pipes, clubs, crowbars, stuff like that. Hammers, anything you could bludgeon with. No guns or knives—they didn't want the fights ending fast. Then they'd dangle a big bucket of food and it would be a fight to the death. Their families had to agree to be right by the cage, so you'd see starving, pathetic kids screaming at their fathers at the top of their lungs, 'Kill him, kill him.' Didn't matter what the language was, you knew what they were saying. It was the highest rated show on the old Execution Channel."

"I guess I missed that one, too."

" 'Twenty-four hours a day,' " Burned Fingers intoned in the deep voice of an announcer, " 'live death, when you want it, *how* you want it.' Doesn't that ring a bell?"

"No, it doesn't."

"There's going to be more than just us on the menu, that's all I'm saying."

"With the dragons?" Jessie asked.

"No, I doubt that. He'll be saving them for us." Chunga roared with such timing it was as if he were agreeing with Burned Fingers. "But I think the Mayor will have something else going on to keep the crowd juiced."

A whole series of bloodlettings sounded so dismal that Jessie figured he was right. They'd never waste the girls by throwing them in the pit. But boys? They'd probably see them as expendable as the dogs. Maybe more so. The older girls, too. She guessed that men with burn tattoos would find lots of entertainment in gladiator girls. Some of the adult women, like Maureen Gibbs and Solana—even with her machete wounds—were plenty strong and could put up a good fight. So they'd be seen as good sport. Same with the men, of course, especially Maul, although Jessie hadn't spied him on the march there, or his little sidekick, Cassie. Burned Fingers hadn't seen them, either.

"Maybe Maul got away," she said. "He's tough. There's some hope."

"I can't believe I've got to pin my hopes on a guy who wanted to murder me a few weeks ago."

"We all did, in case you've forgotten. Anyway, you're here."

"Because you wouldn't let him."

"You were useful," she said, laughing softly, surprising herself. "So be useful now."

"There's no rabbit in this hat, Jess. But let's try hacking up their tongues one more time before someone comes around. You take Tonga, and I'll deal with big mouth over here."

Jessie pulled out her knife from under her pants and walked along the curved wall till she felt the wooden gate. She tapped it and listened to the dragon stir. Then she crouched and waited for the beast to get curious. When nothing more happened, she rubbed the blade against the bottom of the door to try to draw his attention. The opening wasn't much, about five or six inches, but it proved ample for that slimy tongue. Much as she was prepared for it, she almost screamed when it darted out with enough force to knock the blade from her hand. The forked organ enveloped her wrist. She feared the beast would drag her hand under the gate and into his mouth. But he withdrew his tongue and offered a short bellow, modest by Chunga's enraged standards.

She wiped off glops of saliva, then searched for her knife, careful not to impale herself; dragon bacteria could be deadly.

Chunga roared on the other side of the pit. As Jessie wheeled around, the beast smashed the gate once more. She could just see Burned Fingers's dark outline jump up and start dancing with his arms in the air. He looked like a crazy man.

But he knows war. Always reminding herself of this in the worst moments.

When she spied the silhouette of his knife waved above his head, she realized the absolute blackness of night was retreating, and that light, however weak, had invaded the City of Shade.

Only seconds later a soft voice drifted down from the top of the pit. Jessie looked up and could just make out a man crouched above them, but not what he'd said. Neither did Burned Fingers.

"Missed that, partner." The marauder spoke warily.

"I've got food and water for you," the man said in little more than a whisper. "I'll lower it down, but we've got to hurry. I can't have anyone finding me here."

A chain rattled the still air as he lowered a bucket. The prisoners put away their knives. They found a metal canister, a handful of hard round vegetables, and two chunks of meat with a smoky smell. The chicken, Jessie thought.

"Just pull us out of here," she said, taking hold of the chain.

"Not now. We'd all be dead," he responded urgently. "Trust me, just drink the water and put it back in the bucket. And take the food. But *don't* hoard it. You don't want them finding it on you. I'll be back, if I can."

He seemed to look around everywhere at once, but it was still too dark for Jessie to make out his features. "Who are you?" she asked.

"Never mind. And I heard what you were doing to the dragons. It's a bad idea. If they catch you they'll cut off your fingers or hands to even the score. He really babies those monsters."

She and Burned Fingers took turns gulping the water and returned the canister to the bucket. The man pulled it up, put it aside, and scurried away without another word.

"Who is he?" Jessie didn't expect Burned Fingers to

know, and he confirmed this by shrugging his shoulders and taking another bite of the chicken. But then he leaned forward, as if to say something, so she did, too. Their cheeks brushed, sending a shocking tingle through her system. She recoiled, so intent on avoiding a further intimacy that she almost missed what he said:

"That's someone who doesn't have the best interests of that madman at heart."

"I hope he's got some allies," she responded in a tight, quavering voice that belied her fear—or unbidden desire. Or fear *of* unbidden desire; even she didn't know. She looked away, took steadying breaths, and tried to eat.

"Unless he's suicidal, I'm guessing he's working with at least somebody else. I'd say things are looking pretty damn bright compared to a few minutes ago."

Bright? She wouldn't go that far, but the man had brought them more than sustenance. He'd brought them hope. *And you?* Her eyes settled back on Burned Fingers. *You just brought me—*

Chunga roared louder and longer than he had before, shutting down Jessie's thoughts and turning her gaze toward the frightening eruption. The beast was thrusting his entire head through the narrow gap above the gate, wresting chunks of hard earth from the low tunnel ceiling. Then the reptile smashed his heavy chest against the boards, repeatedly driving himself forward on the strength of his huge, powerful haunches. The wood screamed like it would shatter. He whipped his head back and forth, raining more dirt clods into the pit.

Jessie and Burned Fingers jumped to their feet. She backed into the wall, swearing to herself.

Chunga's claws, long and thick and sharp as railroad spikes, gripped the top of the gate. They raked the edge furiously, like a hefty dog trying to scrabble up a big boulder. Wood chips exploded into the air.

The creature bugled and arched his bulky neck, visibly straining against boards and earth. He bulled his head as far as he could and tried to roll his massive wrinkled shoulders into the widening gap. The gate sounded like it was truly splitting apart.

Jessie drew her blade again. So did Burned Fingers. But she knew it was a hopeless gesture. A few inches of flint to face down a raging carnivore at the peak of the food chain?

The giant lizard paused in his wild struggle only to stare at them and probe the air with his long wounded tongue—as if he were already tasting his prey.

Great gobs of drool spilled from his gums.

And then he lunged like a beast that had broken his chains.

Chapter Thirteen

Esau perched on the back of the Harley, hands hanging limply by his sides. The slave had wanted to hold his master through the long night, but found no excuse. Hunt drove slowly behind the disarmed gunmen as they navigated mine fields and tramped around sand dunes that would have bogged down the bike.

Light seeped across a gray, awakening sky, exposing a bald absence of soil, brush, or life. Hunt steered around another dune, and the slave saw the City of Shade for the first time. It stood in the desert a half mile away, colossal and unyielding, as if risen of sulfur and rock salt.

The sidecar creaked brazenly, weighty with food and water, confiscated firearms, and the medieval-looking cage. A moan sounded above the axles and iron. Jester, the defeated gunman with a burned and leaking eye, staggered to keep up with the motorcycle, openly fearful of being chained and dragged in the sand and grit, turned to scab and bone. Ahead of them the short black gunman still carried Hunt's torch, its reach weakening in the looming day.

When the band drew to within a couple hundred feet of the City of Shade, three sentries raised their rifles and shouted for them to stop. The bricks and mortar looked even more massive now, a beastly edifice extruded from earth, heavy as a mountain. Fat columns supported the roof every twenty feet along the broad face, bones protruding rudely like compound fractures. From what Esau could glean of the torchlit interior, many more columns studded the shadows.

Far to his right he spied rows of towering junked cars, taller than any building he had ever seen. In his youth, before he was taken slave, he had passed through a city called Mobile. Thousands of cars had been bombed or burned or discarded like trash amid piles of rubble so thick that finding streets was impossible. Even the city's graveyards, with their cherubs and angels, crosses and chiseled paeans to the dead, lay flattened and shattered, slabs of marble and concrete no stronger than china or ceramic under the crushing weight of the collapse.

But Esau had never seen anything like the wrecking yard. All that destruction so orderly, so neat, as if to defy devastation. Only a God of infinite mystery could have granted such design to such ruin.

Two of the sentries approached. Hunt drew his pistol, then settled his hand back on the ape-hanger handlebar, muzzle pointed casually to the side.

"*He* did this to me," Jester suddenly screamed, jerking his head toward Hunt. "This fucker burned my face. Shoot him! Fucking *kill* him!"

The pair of sentries glared at Hunt, but Esau found it telling that they didn't raise their weapons at his master, who got off his bike, leaving it to idle. Esau, alone on the seat, wondered if he could drive it. He'd watched Hunt touch wires together to start the engine, and use his hand and foot to change gears.

"Shoot him!" Jester screamed again.

"I want to see the Mayor," Hunt said to the sentries. He looked at Jester. "And *I'm* taking him with me."

"No you're not, you fucking—"

Hunt silenced Jester by gripping the back of his neck, as

he had when he forced him to confront his failure to find the girl or the dead man's gun.

"The others can have their weapons back," Hunt announced, glancing at the wary men who'd led them to the City of Shade. "As long as they move on," he added sharply.

Jester tried to wrest his head away from Hunt. "You're not doing jack shit with me, you mother—"

Hunt released him, only to punch his burned face so hard Esau heard a bone crack in Jester's nose. It sounded like a twig snapping. Blood flushed from his nostrils. He put his head back to try to stop the bleeding, reeling away in agony. Hunt grabbed the lone hank of dark hair hanging from the side of the gunman's head and jerked it like a dog's leash. A *pop* sounded—it might have been Jester's neck. "Sit," Hunt commanded, as if to humiliate him further.

Jester collapsed on the ground, blood dribbling from his nose, head tilted awkwardly. Hunt flipped aside Jester's hair. Still holding his pistol to his side, the blond man opened the cage with his free hand and returned the firearms he'd seized from the gunmen.

"I want mine, too," Jester cried.

Hunt ignored him, turning to the others. "Don't think of helping him. He made mistakes. You don't want to."

The short black man actually nodded and hefted his sawed-off single shot. He looked happy. Hunt told him to give the torch to Esau, who jumped off the Harley. The four gunmen walked toward the City of Shade.

One of the two sentries grimaced. The other, more muscular man, stepped closer. His lips were pierced with tiny polished bones. From babies, Esau thought. He had seen that once before.

"Why the fuck are *you* telling them what to do?" the sentry demanded.

Before Hunt could reply, Jester cried, "Because he's a fucker."

Hunt glanced at the departing gunmen. "They're smart enough to listen. Are you?"

The question hung as a challenge. When the sentry didn't respond with words or weapon, Esau saw that his master had taken command again. He behaved as if no one would dare shoot him; therefore, no one did.

"Tell the Mayor the Alliance guy is here," the sentry said to his brother-in-arms. But he kept a defiant tone and an eye on Hunt, who drove the Harley to the City of Shade, cutting the engine only after facing it away from the building.

The slave followed on foot. Jester still sat in the dust.

"Get up here," Hunt shouted to him, "or you'll never walk again."

The gunman climbed to his feet and stumbled toward them, moaning as he lowered himself gingerly to the ground about ten feet away.

A lean African guard stepped from the building, saying the Mayor would "receive" Hunt in the Oval Office. Esau knew the real Oval Office was not in the Great American Desert, much less the City of Shade, built on the remains of a prison. His master had told him that many years ago the actual Oval Office—and the rest of the White House—were looted by a mob of thousands that hung the president naked from the rooftop flagpole, which quickly grew so heavy with her husband, children, and members of her cabinet that the top half snapped off. Hunt said the building itself, stripped of every last plumbing fixture and chandelier, switch plate and knickknack, was finally "blown to bits."

"What's he talking about?" Esau whispered.

"Idiots," was all his master said before telling Jester to get up.

The gunman didn't budge. When Hunt reached down, the African tried to push him away. Hunt shoved him back. As the black man moved to draw his weapon, Jester came to life, screaming, "Kill the fucker!"

Hunt thrust his gun in the African's face, freezing him with his revolver barely out of his belt.

"Put it away," Hunt said evenly to the man, "or I'll kill you." He spoke with the same menacingly calm voice to

Jester. "I'm tired of you. If you make one more mistake, I'll kill you, too."

The African put away his gun. Hunt grabbed Jester by his strange hair and dragged him to his feet, before returning his gaze to the black man. "I know you have a job to do, but don't waste yourself on him. I doubt his life is worth the dust around here. Now let's go see your Mayor."

At Hunt's direction, Esau snuffed the torch and left it by the motorcycle. His master told Jester to follow him—and warned the gunman not to try to run off. The slave doubted that he could; Jester looked barely capable of standing as he got to his feet.

Without a word, the African led them along a torchlit path that revealed a structure unlike any Esau had ever seen, even at the old military base with its huge assembly halls and chapel. Sparse daylight crept into what appeared a mostly open but crowded interior. More than a dozen long rows of sleeping mats disappeared into the shadowy distance, but no one rested. The men were squeezed around cold fire pits eating their morning meal, or pressed hip-to-hip on heavy benches that might once have lined the visitors' gallery in the Ohio state capitol. They stopped talking and stared at Jester and the others.

From stoves in adjoining canteens, the acrid odor of burning coal tainted the air. A cook pounded a long metal cookie sheet, jarring loose a pile of hard biscuits. Esau heard them fall onto a concrete counter. Farther along, five men lifted dumbbells crudely constructed from rocks and metal bars that looked like car or truck parts, or steel studs ripped from the walls of abandoned homes. The weightlifters barely paused to notice the passersby, but the slave was mesmerized by their glistening, well-nourished muscles.

They approached a white guard, who opened a door to a large room lit by several torches. The fumy air irritated Esau's lungs. There were no vents in the walls, empty except for a jagged circle of blue carpet with an official-looking seal. It hung behind a table that dominated the room as wholly as a rapaciously rendered eagle dominated the emblem. The bird's wings were aggressively outstretched, and a red-and-white-striped shield protected its chest. One talon clutched an olive branch, the other arrows. Esau noticed the colors were dull, most likely from smoke and dust and the insults of smuggling.

Hunt studied it, too, as the Mayor entered through a door neither master nor slave had noticed. Both started when the wall opened, and turned their eyes from the carpet.

"Do you like my art?" the Mayor asked in a silky accent. He settled at the table, the African guard standing by his side.

"Fuck that shit!" Jester bellowed, lurching toward the table. "Look what that asshole did to me." The gunman thrust his face at the Mayor to show him his bloody, rheumy wound. "He burned my eye and beat me with a fucking torch."

Hunt nodded his assent. The Mayor stared at Jester. "Be silent. We are discussing art."

Jester trembled, Esau guessed, with suppressed fury.

"It's a replica, right?" Hunt asked the Mayor, who shook his head.

"No, it is the real carpet from the Oval Office. My grandfather brought it back to Curacao when he sailed from this country. He took it from the White House himself on the day it fell. He saved it from certain destruction. I am proud to have brought it back home to the Bloodlands. Do you want to touch it? Make sure your eyes are not dreaming?"

Hunt shook his head. Esau knew better than to respond.

"Then answer another question and tell me why you demanded a meeting with me at this hour?"

Hunt glanced at Jester. "This joker doesn't know how to do his job. He didn't find a small girl who escaped when your men raided the caravan—"

"That's a lie," Jester shouted, but the Mayor sat forward.

"And he did such a lousy job of searching a man he killed, somebody else found the guy's gun and fired at me. None of your men managed to find this one," Hunt held up the pistol he'd dug out of the sand, "after they burned through a bunch of ammo last night, killing five guys. I'm guessing the dead ones were out there trying to claim whatever they could, like the missing girl. Somebody did, too. Probably the same one who shot at me. I don't mind this joker missing the gun I found, because I'm keeping it, but another gun *and* a girl? That's not good for you or me."

"He's a fucking liar," Jester shouted.

"And if he keeps calling me a liar, I'm going to kill him."

The Mayor shook his head. "Do not press your luck, Mr. Soul Hunter, but you must tell me, did my other men see evidence of the girl you say got away?"

"They sure did."

"I will talk to the them—but you, Jester, will not be a happy man if you are lying to me. If this is what you are doing, I will feed you to my pets. So tell me now—this is the Mayor talking to you, not the Alliance—and I will give you one more chance. Is there any truth to what Mr. Soul Hunter says?"

The gunman said nothing.

"Now I will tell you what you will do, Jester. You will go find the missing girl. You may take food and water for five days. If you do not find the property that is mine, you will have stolen from me. So then you should kill yourself because it will be faster than dying without food or water. If you insist on coming back anyway, I will feed you to Tonga and Chunga."

Jester looked stunned. The Mayor smiled and continued. "You can see that finding the girl is your only hope. It is daybreak. The clock starts now. I would go to the wrecking yard. I would search every car, if I had to. Do what you must to find her, but do not set off a rebellion. I do not need that kind of problem. We have a glorious celebration tomorrow night. Do not spoil that for me."

"Why don't I heal up for a day or two, then? I can't even see out of this goddamn eye."

Hunt walked toward Jester, who backpedaled, tripped,

and fell to the floor. "What did I say about using the Lord's name in vain?" Hunt demanded.

"You do not have authority here," the Mayor said. "If he wants to say 'goddamn,' it is okay with me. Now, stand," he ordered Jester, who rose but shrank from Hunt. "When a child is missing, time is of the essence. This has always been true, now more than ever. You have made a most serious error, and you should go before I change my mind and take you to the special pit."

"I need my gun," Jester said sullenly.

"How will I get it back if you fail to find the girl and must kill yourself? Then you will have stolen more property from me, even in death. I cannot have this be. Here." The Mayor pulled a steel knife from the African guard's belt and slid it across the table. "You are a skilled eviscerator. But that is all you get."

Jester grabbed the blade and barreled from the room.

Hunt pressed both fists on the table and leaned toward the Mayor. "I want everybody on that caravan back. The girls, boys, the *demon,* the insurrectionists, and that includes Burned Fingers. And—"

"Burned Fingers?" the Mayor interrupted. "We have the one called Burned Fingers?"

"Don't worry, you'll get your bounty."

The Mayor shrugged like he didn't care. "Is he the one with the burned hand?"

"That's right—"

"I thought he was a strange one. He is in my special pit, so I do not think you can have him."

Hunt, undeterred, pointed his finger at the Mayor. "We must have him *and* the demon. The same goes for the oil tanker and van—it's all ours. Nothing stays with you. You did your job in taking the caravan, but nothing belongs to you."

The Mayor laughed heartily. Esau thought he sounded genuinely amused. But a distant beastly roar brought the black man to his feet at the same moment a spindly Asian guard burst into the Oval Office, yelling, "Chunga's breaking out."

The Mayor darted from behind the table, surprising Esau with how fast a big man could move.

"This will have to wait," the Mayor said to Hunt, "but you may come with me. You might see something you will never forget. Chunga is very hungry."

Hunt and Esau followed him.

The City of Shade became a maze, as dizzying with its sudden enclosures and darkly shadowed paths as the desert was daunting with its vast reaches and burning sky. They made a series of rapid turns, coming quickly to an open arena with a wide round pit. The Mayor slowed. Then he stepped between guards holding torches, their gazes fixed below. The slave inched closer. A creature roared again. "Get us out of here!" a female screamed.

Esau watched a tall woman with a dark braid back into the wall. About twenty feet away a monstrous lizard had jammed his head between the top of a wide wooden gate and the end of a tunnel ceiling. The beast's efforts broke off great clods of dirt and clay from the wall, and his long claws raked the top of the boards. With a sharp *crack,* two of them snapped off, and the reptile jammed a shoulder into the opening. Esau felt weak just watching.

Next to the woman stood a man. Burned Fingers, the slave figured. He noticed both of them held knives close to their legs, and wondered where they got them.

"So you are Burned Fingers, I hear," the Mayor said in a voice the slave found too jovial for the circumstances. "What did you do to my Chunga?"

"Nothing," Burned Fingers shouted, "but he sure looks hungry."

The Mayor chuckled, which Esau could barely hear over the lizard's roars. "Oh, yes, he is a hungry boy. I want him to be hungry, but you must have done something to him because—" He stopped short and turned to a guard. "Take your torch over there and hold it over Chunga."

The lizard, drooling copiously, crashed his heavy body

against the gate. The boards sounded like they were breaking apart.

Jesus, Esau said to himself. Quickly, he begged the Lord's forgiveness for such a blasphemy. And surely the Lord would forgive him because the creature's next powerful thrust wedged *both* of his shoulders between the rupturing gate and the top of the tunnel. Seconds later, when the guard held the torch out over the beast, Esau saw the battered boards actually bowing. The Mayor saw even more.

"Why does poor Chunga have bloody saliva?" he demanded.

"Gingivitis?" Burned Fingers shouted. "Who the fuck cares? Get us out of here."

"I care," the Mayor said staunchly.

"Yeah, you want us fighting tomorrow, you better get us out."

"Do not tell me what I want. What I want right now is a true answer. I do not lie, and I promise you that I will let him eat you right now if you do not tell me what—"

Another hard *crack* silenced the Mayor as the lizard slammed his front leg through the top half of the gate. Then the beast lunged hard enough to force most of his upper body into the enlarged opening. His claws raked the wood again, shaking it violently, before he smashed his other leg through the last unbroken board on the top part of the barrier. The chunk flew through the air, landing in the middle of the pit, not far from the prisoners.

The Mayor resumed speaking in the same steady voice. "I want to know what you did to my pet."

Esau found the Mayor's tone maddening. The animal wanted to *eat* those two people, and if someone didn't move fast, he *would* eat them. *Jesus,* Esau said to himself again, not bothering to beg forgiveness.

The woman spoke hurriedly to Burned Fingers, but Esau couldn't hear her over the lizard's exertions. When the slave looked back at the creature, he edged away from the pit in horror. The beast had climbed halfway out of the pen, and his long abdomen was tented over the wrecked gate. With another mighty effort, the saurian sank his claws into the sand and looked up, probing the air with his bloody tongue.

"You're looking at it," Burned Fingers shouted, pointing to the beast. "I cut him up with my knife."

"You have a knife?" the Mayor asked.

Burned Fingers held it up. "Your men did a shitty job searching me."

"What a surprise," Hunt said.

"Bring him up," the Mayor ordered the African guard, who lowered a chain. It was linked to a metal ring anchored in concrete.

Burned Fingers urged the woman to go first.

"No," the Mayor declared. "There will be no gallantry from you. I did not say anything about the female."

"I'm not coming unless she goes first," Burned Fingers said. Only yards away, the lizard clawed up buckets of sand trying to haul the rest of his body over the beaten boards.

"You are a fool." The Mayor lifted his gaze to Chunga, then he eyed the woman. "Come," he said to her.

She made it halfway up when her foot slipped and she slammed against the hard wall.

Only the lizard's powerful haunches were still behind the gate when the splintering wood collapsed like tinder. The beast floundered, found his footing, and rose up.

The African reached down and grabbed the woman's wrist, hauling her from the pit and taking her knife. But it was too late for Burned Fingers. He turned from the wall and stared at the dragon. Incredibly, to Esau, the marauder raised his blade and stepped forward to fight.

Chunga charged.

"Oh, you are good," the Mayor said. Esau thought he meant the lizard, but then the Mayor yelled, "Look up," and tossed Burned Fingers a blazing torch.

The instant the marauder caught it, he swung the flame in an arc. The beast stopped so suddenly his front legs plowed up sand, then he lurched away from the fire. The momentum shot a gob of drool into the air that landed on the torch, sizzled, and almost snuffed the flame. Burned Fingers raised the torch above his head. Pink drool slid toward his hand. The Komodo spotted the opening and darted at him. Burned Fingers jumped aside. The flame burned up the last of the drool and flared brightly. Burned Fingers held out the torch like a sword, tilted upward. The dragon circled him.

"I want him alive," the Mayor said to the African guard. "He is an exciting fighter." Esau listened closely as the Mayor went on. "My guests will love him. Get the wagon backed into the pen, and find something tasty to tempt Chunga. But not too much. I want him hungry for tomorrow night. Look at him!" The Mayor pointed to the dragon circling Burned Fingers. "He really wants to eat him. Oh, this will be a good fight." He put his hand on the African's shoulder. "Get him a leg. No, an arm," the Mayor said after a moment's reflection. "A smaller one. Female. Just a snack to tide him over. But make sure it is fresh. And then you should help Burned Fingers."

The African ran off, and the Mayor turned his attention back to the pit. Burned Fingers was moving in a tight circle, keeping the torch well before him. The lizard had forced him farther from the wall. The beast seemed to know what he was doing, a cunning starving creature with meat only feet away.

"How about tossing me a gun?" Burned Fingers yelled without looking up.

"You do not need a gun," the Mayor said. "Fire is such a primitive fear. But you should feel honored. I have never seen my pet so agitated. He wants to eat you very much."

The beast lunged forward, shooting out his tortured tongue, as if testing the air for heat. Burned Fingers stabbed the torch at the bloody organ, but the Komodo was quick and pulled it back.

"Yeah, a real honor," the marauder yelled. "How long you want me dancing with you know who?"

"I did not hear that you were a man of such humor, Mr. Burned Fingers. Only that you were a fine killer. Are you a lover, too, in these dangerous times? Is this your lady friend?" The Mayor grabbed the woman's arm and forced her forward.

"Nope," Burned Fingers answered without sparing a glance at him.

The African guard raced out of Chunga's pen with a torch, shouting, "We've got to get him back there. There's a wagon."

An unseen woman in the tunnel shouted, "No, don't. Please don't do—"

Horrific screams fried the air.

The arm, Esau thought. Breathless shrieks might have confirmed this.

Chunga backed away from the torches. Then the beast turned and ran toward the ceaseless cries, as if their meaning had finally registered in his reptilian brain.

"Thanks, bub." Burned Fingers handed his torch to the African guard and climbed up the chain. He looked exhilarated as he dragged himself from the pit, paying no mind to the overarching agony back in the tunnel. Guards closed in on him, demanding his knife. The marauder looked at their guns and handed it over.

"Take them to a cell by the sick ones," the Mayor ordered above the screams, which began to weaken.

Two burly white guards seized Burned Fingers. The Asian grabbed the woman at gunpoint, and the prisoners were marched away.

Esau saw his master turn to the Mayor.

"You have men fighting your Komodos?"

"Yes, but most are not good fighters. They try to run and my pets eat them. I think Burned Fingers will give a good fight." The Mayor nodded. "Come, we must finish this business of ours."

He walked from the pit with a guard on either side of him. Another one trailed Esau and his master. The slave feared he'd be shot if he made one wrong move. Even his master did not appear so commanding in the City of Shade.

More daylight had stolen into the building. Esau saw a group of men cleaning weapons. They had brushes and cloths, and the smell of fuel filled the air.

Once in the office, the Mayor took his seat, but didn't encourage Hunt, much less his slave, to join him at the table.

"No matter what you think," the Mayor said, resuming the conversation as if he'd paused only to sneeze, "the people on the caravan do not belong to you. They belong to us. So does the gas. But," he raised his hand to stop Hunt from interrupting him, "we can negotiate. We want gold bullion. Do not try to pawn off sacks of dust on us," he said dismissively. "Not for a prize so great as the caravan. We know the Alliance has bullion from the old fort at Knox. And," the Mayor raised his hand again, "do not expect Burned Fingers or that woman. They are both going in the pit tomorrow night, and they will never leave it. I do not care about your bounty."

"You'll care about what His Piety wants, and he insists on Burned Fingers," Hunt said. "He led the attack on the Army of God. He killed dozens of our men. He committed horrendous crimes against our people, so there's no negotiating about him. But we'll let you keep the woman."

"Do not tell me what I can keep. I will tell you the terms of trade, and Burned Fingers is only the beginning. We want two used-up girls for each of the virgins. If we had not stopped the caravan, they would have been blown up by now. But your used-up females are not so valuable, so the Alliance also must give us two hundred kilos of food, a Basalt rocket launcher, and five hundred grenades." Basalt was the Russian manufacturer of the RPG and its ammo, before the factory had to shut down in the third decade of the century. "One more thing. We will take half the gas before your return."

"No you won't, and I'm not here to negotiate," Hunt said. "I'm here to take back everything. And that includes *all* the gas."

Esau had never heard his master's voice harden so fast.

"How will you do that, Hunt? You are but one man with one slave." The Mayor glanced at Esau. "And you think we will let you leave here with any of that? You are a mistaken man."

"I will put some in chains and march them back, and I will come back for the rest."

"You are not in a position to make such demands. The Alliance has no gas, and the Russians have taken the Strategic Petroleum Reserve."

Esau detected the slightest tic on Hunt's face. The slave was shocked his master was learning of the catastrophe only now. Esau had overheard the news back in the chapel, but never would have admitted to Hunt or anyone else that he eavesdropped on His Piety. The Mayor must have spotted his master's surprise, too.

"Yes, that is what happened. You did not know this?"

Hunt did not reply. Esau saw tension in his master's face, neck, arms.

"Your wealth is limited," the Mayor went on. "Your need is great, so of course you will negotiate—from a position of weakness. And do you know why? Because we can always ship the girls north, now that we have gas. We are in touch with the Dominion, too. And we control *all* migration across the Bloodlands. What do you control? Gas? Not anymore. You cast your lot with losers. We did our job. We stopped the caravan. We caught everyone with only one man killed. And we will find the girl. She could not have gone far, and Jester is highly motivated. So now you must do your job and tell the Alliance what we demand."

"His Piety will never accept this," Hunt said.

"But he has no choice." The Mayor stood. "Do not confuse a stupid white man with me. We have not had so many talks, Hunt, but do not think you can humiliate me. I will kill you myself. But I am a fair man. That is my code. I will give you a child to take back, to show *your* masters that you have found their prize. But do not expect a girl. I will give you a boy. You may take him to His Piety and tell your master what I require for all the others. This is a grand gesture on my part. If he thinks he can attack the City of Shade, tell him I will hunt him down and feed him to my pets. That is not an idle threat. I have my own allies now. The Russians and I get along very well. They are not so crazy with religion. His Piety placed all his eggs—is that not what you say?—in the wrong basket. He thought the gas would last forever."

"Give me the demon, then. I will take the demon back."

"You do not listen, Hunt. You will take a boy. And why do you call two fine African girls a demon? You are a sad man, Hunt, to say such a wicked thing. I slept with them last night." Esau saw his master startle. "That is right, in the same bed with all the other girls, and look at me." The Mayor tapped his head with both hands. "No horns. Imagine such a thing. So do not call those fine African girls a demon. You are a gullible man, if you believe such tripe. Now, I tell you, go. Leave. I will have a boy brought to your motorcycle. You like boys. I have heard."

The guards shoved Jessie and Burned Fingers into a cell that shared a wall with a much larger brick chamber imprisoning upward of twenty horribly gouged women. Snarls and whimpers rose from their midst. Jessie thought they ranged in age from mid-teens to mid-twenties.

Thick human bones formed a barred window in the common wall. Femurs, Jessie recognized. She peered past them, unsure whether she could see all of the women without moving closer and calling attention to herself. What she did glean looked nightmarish. Several women lay unmoving on the bloodstained floor. Two looked recently slain, with deep bite marks, including half a dozen on each of their faces. Chunks of tissue had been torn away, along with all of their clothes. One had no eyes.

A number of women caught Jessie looking. They stared

back at her, gazes jittery and wild with apprehension or anger. They were tortured by Wicca—limbs, torsos, and faces uniformly red with cuts, blood, and scabs. A few spoke gibberish; one responded nonsensically, then turned her burning eyes to the newcomers next door. But most wandered about without any apparent purpose or pattern, bumping into one another, shouting and striking out at their cell mates.

Two women and a slightly built teenager rushed the window. Each of them had infected bites on their faces and necks. Half the teen's ear had been torn off, leaving another suppurating wound. She reached between the bones with a broken arm, straining to try to touch Jessie, who reared back, fearing the disease. But she was still close enough to see that the fracture had driven a spike of shattered ulna through the girl's skin. Dark blood crusted the opening.

"Fix it!" the young woman demanded. "You broke it, you fix it!"

"I didn't break it," Jessie said after she thought the girl had calmed. "I just got here."

"She broke it," another teen declared. Jessie spotted a white glint on the young woman's bloody forehead, and realized it was expressed skull. "I saw her, too."

They howled together and tried to yank the bone bars free. Burned Fingers crouched. He looked ready to fight, whispering to Jessie, "Don't let them break your skin."

But they're biters, was all she could think at seeing the ravages of the disease after all these years.

"Wait!" screeched a woman with numerous facial wounds. "Wait," she repeated, this time eerily. She clawed her face, scraping thick scabs from her nose. She paid the gore little mind, wiping off her hands on her filthy shorts. "She's bigger than the one that broke your arm." She peered at Jessie. "Did you get bigger?"

Bliss, Jessie thought immediately. But she warned herself to sound disinterested. "Did you see where they took the girl," she hesitated, "who broke that one's arm?"

"Section R."

The response set off an eruption. Women stomped their feet and shouted senseless profanities. Three of them jumped a wire-haired teen next to them, pummeling her viciously. A girl no older than fifteen bit her own hand, tearing off a fat mouthful of palm. She chewed it and smiled at Jessie. Her chipped teeth were the pale pink of her gums, lending the latter a bizarre, elongated appearance. Blood flooded from her lips and quickly dripped from her chin. She held her mangled hand through the bars, as if to share it. Jessie backed away.

"We all go to Section R," yelled the woman who'd casually clawed her own face. "And some of us come back here. You, too."

"She's too old," said the younger one with the broken arm.

"Where's Section R?" Jessie managed to ask.

"Down there," the broken-armed girl shouted. "Down there, and then you go inside." She stared intently at Jessie. "So it was your girlie who broke my arm." Jessie didn't reply.

"She's coming back here," singsonged the girl who'd clawed her face.

"Maybe not," shouted the younger girl, holding her bloody arm. "She could be a porn—"

Her face exploded against the bone bars. A big, older woman grabbed her hair, yanked her head back, and drove the girl's broken, bleeding features into the bones a second time. The wall shook. Then the assailant slammed the teen's face down onto the brick ledge of the barred window, spilling teeth. The two women who had been by the girl's side dragged her away. A fight broke out as others tried to eat her.

The assailant rushed to the nearest wall, screamed, "Why?" and smashed her face against the bricks with such unbridled fury that her legs folded. She fell heavily to the floor, cracking her skull on the concrete with an audible thud.

Weeping, Jessie turned to Burned Fingers. He took her hand and held her close.

Esau squatted in the shade of the building, the Harley parked only feet away. He'd helped Hunt clear the cage of anything that could be used as a weapon, including most of the bike tools. They stuffed screwdrivers, wrenches, pliers, and assorted coils and bolts and chain links into an old leather saddlebag, leaving space for the boy next to food, water, and gas.

Hunt leaned against a brick column, paring his fingernails with a pocketknife. He never let them get long and sharp, which Esau honored when they were alone.

"If the boy touches any of it," his master eyed the provisions, "I'll have to punish him."

Hunt sounded unsteady, maybe excited, and Esau remembered the Mayor's words to his master: "You like boys. I have heard." The slave had always suspected as much, but Hunt had him for company now. He didn't need boys.

Then Hunt said, "True Belief." Just those two words. They could have been a pronouncement of faith, a declaration from on high, reverence of the first order. But the slave knew better. His master's voice cracked, as if the unsteadiness Esau had just detected was a seam splitting open to reveal a side of Hunt so dark, so dense, that the slave would never see beyond the simple rupture. It scared him. But it also sent a sharp thrill down his own spine. The three of them would be alone in the desert. The possibilities infected his feelings, the way unbidden thoughts of unspoken sex can strip a good man of decency—and fill him with the most ruthless desire.

Hunt put away his pocketknife. Esau's eyes fell to ants marching single file into the shade, their brittle black bodies disappearing into deeper shadows. Thousands more stretched into the distance, a dark line in the burning sand.

He and Hunt had been waiting almost an hour. Esau wanted to leave, but not to go back to the Alliance. The thought of His Piety touching him made the slave want to pull out the knife Hunt had given him and kill for the first time. He couldn't even force himself to beg the Lord's forgiveness, only for the chance to sleep under the stars with Hunt. Touch under the stars. Never stop under the stars.

With the boy, too. Don't forget him.

Esau rose to his feet, so restless he couldn't stop his fevered imaginings until his thoughts returned of their own accord to the Alliance. He knew that once he passed back under the shadow of the giant cross—the crucified Christ of cannon barrels and tank treads and bazookas—he might never leave the base again. How much would His Piety care about a slave's freedom—if he cared at all—with the survival of the Alliance at risk? How much would Hunt care? Bad news was never good for freedom. Anyone could see that.

A struggle broke out behind them. Esau turned and saw two guards dragging a sandy-haired boy from the shadows. The white guard had a burn tattoo of a bullet in the cleft of his chin. It was framed by his black beard.

The slave watched his master smile, but the kid was staring at Hunt and trying frantically to back away. He screamed and tried to kick Hunt when he walked up. Hunt choked him till he stopped struggling.

The youth, ragged in chopped-off pants, gagged convulsively.

"Put him in the cage," Hunt ordered the guards.

Instead, they pushed the boy into Hunt, and the guard with the burn tattoo yelled, "Fuck you, you goddamn freak." They backed into the shadows.

Hunt reddened, but held the boy. Esau was stirred by the kid's handsomeness. He looked strong, and even though he was young, no more than fifteen, he already had a perfect V-shaped torso. Perfect teeth, too, and full lips.

Hunt forced him into the cage and locked the door.

"Look at me," Hunt said to his prisoner, who stared at the ground. Hunt shook the cage hard enough to raise the boy's eyes in terror. "I don't care how thirsty you get, or how hungry you get, you don't touch anything in there. You do that, and I'll hurt you. Do you remember what that means? The godliness that sets wrong to right?"

The boy looked too scared to answer, but when Hunt reached into the cage, the kid yelled, "Yes!"

Hunt rested his arm on the bar. His hand, hanging inches from the boy's face, pointed to him. "I remember, too."

Hunt climbed on the Harley. Esau sat behind him. They gained speed quickly, racing across the long black line of ants. The slave reached around his master, holding him at last. He felt Hunt trembling, his powerful body as unsteady as his voice had been. Hunt's excitement made him shudder, too.

"What's his name?" the slave asked.

"Tell him your name," his master shouted over the engine noise. When the kid didn't answer, Hunt braked.

"Jaya!" the boy yelled.

"Not here," Esau said as the bike idled. He whispered in Hunt's ear, letting his lips brush his master's lobe. "Tonight. Under the stars."

Chapter Fourteen

Sunshine spilled through a wide opening in the cavern ceiling, tracked across smooth stone and gawky boulders, and within the hour found Cassie curled-up in a gray blanket on a bed of white sand. The girl welcomed the warmth for the first time in memory. During the night a chill had settled on the cavern floor, just as the woman named Sam had warned, and the sun's arrival added a somnolent layer of comfort. Cassie had slept deeply, blissfully void of dreams.

With a luxurious feeling of rest flooding her limbs, she remembered the long dark climb down the rope ladder, and Sam and Yurgen leading her to the river. She sat up and saw the couple's empty blanket about fifteen feet away. But their absence didn't alarm her. The cavern felt secure, and as she yawned her eyes settled on the colorful spirals she'd only glimpsed last night. In daylight, the rose, yellow, and buff bands of stone were astonishing to see, like swirling galaxies from the night sky rising to the circular gap where the sun poured in a good hundred feet above her. It looked as though water had once defeated the laws of gravity to drain upward, leaving behind these wondrous, mystifying whorls.

I want to stay here, she said to herself. She'd lost her mom, dad, sister Jenny, and Maul. She did not want to lose the stunning world beneath the desert.

But when Cassie stood and gazed at the dark slope she'd crossed last night, she also found it all too easy to imagine a killer climbing down the unseen ladder and crawling out of the shadows. *That's not going to happen,* she assured herself quickly, forcing her eyes back to the sunshine.

The cavern was larger than any enclosed space she'd ever seen. Maybe bigger than a stadium in the long ago, where she'd heard that people saw concerts and games. That sounded like fun, *fun!* But men in her old camp said there weren't even enough people left on earth to fill a stadium now.

Murmurs alerted her to a group huddled around a small cook stove. She couldn't make out their faces clearly, but a woman waved. Cassie waved back and tidied her blanket before starting toward the strangers. Whatever they were cooking smelled good, and as she drew closer, two dark-haired girls eyed her appraisingly. They were older, around twelve, and looked clean. So did their clothes. Cassie glanced down, feeling shabby and shy, and headed toward the woman who had waved. Her dark hair was cut short, like Yurgen's, and she also wore a clean shirt and pants.

"Are you hungry?" the woman asked her with a wide smile. Her face was round and full, like she got to eat every day. All of them looked healthy.

"Yes, please." Cassie's stomach felt as hollow as the cavern.

"I'll have this ready in a minute. I'm Helena." She paused from stirring a dented pot to shake Cassie's hand. Helena's fingers felt hot. Then she turned to the girls. "Come over here, you two, and introduce yourselves."

The one with a ponytail stepped forward. "I'm Miranda." Except for her longer hair, she looked like Helena. "What's your name?"

Cassie told her, feeling even shyer talking to her.

"This is Steph," Miranda said. "She just learned to swim

yesterday. Can you swim?" Cassie shook her head. "Want me to teach you?"

"Let her eat first, child," Helena said, lifting the pot from the stove, which was built from stones and metal rails, and blackened from use. A rusty screen, resting horizontally on four wooden supports, perched above it.

"What's that for?" Cassie asked.

"It spreads out the smoke," Helena said as she scooped a mix of greens and meat into a scaly, blue plastic bowl for Cassie. "We cook with just a tiny bit of coal. It keeps the smoke down, and that way it disappears before it goes up there." She eyed the opening. "We don't want anyone knowing we're down here. Miranda, get your bowl. You, too, Steph."

Miranda led Cassie to a natural stone bench, making her feel welcome. Swinging her feet back and forth, she ate the tastiest food of her life with her fingers, like the older girls. The piquant greens were so flavorful she thought they must have come straight from a garden, and she discovered numerous chunks of meat. She held one up. "Snake?" she asked.

"And nothing but," Miranda said, making big comical eyes. "We raise them for eating, so don't go making them your pets."

"Snakes? For pets?" It sounded ghastly to Cassie.

"I knew a girl once who liked to pet them," Miranda said. "But she died. Not from a snake," she added quickly. "I like dogs, but we haven't had one for a long time. Do you have one?"

"How'd she die then?" Cassie asked.

"She got caught by some guys and they killed her after doing some things. So do you have a dog?"

"No, but there were two on the caravan. One only had three legs. A marauder chopped it off."

"How'd that happen?" Miranda asked.

"They were attacked. It was before they got to the Army of God, where I was." Cassie told them about the big battle to get out of the Army's fortress, and how an older guy burned down walls, crops—"everything, even a bear cage"—with a rocket attack on a fuel supply. "We thought we were all going to die."

"Was the bear in it?" Miranda asked. Steph still hadn't said a word.

"No, it got away."

Helena walked over with the pot. "Would you like some more?" she asked Cassie, who looked at Miranda.

"Go ahead," the older girl urged. "You look like you could use it," she added earnestly.

"Sure," Cassie said to Helena. "Thanks. It's really good."

"I'm okay, Mom." Miranda put her hand over her bowl. So did Steph.

Cassie warned herself to stop gobbling her food. By the time she finished, she figured she was "sport eating." That's what her mom said people did in the long ago—stuffed themselves for the fun of it. It sounded so bizarre that she'd wondered if her mother had made it up. Now, she guessed her mom hadn't.

"Are you sure you got enough?" Miranda asked Steph, who nodded immediately. She was about Miranda's height, but looked like a young woman because she had breasts. With her long black hair and bright blue eyes, Steph was the prettiest girl Cassie had ever seen.

"She doesn't talk," Miranda said to her. "But that's okay. She's real nice."

"Is her tongue all right?" Cassie asked. Callabra didn't try to say much, but her tongue had been cut off by a priest at the Army of God.

"It's not that." Miranda put her arm around her friend. "We found her about six months ago after her people were attacked. Kind of like you. Except something happened to her." She gently hugged Steph. "Right?" The girl didn't respond. "We figure she'll tell us sooner or later. Or maybe not."

Steph rested her head on Miranda's shoulder. Cassie

wanted to do that, too. Miranda already felt like a big sister, caring and comforting. Then she remembered Jenny and struggled not to cry because she didn't want to explain why sometimes she burst into tears.

Helena strolled over and took their bowls. "We'll have you cleaning up after yourself soon enough," she said to Cassie, "but this morning I think you should let these two hooligans show you around." She rubbed Miranda's head. The girl frowned and straightened her ponytail. "Just be sure you have Cassie back here when you can see the sun up there." Helena glanced toward the opening. "We're having a meeting, and we want you guys there. On time! Now go," she said, and laughed.

"How big is this place?" Cassie asked Miranda as they headed out on the broad, delta-shaped expanse.

"Where you came down the ladder," Miranda glanced over her shoulder at the shadows, "that's just the start. This goes on for hundreds of miles. It stops at what used to be Lake Michigan. Only a few people have explored the whole thing. It's a bunch of caverns and tunnels and *pools*." She smiled. "There's even a waterfall, but I don't know if we'll have enough time to get you there and back. It has a really deep plunge pool, so you can't go in till you learn to swim."

"Can I learn today?" Cassie had heard of waterfalls, but nobody she knew had ever seen one.

"Today? I don't know. Depends on how you feel about dunking. Sometimes that scares people. I might be able to teach you underwater swimming, if you don't panic, but you've probably never seen a lot of water."

"The Gulf," Cassie said.

"What's that?"

"The Gulf of Mexico. People got sick if they went in, and they died if they drank it. Sometimes they drank it," she said slowly, "so they *could* die."

"That's not like here," Miranda said. "People drink water 'cause it's good."

She skipped away still holding Steph's hand, and didn't

stop till they crossed the smooth stone to the river. The water sparkled in sunlight reflecting off the rocks, and looked even more magnificent than Cassie had imagined from her glimpses the night before. It was at least twenty feet wide there, and she thought it might not be too deep.

Miranda stripped off her clothes. Steph sat on a boulder and pulled her knees up to her chin. They poked through her jeans, threadbare and holey.

"She won't take off her clothes or go in the water, except with me. You can wear your clothes, or not. Clothing optional." Miranda laughed.

"Are there boys?" Cassie asked.

"Four, but this is the girl's area." Miranda folded her pants and shirt, arranging them in a neat pile. "If you take them off, make sure you keep them by the bank, so you can wash them. They kind of need it."

The water rose to Miranda's belly, but came all the way up to Cassie's chest, reminding her why everyone on the caravan called her "Little Cassie." She couldn't wait to show her friends this place.

But the cool water felt so foreign that she climbed onto the rock she'd just stepped from to make sure she could get out. Then she lowered herself back in.

"You okay?" Miranda asked.

Cassie nodded. "This is *nice*." She splashed water with both hands. "I just can't believe it."

The other girl took a breath and disappeared. Cassie thought she must be dunking. Seconds later, she jumped up with a grin.

"Try it!"

Cassie lowered herself to her chin, then hesitated. The current was slow, and felt like a gentle breath blowing over her body.

"It's easier if you do it all at once," Miranda advised.

"Okay-okay, I'm going to do it," she said, both scared and excited.

She thought she would come right back up, but the water

felt so soothing, so otherworldly, that she stayed under with her eyes shut, letting the flow caress her face. It was as if she'd discovered more than the secret realm below the surface—she'd discovered the real feel of her own skin. After coming from such parched environs, to find herself in water's full, weightless grasp made her deliriously happy. Like a great dream. She burst back up, out of breath. Full of wonder.

"That's incredible," she sputtered. "How did you guys find this place?"

Miranda shrugged. "I'm not sure. Somebody found it after the Big Flood. You can really hold your breath. You had me worried."

"What big flood?" Cassie asked warily. "You mean that stuff about Noah?" She hoped not. Religious crazies had tried to kill her.

"No! Not *that*," the older girl said. "I meant after the earthquakes. The land got so much lighter with water burning up into the air, and then it started moving around and a monster earthquake hit. It split Lake Michigan right down the middle, and all the water came pouring out. It was the biggest flood in a million years, or something like that, and it made a huge canyon, and these caverns got really big. See up there." She pointed to the opening. "This whole thing got filled up with water going round and round like a giant whirlpool till it shot out of the ground. That's what they think anyway."

"Water did that?"

"You bet! Just like this." She splashed Cassie and dunked again. Cassie dunked, too, and opened her eyes underwater for the first time. Miranda looked blurry. So did the river bank, though it was just a few feet away. She surfaced, grabbed another breath, and went back down so she could see the bottom, where long green strands drifted in the current. That's when she realized her feet weren't on rock or sand, but on soft, squishy dirt.

"What's growing down there?" she asked Miranda.

"River grass, but you can't eat it, so don't get any ideas. We use the silt in our garden. You want to try swimming underwater? You seem okay with dunking." Cassie nodded eagerly. "So when I go under," Miranda said, "just stand there and watch me. I'm going to do this." She feigned a breast stroke. "At the same time, I'm going to move my legs. But I'll just have to show you. Ready?"

"Sure."

Miranda dove forward, and with each stroke of her arms she also drew her heels toward the back of her thighs and straightened her legs with a strong thrust. After about ten seconds, she surfaced upriver. "Think you can do it? This is a good place to try 'cause it's shallow."

Cassie took a breath and lowered herself, thrilled when she moved through the water. She made it almost to the far side before she got scared. She stood then, took another breath, and swam back underwater to Miranda as fast as she could. The other bank frightened her. It curved up into the massive rock wall that arched over the river, and felt too close, like it might drop down any second and she wouldn't get air. She told herself that was crazy, but was afraid anyway.

"That's really good," Miranda said. "Now do it again, but try coming up for air without standing, and then see if you can swim some more."

Cassie headed upriver this time. She failed in her first two attempts to get air without letting her feet touch bottom, but when she headed back toward the other girl, she surfaced, went back down, and managed to swim a few more feet.

"That's great for the first time," Miranda yelled. "But it's not really swimming, okay? So don't go throwing yourself in water over your head. But what a start!"

As Cassie beamed with pride and caught her breath, Miranda told her that in the long ago there were special glasses for swimming underwater. "I can't remember what they were called. My mom will know."

"Moms know all that stuff, don't they?" Cassie said, still

exuberant. She patted water with her palms, feeling the sensation of suction for the first time.

"Where's your mom?" Miranda asked.

Cassie stilled her hands. "She got killed by marauders."

"I'm so sorry," the older girl said, embarrassment written across her suddenly taut face. "I forgot, I'm never supposed to ask."

Cassie thought she seemed about to cry, and took her arm. "It's okay. I'm all right now." She dunked to hide her own tears, and didn't see Steph bury her face in her knees on the bank.

Before they climbed out, Cassie soaked her clothes. The water clouded with dust and dirt from her pants and shorts. Miranda helped her wring them mostly dry, but Cassie still felt a chill when she put them back on. She had been cooled to her core for the first time in her life.

"Let's keep heading down along the river," Miranda said, taking Steph's hand, "and I'll show you where we can go, and where you definitely don't want to go."

Oddly spaced gaps in the ceiling lit their path, and Cassie saw where sand had spilled into the cavern. She wanted to hurry to the waterfall, but Miranda stopped when they stood across from a dark cavern on the river's far bank. The opening was taller than half a dozen men.

"This is one of those places in the river you don't ever want to go until you can really swim because it's definitely over your head. So look around you. It's right by this bridge, so it's easy to remember." Two weathered beams lay side by side across the water.

"Okay, I'll remember," Cassie promised.

"And you *never* want to go in that cavern," Miranda warned, glancing at the tall opening. "Not for anything."

"Why's there a bridge, then?" she asked. "Someone does."

"But you don't want to," Miranda replied. "It's the catacombs," she whispered. "Millions of bodies are in there, except they're skeletons now." Steph pulled back, but still held Miranda's hand. "It goes on forever," Miranda explained. "They're piled really high."

"Skeletons?" Cassie's eyes were fixed on the dark opening. She hated skeletons. She'd seen so many in the desert.

"You know most people died, right?"

"Yes," Cassie said somberly.

"They had to put the bodies somewhere, and after the flood they really piled up, and not just from the water. So they used giant bulldozers to push them into the canyon and caverns that had big openings. I guess some of the storms moved them around since then. That was a long time ago. I once had a nightmare about skeletons marching out of there and chasing me. It was pretty bad." She looked at the cavern. "They're supposed to be stacked higher than the wrecking yard."

"Millions of them?" Cassie asked nervously.

"That's what I heard." The other girl stared at her. "Don't be scared, but we use some of the bones."

"For what?" Cassie remembered hearing about a church of bones in the long, long ago.

"A couple of things. We take the dried-up marrow for our garden. You should see it. It's huge, and a lot nicer than here. Let's go."

Before they could turn away, they heard footfalls from the catacombs. Cassie saw a lantern's dim light floating like a ghost in the dark. A moment later Sam and Yurgen stepped from the darkness with a shorter man. Sam waved to the girls.

Each of the adults carried a pick and shovel, their noses and mouths covered with rags coated in dust. From bones, Cassie thought. They shook them out as they walked across the beams. Sam snuffed the lantern candle and smiled at her.

"This is William," she said.

The short man nodded at her. His cheeks were so sunken, Cassie could see their bowl shape despite his scruffy beard. A dirty canvas bag hung from his shoulder with a wire poking out the top. He pushed it down when she gazed at it.

"Did you sleep okay?" Sam asked her.

"Really good," Cassie said. "It's nice down here, except for in there, I guess." She glanced at the cavern, and noticed William staring at her from a few feet away.

She looked back at Sam as he said, "This kid's perfect. She'd fit through there."

"Me?" Cassie jumped. The intensity of William's eyes alarmed her. "Fit through what?"

Neither he nor anyone else answered, but Sam shook her head. Not like she was saying no to him, but like she was sad.

"I'm sure she could," William said. "She's a godsend."

"No, I'm not," Cassie insisted. She didn't believe a god or anything good had sent her down there. She was in the caverns because killers had attacked the caravan and murdered Maul. And *then* she got lucky. She might be only nine, but she knew it wasn't the kind of luck you prayed for.

At last William looked away. But Cassie found little relief because he finally answered her question with his eyes fixed squarely on the catacombs. "It's a tight spot back there, but you'd get through—if you kept your wits about you." He turned to Sam. "We need her, and don't tell me you didn't know that from the start."

Maybe her being there wasn't luck at all.

Screams from the women prisoners woke Jessie repeatedly from a nap riddled with nightmares. They were so hallucinatory, she feared she'd become infected with the virus that was ravaging minds and bodies only feet away. Wicca *might* be weakening in the North, but the disease remained a virulent horror here.

It's only a dream. Jessie had to reassure herself each time she stirred, grateful to find Burned Fingers by her side. He was keeping watch on the clawed, purulent arms grasping for them through the bone bars, or yanking them with unmasked madness. He was trying to protect her, much as she had wanted to help him after a guard pounded him to his knees on the march there. Her instinct to survive slowly grizzled by affection, reeky and alarming.

But now as she limped into consciousness, the din softened, supplanted by a muted voice. She opened her eyes on a straggly-haired teen, pressing her face against the bones to reach toward her. But the girl's cracked lips appeared to move soundlessly, and the voice Jessie actually heard belonged to a bald, beardless man who was talking to Burned Fingers through the bars in their·cell door. He said something familiar to her sleep-addled ears.

"What was that?" she asked, climbing to her feet.

"'I've got some food and water for you,'" the man repeated, sounding kinder than he looked. As Jessie's eyes cleared, she saw that he also lacked eyebrows or eyelashes, which highlighted the unpleasant angularity of his hard features.

"Who are you?"

"The Mayor's special emissary," he said to her. "He wants me to make sure you're both fed so you can keep your strength up." He handed smoked chicken to Burned Fingers, then leaned closer to the door. "Listen to me, I—"

"You're the guy who came to the pit this morning," Jessie said, keeping her voice low. Now she knew why he sounded so familiar.

He looked left and right. "That's right. I was making sure you didn't starve. I had no idea if the Mayor planned to feed you. I wanted to give you some hope, too. Now's different. He told me to come."

"Thanks," Burned Fingers said, "but we're going to need a lot more than hope and chicken to fight those Komodos—if he wants us to last more than a few seconds."

"Listen closely," the emissary whispered, handing Jessie a thick bunch of dried mustard greens. "There's an action set for tomorrow night during the fights. If you last long enough, you could help us and help yourselves."

"What kind of action?" Jessie whispered back. "And who would we be help—"

"If you spit on me again," he shouted at her, "I'll cut your lips off." He backed away, swiping at his arm.

Before Jessie could bellow her outrage, Burned Fingers gripped her arm and shook his head once. Two guards immediately appeared in front of the door.

"What is it?" demanded a brutish-looking white man.

"She spit on me," the emissary said. He rubbed his hands on his pants, glaring at Jessie. "I gave her food and she *spit* on me."

The guard studied him, then turned to Jessie. "You want her punished?" he asked, unsheathing his knife.

"No, the Mayor wants them in one piece." The emissary stormed off.

The guard moved the blade over his lips, elbowed his black buddy and said, "Like mother, like daughter." He pointed his knife at Jessie. "You know where she is now, don't you? The one that looks just like you? Section R. Know what that means?"

Jessie looked away, refusing his cruel game.

"Your little girl's the reward. She's a real porn queen now. Best ever. She's got something *everybody* likes." The guards walked away amused.

Jessie almost collapsed. Burned Fingers eased her to the floor. She forced herself to breathe evenly. Her stomach steadied.

"Sorry to grab you when our friend was here," Burned Fingers whispered, "but he was covering his tracks with the guards."

"I get that." She glanced up and saw the straggly-haired girl still reaching through the bars. With the appearance of food, the teen looked more desperate than ever. Now, fully awake, Jessie heard her say, "Please, please," muttering her miserable plea so softly that she might still have missed it. But she could not avoid the swollen red rims of the girl's sodden eyes.

Jessie handed her the greens. The child shook and wept and nodded her thanks.

She's somebody's daughter.

Jester stopped at the first row of wrecked cars. For two hours he'd plodded across broiling sand dunes, carefully avoiding a minefield. He threw open his pack and gulped water from a steel canister. Every mouthful lightened his load. The wrecks looked steaming hot and utterly empty. He figured the yard scum must be holed-up in the heat of day, dying of envy every time they looked at the City of Shade. No more than a few miles away, but a different universe. This was a hellhole. All he wanted was to get back to the city. Three squares a day, naked bitches for Catch the Queen, raids on dumb shits trying to cross the Bloodlands. Taking slaves. Beating them bloody. A great life! Good as it gets.

But here he was in the suffocating heat because of some iddy biddy bitch. He wondered what she looked like. Had to be skinny—they were all scraggy as snakeskin—and ugly as a dog bite. No sense even looking for her in the desert. If he did find her out there—if some goddamn beast hadn't already dragged off her scrawny body—she'd be dead, and the Mayor would feed him to those giant cocksucking lizards anyway. Jester shuddered at the thought, feeling a chill that defied all logic in the unremitting heat.

She had to be hiding in these cars, the ones not buried in the sand. Maybe with somebody's help. Pity that fuckup. He planned to check all the ones on the ground first, hoping to flush her out. Wherever he found her, that kid was going to pay. And when he dragged her back all broken to pieces, he'd blame the damage on some guy he'd killed for raping her and cutting out her tongue and making her face look so bad nobody would ever want her. Revenge sweeter than Choctaw pie. Then *she'd* get fed to the Brothers Grim. That's what one of his buddies called the Komodos—but never around the Mayor. Wouldn't want to offend His Royal fucking Highness, now would we?

"Get out," he yelled at a lazy hairy bastard in the first car he checked. Didn't have enough respect to move on his own. No, but stared at him like he was a parasite. The gunman knew he looked like shit. Face burned up like an old rag, eye hurting so bad he wished he had the balls to rip it out. He'd like to stab this asshole's eye, hold it up on the tip of his blade and make it stare at *him*.

Now the asshole was moving, climbing out the other side. Be fun to see him stumbling around half blind, hurting so bad he'd bite rocks to forget the pain. But the Mayor wouldn't hear of it. *Do not go starting a rebellion.* The big black bastard's fruity accent haunted him all the way out here. *Do not go spoiling Fight Night.*

Jester trudged to the second car. An ancient Audi. Looked like a carcass picked clean, but on the steering wheel he could still make out four filthy circles, each looped into the next like a chain. He wished like hell he had one. He'd whip these asswipes down to their bones. Someone would talk. Someone always did—right before they died. But mostly the chain made him think about how tightly his fate was linked to the iddy biddy bitch.

And then he thought of the Brothers Grim living the good life only a few miles away.

Getting hungry.

Cassie couldn't leave behind the catacombs fast enough, and was glad to see Miranda hurrying Steph along.

In less than a hundred yards the cavern narrowed to the width of the river, which shocked her by vanishing beneath the rock floor.

"Where'd it go?" she asked the older girl.

"It's right below us." Miranda crouched and put her hand on the stone. "Go ahead, you can feel it."

Cassie joined her, and a slight vibration filled her palm. "What about the waterfall?"

"Don't worry, it's not gone." Miranda stood, letting Steph take her hand again. "The river comes back up. But you just don't want to go in it anywhere around here 'cause there's no getting out for a while."

I'm not going to do that, Cassie vowed to herself. When she was swimming underwater, just thinking about the massive stone ceiling had scared her. The possibility of being entombed in rock and river was horrifying.

The narrow passage opened abruptly to light-colored chambers that appeared to billow larger and larger, like the huge white clouds that could suddenly crowd the sky. Each gap in the ceiling grew, too. Her eyes were drawn to them before she spotted the river again, and the garden. Raised beds were spread over two acres, bigger than the entire camp she'd lived in with her family.

As they walked past rows of lush green plants, Miranda identified a bewildering variety of produce: "Radishes, parsnips, jalapeno peppers, red peppers, green peppers, carrots, spaghetti squash, corn, beans, okra, blueberries, strawberries . . ."

Cassie had heard of berries, but didn't know most of the vegetables. She had an almost insatiable desire to eat everything—leaves, stalks, husks, roots. A hunger, deep and abiding, startled her. Even after breakfast her body felt emptier than ever. And still Miranda went on, oblivious to the most miraculous vision of her life: " . . . cantaloupes, onions, potatoes, leeks . . ."

Tears dampened the young girl's cheeks. All of this, she thought. That was what she kept repeating to herself. *All of this.* Words that came as a prayer, maybe the only one that had mattered in her short life. Then she thought, Everyone should have this. She wiped her face before her new friends could see her sadness and joy.

They came to three farmers forming a widely spaced bucket brigade by a bed of tomato plants near the middle of the garden. Miranda introduced Cassie to the two women and man. They looked up briefly but never stopped emptying the water they'd drawn from the river. None offered more than a simple greeting. Cassie promptly forgot their names. She wished she could forget William that easily. What did he mean about fitting her through some tight spot in the catacombs? *If you kept your wits about you.* That sounded scary. She wanted to ask about him, but Miranda filched half a dozen snap peas from the last of the beds, then ducked behind rocks to divvy up the shiny pods equally. Cassie bit right into one.

The older girl laughed. "You're smiling."

"This is so sweet. It's like candy," Cassie exclaimed. Not that she'd ever eaten candy, but she'd heard about it plenty. Finding a big cache of chocolate or licorice or mints was one of the most popular fantasy games on the caravan. Candy was supposed to be the sweetest taste in all creation, but she told Miranda she couldn't imagine anything sweeter than the peas.

"Raspberries and strawberries," the older girl said knowingly. "But they're really hard to steal, and the farmers get kind of mad. It's a special dessert." Miranda had to explain dessert to her. The concept proved as exotic as an underground river would have sounded twenty-four hours ago.

"You have it really good down here," Cassie said.

Miranda leaned against a boulder. "We do have it good," she said thoughtfully. "But girls can never leave. It's so dangerous for us up there. It's even dangerous for the older women when they go."

"So it's like a prison for you?"

"Best prison ever. You'll see."

"What about the boys?"

"When they're sixteen, they have to start living up in the cars for two weeks out of every month."

"Why?"

"To make those idiots at the City of Shade think that's how we really live. My mom calls the wrecking yard a 'Potemkin village.'"

"What's that?"

"A pretend place, I think. I'm not sure. But it fools the fools. She says they're not exactly the National Brain Trust. The trading we do with them is all pretend, too. We keep them supplied with vegetables, but everything comes from down here. So we have to dry them out and make them look kind of crappy, like they came from far away."

"What do you get from them?"

"They don't kill us." Miranda nodded emphatically. "Really, I'm not kidding. It's not like we get anything else from them. They thought they were doing us a big favor by showing us a way through a minefield so our 'traders' could go get stuff."

"What's a minefield?" Cassie asked. She'd heard about land mines last night when she was falling asleep, but she wasn't sure what they were.

"They're bombs they put under the sand, and if you step on them, they blow up."

That's right. Jessie and Burned Fingers had warned the kids about land mines when the caravan started across the Great American Desert.

"They can even blow up a whole car," Miranda continued. "So that's why our people had to go and steal—"

This time Miranda interrupted herself, as if she realized that she was about to reveal more than she should.

"What?" Cassie pried. "Just tell me. Who am I going to tell?"

"Just that showing us a way through the minefield was a joke. And you want to know why?" Miranda didn't pause for an answer. "Because we'd already taken them all out!"

She beamed, and Cassie doubted Miranda could have stopped herself from bragging about the land mines for all the snap peas in the world. Smiling proudly, the older girl added, "But the City of Shade is still really dangerous. They're killing people and taking slaves, and sooner or later they're going to figure out the mines are missing. Like when you and Sam got away last night? If those idiots see your footprints, even they are going to wonder why the mines didn't blow up. I'll bet anything that's why Sam and those guys were back in the catacombs today. William's our mine expert. Did you see the wire sticking out of his bag?"

"I was going to ask about that."

"I'm pretty sure it's for the mines. And then he said that stuff about you fitting through something in there."

"What do you think he meant?" Cassie asked.

Miranda shook her head. "I don't know. I've never gone in there, and I never want to; they go on and on for a long ways. But sometimes they're in that place for days at a time, and they *never* say what they're doing. I spy on them all the time, and they don't breathe a word about the catacombs. It's the biggest secret of all."

"So you really don't know?" Cassie asked.

"I really don't."

"Maybe it's just a safe place to get rid of the mines," Cassie said. "It's where all the bodies got dumped, right?"

"Except they went right back in there after you guys ran across a minefield, and right when there's supposed to be some big fight or something tomorrow night. And you saw Sam and them. Why would they need shovels to throw away mines? You don't want to bury them. You want to *see* those things. And what about the wires, and trying to squeeze you through something? I think putting in mines is the only thing that makes sense, except I don't know how putting them in there can hurt the idiots. But William's up to something, and Sam and my mom are always saying we can't just sit around hoping they don't find out what's going on down here."

"But would they really use mines?" That sounded horrible to Cassie, to have someone walking along and getting blown up.

"We have to protect ourselves," Miranda said solemnly. "Follow me."

She raced ahead until she came to a fork. On the right, where the river continued, another huge canyon appeared, its walls yellowed by sunshine. But on the left, a separate, dimly lit space loomed with a long, rectangular raised bed. Instead of vegetables or fruit, it held sharp sticks. Each one pointed upward.

Breathlessly, Miranda said, "They're punji sticks, except we make them from bones. That's the other thing we use them for. There are three hundred of them in there. I know 'cause I helped bury them in rocks. If we're ever attacked again, that's our last resort if someone gets past the mines we put up there."

"So you guys are using them?"

"Up there we are," Miranda said. "They were going to use them on us sooner or later, or on people like you out in the desert, so you bet we planted them. We have to protect ourselves," she repeated. "It's the end of the world for us if any of those idiots get a look at our garden. That's why we also have a bunch of warning signs up there."

"For the mines?" Cassie hoped so.

"No, not for the mines. That would give them away. For radiation. They're signs with a weird symbol that tells people to stay away because it's super radioactive." Miranda had to explain about the poison. "Some of our explorers found tons of signs around an old nuclear plant that melted down. It was near where the earthquake destroyed Lake Michigan. We put them by the openings up there," she glanced at the ceiling, "but especially near the ones over the garden."

"And that keeps them away?"

"*Maybe*. Radiation killed so many people, it should scare the crap out of them, but we don't know if they've even seen them yet. There are lots of dunes, and they hardly ever come by. We're always the ones to take the food to them, and the garden's about two miles from the wrecking yard. But even if they did see the signs, they might not believe them. People stopped believing all kinds of scientific stuff a long time ago. Even stuff about the warming. So that's why the signs are just the first thing to keep them away. Then we have the mines."

Cassie eyed the pointy bones. "So how's that the last resort?"

"If the signs don't stop them, and they get past the mines, we have a great plan." Miranda clapped her hands excitedly and pointed to the ceiling above the bones. "There's a long opening up there, except we covered it with wood from an old barn. Then we put sand on it. So guess who's going to make sure those idiots come running across it so they'll fall onto our punji sticks?"

"Who?" Cassie asked, cringing as she imagined the mayhem.

"Us! *Girls.* The only ones they'll come after, no matter what. We'll be heroes. And now guess what? That includes you!"

Jester knew he was down a quart, at least. He'd just finished searching another row and was dryer than a desert toad. Worse, he would have to start rationing his water. He'd been too damned lazy to lug more than he thought he could squeeze by with. Story of his life. He sure couldn't go back to the City of Shade for refills. Showing up without iddy biddy bitch might be all the excuse they'd need to throw him to the Brothers Grim.

There had to be a damn water pump around here somewhere. Now he wished he'd made that lazy, hairy bastard fess up. But he hadn't been so dry then, and it was so much fun running him off. The scum sure hadn't looked thirsty, now that he thought about it. None of them did. They didn't look hungry, either. Jester figured they must do all right trading, and it made him wonder if he'd picked the wrong profession when he decided on killing.

And will ya look at this. Broken glass on the floor of an accordioned Escalade. Every window in the yard picked clean, but nobody had bothered to scavenge glass all ready to use? That was downright strange. He'd always heard yard scum were deprived, broken asswipes, but deprived broken asswipes should look hungry and thirsty, and they sure as hell shouldn't be turning their noses up at broken glass. Nobody did. You could make a knife or spear tips with them. Hell, guys chipped away on rock walls till their fingers bled just to break off a sliver half as sharp as the glass he was scooping up. There was no figuring this, and it stoked his suspicion.

He'd seen lots of desperate people, had the pleasure of killing more than his fair share, and he could always tell at a glance if they were scared shitless. Like the ones on the caravan yesterday. They were running around batshit crazy, almost as much fun as the crew that came staggering through six months ago. Hey, that was a party.

But he didn't sense much fear in the yard scum. He'd tried to stare down a guy with a nice-looking knife. When the bastard actually stared back, Jester knew he wasn't getting that blade without giving up blood. In fact, he had a strong feeling that without the City of Shade nearby, some of those fuckers would have skewered and roasted him for the meat on his handsome bones.

He moved on to a Pontiac Grand Prix, front-ended with paint so blistered he couldn't be sure of the color. Blue? Black? He shrugged. But the wreck still had a rear seat big enough for two skinny ones. But what Jester didn't see was making him look askance. The backseat would have made a nice hovel, like some of the others he'd come across, but there wasn't much evidence of anyone living there, like a hoard of hand tools, or utensils carved out of the dashboard, or nuts and bolts that might come in handy someday. And what about combs, keys, nail files, coins, all the shit you found under car seats? None of those little treasures had been set aside. No tiny altars or crosses. Wouldn't you at least want to scratch your name into something on the car? Make a claim to a spot sweet as this? Jester sure would have.

He thought he might have been the first guy from the City of Shade to shakedown the wrecking yard since they slaughtered a bunch of scum six years ago. They could be up to all kinds of trouble. It didn't pass his notice that if something were amiss, and he figured out what, he'd move back up the city's food chain, which would put a cozy distance between the Brothers Grim and him.

He climbed out of the Grand Prix and edged into a crumpled VW Camper. Even weirder in there. This was a home on wheels, and, sure, it had been T-boned, but he found plenty of living space for an enterprising guy, even a blanket and small pile of rags that might have served as a pillow. Sure signs of habitation. Or were they?

Jester wasn't long on brains, but he'd survived with the feral instincts of a predatory creature; and while his gut had failed him of late and left him burned and half blind, he'd always had an unerring ability to look at a nest of any size and know whether it was abandoned, or empty on a strictly temporary basis. Even better, if a good nosing around would turn up some tender young ones to eat, he could suss it out in seconds.

He hadn't been dwelling on how strange everything was. He'd just been noticing the disconnects. But all that noticing was forcing him to think, and he couldn't help thinking the wrecking yard might be nothing more than a big shell game. And where was the prize in a shell game? No secret about that. It was always under something. Just like water.

Find it, he told himself, *and you've got a good shot at finding iddy biddy bitch.*

Chapter Fifteen

Bedlam in the sidecar drowned out the Harley's throaty rumble. Jaya had suffered the shriveling desert heat quietly, but now banged his elbows against the cage and began to babble. When Hunt glared at him, the fifteen-year-old gripped his own arms, as if to still himself. But then he started rocking raucously from side to side, and his gibber grew louder. Esau, holding his master's hips, watched to see what he would do.

Four times Hunt had stopped the old motorcycle, grabbed one of the steel canisters stored inches from the kid, and made a splashy show of satisfying his thirst. Four times Hunt shared water freely with him while Jaya begged. Four times Hunt leaned into the cage, seized the teen's neck and warned him not to touch a drop, "Or I'll punish you in the name of God Almighty."

The clamor in the sidecar now ended in a frenzy: Jaya grabbed a canister, twisted off the top in a single frantic motion, and drank greedily, gasping loudly between gulps.

This time Hunt shut off the Harley, easing off the seat without haste. They were surrounded by endless reaches of white sand and undulating waves of heat. Hunt once told his slave that a temperature of 137 degrees had been recorded in the Great American Desert. The dead zone only became hotter since anyone had seen a working thermometer.

Hunt grinned, looking pleased that the heat had wreaked horror on the kid. He drew his short knife, the one he used for paring his nails and other cuts of a precise, implacable order.

Esau trailed his master around the motorcycle. Hunt unlocked the cage once more. Oddly, Jaya appeared happy, or relieved, legs a-sprawl in his chopped-off pants.

But when Hunt swung the door open, Jaya shrank back. The creaking metal might have shaken him from a stupor.

"Don't hurt me," he croaked. He held out the canister to Hunt, who swatted it away, letting the last drops drain.

"Get out," he ordered, brandishing his knife.

Esau watched his master step back, perhaps to give the boy room—or the chance to make another mistake. The sun felt corrosive, like it could blister the backs of beetles.

Jaya didn't move, his fear palpable. Esau had suffered similar dread many times, but the slave also anticipated the youth's punishment—and the wanton role he himself would play. Pleasure filled his belly and weakened his legs. They trembled, and he wondered if Hunt was shaking, too, as his master had on the bike when he first warned the youth about touching the provisions.

Jaya stared at the slave's obvious arousal. The boy looked scared. Esau smiled at him. The kid turned away, like he wanted to explode from the cage and never stop running.

He was young and strong. *A man,* the slave assured himself. *Not a boy, not anymore.*

"Fair skin, fair hair, fair game," Hunt said, marking the moment when the punishment would begin.

He leaned into the cage and coolly knifed Jaya from his knee to his foot. The kid bled profusely but uttered no cry. His blue eyes appeared dry, large, unblinking, already retreating to the mortal anonymity of sand.

Esau watched his master grip the red blade in his mouth sideways. The slave had never seen anyone do that. He wanted to kiss Hunt where the steely edge parted his blood-reddened lips. In that sudden madness, he wanted his master to cut him, too.

Instead, Hunt dragged the boy out. The youth seemed drained of resistance, or fearful that to fight would only add to his terror. A moment later he vomited, spilling clear sickness onto the sand. The water that had swelled his stomach left him steeply fated. Any fool could see that.

Hunt slammed the cage door and stepped away from the bike, staring at the bent-over boy. He whipped him around and jammed his face against the metal bars. Then he forced the kid's arms up and cinched his wrists to the cage with tightly wound wire. When he wailed, Hunt grabbed his silky hair and jerked his head back. "Dead or alive, your soul is asunder," he whispered, though no one but Esau and the youth could have heard him. The sun had silenced the land and almost all its trespassers.

The Harley's engine cooled and ticked—the only sound before Hunt tore off Jaya's shirt. Esau stared at the bite wounds on the boy's back. A beast had attacked him. Ragged cuts, barely scabbed.

Hunt slid the tip of his knife under a crusty red pane on the kid's shoulder blade, prying open an inch of dried wound—till it broke off and the bite bled.

"Damocles. Remember him?" Hunt said, still whispering.

The slave now understood the damage and his master's cruelty, but could not stanch his own accord. Helplessly, his hand fell and he squeezed himself when Hunt placed the blade back between his teeth and kissed Jaya all the way down to the base of his spine. A trail of red cuts appeared, each as precise as the next. Small drapes of blood hung from all of them.

Hunt opened his mouth and dropped the moist knife into his hand. With great care, he sliced off the boy's pants and knelt behind him, gripping his pale buttocks. Esau stiffened. He felt like steel reaching for the sky.

His master spoke loudly to him: "I'm a spy in the world of sin. We find the blight and destroy it."

Hunt rose and shed his boots and pants, leaving only his shirt to shield him from the sun. Esau, cued by his master's desire—and fired by his own burgeoning needs—stripped off all his clothes. He wanted the full pleasure of skin on skin, and though the kid's back bore those wretched wounds and fresh blood, they didn't unman the slave. They made him seethe.

The three of them stood naked, or nearly so. Nothing remained of mystery. Only completion. Esau's hands moved purposely as he watched his master return to his knees, lavishing his lips on the boy's softest skin. A worshipper, an acolyte at an altar.

Hunt scooped up fine white sand and with sacramental care spilled it carefully over an exposed cheek, as if aware, in the midst of his mesmerizing display, of the pain of a single displaced grain. Sand clung to the damp spots, sparkly in the bright light.

This unexpectedly consuming vision dropped Esau to the ground. His legs had never stopped shaking, nor his hand moving, but the white flow on the boy's perfect bottom keeled the slave forward till his brow smacked the sand and his semen left gummy gray dashes.

Hunt told him to sit up. Esau steadied himself with a breath before settling back on his heels.

"You've nothing left for the boy," his master said dismissively. "Nothing to test his needs, his sickness and sin."

Hunt turned back to Jaya. The slave felt his master's judgment keenly. But with his seed now squandered, a swift unwelcome clarity made him see that Hunt's disdain did not arise from a need to test Jaya further. It arose from his own inability to immediately gratify his master with the same voyeuristic thrills that had driven his face to the sand.

Although numerous men in the Alliance, including His Piety, had forced themselves on Esau, he himself had never committed rape. As he rested on his heels, drained of desire, he sickened at what he now saw plainly: a boy—not a man, no matter how dearly he had wished otherwise only minutes ago—was brutally bound to a cage and about to be assaulted even more savagely. Hunt wasn't a spy in the world of sin. He was a spy in a pitiless world of his own making, ducking in and out of desire under the clumsy cover of faith.

The slave stared at a distant mirage, wishing it could wash away his treacherous understanding—and all it might portend.

Hunt rose to his feet and pressed against the boy, who cried out. Esau had never known for certain what his master did when he journeyed from the base and left him in the coarse hands of other men. But now the evidence was as indisputable as the slave's irrepressible jealousy, which fueled his revulsion and sparked his only hope.

He walked to Hunt and took hold of his master's hardness, as he had many times. Hunt gave him a smile of forgiveness, and said, "Yes, do it for me." Hunt then used both of his hands to spread the kid open.

The slave knew the warmth his master desired most. But with Hunt in his firm grip, Esau tried to lead him from the youth, whose wrists bled from the wire, and whose slashed leg and foot spilled a steady red stream onto the sand.

Jaya, momentarily free from Hunt's grasp, mule-kicked him, catching his shin. Hunt ignored the boy's blow and struck Esau across the face, yelling, "Don't you dare." He pushed his slave away and turned back to Jaya, reaching through his legs to crush his testicles.

The kid's agony tightened Esau's own groin. His Piety had committed the same violence when he raped the slave in the church office. Esau wondered if the cleric had taught Hunt the same crippling technique, and how the lesson might have been learned.

Jaya convulsed, howled, and thrashed against the cage, rattling it loudly before all his weight hung from the wires. Hunt grabbed the boy's hair again, pressed his teeth to his bare neck and bit him hard enough to leave marks.

Esau glanced at Hunt's pants on the ground. The butt of one of his guns poked from the pile, which lay right behind his master. The slave gazed at his own clothes, inches from his side. He reached down slowly and felt around his pants and shirt without taking his eyes off Hunt. If his master looked at him, he'd say he wanted to get dressed. But he knew Hunt would never accept the lie—once he held a knife.

Still reaching blindly, Esau found the handle of the long steel blade his master had given him. The slave straightened. He stood at least five steps from Hunt, whose knees bent to force open the boy's thighs. Jaya squirmed, tried to resist, and Hunt yanked back his head, shouting threats into his ear.

Esau closed his eyes. Foolish, but he could move no other way. When he opened them, Hunt started to turn his head. Esau lunged and sank the blade into his master's back, feeling it glance off a bone.

Hunt didn't fall. He stared at Esau. If he was surprised by his slave's attack, he didn't show it.

Esau backpedaled, frantic and stumbling, naked and starkly crazed with fear, shocked beyond measure that his master lived.

Hunt took one step toward Esau before dropping heavily to his knees.

He's dying! Esau thought, nearly hysterical with hope. But Hunt now reached for one of his pistols.

Esau tried to race away, hitting deeper sand in seconds. Cursing it wildly, he thought of hurling himself to the ground and rolling, but Hunt was an excellent shot. His only hope was distance—or his master's death.

In silence punctuated by his own panicky breaths, Esau heard Hunt cock the hammer of a revolver. Then a grunt and a shot. Esau clutched himself, expecting piercing pain. When he wasn't struck, he looked over his shoulder. His master was pitching forward with two inches of the shiny knife tip sticking out of his chest. The boy was pulling back his bloody foot after mule-kicking Hunt again, this time driving the full length of the blade into the rapist.

"Help me!" the boy cried.

Esau stared at his master. So did the youth, twisting as far as he could, shredding his wrists as he tried to wrench them free.

Both of them froze when Hunt's head rose.

"Get that one," the boy screamed, jabbing his heel at the other handgun. It lay on the sand a couple of feet from Hunt, whose eyes blinked open on Esau.

The Mayor and his hairless emissary, Linden, walked toward a round pit near the rear of the City of Shade. Late afternoon light spilled across their path, throwing long shadows from the tanker truck and van baking nearby in the sun. The self-styled officials were trailed by two guards.

The pit was divided into two large cells by a concrete wall. One side imprisoned the girls from the caravan, except for Bliss; the other held the adults and boys.

Ananda had spent a long night listening to the Mayor snore—yet hoping he wouldn't awaken and hurt her. He did sleep till morning, but the new day brought little relief. As guards herded them from his chamber—and she relished the possibility of leaving the Mayor's side for good—he announced that a few "lucky girls" would sleep with him again that night.

At least water was plentiful. The city had more of it than anywhere she had ever been.

Solana stopped finger-combing her black hair as soon as the Mayor and his entourage came within view, then scrambled to her feet, shouting, "How long are you going to keep us here?" Maureen Gibbs simply swore at him, anger sharpening her pointy features, perhaps scaring her nine-year-old son as well; he clung to his mother's arm. Her two daughters were jailed on the other side of the wall.

The Mayor ignored Solana's question, and shook his head at Maureen. "If you insist on cursing me, I will insist on taking your children where you cannot see them, and where

I cannot guarantee their comfort, or even their safety. I have been a most gracious and accommodating host. I give you food and water and—"

"It's *our* food," Maureen yelled, interrupting him, which the Mayor ignored.

"—and a fine roof over your heads. The finest in the world. I am generous with our shade." The Mayor's tone hardened. "But if you insult me, I can enforce the most rigorous discipline." He stared at Maureen, as if daring the furious woman.

Her husband, Keffer, stepped to her side and placed a cautionary hand on his wife's shoulder, which she shrugged off. But Maureen said nothing more, and the Mayor turned his eyes to all of them.

"There will be a great fight tomorrow night." Girls all around Ananda tensed-up. Imagi grabbed her arm, and M-girl pulled them both close. The Mayor must have noticed the reaction he caused: "Do not worry, you girls will not be fighting. In the big fight of the night, your leaders, Jessie, and the one called Burned Fingers, will battle my two Komodo dragons."

What? The animal that ate that girl? Ananda backed into the wall, dragging Imagi and M-girl along, before she realized she was retreating on her mother's behalf.

"I am so sorry, but most of you will not get to see this battle. It is a most special treat for my most special guests, but Ananda, Leisha, and Kaisha will take part in the festivities. Yes, you girls will have most special roles. It is a great honor."

"You're not touching my daughters," Augustus said, walking within feet of the wall below the Mayor.

"Stop your fretting, black man. I will not hurt your girls. They are our crown jewels for the Alliance. Come to your senses. If they do not come up tomorrow when I have the ladder for them, I will send my men after them, and you will not like that. Your daughters will be of great interest to my guests. Do not try to deny me this small pleasure." He turned to the girls' side of the pit. "Leisha and Kaisha, you will be very busy tomorrow night. It will be most exciting, and I promise it will not hurt too much. I say the same to you, Ananda."

Not hurt too much?

He smiled at her. Perhaps he considered it a "most special" kindness. She just wanted to kill him—before he murdered her mom. That would be most special to her.

Hunt tried to pull his gun out from under his body, but the barrel caught on the blade sticking out of his chest. Esau stared, hoping his master would collapse, *die*. But Hunt groaned, straining to push himself higher, offering a chilling view of the blood-streaked steel. Slowly, he began to slide the pistol out from under him.

Esau thought he might have time to grab the second gun. The weapon lay next to Hunt's pants. The fully naked slave raced only half a dozen steps before his master started to raise the weapon in his hand. Esau gulped in terror and kicked him in the face, flooding with animal fear even before Hunt's arm locked around his ankle. The slave slammed to the ground.

His master's hold tightened, but Hunt had dropped his gun when he grabbed him. Hunt's other elbow, supporting his weight, pinned the slave's right leg. The bone-on-bone pain was excruciating. Esau lunged for the gun by Hunt's pants, but it lay inches beyond his grasp.

He looked back, finding Hunt desperately trying to pick up the pistol he'd dropped. But Hunt couldn't hold his leg and also make the grab. When he maintained his fierce grip, the slave realized his master had made the same calculation as he: if both of them scrambled for a gun, it was he who would win the deadly race.

Hunt began to claw his way up his leg. Esau tried to drag himself away, breaking fingernails on the hard ground just below the sand. He made no progress.

Esau lunged again for Hunt's other gun. He failed. His master tried to force his hand between the slave's legs. Esau squeezed them together as Hunt's fingers grazed his testicles. The slave rolled onto his back, prying Hunt's hand farther from his privates. But his master hauled himself a foot off the ground and slammed his chest down on Esau's calf, stabbing him with the knife protruding from his blood-soaked shirt. The slave shrieked.

Hunt pushed himself forward, knifing the younger man's lower leg as surely as he had the boy's. His next thrust drove the blade up into Esau's kneecap. The slave screamed and beat Hunt's head, to little effect.

Grunting almost as loudly, Hunt grabbed two fistfuls of the slave's belly and heaved himself forward, plunging the knife into Esau's inner thigh. Clawing now at his chest, Hunt plowed the blade up the final length of leg, cleaving the meaty muscle.

Esau, screaming hoarsely, tried to push Hunt away. But he remained pinned by his master's size, and paralyzed by the grilling pain of the knife.

Hunt tightened his grip on the slave's chest, tearing skin. Then he jammed his elbows into Esau's hips and rose over him. Struggling mightily, Hunt aimed the blade sticking out of his chest right at the slave's sex organs.

A gun was fired from inches away, and Hunt collapsed. Esau, ears ringing, twisted violently from the plunging knife. It struck his hipbone with enough force to drive the handle halfway out of his master's back. The pain from this final assault felt crippling, though even in his misery Esau knew how much worse it could have been.

Jaya stood over him, revolver shaking in his damaged hand. He'd ripped open the big knuckle at the base of his thumb when he tore himself free from the wire. The exposed bone burned white in the sun. A flap of his bloody skin hung from the cage like a peeled-off glove.

"Get him off me!" Esau cried.

Jaya kicked Hunt's body as ruthlessly as he had the knife

handle only minutes ago, forcing the lifeless torso to the side. Esau spied a bullet hole in Hunt's temple, blood matting the dead man's hair.

The slave climbed to his feet, shaking terribly. He stared at his leg wounds. "Did you see what he did?" The savagery astounded him.

Jaya shook his head no, but eyed the long, deep cuts. "They're bad."

"They hurt. Oh, God," Esau cried, "they hurt so bad." He bent to pick up Hunt's weapon.

"Don't touch it." Jaya raised his gun hand. "You were going to hurt me, too." He glanced at Esau's crotch.

"I saved you." The slave hugged himself. He couldn't stop shaking.

"Get away from the gun."

"You're a kid. You don't now what you're doing."

"I sure saved you." Jaya never lowered the barrel.

Esau stepped aside. The youth grabbed the weapon. He was still bleeding from his own knifing and brutal unfettering.

"Get dressed," he told Esau. He sounded older than the weakened slave. "I'm taking his pants." His own lay shredded on the sand.

"Mine will fit you better. I can wear his."

The boy considered this, and nodded.

The sun's edge appeared in the cavern ceiling. Miranda studied it, shading her face with her hand.

"Do we have to go?" Cassie asked anxiously. More than anything, she wanted to keep walking to the waterfall.

"Do you think you could run all the way back?" the older girl asked.

"I guess. Sure." Cassie tried to hide her disappointment, but it felt heavier than the boulder she leaned against.

"Then we better go now."

But instead of turning around, Miranda grabbed Steph's

hand and darted ahead. Delighted, Cassie hurried after them across narrow chasms and long stretches of unseamed rock, excitement building in her tummy.

A pounding noise forced its way into her awareness, the ground vibrating. She slowed, uneasy by what she felt but could not see. The water flowed faster by her side, as if it were scared, too. She looked ahead and saw Miranda and Steph stop where the water disappeared over the edge of smooth pale stone. Mist billowed up around them.

That's it!

Cassie rushed closer, exhilarated again, as the sound of the falls grew louder and the ground vibrated even more. But now it seemed to shake the fear from her body, filling her with the sweetest anticipation.

She looked out over the edge and watched the river whiten where it exploded more than twenty feet below. It surged into a wide, emerald-colored plunge pool. Mist now coated her skin with its soothing velvety touch. She'd never felt that before, only hard rain, and then only rarely. The cool moist air was calming, like she was standing in the middle of a cloud. Her face felt clean and wonderfully alive.

She stared at the waterfall so intently that she startled when Miranda grabbed her arm.

"Watch this!" the older girl shouted above the roaring river.

She jumped, fully clothed, but raised barely a splash in the churning water at the base of the falls.

Cassie waited nervously for her friend to surface. So did Steph. The mute girl took her hand for the first time, a firm grip that didn't relax until they saw a head full of dark hair bobbing up. Miranda cleared it from her face, smiling ecstatically.

She swam to the middle of the pool, where she stood with bubbles eddying around her chest. Steph released Cassie's hand, and the towhead wanted to take it back. She liked Steph, even though the girl hadn't said a word to her.

"It's really deep, but there's a tiny island I'm on," Miranda shouted above the waterfall. "Kind of like a stalagmite."

Cassie didn't know what she meant. "I want to jump!" she yelled back, even though her stomach fluttered at the very thought.

Miranda shook her head forcefully. "No! You'll drown. Wait till you can at least swim underwater."

But I can. You showed me.

The older girl floated on her back, gazing at a wide streak of white stone in the high ceiling. When she neared the far side, she swam forcefully to a large round stone and pulled herself out. Then she scaled steps that had been pounded out of a rock wall, and made her way through a stretch of small sharp rocks to the two of them, who stood watching.

"Where's the river go?" Cassie asked. She couldn't see any water beyond the plunge pool, only the end of the enormous cavern catching scattered streams of light from small openings.

"It goes underground for five miles. You can see where it gets sucked under when you're over there. That's another reason for not just jumping in till you're a strong swimmer." Miranda walked closer to the falls, dripping on the mist-covered rock. "We've *got* to go."

Cassie also paused for one last look at the waterfall, then the three of them dashed back through the caverns, Miranda and Cassie hooting and hollering. Their echoes chased them all the way to the garden. The farmers looked up as the girls burst into the bright sunlight and raced madly past the raised beds. They didn't stop till they reached the encampment. Cassie thought she'd keel over from breathing so hard—and she'd been one of the strongest runners on the caravan.

Eleven adults were congregating around the stone bench where she'd eaten breakfast with Miranda and Steph. Four boys stood outside of the gathering. Only one looked about Cassie's age, and she noticed he was taller.

Sam, Yurgen, and William had washed and changed into fresh clothes. Cassie realized they must own two pairs of pants and shirts. *Maybe more.* But the adults looked worried, except for Sam, who smiled so warmly at Cassie that she thought of her mom again.

Sam had her sit on the bench. Miranda and Steph settled to her right.

"We have to ask you some important questions," Sam said to her, "but do you need anything before we get started? Are you hungry?"

Hungry? Cassie shook her head, amazed that Sam had offered her more food; she'd eaten a few hours ago.

The woman crouched in front of her, as she had by the catacombs, and pushed long white curls behind her shoulders. "Do you know how many people you were traveling with?"

"A lot," Cassie said. She wasn't sure. There were three little babies, and Leisha and Kaisha. *How do you count them?* "Maybe thirty?"

"Do you know how many were children?"

"Most." She stared at her hands, as if counting her fingers. "Twenty? I think that many. I don't know how you count Leisha and Kaisha. They have two heads, but just one body."

"Conjoined twins?" William asked, scratching his sparse beard. His dirty canvas bag still hung from his shoulder, even after he'd changed clothes.

"Yes, that's what they called them," Cassie said. She noticed everyone was paying close attention. Even the boys.

"Were you the only one who got away?" Sam asked.

Cassie told them about Maul. It hurt to think about him. Sam said she was sorry to hear about her old friend, before asking what the caravaners had been doing for food.

"We had lots." Cassie described the provisions they'd taken from the Army of God. "It was all stuffed in the van."

"Were people pretty healthy, or were some of your friends sick?" Sam asked.

"Mostly, everybody was okay," Cassie said, but with a questioning lilt. "Sometimes Ananda was kind of sick. She was tired a lot. But she was the only one. Her mom was the leader with Burned Fingers."

Yurgen asked about him.

"He's a marauder, but now he's a good guy. He's got two burned fingers." She showed them which ones. "But he sure keeps things moving."

"I've heard of him," Yurgen said. "And you're sure he's helping you?"

"You bet he is. He burned down the whole Army of God. I saw him do it with my own two eyes," Cassie said, clearly awed.

Sam smiled. "Do you know why you guys were heading north?"

"Green things. They grow up there, like down here." When no one responded, Cassie sounded a panicky note: "They're growing stuff there, right?"

"We don't know much about the North," Sam said. "We just know that somebody doesn't want anyone going there because every time people try to cross the desert, they're attacked. You're the second girl we've rescued. Steph was the first. Up till then, nobody ever got away."

"Are you going to rescue my friends?" Cassie asked.

Sam took Cassie's shoulders and held her eyes with an intense stare. "For a long time, almost a year, we've been planning to stop what they're doing up there. It's cruel. And if we don't stop them, sooner or later they're going to find out what's going on down here. We're living on borrowed time. Do you know what that means?"

Cassie shook her head.

"It means every day counts because they could have found all this," Sam glanced around, "a long time ago. Tomorrow night a lot of people are going to be up there for a big party. They're really bad people. Have you seen the City of Shade?"

"No."

"It has a huge, heavy roof over it. We're planning to drop it down on all of them."

"But my friends!" Cassie cried. "Ananda and Bliss and Leisha and—"

"We know where most of your friends are, so they should be okay."

"How do you know where they are?"

"We can't tell you that," Sam said.

"How can you make the roof fall, but not on them?"

"It was built in sections, and we know most of the men are going to be by a big pit. We've planted a lot of land mines under the city. When they go off, the sections of the roof right over them will fall down. The roof looks very strong because it's made of bricks, but its actually very heavy and very fragile."

"I knew it," Miranda exclaimed. "That's what you guys were doing in the catacombs."

Sam nodded and said, "You're right. And everything's just about ready to go."

"Not really," William said, pointing to Cassie. "Tell her. We have no time to lose."

Sam frowned at William, but she did turn back to Cassie, saying, "We need your help. The City of Shade is built over an old prison that was buried under sand and dirt during a big flood that tore through here a long time ago."

"I told her about it," Miranda said.

"That's great, so you know all about that," Sam said to Cassie. "We've dug our way into the old prison and planted a lot of land mines, but we need someone who can squeeze past some bars to get the last ones in. They're bowed out in one place." Sam demonstrated with her hands. "But they're still not wide enough for any of us to get through. We've tried to break them, and dig around those places, but we can't. And we can't blow them up because it might give away our plans and collapse the wrong part of the roof, and that could hurt innocent people, like your friends or the slaves. So we need you to go in there with the last few mines and put them right under where they'll be having that party. You'll be inside the old prison."

"Is it dark?"

Sam told her it would be. "But you'll have a lantern."

"Are there going to be skeletons in there?" Cassie asked uneasily

"Nothing like the catacombs. There are—"

"But I have to go past all of them to get in there, right?"

"There are a lot of them in the catacombs, but we'll be with you then. There are some skeletons in the prison, but from what we can see, they're all behind bars, and you don't have to go near them. But it's possible you'll run into others. We have an old map of the prison, but we don't know for sure what you'll find."

"Snakes?" Cassie asked.

"Probably not," Sam said.

"But maybe?" Cassie persisted.

"Maybe, but I don't think so. You'll be helping so many people, Cassie, and you'll be saving your friends' lives."

"I hate bombs," Cassie shouted. "And I really hate snakes."

Sam hugged her. "I do, too," she whispered in her ear.

"Is this why you saved me?" Cassie asked. "So I could fit through some bars?"

Sam shook her head and took Cassie's hands. "I would have saved you a thousand times over, even if I'd known you'd say no. I saved you because I saw a wonderful girl trying to hurt herself, and if you had, the world would have lost someone very special." Tears spilled down Sam's cheeks. "I didn't want to lose another girl."

"Do you have a girl?" Cassie asked hesitantly.

She barely heard Sam's soft reply: "I had one. She was taken from me."

"We don't have time for this," William said.

Yurgen pressed his hand against the smaller man's chest. William pushed past him and raised his voice. "I'm asking the kid flat out: Will you help us?"

Cassie stared at William, then turned back to Sam. "Yes," she told her, "I'll help you. But can I go up and get my friends after the roof comes down?"

"We'll find them and bring them down to you," Sam said,

wiping her eyes. "It won't be safe up there, not after the roof collapses. There's going to be fighting. Maybe a lot of it. We're going to have to take control of the whole city. It'll be much safer down here."

No sign of iddy biddy bitch. He had spent the whole goddamn afternoon scouring the junkers in the first three rows, still working the ground level, still hoping to flush that rancid kid from one of those wrecks. Couldn't find her. Couldn't find a water pump. Couldn't find a pipe that might lead to a water pump.

Somebody was helping her. At this point, he would have grabbed the scum and carved the truth out of their thick fucking skulls—if he could. But he was in no condition to run them down, not half blind and with his tongue thickening from his measly water rations.

The last few cars of the day proved grueling for Jester. Sweat kept pouring into his one good eye, salt nearly as fiery as the torch that had scorched the other one. He felt delirious, rage a bright red coal burning through his brain.

Time to hunker down, he thought. Jester looked around carefully, saw nobody. *But who knows, right?* He shouldered his pack and climbed to an El Camino that looked like it had died a peaceable death. A pulse of envy ran through him. He squirmed into the cab. Not a sound rose to his rusty aerie, the wrecking yard as quiet as the pumps that once fueled these cars. No one would get the jump on him up there without making a racket, though it pained him to have to worry about the scum—they'd always feared gunmen from the City of Shade. *What gun?* His disgust bristled with so much hate it could have been a bomb. The blond bastard had taken his gun, and his Royal fucking Highness refused to give it back.

As evening shadows fell, he crawled out the Camino's passenger door into the backseat of a Suburban stacked next to it, upholstery oozing like guts from some loser's belly. He studied the fourth row. Yard looked no different down there, empty as a ghost town. He'd seen a ton of those. Helped make a few, too.

Jester bit into a biscuit so dry it crumbled in his mouth. It could have been gravel, for all the moisture he could muster. A sip of water turned it to mush. Revived, he looked down again. In the creeping darkness he spotted a truck trailer across the way. He wondered what it once hauled, certain that water had been its most valuable load in the end, when anything that could move was packed with barrels of it. No matter the price, no matter how murky, people ponied up—in all kinds of ways. Great sport selling that stuff. Made him King of the World.

Darkness sealed the last of the light, and his eyes settled. He dreamed of oceans he'd never seen, tasting the salt on his lips, then filled with a vague sense of loss and a sudden longing that almost woke him. He slipped back into one of sleep's infinite interludes until a little girl appeared. She stared at him, eyes big as bowls. She didn't blink, not once. It was like she was dead, but wasn't. Not yet. Even in his sleep he had swift intimations of blood. He asked if she knew what an eviscerator was, saying the word slowly so she'd understand him. She shook her head, scared, like all the kids he'd ever asked in real life, including the one who got away. He smiled at the girl with genuine pleasure and showed her his knife. She tried to run. He grabbed her, then awoke with a start.

Too dark to see much at first. But down below he heard three soft knocks, a pause, then two more. A door opened slowly.

His one good eye adjusted to the starlight, and he spotted four dark figures stepping from the trailer. They hurried away, like they were up to no good. He thought he saw someone else step back inside. No telling, for sure, but the door closed as slowly as it had opened. Someone didn't want to make noise, but someone sure did.

He kept watch for several hours but never spotted any other movement.

Tomorrow, he promised himself, *you're gonna find out what the fuck's goin' on.*

Three knocks, then two more. Some kind of code. Maybe the keys to the kingdom for the King of the World.

Chapter Sixteen

Hunt's half-naked body festered on its side in the strong morning sun, wounds drawing flies. Their squat shapes clustered thickly on his gaping chest, a bristly buzzing mound.

Where do they come from? Esau wondered. Nothing but sand and hardpan and dunes as far as the slave could see— yet the hidden world of flies everywhere he looked. They came alive, as if from air. You never saw them, and there they were, laying their eggs, smearing your skin.

Esau felt them under his pants. He unbuckled and brushed them from his thigh, split and swollen like a grilled intestine. The severed muscle throbbed.

Flies fed on the kid, too. Jaya twitched in his sleep as his body tried to flick them off his hand, shin, and foot. Esau envied the boy's oblivion. No pain, not really. Not yet. As he eyed him, Jaya rolled over, turning his back on one of the two pistols he'd clutched the night long.

The slave shrugged. He needed Jaya's help more than he needed a loaded weapon. No different for the boy. The motorcycle was their only lifeline, and Esau knew how to use it. Well enough, at least. He'd watched Hunt carefully, saw him work the touchy throttle and sticky shifter, and he'd thrilled with the bike's raw speed.

But where? Esau knew his way only to the Alliance and the City of Shade, where they'd pluck out his eye and put him to work—or force him back into the hands of His Piety. The black S on his brow did more than scar his face. It placed an indelible bounty on his head.

Jaya awakened on his belly, patting the ground in panic. He coated his bloody hand with sand before sitting up and finding the missing revolver behind him.

"I could have taken it," Esau said. "It would have been easy."

The voice startled Jaya, but one glance made him doubt the slave's words. Nothing would be easy for him with his wounded leg, bloodstains down the front of his pants.

"So stop worrying about me doing something to you," Esau went on. "We've got to get moving."

Jaya climbed to his feet, shoving the guns into his belt. He wished he'd waited to chop off his new pants. Hundreds of flies seamed his shin, feeding on scabs. His sand-crusted hand, burning less than before, raised a dark cloud that landed right back on him.

"They're not leaving us alone till we get going," Esau said. "And you better keep that thumb turned in."

It hurt like a son of a bitch. The slave had told him to heal the broken knuckle so he could hold a pistol.

Jaya headed to the sidecar. He hadn't spoken, mouth and throat parched. As he reached for a water canister, he recalled Hunt slamming him into the cage, spreading him open. He wished he could have kicked the blade through the bastard's back all over again. One of the greatest feelings of his young life.

He drank and held out the canister to Esau, who leaned on his elbow, looking pained.

"I could use some." Esau took the water.

"Food?"

They both ate smoked snake.

"We can't stay here," Esau said.

Jaya drank more water, loosening his lips. "I'm not going back to the Alliance or that damn city, or whatever they call it."

"I'll end up back at the Alliance no matter what." Esau moved aside his hair and pointed to the S. "They'll make me tell what happened, and then they'll really hurt me. His Piety raised him." He nodded at the body.

"Who's this piety guy?" Jaya capped the canister.

"A fucker," Esau said, smiling when he swore. "A *god-damned* fucker!" he shouted.

"We could go to that wrecking yard," Jaya said. "We don't have to go to the City of Shade. I've got guns and you've got a motorcycle. They must have food and water. Maybe make our peace with them."

Esau struggled to his feet and hobbled to Hunt's body. Jaya called after him.

"You think you can drive that bike there?"

Esau nodded without turning. Half of his knife handle protruded from Hunt's back. He failed to pull out the blade until he braced a hand on Hunt's shoulder and jerked hard. "I'm keeping it."

"You put it to good use sticking him." Jaya knew he would be riding on the rear of the saddle, so he wasn't worried about the slave stabbing him in the back.

Esau held up Hunt's knives, offering the boy a choice.

"The smaller one." Jaya liked the idea of something handy.

Esau tossed it to him. "We've got to get rid of him before we do anything else. Somebody finds him, they're coming for me."

"I want to burn him up," Jaya said. "Leave what's left for the animals. Maybe that dragon."

"Burning him's a good idea. I don't want anyone knowing who he is. But we got to bury him, just in case."

"Sounds good to me," Jaya said, mostly wishing the bastard was alive so he could burn him to death. He pulled a gas can from the sidecar. "We got enough of this?"

"Plenty," Esau said. "But hold on. We have to move him first. I don't want to blow up the Harley. And you should take his boots. No sense burning them. They're old army boots. No one's going to know they're his."

Jaya pulled them on, not caring that they were too big. "My first shoes." He beamed, feeling like a child. Then he grabbed Hunt's feet and dragged him from the bike. Esau wasn't much help.

The youth sloshed gas on the body "Where's the flint? I want to do this."

"In the saddlebag. The one on the right," Esau said. "Hurry up, we don't want the gas evaporating."

Jaya hustled to the bike and found the flint, making sparks as he turned back. Hunt's knife, Hunt's flint, Hunt's gas. The boy grinned, ready to make Hunt burn.

"You hear that?" Esau said, limping toward a nearby dune.

"Hear what?" Jaya asked, setting off the biggest spark yet. *Whoa.*

The slave didn't answer him. Maybe he hadn't heard. He caught up with Esau near the top of the dune. He was crawling fast.

"Get down," Esau said to him.

Jaya didn't want to, not with his leg, but he heard loud cars and ducked. A half mile away four vehicles churned up a dust plume. The one in front flew a large red, white, and blue flag.

"Those are Russians," Jaya said.

"How do you know that?" Esau asked.

"We had a school. Their flag's the ones with the fat stripes. There aren't many countries left. The Russians are one of the winners."

"Of *what*?"

"They survived," Jaya said. "Not a lot of them, but a lot more than us."

"Who's 'us'?" Esau asked.

"That's what I mean. Most of us don't even know we're an 'us,' 'cause we're not anymore."

They stared at the dust plume.

"Good thing we didn't go burning him yet," Esau said. "Last thing we need right now is—"

"Shit!" Jaya moaned. "I didn't know."

They both turned around. Thick black smoke blotted the sky.

"Oh, God, we gotta go." Esau started hurling himself back down the dune.

Jaya stole another look at the cars. They were already turning toward them. "They're coming!" he shouted. He spotted armor plating. They looked like monsters. "I'm sorry," he yelled, bounding toward the bike.

"Grab everything," Esau screamed, "and throw it in the cage!" He was hunched over the front of the Harley, fiddling frantically with wires.

Jaya shoved food, gas, and water into the sidecar. He looked around. Nothing left but Hunt's burning body, blood boiling from the wounds, skin crackling—eerie death knells quickly engulfed by the roar of car engines.

He drew his guns and backed up to the bike, where the only sounds were Esau's prayers and violent imprecations.

Cassie hurried off with William to a sealed-off storage area for a primer on land mines. Sam and Yurgen watched the odd pair leave the main cavern. The girl needed to learn to carry the mines safely, Sam thought—if that were even possible for such a tiny child—before carting them across the treacherous terrain of the long-buried prison. Unless, of course, Cassie had the strength to pull out the pins, which was also doubtful. While a training session with live mines was risky for anyone, much less a nine-year-old, she, Yurgen, and William knew it was essential to teach Cassie the basics about the bombs before having her place them under the City of Shade.

Sam and Yurgen settled at a grayed wooden table where their battle plans lay sketched in charcoal on a stone tablet.

"She's a gutsy kid," Sam said.

"You mean working with the mines, or being with him?" Yurgen joked.

"Both," Sam said without a smile. "He's not exactly kid-friendly."

"We'd be lost without him."

"We'd be lost without *her*," Sam responded.

As she lowered her eyes to the plans, bare feet smacked on the cavern floor. Both of them turned toward the shadows. Someone had leaped from the rope ladder.

They sprang to their feet. Yurgen dropped his hand to his holstered pistol and stared into the darkness, relaxing his grip when he spotted Keegan racing toward the encampment. The young man's black ponytail peeked out from behind him with each of his long strides.

"We lost the guy with the burned eye," Keegan said in a startled voice, as though he were just hearing the news about the missing gunman, rather than delivering it.

"How did *that* happen?" Yurgen demanded. The closely cropped man looked past Keegan, perhaps worried the half-blind gunman would stumble from behind a stalagmite or boulder.

"Our guys were keeping their distance, switching off, trying not to be too obvious," Keegan said in a rush, "but he must have gotten ahead of them, or backtracked. It's not the only thing they've been doing up there," he added in an even faster note of reproach. "He must have climbed up one of the stacks."

"We needed to know this right away," Sam said. "He could have seen everyone deploying."

"You *are* hearing it right away. I just found out. I took a risk just slipping back down here."

"He's got to know what's going on," Yurgen said, raising his spectacles when he pinched the bridge of his nose. "Only a moron could have missed our people moving out."

Sam took a deep breath. "We've got to find him."

"No, we don't," Yurgen said. "We can't take time for that. He can see all he wants, as long as he doesn't get back to the city."

"He's definitely not getting back there," Keegan stated. "I've got Mika, the Donatos, and MacKenzie making sure no one crosses till we head out. They're patrolling every last inch of the perimeter. And he is kind of conspicuous."

"Not *that* conspicuous," Sam said, flipping her white curls behind her back. "We lost him! What if he starts wondering where everyone is coming from? We're leaving girls down here. And Denton." A nine-year-old boy.

"William will be down here," Yurgen said, "and he's armed."

"But he's going to be busy with Cassie," Sam countered, "and definitely doesn't need to be dealing with a guy who's clearly looking for something. Probably her. We should have killed him when we had the chance."

"That could have been a disaster," Yurgen said. "What if someone showed up looking for him, right when we're getting ready to attack?"

"Or several someones," Keegan added. "Look, he's a gunman, right? But I don't think he even has a gun."

"What about in his pack?" Sam asked.

"They always have their guns out when they come here," Keegan said.

Yurgen nodded.

"Even if he doesn't have a gun, it doesn't matter," she responded, "because now we've got to put someone in the trailer when we head out. We can't have some guy finding his way down here." She glanced at the battle plans. "It's going to leave us one short, with one less gun."

Yurgen tapped the stone tablet. "Let's leave Helena in the trailer. She'd rather be closer to Miranda." He looked up and lowered his voice. "And we'll give her the derringer. We're only losing two shots that way. Let's be honest, she's not our best fighter."

"Which is why we should leave someone else," Sam said. "These are our kids we're talking about—and all our water and food, our entire support system."

"Wait a second," Keegan jumped back in. "Let's just slow down and look at this. We've got a one-eyed guy stumbling around with a knife, versus Helena, a real mama bear, with a gun. *And* we've got William, if we need him, with his .38." Keegan looked intently at Sam. "I think you're overreacting."

"We either take them down tonight, Sam, or we're finished anyway," Yurgen said. "That's the truth, and we all know it. Helena is the only one we *can* spare."

Maybe so, she thought. But when she stared at the shadows hiding the rope ladder, she imagined only more feet landing in the cavern—to hunt children and plunder paradise. "Where is our mother bear?" she managed to ask Yurgen.

"She and the cub are pulling the plug."

Loud jostling and raucous laughter woke Jessie. Burned Fingers, too; his arm fell from her shoulders when he turned to the cell door. Five guards appeared, including the bullishly built white thug who told her they'd turned Bliss into a "porn queen." He pointed to Burned Fingers: "Get out here with your arms straight out. You try any shit at all, we'll break every one of your goddamn fingers. The Mayor's pissed about what you did to Chunga, asshole."

Burned Fingers stepped out as ordered. They chained his hands and ankles.

The same brute pointed to Jessie. "Now you get your witchy ass out here or we'll break your *girl's* fingers."

The guards led them past the infected women. None of them reached through the bars. A few muttered curses, but with barely the breath to be heard.

"Maybe we should feed those bitches," said the lean African, who generally teamed up with Jessie's tormentor. "They're more fun when they're fed. There must be some kind of truce going on. No one's getting eaten."

"They're tired, that's all," his buddy said. "Lots of excitement." He slapped Jessie's back. "We'll toss them some bones later, and then we'll have all kinds of fun seeing them in the pit tonight."

Doing what? Jessie wondered.

The guards hurried them through a labyrinth of shadows to the Mayor's office, where she noticed a dirty carpet with the presidential seal hanging on a wall.

Guards pushed them onto chairs at a large table. The African opened a door on the other side of the room. "They're here," he announced.

A moment later the Mayor stepped into his office. So did his emissary, Linden, who avoided Jessie's eyes.

"I trust you have eaten well," the Mayor said, standing across from them.

"We haven't eaten at all this morning," she answered evenly.

The Mayor turned to Linden. "Why have they not been fed? These are my finest gladiators." He chuckled, holding up his arm as if looking at a watch. "It is almost noon."

"She spit on me last night when I fed them."

"That is not good." The Mayor's exchange with Linden sounded rehearsed to her. "But they must be fed," he said tiredly, as if speaking of household chores. "Give them their chicken, and make sure they get vegetables and biscuits, and a lot of water."

He turned back to his prisoners. "Is there anything else you would like for your last meal? Chateaubriand? Grilled asparagus spears in wine sauce? Peach mango sorbet?"

He laughed so hard he had to sit down. After he coughed and cleared his throat, he leaned forward. "It was the custom in your country, was it not, to give the condemned the right to choose their last meal? I always liked the story of the retarded man who asked for ice cream, and then saved it for later. He was black, so they killed him anyway. Savages. But you two, you are smart. You will eat your smoked chicken. Maybe you have even figured out how to kill Chunga and Tonga."

Burned Fingers nodded. "Got it wired, boss man."

The Mayor clapped happily. "I like this man. He has mighty balls. So how are you going to slay my dragons?"

"I'm going to throw you in the pit, and watch them choke to death on a big fat asshole."

The Mayor didn't laugh. "You should not make such jokes. I do not like them."

"Who's joking? And what are you gonna do to me, boss man? Toss me to a couple of man-eating lizards?"

Nobody spoke. They Mayor stared at Burned Fingers for the longest minute Jessie could recall before he laughed again, but this time his mirth sounded forced.

"I could send you to the larder and take your arms and legs and testicles one at a time, all fresh and juicy for my pets."

"But you know I'll put on a show for you. And you want to know why? Because I can't wait to finish off that stupid god-damned freak. I started on his tongue, and I'll finish with his tail. You wait and see."

"If you do not watch what you say," the Mayor unsheathed a foot-long knife from his belt, "I will start on your tongue and finish with *your* tail."

Burned Fingers tilted his head and peered down his nose at the Mayor, jaunty mood undiminished.

Tempting fate, Jessie thought. She wished she could kick him under the table, shut him up. He'd been just as maddeningly cocky before the assault on the Army of God. But they'd been attacking depraved men then, and now they were prisoners facing monstrously powerful reptiles.

"You are going to meet my guests," the Mayor said. "It is a perk I extend to some of them for Fight Night. Watch *your* tongue, or I will start the festivities here." He laid his ample blade on the table. "Go get them," the Mayor said to the African.

The guard darted out the door behind them, returning in moments with five men. The biggest wore an open, sleeveless leather vest. His thick arms and naked chest crawled with crudely rendered tattoos of spears and knives, barbed wire, and chained women raped by armor-clad beasts with long claws.

"I would introduce you," the Mayor said to Burned Fingers, "but I don't think this is necessary. When your old friends heard you were going to fight my dragons, they could not get here fast enough. Is that not right, Pie?"

The large inked man offered no response, tiny pink eyes already pinned on Burned Fingers. His bald pate was encircled by a moat of frizzy blond hair, but the most prominent feature on his round, bearded face was his rapidly reddening skin. Jessie watched him flush all the way to the crown of his head before he exploded with anger.

"You fucked-up, asshole," he yelled at Burned Fingers. "You burned down our best customer. You fucking killed them. I would have swam through a lake of your stinking piss to see you get eaten alive. And we got nineteen more guys coming, and every one of them wants to see you die."

"Nice to see you, too, Pie. When I'm through with the Komodos, I'll waste you."

Pie lunged across the table, bringing the reek of booze with him. Burned Fingers jumped to his feet and smacked his forehead—his only weapon—into the much larger man's face, mashing his lips. Pie rolled away and spilled to the floor. Guards seized them both. The Mayor chortled.

"Oh, it is good to see men with such fire in their bellies. But I urge you to calm down. We will have our entertainment tonight. And this one," the Mayor nodded at Jessie, "will have motivations galore. Bring in the girl."

Jessie scarcely had time to register the Mayor's last words when Ananda was hauled into the room by another guard.

"Mom," she cried out, but the rugged-looking man held her firmly.

"No, let her go," the Mayor said. "This is a good thing."

Ananda raced around the table, breathless when she hugged her mother. Though fettered, Jessie tried to hold Ananda close while her youngest gripped her tightly and wept. Jessie's eyes also moistened. The marauders laughed, and Pie turned away in head-shaking disgust.

"There is a good reason for the mother and daughter reunion," the Mayor said. "And these tears are good, too." Jessie looked up. "I like your little one very much."

"Don't you dare touch her." At the Army of God, the Mayor's comment would have been followed by a marriage announcement.

"Do not speak to me like that. You have no power. Look at your chains. But what I said is not what you think. I like her so much that I am sad about what I will have to do to her tonight."

"Do what?" Jessie demanded.

The Mayor peered at her for several seconds before shaking his head. "You do not listen when I talk. You still speak to me like I am your slave, so I will tell you nothing."

"You're the one with slaves."

"Because I have earned them. You have earned nothing, not even word of what I will do to your daughters tonight."

Ananda hugged her mother in terror. Jessie whispered, "Don't worry, nothing's going to happen. It's just talk," wondering how many more lies she would have to tell before death ended her duplicity.

"But I will tell you this," the Mayor added. "You will see your girls once more, before the fight. And maybe *during* the fight."

What are you talking about? But she didn't ask the question aloud. Ananda didn't need details. Instead, Jessie tried to live forever in the touch of her daughter. Ananda suddenly seemed so young for a girl who had been so brave and endured so much.

A stout guard burst into the room. The Mayor glared at him. "What is it?"

"There's no water."

"What do you mean?"

"Nothing's coming out of the taps. We didn't want to bother you, especially today, but we can't get it going, and the men are getting thirsty."

"Who gives a shit about water?" Pie bellowed. "We've got hooch." He pulled out a dented metal flask and offered it to the Mayor, who brushed past him, stopping at the door only long enough to order the prisoners returned to their cells.

As Jessie's tormentor hauled her from the chair, she saw Pie drinking. His faced flushed again; but with his tiny eyes fixed back on Burned Fingers, she couldn't tell whether he reddened from liquor or rage, or the unruly eruption of both.

Helena crawled into a tunnel off the main cavern, ducking dozens of stone roof supports. River water no longer rushed through a five-inch pipe by her side. Earlier, she and her daughter had shut off the flow to the City of Shade. Now, pale light from her candle-fired lantern reached Miranda, who rested where the coupled pipe formed an el and ran straight up to the city.

"Have you heard anything?" Helena asked. Miranda was monitoring the pipe for any sounds of digging.

"Nothing. They're not even cranking the pump anymore."

"They've given up, then. They'll start digging any time now."

Almost a year ago, after the cavern people had hatched plans for an attack, they cut off water to see how long it would take the city to drain the old prison pipe. Just two hours. As soon as Helena had heard the pipe ring from shovels, she'd released the flow. The digging stopped almost immediately, which was no surprise, given the arduous task of hacking through almost twenty feet of earth to investigative the short-lived shutoff. Besides, most systems had a blip sooner or later.

The Mayor had seen it as a "one-off," according to his emissary, Linden. The dry run had told Linden and his co-conspirators in the caverns that cutting off water could be their first salvo on the city, a silent, invisible assault.

Helena rested the lantern on the ground. "You okay?" she asked Miranda. "Not too cold?"

"No, it's nice in here. But I've been wondering if cutting off the water is really a good idea. Isn't it going to make them think something's up?"

"Sure, that they've got a water problem. But that's happened before and the problem went away, right? So they're probably hoping that'll happen again. Only this time it's not going away, and they're going to have to figure out what's wrong at the same time that we're planting bombs. But this isn't just a diversion, hon. It's going to force a lot of slaves to start digging, and as soon as the slaves have picks and shovels, they're going to have to put guards around them. Which is great because it uses up manpower and makes them work harder in the heat, and that'll use up whatever water they have even faster. We figure it'll take at least a day and a half to dig all the way down here, and they don't have that much time."

"Don't they store any water?"

"Not from what we've heard."

"That's stupid."

"Hold on," Helena said. "Do we store water?"

"No, but we've got a whole river."

"And they've had all the water they wanted for as long as they can remember. From everything we've been able to find out, they don't even bother to keep their canteens full, unless they're chasing people on the desert. They'll get thirsty." Helena patted the silent pipe. "Real thirsty. And then they'll start drinking other stuff. It'll be one big party, and that's exactly how we want them—hot, dry, and drunk."

"For the extermination," Miranda said excitedly.

Helena nodded, wishing more than anything that her child had not inherited this earth.

Jester figured he'd all but found iddy biddy bitch. He hadn't seen her yet, but she was in that trailer. Had to be. Along with a bunch of other secrets.

He couldn't be happier. He'd just keep hiding and biding his time in the old Suburban, as long as no one came apeeping. Sipping his water in a shady backseat. Getting his strength back.

Would you look at that.

Damn if another group wasn't oozing out of that thing, looking around like they'd jump if he said "Boo." Four men and three boys. Even the kids had guns. Jester hated little bastards with guns. They didn't have any maturity. They might go blasting your head off for the fun of it. Who raised those monsters? Anyway, that's why you had to shoot them first. Fact of life. *And there they go.* Running off like there was a fudge factory around the corner.

Nothing came quickly to Jester, so he had to sit there awhile longer before it occurred to him that a rebellion might be getting under way—and that he ought to hightail it back to the city and warn everyone. Be a hero. But then his coolest reasoning prevailed. If the yard scum caught him while they were heading out to attack the city, he was as good as dead. And if his Royal fucking Highness saw him without iddy biddy, same difference.

Nope, he'd be better off taking his chances with the trailer. Least he could get the jump on someone down there—and get himself a gun. Looked like they had some kind of arsenal in there. Even the kids got guns. How fair was that? But he had the keys to the kingdom—and perhaps a joke only he could appreciate.

Knock-knock . . . Who's there? . . . Jester . . . Jester who? . . . Jest you and me, iddy biddy.

Jaya raised his guns as Esau tried again to start the motorcycle. The slave's hands trembled as he held the battery wires together. The tips crackled encouragingly, but the Harley's engine didn't turn over.

Thunder from the armored cars rose from the flank of the broad dune that he and Jaya had run down moments ago. Hunt's body burned only feet away, a steady stream of oily black smoke.

The youth hoped the Russians would bog down, but based upon their detour around the dune—and the healthy growl of their engines—they understood desert terrain.

He cocked the hammer of his revolver and racked back the slide on the semiautomatic. He hadn't checked his ammo, and didn't dare now because the lead car, flying the Russian flag, raced into view, churning up large chunks of dirt and sand as it pivoted furiously around the dune. In a flash of armor, it fishtailed and sped straight at them.

The Harley rumbled to life.

"Get on!" Esau shouted.

The slave already had his foot on the shifter when the boy jumped onto the back of the saddle, but Esau clearly didn't know much about the motorcycle. It took him critical seconds to engage a gear, then the bike lurched forward—and stalled.

Jaya swore desperately, but before he could look back, Esau sparked the wires and the warmed-up engine snapped back to life. He let out the throttle, and the motorcycle's front wheel rose up. The bike listed left, so unwieldy with the sidecar that it felt like they'd spill over or flip onto their backs. But the wheel slammed down, Esau shifted, and the bike gained speed.

The slave looked over his shoulder and screamed, "Shoot them."

Jaya twisted around, finding the lead car so close he could see the driver's bearded face and eyeglasses. The passenger was leaning forward, revealing only the top of his head. Jaya feared he was reaching for a weapon, but a metal shield with a narrow horizontal opening, like a knight's eye slit, started lowering over where the windshield had once been.

He fired the semiautomatic three times in rapid succession, so adrenaline-driven he never noticed the pain of his broken thumb. He was shocked when the driver clutched his face and knocked off his glasses, drenching his hands with blood.

"I hit him!" Jaya bellowed in bald wonder, before real-

izing that a quick death was now preferable to being taken
alive.

The driver slumped onto the steering wheel. He must have
weighted the gas pedal because the vehicle never slowed as
it veered wildly left, heading for a distant dune.

The second car gained on them. With its shield in place,
Jaya didn't dare waste any bullets.

"Faster!" he cried, the blood of Russians heavy on his
hands.

Esau risked certain capture to try to grab a higher gear. A
horrible grinding noise erupted from beneath the seat, but
when it ended the bike accelerated swiftly. For the first time,
Jaya saw them speeding away from the cars. The last in line
turned toward the vehicle peeling off into the desert, but the
car in the lead never paused. Neither did the larger one right
behind it.

The cage rattled loudly, incessantly, canisters and gas
cans banging around. Jaya hoped nothing was leaking; they
needed all the fuel and water they carried.

"See that?" Esau yelled, nodding toward what could have
been a solid horizon of dunes.

"Yeah, I see it," the boy shouted back, realizing most of
his attention had been on the cars.

"You see that opening?"

"No."

"You will. I'm going to drive this thing right through
there. If we get stuck, they'll get stopped for sure. Just grab
ammo, food, and water—whatever you can—and run."

Jaya saw a narrow valley now. It didn't look promising
to him. He turned back, finding the Harley a quarter mile
ahead of the two cars still hounding them. As they sped
closer to the dunes, Esau increased their lead to almost a
half mile. Not nearly enough, as best Jaya could figure.

"Hold on!" the slave yelled.

Jaya braced himself against Esau's back. The dunes
loomed large, the valley tight. They hit deep sand almost
immediately. The bike slowed so abruptly that Jaya pressed

hard against the slave, who fought to keep himself from slamming into the ape-hangers. But they both spotted hard-pan about four hundred feet away, a viable-looking corridor between the dunes' soft white shoulders.

"Go-go," Jaya pleaded, so anguished he squeezed his thighs almost bloodless against the saddle.

The bike labored, rear wheel spewing a furious stream of sand. But it kept rolling, first on momentum, then torque. In moments, though, it floundered. The slave screamed in torment, pushing on the tall hand grips as if will alone could force the cycle forward. The rear tire did find just enough traction to lurch ahead again, jerking along on its few nubs of tread.

Jaya whipped around and saw the lead car slowing, too. Then it stopped, forcing the one behind it to brake. He would have shrieked with joy, but the doors burst open on both cars. A scramble of men jumped out.

"They're coming after us!" he yelled into Esau's ear, panicking when he saw the Harley wasn't moving any faster than the men now chasing them on foot.

Gunshots screamed past the cage. Despite the distance, a bullet ripped away one of the metal bars, setting off a loud clang—and Jaya's intense fear that the Russians would also get lucky with their shots.

He fired back. Now his thumb ached horrendously. The men dropped to the sand. He saw no evidence that he'd hit anyone, but the bike was inching closer to firmer ground. Dead earth had never looked more inviting. Just as he let himself believe they'd speed off unscathed, the rear wheel mired itself in sand—less than fifteen feet from the hardpan.

Jaya jumped off. So did Esau. The slave started pushing the bike, making little progress. Jaya turned, aimed, and fired twice more, emptying the semiautomatic. Then he threw his shoulder into the back of the saddle, but moving the Harley was much harder than dragging away Hunt's body. And he had to keep looking back. When he spotted the Russians running boldly toward them, he drew the revolver, worked his swollen thumb around the butt, and kicked up sand near their feet. All three dropped back down, returning fire with their own pistols.

"Help!" Esau gasped.

The slave's badly wounded leg shook visibly. Jaya slammed himself against the bike, torturing his knifed shin to dig his foot into the sand and force the Harley forward. Esau dragged himself onto the saddle.

"Wait!" Jaya shouted when he saw Esau move his foot to shift. The youth barely climbed aboard before the bike roared off.

"Cover us," Esau said in a voice so weak Jaya hardly heard him.

He fired the revolver's last load at a muzzle flash, doubting he hit his target. Another bullet clipped the cage, but the growing distance silenced the Russian guns.

Esau didn't slow. Jaya was grateful. Every second of flight made him feel safer. And he'd killed one of them, all by himself. Not confirmed, and maybe the man wasn't dead yet, but nobody survived a head wound anymore.

My first real kill, he whispered to himself.

No remorse. Only relief.

Sam and William crossed the gray beams to the other side of the underground river. Cassie tarried on the jury-rigged bridge, staring at the water flowing under her feet. She remembered its cool velvety touch, and wondered whether she'd ever feel it again.

She looked up, saw the grown-ups waiting, and walked toward them. But as soon as she glimpsed the catacombs, she closed her eyes, imagination feverish with all the death hiding in the dark.

Sam rested her hand on Cassie's shoulder. "It's going to be okay, and it'll be over before you know it."

She wanted it over now. Dread thickened her limbs, made them heavy with the imminence of bombs and battle—and all the shooting and killing and screaming and crying to come. Like the Army of God. Her eyes lifted to the colorful cavern ceiling. Rock. But it looked thin and fragile to her, and she worried it would shatter and fall like the roof they planned to blow up.

Sam crouched and hugged her. William watched them, weighted down by a backpack stuffed with land mines and a spool of wire as big as a small boulder.

"I can't wait to see you again." Sam ran her hand over Cassie's short, light-colored hair.

"Me, too," the girl said longingly, expecting William to butt in any second to say they had to leave. "Are you going to get hurt?" she asked Sam, who shook her head.

"I promise you, I won't."

But how do you know? Cassie was scared for herself, too. There were so many ways to get hurt and die. She'd seen it happen lots. To kids even. And she knew it *would* happen to her if she dropped a land mine. She didn't have the strength to pull the pins, so William would have to get them set to blow up, and then she'd have to be supercareful. Even after she laid them down—"Like they're babies," Sam had said—she knew she couldn't so much as breathe on them. What if she happened to hiccup or sneeze?

"Can I . . ." She couldn't find the words for the most important question of her life.

"Can you what?" Sam said, smiling.

Cassie shook her head. *Never mind.* Why was she even asking?

Sam cupped Cassie's cheeks with her warm hands and looked into the girl's alert blue eyes. "Ask me. There's nothing you can't ask me. I promise you that, too."

Nothing? She wasn't so sure of that. She'd never gotten what she wanted most: Mom, Dad, Jenny, Maul. Why would asking for this make any difference? But the words to finish her question did come to her: "Can I stay with you when it's all over?"

"Yes," Sam said. "I'd love that. I *want* you to stay with

me more than anything." Sam hugged her again, this time
long enough to moisten both their cheeks. Then she stood,
and Cassie knew it was time to follow William into the catacombs.

When it's all over, she repeated to herself, looking back
one more time at Sam and the river.

After only a few steps, William asked her to walk in front
of him. "I know bones bother you, but we can't have any
surprises, as far as my footing goes."

Cassie led them deeper into the catacombs, glad the lantern didn't light more than a strip of darkness. The path
narrowed quickly, and she caught sight of small skulls
and bones piled hip-high on both sides. She couldn't avoid
brushing against them, cringing each time. It felt like she
had bugs crawling on her body. She didn't let herself think
of snakes at all.

William warned that the path would steepen, and in minutes she had to lean forward to climb the trail. Even so,
she slipped and bumped the lantern against the bones. The
candle almost went out. She held her breath till the flickering flame bloomed again, afraid exhaling would somehow
snuff the precious light.

"You okay?" William asked. She nodded. "Go ahead and
use your free hand to get up this last bit. It's going to get
harder. We braced some things in the ground so we could
get a better grip."

Things? They were *bones,* placed evenly, like rungs on a
ladder. Sickening to feel in bare feet, but they did keep her
from sliding backward. She made her way up into a wide,
dug-out space that resembled a cave. Tall enough for her to
stand, but William had to bend over.

Waving her away, he carefully slid off the pack. Then he
asked her to move straight ahead. She took a few tentative
steps before spotting the two bowed-out bars in the middle
of a wall built of them. The two didn't appear wide enough,
even for her. And when she peered past them, the darkness
looked black as death.

Duck walking, William lifted the pack and eased it down ahead of him. In this awkward manner, he moved up beside her.

"Just squeeze through there," he said to her. "I'll hold the lantern for you."

She stared at the tight opening and shook her head without realizing it.

"Cassie, you *have* to do this."

In his sudden desperation, she recognized the panicky words of so many adults she'd known. Or maybe—and this frightened her far more—she'd just heard a man who didn't want to do anything violent, but would.

She lay on her side and slipped between the bars, more easily than she wished until her bottom lodged against the cool metal. Relieved, she said, "I can't. It's too—"

William shoved her buttocks through, scraping her hip on the hard ground.

"That hurt," she cried out.

"I'm sorry, but we don't have time for games. From now on, if you tell me something's wrong, it had better be wrong. My life and yours depend on you being straight with me."

Cassie was angry, but shifted her head to the side to slip all the way through. She took the lantern from him. Slowly, she raised it, revealing a cracked concrete ceiling pressing down on the two bars that had let her pass. Then she turned and spotted her first cage. She didn't know what else to call it. Two skeletons lay with their arms entwined, as if they'd died hugging.

"Cassie." She jumped at the sound of her name. "Look at me."

She turned back to him, staring through the bars, realizing *she* was in prison, like the skeletons she'd just seen.

"You have to get started," he told her. "Think of the maps I showed you. You have to walk through this room. You'll see all the cells on your right. When you come to the end, try to find the stairs. They should be on your right, too. Remember? Unless they've collapsed."

"You mean you don't know?" *How did I miss that?*

"No, we don't, but there's a good chance they're there because that's where the tower was, and we're sure this is the top tier."

"So anything could be here. Snakes. Animals. Somebody else." Her throat pinched tighter with each new threat.

"Cassie, move. We don't have any time. You need to make sure you have a clear path up into that tower, and then you've got to come back and get the mines."

Stunned by every terrifying possibility, she stood as still as the earth that surrounded her. William reached through the bars and took her arm. She flinched, expecting another shove—or worse—but he held her gently.

"Listen to me, Cassie. What you're about to do could be the most important thing you'll ever do in your whole life. I don't know how else to tell you that."

She believed him. She didn't want to, but his words rang with an honesty so raw they could have peeled her open. He wasn't just desperate. He was pleading for his life and the lives of everyone he cared about. Cassie nodded. As a child of privation, she grasped all the feral underpinnings of extinction.

Without another word, she forced herself into the black unknown.

Chapter Seventeen

Cassie's arm shook from holding the lantern up like a shield. She changed hands, but didn't dare lower it. For the nine-year-old, the candle might ward off more than darkness. It might be the only way to keep all the unseen dangers of the long-buried prison at bay. Men had died horribly there. She sensed this in *her* bones. But even that instinctual understanding could not keep her from dwelling on the most grievous threat of all—the land mines she would soon have to carry.

She tried counting the cages, but the distraction proved unbearably grim: each held two skeletons, picked so clean they glowed white as the moon.

Who ate them?

Rats, she decided with a small measure of relief.

And who ate them?

Snakes. Her dad had told her all about the reptiles. But she didn't see any rats.

So what are the snakes going to eat now?

Me. Me!

She stumbled across a chunk of concrete and saw rubble spilled across her path. A massive ram of earth had battered open the left side of the cell block, leaving bricks and mortar scattered like pebbles. Just thinking about the planet's power to grind mountains into motes gave her a nightmarish chill. It was even worse than the cages—the bones that appeared behind bars every ten feet.

Cassie turned around to make sure she hadn't missed any debris that could trip her when she came back through with the mines, then moved on, tossing aside what she could until broken concrete hunks half her size blocked her way. She had to clamber over them, avoiding spikes of rebar as she tried to memorize each hand and foothold. That's what William had urged: "You've got to make sure you know every step you'll take. You want to be able to walk right through there." But some of the blocks were too big to move, even for grown-ups, and other wreckage looked murderous, like a severed length of prison railing sharp enough to impale her. She lifted her leg over it carefully, knowing that once she started her mission, the cell block itself would become a minefield.

She passed sixteen cages, and twice as many skeletons, before coming upon a solid steel door folded almost in half by an outthrust of rock. She was so shaken by another demonstration of the earth's raw power that she mistook the mangled door for the one to the tower, which hung open a few feet away. When she finally spotted it in the candlelight, she imagined guards fleeing the prison in such terror that they didn't care if they left the tower open—or the prisoners to die. She wondered if any of the men had eaten their cell mates. Only the skeletons behind the first set of bars looked like they were hugging. Were they? she wondered now. Or were they killing?

The stairs were also concrete, broken apart as if the orange clouds that blew up the sky had breached the earth. Even the empty stairwell was filled with the gossamer presence of the dead, the unburied bones gathering dust that would inter them over centuries. And as she climbed the ruptured steps, starkly fearful of the evil that could issue from every crack, she worried about ghosts already risen from all the brittle remains of the prison. Mom, Dad, Jenny, and Maul had said there were no such things as ghosts, but the older girls on the caravan stewed about them whenever they spotted bones sticking out of the sand—and her parents and sister and Maul had never walked past cages with skeletons, or known the final enveloping darkness of the earth itself. No light. Just the candle. And as soon as she moved on, blackness surged behind her like a flood, sealing her off from the visible world, leaving her as unmoored as the ghost ships of the Gulf, sacked by thieves, soaked in oil, adrift on marbled tides and unsteady winds.

Nothing's living down here. But instead of reassuring her, the thought gave rise to a question: If the dead had a home, where would it be?

The answer came with dreadful certainty. The dead always claimed the blackest, densest depths. They would gather in a compressing universe of prison cages and rubble and skeletons, where even walls burst apart with hidden rage.

The silence itself spoke of dark wands and brutal intent. Had she ever heard such quiet? Her heartbeat and nervous footfalls registered with unsheathed clarity.

That's good, she tried to tell herself. *You'll hear them.*

Them? Ghosts and snakes. *But they don't make noise.* A frightening reminder. And then, two steps from a black opening at the top of the stairs, she heard a scary pounding. Not her heart. A heavier, harder thunder above her. There it was again.

She froze. A smell, worse than any she had ever suffered, threatened to strangle the little air she could take.

Cassie felt a touch on her neck then. It slid down her back. She wanted to scream, but fright alone forced her silence. She spun to the side and the sensation vanished. She looked down. No snakes. Then she raised the lantern and spied a thin stream of sand spilling from the stairwell ceiling, so fine it might have been mist. As she watched, the flow thickened, as if it had broken through its own obstacles to empty the world above, grain by grain, enough for all eternity.

The pounding resumed, a loud *boom* right over her head. More sand poured down, a wider, faster stream. She worried about a cave-in.

Boom. Boom.

The stairs vibrated. So did the ceiling. And the awful odor grew worse, infecting more than her nose. It left a feculent taste on her tongue. She wanted to run until she could hurl herself into the river and rub her face frantically, rinse out her mouth, and scream below the placid surface. Empty her anguish into a silent, soothing flow.

The noise stopped. Now she heard only her heart.

Find a place for the mines, she told herself sternly. Close to the ceiling was best, William had said.

She climbed up the last two stairs. Her lantern opened the tower's darkness. Rock and dirt had broken through the tall windows, forming a head-high ledge directly in front of her. It angled out like an anvil. She thought it could hold the biggest mine, and maybe a couple of the smaller ones. She pointed the lantern around the defeated post, compacted to half its size by the flood, gravity, and the enormous pressures of earth's fitful crust.

No other place looked as suitable as the ledge. But would the pounding set off the mines? She'd ask William.

It felt wrong to Cassie that a device so delicate should be so deadly. A delicate device should heal the sick, or store the sun to light the darkness. That's what she wanted most of all—to light the darkness. Not to kill. She was sick of the killing, first at her camp, then at the Army of God, and now here. She wanted all the guns and bombs to go away so she could live in caverns filigreed with sunlight, and swim in the river and enjoy good food and drink all the water she wanted.

And not kill.

She turned back for the land mines, led not by her heart, but by her feet in rapid retreat.

Jessie clutched herself at the boisterous approach of the guards. She and Burned Fingers had eaten, and spent the afternoon and early evening hoping for whatever action Linden had promised. They hadn't glimpsed a hint of resistance, and now faced her tormentor and his goons.

She tried to brace herself for more abuse, but could not have prepared for what followed. As she stepped past the barred door—and two of the tormentor's minions slapped chains around her ankles and wrists—the thickly muscled guard described in excruciating detail what would happen to Bliss after Fight Night ended. "But by then you'll be in a big dark belly," he said to the amusement of his fellows. "Wonder which one." That brought more laughter. "But you'll still be hearing your kid, because a porn queen always gets to *scream*-ing."

As eager as he was to talk, the tormentor said nothing of why she would see Bliss and Ananda before the fight, as the Mayor had revealed only hours ago, much less why Ananda might show up during it. Jessie figured the guard's prerogatives didn't extend beyond celebrating the savage death of her older daughter.

The guards rushed Burned Fingers and her through the city's darkening shadows, a route that offered brief views of dusk graying the desert beyond the massive roof. The men held them so tightly and moved so fast that Jessie's chained feet were lifted from the ground as she was swept into the open arena with the "special pit." Tall torches were sunk like stakes along its broad perimeter, casting shadows on the sand where she and Burned Fingers had barely escaped Tonga.

The dragon's gate had been repaired, but what seized Jessie's attention was the gruesome spectacle a few feet from it. Two women maddened by the virus were beating a third to death with rocks, crude weapons that must have been tossed into the pit for the entertainment of about seventy men shouting and crowding the edge.

She recognized the larger, older woman as the prisoner who had smashed the girl's face into the bone bars then screamed, "Why?" before knocking herself out against a brick wall. A smaller, wiry woman didn't look familiar. With only a few patches of white hair, and a horribly scabbed scalp, Jessie knew she would have sparked her memory.

Sickened by the sight, she turned away. Her tormentor snapped his fingers in front of her face.

"You don't keep watching, you'll lose your damn eyes before it's your turn." He squinted and held out his arms like a blind man lost in a crowd, drawing more laughs from the others.

Jessie forced herself to look into the pit. He leaned close to her ear. "It's a fight to the death. I don't think your girls would do real good down there."

The possibility ignited her blood pressure so fast she thought the top of her head would lift off, but she stifled an impulse to demand to know what he meant. Cruelty was like blood, always seeking an opening.

He forced her closer to the edge. Pie and a large, unruly contingent of marauders were screaming at the surviving combatants to go at each other. Six other men, dressed alike in what might have been rudimentary uniforms, ran up and joined the fray. They were surprisingly well-groomed, with short black hair and closely trimmed beards. Three of them quickly merged with Pie's ragged-looking crew, running alongside the pit and bellowing in a language Jessie didn't understand, though their meaning was as clear as the marauders' barbaric demands.

"Russians," Burned Fingers said a moment before one of them tripped and tottered over the edge, gasping for help. The comrade beside him calmly grabbed his arm, saving him from the fifteen foot fall. But the third Russian, whose eyes had never strayed from the carnage—or the two women now circling each other—stumbled and bumped him. The first two fell.

The surviving women raced to attack the stunned Russians,

who were trying to drag themselves upright. Jessie almost cheered the prisoners. One of the Russians' compatriots shot the smaller, scabbed woman. But before he could kill the older one, a Latino guard shoved his pistol into the man's back.

"You do not shoot anyone in the City of Shade," the Mayor said. "It is not yours to rule."

A tall Russian appeared to understand the Mayor. He nodded at his comrade, who lowered his gun as the big woman turned from the first man, whose skull she'd meanwhile bludgeoned. She then advanced on the second man, who favored his right side as he squirmed like a one-legged crab toward the center of the pit. Wincing, he tried to draw his gun, but failed; his shoulder looked injured as well.

"If she gets his weapon, kill her," the Mayor ordered the Latino.

But the insane woman smashed the Russian's face so hard the *crack* from rock and bone carried beyond the bleachers. Someone moaned in sympathy; Jessie's still lay with the woman, who whirled around, eyes glazed as she spotted the man she'd left bleeding by the wall. He looked woozy, but pulled out his gun. When he started to raise it, she threw her rock, missing him by a wide margin.

The Mayor nodded once more at the Latino, who had prevented the woman's death moments ago. Now he executed her with a clean head shot before the blood-streaked man could violate the Mayor's edict.

None of the Russians spoke. They looked as shocked as their battered comrades. Only the marauders carried on, laughing and toasting the monstrous turn of events. Three women lay dead in the pit.

Fight Night had begun.

"I heard something," Cassie exclaimed to William through the steel bars. "Something really big." She spoke to him so fast she had to catch her breath. "And there was a really bad smell."

"That's good, Cassie," he said smiling. Till then, she'd never noticed that he always frowned. "If you're really careful," he went on, "this will work."

He had the land mines laid out next to his pack. She gazed at them. One big round antitank mine—which he called an AT—and four smaller ones disguised in the long ago to look like teddy bears.

"So what was that thing I heard?" she asked him. "Do you know?"

"Don't worry about that. It's not going to matter as long as you can get these there without dropping them."

"But it sounded really close." William lifted his gaze from the ball of wire he'd started to unwind. "I *want* to know what it was," she said insistently.

"A Komodo dragon."

"A dragon? Right *there*?"

"It's just a big lizard, Cassie," William said patiently. "They've *never* gotten down here."

They? "There's more than one?"

"There are two of them. What we're doing will kill them."

"What we're doing will make a big hole. You told me yourself," she sputtered. "They could escape."

"That's not going to happen, and they're the least of your worries."

The least of my worries? "You mean the ground shaking? Will that blow them up when I'm there?" She'd wanted to ask him about that.

"The ground was *shaking*?" The way he asked scared her. "Yes!"

William collapsed from his crouch, shoulders drooping as he sat on the dirt. "How bad was it shaking? Did it make the ground look blurry?"

"I don't think so."

"Okay, here's what we've got to do. The first mine, the AT, won't go off from that kind of vibration, but the smaller ones will." He glanced at the mines disguised as toys. "But we need to get at least one of the bears in there to get the big one to blow up."

"You said we needed four of the teddy bears."

"Not anymore. It's too dangerous. If you can get one of them in there when the dragon's not walking around, that'll be great, Cassie. And then you've got to get back here as fast as you can because if that dragon comes back with you in there, you're going to die. Did you see a place to put the AT?"

She told him about the ledge. He shook his head.

"No good. You've got to get the big one into the wall so the mine sends all its power upward." He handed her a metal knife. "Use that to dig out a place for the AT. You can dig right into the wall. The small one can go on that ledge. You hearing everything I'm saying?"

"Yes." She slid the knife into her rope belt.

"How's your path? Is it clear?"

"Uh-uh. I had to climb over some big stuff where the wall got crashed in."

"There's no way around it?"

"No."

"Are you sure? Because you can't fall with these things, Cassie."

"I'm pretty sure I know where to put my hands and feet."

"You're only going to have one hand, at best. You'll still have the lantern."

"I know that."

He picked up the AT. "Remember, it's heavier than it looks."

He'd made her hold it back in a storage area so she could "get a feel for it." But now it was activated because pulling the pin took William's strength. He slowly turned the mine on its side and threaded it through the bars, careful not to jolt it, even though he'd said it needed a big thump to go off.

Like dropping it.

Jessie watched slaves lower a dented aluminum ladder into the pit. The bludgeoned Russians crawled toward it, while their four comrades scurried down the rickety, paint-spattered rungs. She wondered if the Komodos smelled blood, or otherwise sensed it. Chunga seemed to confirm this when he crashed against the gate; to keep him hungry for Fight Night, the creature had been fed only freshly butchered arms from the human larder. The four Russians scurried back up the ladder, leaving their injured friends rigid with fear. When the barrier held and Chunga settled, three of the rescuers resumed their efforts. The fourth kept his eye on the pen.

Moments later a scuffle broke out above the other side of the pit. Jessie saw Ananda struggling to shake off two guards dragging her toward the Mayor.

"Don't hurt her!" Jessie screamed. Her tormentor grabbed her hair and snapped her head back, silencing her.

"Little one," the Mayor said, smiling at Ananda, "stop your foolishness."

Two more men held Bliss, who offered no resistance.

Jessie, still in the tormentor's painful grip, worried more about Bliss than her younger daughter. Despite the tyrant's attention to Ananda, the girl's youth and sex would protect her—in the short run—from the most dire reprisals. But her sister, always so fierce, appeared deeply shaken and strangely passive.

"Where is my crane team?" the Mayor demanded. Four slaves hurried toward him. "Bring it out and strap them down." He nodded at the girls.

What? Jessie watched slaves wheel out a huge, ungainly looking wooden contraption. A cable ran from a hand-cranked spool up along an arm that extended about six feet. The line ended in a rusty, foot-long hook that swayed menacingly until a short, skinny, one-eyed man grabbed it. The hook looked like it might have been salvaged from a slaughterhouse. If so, she thought it hadn't traveled far, regardless of the distance.

The slaves rolled the crane to the edge of the pit. One of them, sporting a full-size tattoo of a rib cage on his back with *X-ray* inked below it, hurried up to Ananda and Bliss with a harness made of burnished leather straps. One gave off a suspicious glint that Jessie hoped was nothing more than an odd reflection of torchlight.

For the first time since she and Burned Fingers arrived, the Mayor turned to her. "Your girls will earn their keep tonight. And you are a lucky woman to see such a sight. Not all mothers are so fortunate as you."

Ananda screamed.

Jester snorted at the sight of the last guy to leave the trailer. Ponytail all the way down to his bony ass. And of course, *he* had a gun. Everybody in the whole fucking world had a gun 'cept him. But he finally caught a big break when a woman's delicate hand reached out and closed the door after Ponytail galloped off. One glance and Jester knew it wasn't a guy. How sweet was that? Leaving a damn female to guard the fort, or whatever it was? *Sweeeeet.*

Two hours had passed since then. Not another scum coming or going, or even in sight. Johnny got his gun and went a-marching, near as Jester could tell. He would have bet hollow points to hardtack on that one. From what he'd seen of their weapons and numbers, they'd be no match for the City of Shade. And they didn't even know about the Russians and marauders.

Just like that female had no idea who was gonna be a-knock-knock-knocking on her door. Jester was already climbing down the stack on the row three side so she couldn't happen out and see him. He was feeling much stronger than yesterday when he'd climbed up. Tongue only half as thick as boot leather now, and he had himself a belly full of biscuits. All ready to do battle. He just felt sorry to have wasted all his fine reviving on a woman. But the place held secrets, and he aimed to find out what they were.

Hey, iddy biddy. I'm a-comin' just for you.

He hustled around the crashed cars and looked across the thirty-foot-wide strip of sand separating him from the row with the trailer. Then he scooted over to the wide metal door, wondering what she'd try to do first. That was the great thing about having fun with a female—there were all kinds of ways of doing it. He wasted no time: *Knock-knock-knock.* Pause. *Knock-knock.*

The handle shifted, creaking when it turned.

Open sesame.

Her fingers reached around the edge, and he grabbed her hand fast as a snakebite. Soon as he tried to pull her out, something banged the inside of the door, inches from his head. Sounded like a gun. But he had his knife ready, and that was a smart move because when he twisted her wrist and cut her deep, she shrieked and fired.

Idiot. What did she think she was aiming at? She hadn't seen more than his hand, and it was on hers. She'd panicked. That's what she'd done. He sniffed that out. Just as quick, he seized the arm with the gun and bent it away from him like it was nothing more than a flap of sun-rotted tire.

But he had to move 'cause someone with big ears might be around, so he kicked her belly, left her breathless, then forced the bitch onto her back and pressed his body into hers. Nice and comfy. He gave a good listen for snoops, keeping her gun hand flat on the ground and pointed away from him. Not a sound, 'cept for her trying to breathe.

The door was open enough to throw some light. Turned out there wasn't much to see in that old trailer. A few rusty jacks holding up the roof and all the cars on top.

He'd been hoping for a whole goddamn arsenal, but at least he was going to get a gun. An old derringer, he saw now, an iddy biddy gun for hunting down an iddy biddy girl. Had the one barrel atop the other, which was kind of how he was with her, and how he might have stayed for the hot stirrings in his pants—if the lay of the land had been different. She was a looker. No denying that. Short dark hair that smelled *good*. But it was her skin that made him want to take a bite. She had the whitest damn skin ever. Like it had never seen the sun. White as sand. No kidding. *How'd she do that?*

No time for asking. He pressed his knife into her neck. Blood seeped along the blade, changing the color of things fast. "I'm going to cut your head off, you don't let go of that gun."

No way in hell that pistol was getting away from him. Not like the one some dying scum had buried in the sand just to make him look bad with the Mayor, no thanks to that freak, Soul Hunter. Nope, she was going to the grave knowing she'd fucked up bad in the end, 'cause he couldn't wait to get that gun and tell her that he'd be sure to use it on her kith and kin. Might only have the one load left, but that bullet was his grubstake. It would make his every threat real. When he got the drop on another gunman—and no yard scum could match up to him; look at her, living, make that *dying*, proof—he'd start building his own arsenal.

He slid his hand up to the derringer. Her fingers tensed, but he'd already figured her to put up a fight. *Good luck with that shit.* But the gun went off. For a full second he stared at the little pistol, a sneeze of gun smoke hanging in the air, dumbfounded by what she'd done. She'd emptied the derringer. Taken away *his* only shot. Done it knowing she would die.

Greedy goddamn bitch. What was *she* going to do with it? She was finished. But *he* could have used it.

Jester shook with rage. He pinned her arms with his knees and raised his knife, watched her face flatten with fear. At another time, with another woman, he would have had the patience to make the most of the murder. But not with her. Not now.

The first stab killed her, but he couldn't stop there, not after what she'd done to the King of the World.

"You . . . fucked . . . me . . . over!" With every word, he hammered the blade home, until there wasn't a speck of white skin on her face.

Or his.

Ananda couldn't stop screaming, and Bliss wheezed a non-stop stream of profanities. The harness had barbed wire embedded in the leather strap cinched around their thighs. The tiny spikes drew blood as soon as the slave Ananda thought of as "X-ray" tightened the buckles on their legs. Now he bound them back-to-back.

Jessie, shaking off the tormentor's grip on her head, yelled, "Stop it!" from across the pit.

Her outcry shocked Ananda into trying to control herself; their chained-up mom might get hurt trying to help them, and there was nothing she could do to stop whatever madness the Mayor had in mind. Ananda managed to reduce her screams to gasping whimpers.

The short skinny slave slipped the large iron hook through a metal O-ring attached to three straps. A more muscular member of the crane team cranked on the spool, reeling in the cable, which lifted the ring and straps above the girls' heads.

In spite of his weak appearance, the skinny slave pushed the sisters over the edge with ease. The operator let the cable unwind for several feet, before arresting their flight with a brutal jerk that drove the weight of their bodies forward. Each barb harrowed a full inch of their flesh. Ananda and Bliss both shrieked.

The crane's long wooden arm moaned. Ananda hoped it would snap. Her legs felt incinerated, and she was sure a fall to the sand would be less painful than the razor-sharp barbs.

But the crane's moaning belied no greater weakness in the wood, and they spun about ten feet above the sand until the O-ring straps twisted so tight they released in the opposite direction. Men toasted them with mugs and metal drinking containers.

A marauder yelled, "I'll bet on *them*."

But when guards shoved Leisha and Kaisha toward the pit, attention quickly switched to the conjoined twins and a second crane. X-ray strapped the girls down only feet from the stands. The men pressed close, screaming "Freak show, freak show" so loudly they drowned out the twins' screams when the barbed wire tore into their burns. But Ananda heard Leisha and Kaisha's escalating agony when the skinny slave pushed them over the edge—and the cable snapped tight. Her own pain had subsided slightly, another red tide drawn back from the shore.

A tall slave moved the crane's arm that held Ananda and Bliss, sending them swinging in wider and wider arcs, like a wrecking ball before mobs, marauders, and soldiers saw to the leveling of cities and towns.

Across the expanse, Leisha and Kaisha swung back and forth just as fast, whirling wildly. With both sets of sisters in full motion, the Mayor ordered them raised. His command left them swaying a couple of feet above the top of the pit. Ananda spotted blood drizzled on the sand.

"We will now have our first real contest of the night," the Mayor announced. "Two slaves will race to open Chunga and Tonga's pens. The loser will pay with his life and limbs. Place your bets."

Linden, bald head gleaming in the torchlight, stood at a broad table where men dumped their loot, arguing loudly about the value of guns, bullets, a rocket launcher, weapons of all types. They also shouted out the weights of gold nuggets and debated the relative worth of fuel, engine parts, tires, and luxuries like sunglasses, watches, boots, a neck brace, prostheses for arms and legs.

When the betting settled down, the Mayor motioned to guards stationed over the dragons' gates. Each group lowered a slave, roped around the waist, until the one-eyed men hung directly in front of the barriers, legs dangling like bait inches above the ground.

"When I say, 'Open them,' we will see which slave gets

to live, and which one goes to the larder. Keep the girls *moving*."

His command sent both sets of sisters swinging so hard the cranes' wooden arms moaned.

"Open the gates!"

Ananda caught glimpses of the slaves' frantic attempts to push aside a heavy wooden bar. The man at Chunga's gate shoved it all the way out first, but before he could clear the barrier, the beast smashed it open, slinging the slave into the wall. But he recovered immediately, pumping his legs madly as he pulled himself just beyond Chunga's snapping jaws.

Then the dragon pivoted and spotted the slave still struggling to slide the bar from Tonga's gate. Chunga sprinted with shocking speed across the open pit.

With the beast halfway across the sand, the slave slid the bar free and started hauling himself up the barrier with the help of guards who knew better than to sate a dragon's appetite before the big fight. Tonga slammed into the wood at the same moment Chunga smashed against it, raised up, and tore most of the meat from one of the slave's legs. Screaming in pain and horror, the man pulled himself over the edge. The guards looked uneasy.

The slave's howls were quickly eclipsed by Tonga bursting the gate open. The beast swaggered out, swishing his thick tail and leaving long serpentine trails in the sand.

"Lower them," the Mayor yelled, pointing to both sets of girls. "Give Chunga and Tonga something to play with."

The harnesses dropped quickly, barbs tearing once more at their legs; but Ananda's pain was overwhelmed by acetylene panic when she saw they were deeper in the pit than the slave when Chunga ripped his leg apart.

As the dragons squared off with each other, the tall man working the arm of Ananda and Bliss's crane swung them deftly above the beasts. The Komodos looked up as a stream of blood painted a red stripe over Chunga's head.

"Bull's-eye. Perfect," the Mayor exclaimed. The slave nodded in appreciation.

The blood incited the beast, and the reptile chased the girls.

"Higher," the Mayor shouted. "Quick!" But the cable rose much more slowly than it fell.

The sisters jerked their heels to their hamstrings a blink before Chunga's mouth closed. Only then did Ananda become aware of her mother screaming, "You bastard!" over and over.

"You see," the Mayor roared to the men who'd stepped back from the edge when the Komodos charged into the pit, "the girls and dragons get my gladiators all worked up." He pumped his arms as if running in place. "Everybody gets so excited."

He pointed to Ananda and Bliss, yelling, "Go, Chunga, go!" Then he screamed "Tonga-Tonga-Tonga" like a war cry and slapped his thighs, shaking with laughter.

The lizards needed no encouragement but blood. It dripped from both pairs of sisters spinning and swinging within teasing reach of the giant reptiles. The exertions of the beasts turned furious, frenzied. Chunga rose on his hind legs, lurching upward to try to bat them down. Ananda shrank back as the creature's long hard claws swiped perilously close to the side of the harness.

Just feet away, openly awed men argued loudly whether anyone could last more than a minute with the Mayor's monstrous pets.

Ananda, twisting away from another of Chunga's lunges, knew the odds of survival were dismal—and falling as fast as blood on the sand.

Cassie gripped the heavy antitank mine in the crook of her arm. The initial stretch of cell block didn't worry her much, but now she came to the rubble. She let the lantern hang by her side so she could see whether she'd missed any little chunks, but she'd done a good job of clearing her path.

Quickly, though, she arrived at the first bulky length of

broken concrete. It formed the end of an extrusion that extended to the bars of a cell door.

She placed her buttocks against the rough surface, as she'd planned, and swung her left leg up, using momentum to lift herself. The hard, uneven surface dug into her bottom, but she remained so focused on protecting the AT that she didn't notice the pain—or the lantern banging into the rubble. A five-inch shard of leaded glass broke off.

Cassie winced, then told herself not to worry. *Better than me all blown up.* But she reminded herself to pick up the glass on the way back. It was too precious to lose.

She eased herself down the other side, scaling three more large pieces of debris—avoiding falls, rebar, and the sharp severed railing—before nearing the stairs.

A cramp seized the arm holding the mine, forcing a sharp breath. Jaw clenched, she rested the lantern, then carefully shifted the AT so she held it in both arms. The right one, she noticed, trembled badly from fatigue. She straightened it, and the cramp lessened.

Get going. There's no time.

After switching the mine to her left arm, she retrieved the lantern and navigated the cracked and broken stairwell without stopping until she came to the tower. Setting the lantern to the side, with the AT once more resting on both arms, she crouched and leaned forward until her forearms pressed against the ground. With enormous care, she slipped her arms from underneath the deadly device and backed away as if it would bite. Standing, she gazed at the head-high ledge with regret. It would have been so simple to place the big mine on top of it, but William had been firm about positioning it so the force would explode upward.

Raising the lantern to look for another berth, she saw a gap between the back of the ledge and the wall of dirt from which it protruded. It looked large enough, but setting the mine there would be dangerous. She'd either have to slide it into the opening, bumping it over dirt and rocks, or try to lift the big mine above her head and reach forward with it. She didn't think she had that kind of strength.

Cassie searched the rest of the tower before taking out the knife and hacking at the ledge—the only way to reach the hole. The dirt crumbled easily, and she worked diligently until she heard an appalling metallic *ping*. For several seconds she stood unmoving, terrified, expecting to die. Then she looked over and saw a small stone lying next to the mine. If it had struck one of the teddy bears, she would have been dead.

She placed herself between the AT and the ledge, sweating for another five minutes before she could snug the mine safely into position.

Perfect.

Almost. She didn't grasp the possible danger until she hurried to William, pausing to retrieve the broken glass, and saw a teddy bear waiting for her on the other side of the bars. It looked longer than she remembered, and made her worry aloud whether the hole for the AT was wide enough for the bear.

"That's a good question," William said, sitting with a squat candle burning by his side. "I think so, but I should have double-checked." He gripped his chin, then told her what to do. "It'll take more time, but if you're not sure the bear's going to fit, you can dig another hole in the wall. But first, let's measure the bear against your arm so you'll have a good feel for its size."

He held up the mine, and she pressed her arm against the bars.

"It comes almost to your elbow from the tip of your middle finger. Can you remember that?" She nodded. "When you get to the stairs, put the bear on the ground very, *very* carefully. Then go on up to the tower and measure your arm against the hole for the AT. If you don't think the bear will fit easily, dig out a space a few feet away. Make sure you check that one against your arm, too. Don't worry about digging near the AT, but the bear's another story. That's why you have to leave it till you're ready. Be extra gentle when you go back to pick it up. And don't take it into the tower if you hear the dragon. Did you hear it this time?"

"No." She'd been so preoccupied, she hadn't even thought of it.

"Good. Maybe it's in the pit already. But keep listening for it."

He pointed to the bear's belly, tied in wire that she would trail all the way to the tower. "I'll feed that out as you go. Just don't go getting ahead of me. I don't want it jerking out of your hands." Once she returned, he would give the wire a tug, pulling the smaller mine to the ground so its blast could set off the much more powerful AT.

William slipped the teddy bear through the bars. It was a lot lighter than the antitank mine; but all of its extremities were wired, and she had to be careful not to brush it against herself or anything else.

Alarming as that was, Cassie still had to force herself to concentrate on her way back into the prison. She was exhausted from chopping off the ledge to get the big mine into position. William had warned her that they had the hardest job. After they set off the AT, two other teams would trigger land mines in more accessible areas. Places without bars, Cassie figured. But he'd also said the tower was the most critical location, "especially tonight."

"Go on," he called to her softly. "We'll be out of here in a little bit, and then you can hang out with Miranda and Steph."

The girls had promised to wait by the entrance to the catacombs, probably with Denton. The boy followed them everywhere, but no one followed anyone into the catacombs unless they had to.

Like me.

Cassie held the teddy bear in the crook of her right arm, as she had the bigger mine, with the lantern back in her left hand. She thought she knew every step by now, but still moved cautiously, though not slowly enough: the wire pulled on the bear's belly. She halted in mid-step.

"Stop!" William hissed at the same instant. "Think, Cassie. *Think!*"

Slower than ever, she advanced down the cell block, no longer looking at the remains of men. Right by the stairs, she thought she caught something move. She held out the light but saw nothing. *Shadows,* she told herself.

She set aside the lantern, this time near the door to the tower. She pretended she was putting a baby to bed when she laid the teddy bear on the ground. But she still held her breath when she pulled her hands away.

Hurrying, she scaled the stairs with the lantern, burdened with little of the fear she'd faced on her first trip. *I'm almost done!*

When she reached the tower, she placed her arm against the hole with the AT. *Yes!* She could have clapped.

Cassie hustled down the stairs, lifting the bear as gently as she could. In fact, she held her breath so long as she slowly stood that she became dizzy and staggered sideways. With two deep breaths, she steadied herself.

Scared, but balanced, she ascended to the tower. She wasted no time moving directly to the opening with the antitank mine—and saw her mistake as soon as she managed to angle the bear's ears and feet in without brushing them against the edges of the opening: the space was just wide enough, but it looked too shallow; she might not have left enough ledge to hold it. One of the bear's arms stuck out, along with the bottom half of its leg. Then she noticed the wire hanging from the bear, and felt an almost imperceptible pressure against her hands—a few grams of weight that could spell her doom.

She was too frightened to let go, and too afraid to withdraw the extremely sensitive mine, fearing it would blow up with the slightest shock to any of its intricately wired limbs or ears. She felt like someone who'd climbed into a tunnel but couldn't get back out. In this horrific borderland of indecision and terror, when she knew nothing but the power of a child's consuming panic, she heard the dragon. Its pounding steps were muffled, but grew more distinct every second.

She stared at the teddy bear, imagining the blast.

Go! Get out of here.

No. Don't.

But she had to move, first dropping her hands so she could catch the bear if it fell. Even that impact might blow up the mine, but if it hit the ground, she'd surely die. The cheerful-looking bomb tottered on the edge of the opening. Cassie feared the weight of her own breath. She picked up the lantern, aware again of the dragon—the *pounding*. But at this moment, the wire scared her more.

Don't touch it, she warned herself as she headed for the stairs, knowing just brushing the strand could pull the bear down.

She moved alongside the wire, eyeing it intently with each step she took. One stair shy of the cell block, the wire crossed her path. She stopped.

As she lifted her foot to clear it, she spotted what she thought was the same odd movement she'd spied on her way back to the tower. But she was closer to it now. She held out the lantern, shivering sharply when it illuminated a huge black snake with yellow spots glowing eerily in the candlelight. The reptile slithered slowly under the wire, where the strand draped diagonally across her path from a chunk of concrete onto the stairs. She closed her eyes as hard as she could. She never wanted to see the creature again.

Go away. Go away.

Still clamping her eyes shut, Cassie cried out, desperate to drive off all the horrors descending on her at once. But her outburst added a new fear—of a fatal vibration—that pried them back open.

In the breathless quiet, the mines didn't go off. But the snake was *still* moving. It had to be at least ten feet long. *Is it going to get me?*

Her hands shook worse than ever. The lantern's unprotected candle flickered precariously by her side. She smelled the dragon and almost choked. The pounding grew louder. At any second the mines could blow up, burying her in the prison. She'd turn into bones like the ones she'd seen in the cages. Her head felt crushed by pressure, crazed with the darkest dread. She wished she could tear it off.

Her gaze lowered to the wire, as she knew it must. She had to step over it and hurl herself past the snake. But where was the serpent? It had stopped moving. Was it gone?

Alive with hope, she held out the lantern again. At the shadowy edge of its throw, no more than six feet from where she trembled, the reptile's thick head turned and looked right at her.

Cassie jerked backward, tripping on the stair behind her. She fell to her bottom, just missing the wire with her hip—the last thing she saw before the candle went out.

"William?" she said, wishing she could shout his name. "William?" Whimpers that brought no response.

The dragon's incessant pounding made her heart race.

Stand up.

She was dead if she didn't. At any second the snake could brush against the wire and set off the mines. Or it could be heading toward her now.

It was staring at me.

Fear of being buried alive with the snake brought Cassie to her feet. She tried to remember where the wire crossed her path, the big step she would have to take—the one that could spill her onto the horrifying snake. She was petrified it would whip around, wrap her tightly in its chilly grip, and eat her head first. That's what they did. Head first.

Terror of the snake, dragons, and land mines launched Cassie wildly into the blackness. In the eternal second before her foot could touch down, she felt a lacerating emptiness that could have been death for all its final desolation—and heard a moan erupt from the tortured shell of the joyous child she once had been.

Mom, Dad, Jenny, Maul.

The dragons were back in their pens, each lured by an arm of the slave who'd lost the race to open their gates. Jessie had turned from the man's butchering, delivered in full view of the appreciative crowd in the stands. Her tormentor watched so intently, he never noticed her looking away. The slave screamed but once. She hoped he'd been shocked into oblivion before he bled to death. She wished no less for herself.

Jessie's daughters, and Leisha and Kaisha, were hauled from the pit and lowered to the ground. X-ray unbuckled the harnesses. Blood covered every inch of the girls' legs and feet. Ananda and Bliss staggered when they walked, and held each other up. *They'll be together, at least for this.*

Jessie gazed at the pit, where blood appeared in clear crimson lines, or smudged by the dragons, then raised her eyes to the gates and the men in the bleachers. Everything seemed surreal, as if she were no longer living her own life, but a horribly imagined one. She could make no rational sense of what she was witnessing in this glut of bricks and mortar in the Great American Desert, only that it had emerged from the devastation of her species and reflected that holocaust with harrowing fidelity.

She heard the Mayor speak. His words didn't register fully, but numb with terror she followed Burned Fingers down the ladder. Two swords stood upright in the sand. They looked medieval, and gave her no hope. Short of a rocket launcher, she would soon be dead, and Ananda and Bliss and the other children would be left to the desires of these abominable men.

The Mayor towered above them, holding a short torch in each hand, no doubt to better light the bloodletting.

"Put the slaves in place for our big fight," he ordered with unfamiliar formality.

Guards once again lowered roped-up unfortunates to the front of the gates.

"Show our female gladiator how you will count down," the Mayor commanded a guard with sparse facial hair.

Dutifully, the man spoke up: "Three hundred, 299, 298, 297—"

"Stop," the Mayor interrupted, directing his attention back to Jessie. "If you are still fighting when he gets to zero, Ananda will live. But if one of my dragons gets to you first, the last thing you will see will be me throwing your little girl into the pit. Just five minutes saves her life." He smiled at Ananda, who looked shocked. "If a mother cannot save a girl's life, what good is she?" Then he shook his head at Bliss. "I am sorry to say that nothing can save a porn queen's life. But Catch the Queen is very much fun for my guards, and life is difficult for them."

Jessie hefted the weighty sword, wishing she had the strength to throw it through him. That was what she wanted for her dying vision.

The Mayor turned to the bleachers. "Men, place your bets on who will win: Jessie and Ellison, or Chunga and Tonga?" He laughed heartily. "So now that we have had our good joke, bet the times each will survive. Will they last to two hundred fifty? Two hundred? *One* hundred?" he said incredulously. "You can bet the number of wounds they might give my pets, too, but I think a better bet is who will be eaten first. And do not forget the little one." He waved at Ananda. "Will Jessie save her, or will my pets get an extra sweet treat tonight?"

Bliss raised her arms, smeared with blood, and thrust her middle fingers at the Mayor. A guard grabbed her. She pushed him away. He stumbled as she whirled back around and jabbed both fingers even higher, staring defiantly at the despot.

The Mayor whooped with delight, calling off the men who were seizing her.

"Oh, you will be a great porn queen. I can tell."

"Fuck you," Bliss said in a voice so steely that it startled Jessie, but it thrilled her, too. "Fuck every last one of you," Bliss yelled, shoving her fingers at the men in the bleachers.

She darted to the pit and leaped. The Mayor glared at Bliss as she picked up the second sword. Then he ordered her out.

"I'd rather die," Bliss said, placing her wrist on the weapon's sharp edge.

"She stays," the Mayor announced, as if it were suddenly his idea. When the tormentor started to protest, the Mayor cut him off: "There are others. Take your pick. Take two. I like her down there." His gaze returned to Bliss. "She may be a good fighter. And there is more to bet on."

His words were met with cheers from the stands. The Mayor took a sword from a guard and tossed it into the pit so all three of them would be armed. Burned Fingers grabbed it.

Jessie edged over to Bliss, asking her softly, "What are you doing?"

"I'm changing the odds."

"Not enough. We're all going to—"

"Die. I know. But I'm dying down here with you. Not up there with those fucking bastards." Tears ran down Bliss's cheeks, the flames of her rage. Jessie couldn't remember the last time she'd seen her cry.

"Come here." Jessie took her firstborn in her arms and held her as tightly as she'd hugged Ananda hours ago. With death so imminent, her life as a mother felt strangely complete.

She looked up at Ananda, gripped by a guard since her sister had jumped, and mouthed, *I'm sorry.*

For everything, Jessie added to herself. *For your rotten life. For the world. For the days and weeks to come.*

Her youngest shouted, "I love you, Mom. I love you, Bliss."

Jessie yelled back, "I love you, too." Bliss tapped her heart and pointed to Ananda as strongly as she'd pointed her middle fingers at the Mayor.

While men finished their raucous betting, the Mayor threw his torches to Burned Fingers and Jessie. The marauder caught his, but she fumbled hers, almost singing her hand. It sizzled out on the sand.

"Grab it quick," Burned Fingers said to her.

She picked up the torch, and he lit it with his. Then he gave it to Bliss.

"It'll keep the beasts away," he said to her, "till it burns down. When that happens, throw it at them. Try to hit them in the face. Blind them. Whatever you can do."

The handle of Jessie's torch already felt so hot she doubted she could hold it for more than a minute or two.

"Everybody get ready," the Mayor bellowed. When the bleachers quieted, and he held the gaze of dozens of men, he yelled, "Open the gates!"

The roped-up slaves struggled furiously to slide the wooden bars aside. Jessie didn't believe in God. She didn't believe in heaven. But she did believe in hell.

Chunga exploded out first again, smashing the gate into the wall so hard he knocked the slave unconscious. The man hung limply from the rope, but the guards pulled him up unscathed. The lizard swung his long neck around, surveyed the pit, and bolted. He shunned the flames of the torchbearers for the slave who had just opened Tonga's pen and was climbing up the barrier, escaping with his limbs intact—for now.

Frustrated, the beast bugled. Then he turned and swept his thick tail over the blood-streaked sand. Tonga slammed open his gate, moving up alongside his brother. The two giant lizards separated then, without hesitation circling wide of their prey. Jessie guessed they had done this many times.

"Stay close," Burned Fingers said. "Back-to-back."

The three of them formed a tight circle. Then Jessie heard, "Two hundred eighty-seven, two hundred eighty-six . . ." and knew the countdown had begun. She didn't know about Burned Fingers, but she was sure that she and Bliss were fighting to save Ananda. She had told her girls many times that she loved them more than life itself. Now she wanted to show them the meaning of those words for as long as she could.

Sweat lines formed in the blood on Jester's face. He was so angry he could have killed her all over again. He grabbed the crappy derringer from her lifeless hand and almost threw it at the trailer wall, 'cause there sure weren't any other guns around there. *Arsenal? My ass.* He searched her for ammo. Didn't find any, and tossed aside the empty derringer.

But in the corner of his eye he spotted a dark patch on the floor toward the end of the trailer.

What the hell? A wooden hatch cover lay closed before him. He opened it, worrying about a booby trap, but felt a wave of cool air instead. *Moist* air. Like you could drink it. He smiled when he spotted a ladder made of rope and bones. He was going to like this place, even if the reception so far hadn't been the best. Using up that last bullet was a crime. He'd never met anyone so selfish.

He tested the rope with his foot. Felt pretty damn strong. But before he started down, he heard an explosion. Kind of muffled. But a big one. Then two more.

Jester didn't know what they were for a few seconds, but then he heard the telltale signs and almost ran out of the trailer. A thunderstorm! Just the way people always said they sounded—like bricks tumbling in the sky. *Exactly.* Must be a lot of lightning 'cause those bricks were still a-tumbling.

He hated to miss a good thunderstorm, fat drops splashing on his parched skin. Enough to make a man run around naked hooting at the sky. But the wet air down below promised the sweetest rewards of all.

Chapter Eighteen

A deafening rumble raced through the cavern. William grabbed the steel bars, trying to steady his arms and legs. His lone candle flickered as the ground itself seemed to run from the coming onslaught.

The teddy bear mines he'd just disarmed jiggled eerily, insentient creatures come brazenly to life. Only William's gaze remained fixed, staring in shock at the ceiling as the violent reverberations heralded a screeching rupture. He glimpsed a torch whirling through the air—a falling star in the belly of earthen blackness—then tried mightily to shield his head from rocks and dirt and bricks and mortar—and the ubiquitous bones that formed the crude rebar of the City of Shade.

He yelled Cassie's name, but glimpsed neither her slight shape nor heard her cries as rubble pelted him mercilessly and put out his candle. He could not even hear his own screams.

Where is she?

It was his last thought in the ruin of darkness. Tons of cavern ceiling collapsed the bars and slammed him to the ground, caging him forever in death.

After the big black snake tripped the land mines, the reptile whipped around and wrapped Cassie in its monstrously powerful grip, pinning her arms to her sides, leaving only her head free. She shrieked from the crushing pressure, bulging eyes on the dark ceiling as it opened wide to a fiery show of cascading torches, tumbling flames that flashed on the creature's open mouth. The snake's gamy breath coated her face as it reared back its head to strike. The girl bent forward, trying to bury her features in the dark scaly skin. The serpent's forked tongue flicked the back of her neck as rock and dirt and sand pummeled the beast. It snapped at the assault, its thick body shielding Cassie from an initial deluge that surely would have killed her. Then it released her and tried to fight the ferocious, all-encompassing enemy.

Cassie rolled away blindly, sickened and nearly insane with terror. Rocks and bricks struck her back and dropped her to her knees. She rose and staggered away with her hands clamped on her head, veering from a ball of flame that landed by her side before seeing it was a torch. She snatched it up as a hollow voice echoed, "Run! Run!"

"Where?" she screamed, before realizing the distant command issued from the collapsing world above her, not the death-riddled confines of the catacombs.

She swept the torch through the air to try to find a familiar marker—the bent steel door or cracked stairwell—but saw only that the torrent of shattered ceiling had slowed. Then she lowered her stricken gaze and spotted a glint in a great creature's eyes, and saw at once that they weren't the snake's distinctive slit-shaped horrors. These were dark circles.

"Dragons," she whispered, loathing the word, never again a fanciful wonder of childhood fantasy.

What she'd heard about the giant man-eating lizards frightened her as much as the snake, and she bolted in a direction that she hoped would take her to William. The Komodo would never fit through the bowed-out bars, but the torch illuminated so little of the destruction—and left her with so much fear—that she considered climbing the rubble up to the City of Shade. But the piles fell short of the gaping ceiling, and she knew little more than the cruelty of that dark realm with its fallen torches, ruled by men who'd imprisoned her friends and murdered Maul. She wanted to return to the river, the waterfall, the sun-splashed gardens, vivid memories that sparked her greatest worry: that she would never live long enough to see her Eden again because she was trapped forever in a cave-in with a dragon and a monstrous snake. Her fear worsened as the glinting eyes drew closer.

Stumbling away, petrified that she'd fall and the torch would go out, she came to a broad hill of dirt, sand, and stones. She scrambled up the gritty slope and slid down the other side, looking back quickly. The dragon's head loomed over the short crest, so close she could see his rough, wrinkled skin and forked tongue.

Cassie backed up, instinctively thrusting the flame out in front of her. It didn't stop the dragon's advance. The animal romped down the rubble, looking left and right, his hideous yellow tongue snapping in and out, a ravenous creature trying to find a way past a lone flame.

She gashed her foot on rebar, bleeding on broken concrete. It was painful, but she was grateful that she might be working her way out of the catacombs' scariest recesses. But with the Komodo trailing her relentlessly in the darkness—and a sudden avalanche of rocks that could block her retreat at any moment—the exit to the river felt miles away.

The beast moved closer, then lunged. His tongue grazed her pants. She brought the flame down, searing the dragon's moist flesh. It sizzled loudly and disappeared into the Komodo's mouth as Cassie, shaking, backed into a large rubble pile. She stabbed the torch once more at the dragon, and watched him move only his head aside, keeping his feet solidly planted. But when the creature shifted she had a chance to look behind her, and was startled by the daunting slope of dirt, boulders, and bricks.

In desperation, she risked raising the flame from the beast, and spied a small opening below the ceiling. She began backing up the slope, holding the torch out with one hand while using the other to steady herself. The Komodo watched her intently, then tracked her closely.

Hurrying, shaking worse than ever, Cassie reached the top with the dragon so near she was afraid he would claim her with a single lunge. She poked her legs into the opening—the unknown blackness and whatever it held—then wriggled the rest of her body through the breach, never shifting her gaze from the eyes that fed on her. She had to withdrew the torch to crawl backward over the bricks, then raised the flame again and saw the Komodo's thick head poking through the gap. He strained to break all the way through, powerful exertions that tumbled debris toward her. Not far above the beast, she spied a much wider hole in the ceiling, from which the rubble had formed.

Go up there, she pleaded to the dragon silently, but he had eyes only for her.

Backing away once more, she spotted the steel bars bent to the ground, twisted like candle wax by huge slabs of stone.

Where's William?

Her harrowing question vaporized at the sight of the dragon methodically digging away the last of the stones and bricks blocking his massive shoulders. With little effort he muscled his upper body through the enlargement, forcing aside other ruins to accommodate his girth. In fraught seconds, the beast crouched above her, a gob of saliva dripping from his pebbly lips.

Then the Komodo started down after her, crunching the debris, hurried steps that sounded like the busy jaws of a voracious beast.

The land mines sent shock waves across the arena. A vicious shudder raced up Jessie's legs and shook her upper body, the sword and stubby torch vibrating visibly in her hands. She registered all of this with piercing clarity as Bliss hurled her torch into the mouth of Chunga, the larger Komodo, then slapped her singed hand on her pants. The beast flapped his jaws, and the short smoldering post fell out. Before the giant lizard reeled away, his mouth opened again, wider, like he was bellowing; but Jessie heard only the earth ripping open from the middle of the pit all the way to Tonga's pen, and watched the beast himself slip into the vast hole.

Stunned, she backed away. Support columns broke apart as easily as ancient urns, then the brittle roof crashed down in bucket-size chunks. She grabbed Bliss and dragged her to the pit wall, seeking the limited shelter she could find in the first seconds of devastation.

She still gripped her own tiny torch, enduring burns because she assumed that Chunga was rampaging somewhere in the darkness. Hard as she peered, she couldn't see the Komodo, and wondered if, like the other dragon, he had slipped away, too. But she did spot one of the torches that had fallen from the pit's perimeter, snuffed out by the sand. She quickly lit it with the short one still torturing her hand, then cast the agonizing flame into the pitch, hoping to spot a gun or rifle that might have fallen in the attack. She saw no weapon, but gunshots rang out above. Looking up, she spied the silhouettes of marauders and guards running past the few torches that remained upright. Not for long: even as she watched, they were uprooted by men frantic for light in the darkening chaos. A hail of bricks knocked a guard to the ground. His torch, so briefly held, fell to the pit and rolled into the hole, still ablaze.

Chunga's elongated head leaped from the darkness just feet from Jessie and Bliss, as if he had sniffed out the humans, the tips of his forked tongue testing the air inches from them. Bliss raised her sword, and Jessie stabbed at the creature with the torch.

Then they ran. But a clump of bricks broke apart on Bliss's back, halting her escape. She tried to stifle a scream as her mother hauled her toward Chunga's pen, thinking it might provide protection from the falling roof—and the rapacious dragon.

Burned Fingers shouted her name.

"Over here," Jessie yelled back.

Like the Komodo, he sprang from the darkness, but from behind them near the wall—his appearance almost as shocking as the dragon's. Blood spilled from his scalp and streamed down his face. He wiped at it roughly, and jabbed at the beast with his sword.

"Let's get to the pen," Jessie shouted.

"Right," he agreed, as if he'd been working on the same plan.

She looked up as another rumbling sound erupted, this time from above. Enormous sections of roof peeled away and shattered randomly across the arena, revealing patches of stars in the night sky—heaven's bright incurious indifference to hell.

A twelve-foot length of bricks, mortar, and bones battered the sand inches from Chunga. The hunkering beast didn't shift his dogged eyes from his quarry, sloughing off smaller chunks as if they were raindrops.

When the dragon probed boldly with his tongue again, Burned Fingers sliced off a half foot of the yellowy organ. The lump of flesh fell soundlessly amidst the constant clatter of bricks. The beast opened and closed his mouth several times, as if pained and confused.

The three of them backed out of the pit into Chunga's pen, and Burned Fingers closed the gate. As he searched for a means to secure it, the Mayor jerked it open and slammed it just before Chunga banged against the wooden barrier. Before the Mayor could pivot toward them, Burned Fingers pressed the sword to his spine.

"Drop your gun or I'll cut right through you."

"I think I have a decided advantage," the Mayor replied coolly. But he had yet to turn around, and the hand holding the pistol remained by his side.

"I'll die fast, you'll die slowly. Probably eaten by one of your pets."

The Mayor glanced at his gun. Burned Fingers pressed the sword hard enough to draw a spot of blood through the Mayor's faded blue shirt. Jessie looked from him to the marauder, who appeared intent on goring the tyrant.

The gun dropped to the sand. Jessie retrieved the chrome-plated Smith & Wesson .45 revolver, hammer cocked, and aimed it at the Mayor's head.

"See what else he's got," she said.

Burned Fingers pulled a long shiny knife from a sheath hanging by the Mayor's hip. He used it to cut off the man's belt and tie his hands behind his back. Jessie felt unmitigated pleasure at seeing him so clearly at their mercy.

"Kill him," Bliss said, raising her sword.

"No!" Jessie replied sharply. "Not yet."

"How about you put your sword right on his belly when I turn him around," Burned Fingers said to the girl, "and cut him wide open if he moves?" She nodded, and the marauder forced the Mayor to face them. "I'm searching the front of you head-to-toe," he said. "She'll stick you, and her mom will shoot you."

Chunga banged the gate again.

Burned Fingers patted down the Mayor thoroughly, handing his knife to Jessie. "Now, how does this lock from the inside?"

"It does not." Incredibly, the Mayor chuckled. "And my dear Chunga has not learned to open doors, or even to knock politely," he added in the same amused tone, as the Komodo banged the barrier once more. Then he turned serious: "So before we leave, we will have to open it to save his life."

"Dream on, asshole," Burned Fingers said.

Jessie thought the dragon might be figuring it out on his own. She noticed that the third time the creature banged the gate, it opened inches farther before smacking what sounded like Chunga's head, which the beast appeared to be using as a battering ram. And when the reptile repeated the pounding yet again, she watched the gate swing open more than a foot, wafting the creature's horrendous odor over them.

"You should let me lead you to safety," the Mayor said, "and then we can talk about—"

"Why do you think you're still alive?" Burned Fingers interrupted, putting his knife to the man's throat. "Now turn around and show us how to get out of here. And if you give me any excuse, I'll saw your spine right out of your back."

They hurried through the pen, the gate banging at longer intervals behind them. With the Mayor in front, they eased by the old rickety circus wagon, where the mauled young woman had been used as bait for the beast.

"You see, even if he gets past the gate, he will run into this," the Mayor said, sounding pleased with himself. "But we should leave something tasty so he does not get any wicked ideas. He will expect his usual treat."

"How about *your* arms this time? You like that idea?" Burned Fingers pushed him. "Keep moving."

Jessie would have preferred to lop off the Mayor's head and toss it in the wagon.

The big man remained uncharacteristically mute as they edged into a wide tunnel that rose a foot higher than her head. Only their footsteps violated the quiet of the enclosed space, an unnerving hush after the violence and mayhem of the wrecked arena.

She pointed the Mayor's gleaming gun into the darkness, knowing that even though she looked like a hunter, the torch she also carried made them easy prey for anyone—or any*thing*—lurking in the blackest shadows.

"Bliss," she said softly, "stay back. Out of the light."

When the mines blew up, Linden watched everyone above the pit freeze. He also waited, wondering how long it would take for drunken pandemonium to break out. Only seconds. The Mayor triggered it by rushing to the edge, staring intently at the opening earth. Men rushed everywhere at once, giving the emissary the opportunity to walk up and casually knock the despot into what looked like a blackening abyss.

Then the hairless man bolted toward Ananda, Leisha, and Kaisha, who were lifting their eyes to the roof as it started to crumble.

He grabbed the girls, whispering, "Run fast. I'm getting you out of here, somewhere safe." When they failed to move, he forced them forward, glancing back every few seconds. Gunfire ricocheted all around them.

Ananda hated the bald guy. The Mayor's best buddy was pushing her away from the pit, and she desperately wanted to see that her mother and Bliss were okay. But the falling torches gave her only a glimpse of the Mayor with his pistol. She wondered what he was doing down there. Was he going to shoot her mom and sister? It seemed that he and every man in the arena had a gun and a reason to fire wildly in the melee. But there were also screams and curses, and the howls of the maimed and dying.

She wanted to escape Linden but didn't know where to go. His pushes were keeping them just ahead of the falling bricks. She heard rubble hitting the ground just feet behind them, like hungry hounds chasing ever closer to their quarry.

Now Linden ordered them to hold hands. He pulled them along faster for several minutes, offering encouraging words with almost every step. "Don't worry," he said. "I'll get you away from this." Then he rushed headlong into a brick column and dropped Ananda's hand, cursing and groaning. "Come here!" he snapped, herding the kids into a corner, where he pushed their heads down and forced them into what felt like a cubbyhole. "Stay there. Don't move." Linden sounded angry now, like most men. "I know where you are. I'll come back for you. Just stay put. I mean that."

Ananda listened to him run off. When she was sure he was gone, she turned to the twins. "We've got to get out of here."

"But he said to stay," Leisha quarreled.

"Of course he did," Ananda argued back. "He's one of

them. He wants us safe because we're worth a lot. We're *not* staying."

She crawled out, blinded by the darkness, then she pulled the girls to their feet. Just as she was about to lead them away, heavy footfalls made her freeze. The terrifying sounds hurried toward them.

Ananda heard the twins move. *Quiet,* she wanted to warn them, but couldn't. She put her hand on their chest, hoping they would stay still as the walls and that the men would pass. She smelled a rank odor, and feared her own scent would give them away.

We're animals, she thought, sniffing the air silently.

The footfalls grew louder, and she smelled sweat.

But they're worse, she told herself as the hairs on the back of her neck prickled her skin. *They're beasts of the night.*

She didn't understand how she could be so sure of this—and wondered where those exact words came from—but she knew it was true. And then she knew why. The answer came to her as simply as it had moments ago: *Because we're animals. We sense things.*

The beasts of the night, invisible as phantoms, stepped so close that her nose now filled with their sour, boozy breath.

Linden wondered whether he'd told the girls that he was working to free the caravaners. He'd been in a rush to get them out of the target zone, and then smashed his head into the brick column so hard it had left him dizzy. He was still reeling when he hid them in the empty weapons cache. But everything he'd said about taking them somewhere safe was hardly the message of an enemy. And he'd promised to come back for them.

Still, his doubts needled him, and he wanted to turn around. But he knew it was more urgent to get word to Sam and Yurgen and the others that while the roof did collapse, it looked like many of the guards, marauders, and Russians had been spared. The extermination must begin at once.

They'll be okay, he decided. They're too scared to move. Who wouldn't be in this madness?

But nothing felt certain in the City of Shade. Not his life. Not theirs. Especially if drunken men grabbed them in the darkness: those girls couldn't possibly imagine what that would mean. No one with a heartstring of decency could fathom the deranged mix of desire and murder that swirled through the minds of men so long denied the objects of their lust.

Tonga shifted his weight from foot to foot, and it seemed to Cassie that he was about to pounce. She jabbed her torch at the reptile—which appeared less frightened of the flame now—and backed up.

Behind her, deep layers of bones rose halfway up the slope she'd climbed with William. She thought he must be dead, or he would have waited for her. She checked the ground and saw a teddy bear mine about five feet to her right. Inches away, she spotted William's hand protruding lifelessly from a heavy pile of rubble, as if he'd pushed the bear away in his last seconds.

The sight of his hand startled Cassie, and made her feel more alone—more vulnerable—than ever. Even William had died.

A lifetime seemed to pass as she looked from the bear to the dragon. Finally, she forced her gaze back on the mine and screamed, *"Get it!"* to try to make herself move.

She edged toward the bear, guessing William had pushed the pin back into the mine to deactivate it. Otherwise, the explosions would have set it off. But she hoped not, because she hadn't been able to budge the pin when he'd given her the chance to pop it out in the storage area. That was why she'd had to carry both land mines ready to explode.

Tonga's tongue moved in and out of his mouth almost continually now, dripping strings of saliva, as if he were already digesting her. When he thrust out his tongue again, it darted so close, spittle landed on her pants, inches from her foot.

She parried with the torch. Despite her shaky hands, she fried inches of the organ, withdrawing the flame just before the beast bit down. The Komodo shuddered, perhaps with pain, but mostly, Cassie thought, the beast looked angry.

Almost choking with panic, she gazed down and saw that she'd managed to move within inches of the teddy bear.

With a halting breath, she reached for it, still holding out the torch, and dug her fingers into the ground to try to scoop the bear up gently. Even in fear's densest fog, she knew better than to seize the land mine.

Please be ready. Please.

She rose, fingers feeling the back of the bear to determine whether the pin had been pulled. *It has to be.*

Holding out the flame, Cassie fended off the giant lizard while retreating to the very edge of the slope. Then she clenched the torch between her knees, moaning when she found the pin in place. Tears clouded her eyes.

She blinked away the blurriness, threaded her thin index finger through a metal loop, and pulled, with little hope of success. The pin didn't move, but the beast did, lunging within feet of her. She had to grab the torch and stick it in the dragon's face, unsure it would even stop him. The reptile did back up, but only a foot, more a dodge or feint than any sign of defeat.

You have to do this, she pleaded with herself, knowing that if she failed to free the pin, the slobbering lizard would devour her.

Again she squeezed the torch between her knees, and with a strangling sense of panic grabbed the ring and jerked as hard as she could. Nothing. "No!" she burst out. "No!"

She tried again, so hard she thought the ring would slice off half her finger. It gave, but only slightly. Furious, she jerked it once more, and to her surprise freed it. But the force of her effort nearly whipped her hand and the bear into the torch handle. She stared, shocked at how close she'd come to killing herself.

The dragon attacked, and Cassie dropped the torch and

saw it glance harmlessly off Tonga's open mouth. Panicking, sure she'd waited too long, she tossed the mine at the Komodo and hurled herself over the edge.

As she plunged toward countless bones, she looked back at the bear falling end over end in the last of the dying torchlight—and saw the enraged dragon diving after her.

Jester climbed down the rope ladder into the dark cavern. Moving only by touch in a lunar silence, he descended into cooler, ever more moist air. The soothing temperature and humidity made him smile. And he felt confident, an invader well-equipped with his knife, to use the night to his favor. So strong and sure of himself that he wasn't prepared for the missing rung on the rope ladder.

He slipped so fast, the front of his feet snapped upright on the next rung and failed to arrest his fall. He plummeted past two more rungs before getting a death grip on the rope with his right hand, his only hold as he swayed over the black void.

Slowly, he looped his left leg around the ladder and found another foothold. Only then did he hear the echo of his terror—"Fuck-fuck-fuck-fuck"—and realize he must have screamed to set off such a long shadow of fear.

He looked down, wondering what else he'd set off. *Who's there?* He wasn't worried about iddy biddy bitch. He *wanted* to find her. But he knew you were a fool if you didn't worry about the threats you couldn't see—and he couldn't see a damn thing.

"Ananda?" Linden called gently. "Leisha? Kaisha?" He'd searched the cubbyhole closet where he left them, and where they once secured the guns before the Mayor permitted the men to carry them freely. Linden had warned him to keep the firearms locked up, but the Mayor dismissed his concerns, saying airily, "Men must have guns to keep us safe at all times." He wondered what the Mayor was thinking, with his men shooting drunkenly in the dark. *Feeling safe now?*

"It's okay," he whispered, hoping the girls were huddled nearby. He didn't think they would have traveled far in the chaos. He hadn't grabbed a torch, preferring the cover of night. "It's me, Linden." He listened closely before going on. "I'm with the good guys. I'll get you back to your people. I promise."

No response. All he heard was a spate of distant screams. *Where the devil did they go?*

He stepped forward, ready to call softly again, when a hammer cocked on a pistol. He ducked and reached for his Ruger.

The tunnel from Chunga's pen was ending. Jessie held out the torch in alarm before seeing they'd come to a T-shaped intersection.

"We've got a decision," she said to Burned Fingers, whose blood had dried in rusty streaks on his face.

The marauder pressed his blade into the Mayor's back. "Which way is out?" he demanded.

"We will go to the right," the Mayor said in an imperious voice. The regal tone made Jessie want to beat him to death with a stick.

"I don't trust him," Bliss said, still in the shadows a few steps behind them.

"And going right takes us where?" Burned Fingers smacked the Mayor's head with the butt of his knife.

Wincing, the Mayor said, "To the back of the city, near your big truck and van."

"Isn't that convenient." Burned Fingers shook his head in the dim light.

Too convenient, Jessie silently agreed.

"You can trust me," the Mayor said loudly. "Always, I am a man of my word."

From the dark recesses they'd left behind, they heard a

creak—and the unmistakable racket of the dragon thrashing the circus wagon.

The teddy bear mine exploded, ripping a gaping wound in the Komodo's thick neck. But the shrapnel missed Cassie, streaking millimeters above her head as she fell just below the edge of the slope. With no torch, in utter darkness, she hoped to luck out and land on the narrow path she'd taken up there with William—and hit dirt on the higher part of the rise—but then she barreled right into the bones. The blunt impact scraped her back and legs and hurt horribly.

She balled up, trying to squeeze away the throbbing that overtook her. She hurt so much she didn't even listen for the dragon. And she was sure the bear had destroyed the beast.

So when Tonga trod heavily in the darkness, Cassie, filled with disbelief, forced herself to stand. *Just in case.* She backed up only when the dragon crunched bones less than ten feet away, finally conceding the nightmare of the giant lizard's continued existence.

Her heel smacked a skeleton, and it rattled so loudly she feared—as she would have with ghosts—that it would reach up and seize her for the reptile. Looking around, she saw nothing in the blackness, but heard a frightening snort from the creature as he lumbered close. She had to flee—*now!*

She ran blindly over the endless, unknown dead, stumbling and falling on the bones, horrified that she would leave the catacombs in the belly of that hateful beast.

Sam tightened the knot on her white braid and pressed her shoulder against the edge of a dune, straining in the starlight to study the city. Much of it lay in ruins, but the roof still stood about one hundred yards ahead, including an area over a smaller pit where the caravaners were imprisoned. The shaky-looking scaffolding along the edge of the structure also remained in place.

"Where is he?" she whispered to Yurgen, although Sam knew only Linden could attest to his actual whereabouts. Gunfire in the city had lessened, but they needed the Mayor's chief emissary to free the caravaners, and give them an estimate of the damage and the dead—and the number of men they would now have to exterminate.

"I don't know, but he better get out here soon," Yurgen said impatiently.

Sam spotted sudden movement in the corner of her eye and turned in terror.

"What is it?" Yurgen asked, alarmed. With his poor night vision, he could not see far.

"A dog," Sam said, relieved. She watched it limp away from the rubble.

"I didn't think they had any dogs."

"*They* don't, but Cassie told me the caravaners had two of them. This must be Hansel, the one missing a leg."

Yurgen called to it. The dog started in their direction, but stopped and stared at them, eyes reflecting two stingy spots of starlight.

Sam tried calling him by name. The big mastiff mix hopped within a few feet of her. She put out her hand so he could sniff it.

"There you go," she cooed, rubbing under his chin. Hansel wagged his tail, and Sam drew him behind the dune. "Somebody's going to be glad to see you," she said to the dog.

"If Linden can get them out of there. Where *is* he?"

"We can't wait any longer," Sam said. "I'm going in. You stay and give—"

"They're guarded all the time. That's why Linden's got to handle this. He can walk right up to them."

"Maybe he's shot. And there might not even be guards there. Would you hang around with a roof falling down?"

"I would if the one over my head was okay, and if the Mayor was going to feed me to his dragons if I left."

"It's not just Linden," Sam said. "We can't give those goons time to sober up and get organized. And we need help. If we get those prisoners, they can start fighting." She glanced at a worn leather satchel packed with pistols already confiscated from guards and marauders whom they killed trying to escape the city. "We've got to move while we've still got the jump on them."

Yurgen took her arm. "I'll go. You—"

"No. That doesn't make any sense. You can't see twenty feet at night. I can do this."

"I know you can, but I'm worried. It wasn't going to be easy for Linden, and he knows these people."

"So do we," she said darkly. She kissed Yurgen's cheek. "Nothing's going to happen to me. We've got a kid to take care of," she added, alluding to Cassie.

Sam headed around the protected side of the dune, lugging the satchel and skirting the deep sand while she could. She planned to advance on the rear of the city, and tried to recall what Linden had said about the layout near the smaller pit.

Despite the assurances she'd given Yurgen, the mission scared her. The city's gunmen were merciless. Yet a smile snuck across her face, testament to the prospect of raising a girl again. But the grief-stricken memory of her daughter's murder intruded quickly, and Sam vowed to never lose another child to the City of Shade—and to fulfill a blood oath that she and Yurgen had sworn years ago.

The tormentor, a husky guard, seized Linden's hand before he could grab his gun from his belt, then pressed his own pistol to the bald man's head.

"You got a choice," he said to Linden in the darkness. "You want to die?"

The Mayor's emissary let him take the Ruger. A moment later the other man, a lean African guard, lit a torch and the husky guard patted him down, finding a long knife inside his boot.

"This is a beauty. That real bone?" He ogled the handle. "Human or animal?" Linden didn't reply. "I can do things with something like this," the man went on. "I can make you talk."

"You better quit now," Linden said. "You're going to end up dead if you keep this up. You, too," he warned the African.

"He thinks *we're* going to die," the husky guard said to his buddy, who smiled and held the torch close to Linden's face, which reddened in the firelight. He turned from the heat. The lean guard laughed.

The tormentor chuckled, too, but humorlessly. "I heard it all: 'I'm with the good guys.' Then you said, 'I'll get you back to your people.'"

"I was saying those things so the girls would come to me, you idiot. Now give me my weapons and let's go find them, or the Mayor's going to have your heads." He looked at them both.

"The Mayor? You mean the guy you shoved into the pit? You tried to hide it, but I saw you push his fat ass in there first thing. That's okay with us, 'cause we're taking over. But it's bad for you, 'cause you're done."

"What?" Linden tried to grab his Ruger. The tormentor pistol-whipped him so hard and fast he drove him to his knees.

"Yeah, you really hung around to help the Mayor," the husky guard said with only a brief show of breath for his violent efforts. "About as long as I did. Except you took off like you knew exactly what was going to blow, and when it was going to happen." The tormentor dragged Linden to his feet. "How come you're so smart?"

Blood dripped from Linden's nose and lips, and from a gash high on his cheekbone. "I just ran. Like everybody else. Look, I'm sorry I called you an idiot. The girls must be—"

"Shut up, *idiot*. You're not sorry, you're scared." He raised his gun to hit Linden, who tried to pull away. Instead of striking him, however, the tormentor grinned. "See what I mean? Scared. You should be 'cause you've been working with them all along. Soon as those bombs went off, with

everybody in one fucking place, I knew a spy was setting
us up, and I figured it was you. I saw you whispering to
that bitch yesterday, and then rubbing yourself and trying
to tell me that she spit on you. You think I didn't check?
It was right here." He flicked Linden's right arm. "And it
was dry as bone. Go ahead," he said to the African, who
jammed the flame onto the spot the tormentor had touched.
Linden swore and tried to grab the torch. He failed, and the
lean guard stiff-armed his bloody face. Linden whirled on
the tormentor.

"You guys are screwing up bad."

"Shut the fuck up," the tormentor said, "or I'll burn your
tongue out of your head." He shoved Linden toward the
Mayor's office. *"Now move."*

The African raised the torch and looked inquiringly at his
buddy, who nodded. The flame landed on Linden's back. He
screamed for the first time.

"Oh, shit, he's going to be motherfucking fun," the black
guard said.

"Just the start." The tormentor pushed Linden into the
office. The emissary scrambled around the table and reached
for the unmarked door behind it, but the African kicked him
toward a corner.

"You aren't going anywhere," the tormentor said. "Now,
where are they?" he demanded. "Don't hold out on me."

The black guard advanced on Linden's left. The tormentor blocked the other way around the table, aiming his pistol
conspicuously at Linden's privates. "Don't want to kill
you—yet."

"I don't know where they are," Linden said haltingly, gripping his arm. His eyes darted from one man to the other. "I
swear it."

"Go ahead," the tormentor said to his cohort.

"No!" Linden yelled as the African burned his left arm,
forcing him back to the wall bearing the Oval Office carpet
with the presidential seal. The guard jammed the flame into
the emissary's belly, but held it there only briefly before the

tormentor waved him off. Linden grabbed the carpet to hold himself up.

"The *girls*?" the tormentor said.

"I don't know. I came to get—"

The tormentor shook his head, and the African thrust the flame into Linden's face. He screamed and jerked away, and tried to hurl himself across the table. The tormentor shot him in both legs at close range, and his friend burned Linden's back all the way down to his buttocks, then dragged him squirming and shrieking to the floor.

Linden, still bellowing, tried to stand. His legs, bleeding from bullet wounds, buckled. Smoke rose from his clothes. He grabbed the carpet, tearing it loose. The seal side landed on him.

" 'I don't know' is the wrong answer." The tormentor spoke as if none of this was happening, then nodded at the African. "Have at it."

Linden's screams never stopped, but they faltered horribly.

When the African stepped away, the torch blazed brighter, with bits of flaming carpet, pants, and skin falling from it. The air reeked from burning flesh and fabric.

"He alive?" the tormentor asked.

"Yeah," the guard laughed, "but he don't want to be."

"I think it's time I had a talk with you," the tormentor said to Linden, who didn't appear capable of responding.

He grabbed the emissary's chin, pulled it from his scalded neck, and probed the puffy burnt tissue with the tip of Linden's knife. The brutalized man started to spasm. His eyes rolled and a seizure stiffened the length of him for several seconds. His groans sounded like they came from a wild animal. Then his teeth chattered violently.

"Looks like you're cold," the tormentor said. "We've got something for that."

Linden's savaged lips moved.

"I can't hear a word you're saying, but it doesn't matter, and you know why? 'Cause I know you're telling the truth. I knew it from the start. You don't know where they are, but I do 'cause I found the bitches and put them there."

He used Linden's own knife to slice deeply into the man's neck. Then he dropped his head, leaving him to bleed to death.

"Let's go," he said to his buddy. "Those honeys are waiting."

"Hey, I don't know about that." The African scratched his head. "If the Mayor makes it, he's going to be—"

"Pissed at Linden for fucking over those bitches," the tormentor interrupted with a laugh. "That's what he's going to be. And all the terrible shit he did to them before they died?" he added in mock horror. "But we caught him dead to rights and brought him straight to the office, didn't we? And then he tried to get away, so we had to show him a thing or two, *didn't we*?"

The African's smile broadened in the torchlight.

"Besides, the Mayor's not going to make it, so let's go. We've got virgins, hooch. We've even got us a nice bed, so let's burn it up."

X-ray waited beneath the bleachers for more than an hour, astounded that only a handful of men had taken cover under them. The slave figured the booze hadn't made for much clear thinking when the roof came down. He heard the last of the ones who'd taken shelter run off a few minutes ago.

Reaching out, he searched the ground for a guard who'd been clobbered in the first minute after the explosions. He came across numerous bricks before he found the man still breathing. His touch raised a moan and a weak plea for help.

X-ray listened closely in the darkness. Other men moaned, too; but the ones who'd been screaming earlier had quieted or died. Just now a man on the other side of the pit cried out, "Mom," three times, but then stopped.

"Help," the guard pleaded again. X-ray crawled up beside him and placed a hand on his brow. The man might have found this comforting because his moaning eased and he whispered, but so softly the slave could not make out what he'd said. Maybe thanks.

X-ray removed his hand, picked up a brick, and crushed the guard's skull with five powerful blows. No remorse, only ragged satisfaction. He would have felt even better if he'd killed the guard who'd gouged out his eye.

It took only seconds to find the man's pistol and knife. X-ray checked the ammo by feel. Six bullets. That should do, at least for a start. He slipped the blade into his belt and raised the gun as he headed out of the arena.

Twice he stumbled over dead men. Both times he found a knife and handgun, and ample ammo.

After he made it to a hallway, he walked quickly, placing his left hand on the wall to guide him; the right still wielded the murdered guard's gun. He passed only one man in the hall, a supine Russian wailing and babbling loudly in his strange tongue. X-ray had no beef with him and moved on, finding his way to a narrow stairway that he and other slaves had carved from rock over five months.

The path led deep underground. Halfway down, the pale glow of torches gave him a glimpse of the entrance to a warehouse-sized storage area that had once been part of the prison. Now, he readied a gun in each hand; the narrow passageway made him an easy target, and someone had either kept the torches lit or found no reason to flee with them. Both possibilities suggested guards were down there, but so was the prize he sought most of all.

The last few steps opened a view of towering stacks of recovered wood filling a full acre of the storage compound. "Enough to last a century," the Mayor had once bragged in his presence. X-ray doubted that, but he was grateful for the cover as he slipped past thousands of planks, beams, studs, sheets of plywood, even tree limbs, all separated by length and thickness.

He crept past the stacks for several minutes before spying a brightly lit open area. Peering with his lone eye, he spotted an armed guard with fine blond hair standing near a wide hole. Two men with swarthy complexions and rifles slouched on the edge of it, legs disappearing over the depths.

A water pipe the color of dried blood rose from the center of the dig to the ceiling a good fifteen feet above them. On X-ray's side of the hole, a pair of slaves pulled on a rope, raising a bucket of dirt that they dumped on a pile a few feet away. He saw no other cover, and knew better than to try to shoot three guards from this distance, not with a handgun and his one eye. No, he would have to get as close as he could.

But he'd planned for this contingency; slaves were often bound for the smallest infractions. So, he hung his head till his chin grazed his chest, rolled his shoulders forward, bent slightly at the waist, and placed his hands, each holding a pistol, behind his back. Before taking a step, he studied the throw of firelight to make sure a shadow wouldn't give away the guns.

Meek in appearance, he walked toward the guard standing by the hole. "Sir," he said simply, pleased the slouching men paid him barely a glance.

"What do you—"

X-ray shot him in the face before he finished, gunning down the other two guards before they straightened their rifles.

"Any more down there?" he asked the slaves who'd been hauling up dirt. One of them shook his head, the other squeezed the bucket to his bare chest.

"How many of us in the hole?" X-ray asked, snatching up the first guard's revolver.

"Five," a man answered from below.

Keeping his guns raised, X-ray walked to the edge, the scent of cordite trailing him, ambrosial in its effect. "Okay," he said after looking down at men covered in dirt, "grab your picks and shovels and get up here. You're going to need them."

A tall brawny man scooped up his tools and scaled the

ladder first. X-ray pointed to the dead guards by the hole. "Go grab yourself a rifle, knife, whatever you like."

When the rest of the men followed, he told them the same thing, adding, "I've got two extra guns. One's a little short of bullets. They're in them." He nodded at the guards. "We've all got some payback coming."

He handed the fully loaded gun to one of the slaves who'd been on bucket duty. The man nodded his thanks, popped the cylinder and eyed it with authority.

"We're going to be slaughtered, is what we've got coming," said a hairy-faced man who reached for the gun X-ray had fired.

"Don't you know what's going on?" X-ray asked him. He looked at the others. No one answered. "The explosions? Didn't you hear them?" He guessed not, which explained the guards' casual manner.

"We can't hear shit all the way down here," the brawny man confirmed. His eyes never left the blond guard's body when he spoke, and he went on quickly, "I hated that bastard's guts. I wish I could've shot him."

"I did hear something a while back," said the hairy slave. "I just thought it was their big Fight Night party."

"Ain't a party," X-ray said. "At least not the one they planned. But it's a helluva chance to get even, and let me tell you something." He pointed a gun at the dead guards. "It feels good."

It seemed to take hours for Jester to climb down the ladder, wary now with every step. As he neared the bottom, a soft sighing rose from the silence that had followed his echoes. The murmur increased until he was certain he was listening to something alive, something *moving*.

What the hell is it?

Jester stepped from the ladder onto smooth stone. He still couldn't see his own hand, took only a few steps before walking into a stalactite and almost swore before remembering what his last outburst had set off. He didn't know if there were any creatures down there, but guessed all kinds of animals could use echoes to find their prey.

It took him another ten minutes to make his way to the source of the gentle noise. He'd never seen a river, much less heard one in total darkness, so he learned only now that it had a whisper all its own. When he put his hands into it, he found that flowing water even had a rhythm and a pulse.

Just like blood.

As the four of them hurried down the tunnel, Jessie could still hear Chunga trying to smash his way past the circus wagon. Judging from the racket, the dragon worked in fits and starts. But her thoughts remained fixed on Ananda. When the bombs went off, her youngest child and the twins were near the side of the pit—along with dozens of drunken men. Then the blazing gunfire erupted, as if those fools could have shot their way out from under a collapsing roof. But Linden also had been up there, so maybe he'd had a plan. She couldn't allow herself to think otherwise.

They came upon a body. From his appearance—two eyes—he had been a guard. Jessie paused, but the Mayor stepped over it with hardly a glance. Burned Fingers grabbed the back of the prisoner's shirt, forcing him to halt.

She checked for a pulse, then rolled the body over, finding an empty holster. She stood, shrugged, and they walked on. But several steps later, after Bliss made a wide pass around the dead man, Jessie said, "Stop," and turned back.

Burned Fingers once again had to grab the Mayor's shirt.

"This doesn't make any sense." She glanced from the body to the tyrant. "You said this was the way out. Who comes running *into* a place with a collapsing roof?"

"My men. They are loyal to me," the Mayor said. "But what would you know of such things?"

Burned Fingers cracked the butt of his knife against the

back of the Mayor's head. The man's shoulders snapped toward his ears.

"I'll tell you what I think," Jessie said. "That there are other ways in and out of this thing. *That's* what makes sense."

Burned Fingers nodded, but before anyone could speak another word—in the blank stillness of unanswered questions—they heard the galloping footfalls of the giant lizard.

Cassie couldn't run another step. Her chest heaved painfully. She could barely breathe. It was like the night Sam had saved her life twice, first when she'd been ready to kill herself, and then by leading her from the gunmen. They'd run from the battle so hard that her breathlessness had forced her to stop on a dune, and Sam asked if she had asthma. It felt worse now. She was wheezing and making strange whistling sounds.

Stop it! she silently ordered herself. But she couldn't stop because the dragon was tracking her. She heard him clearly. The beast was making loud throaty noises, but not giving up, like if he could just eat her, he might survive. With every lunge, he rattled more bones. Cracked them, too. *Baby bones.* They must be. She'd run over them herself. They broke like dry sticks.

Breathe, she implored herself. *Breathe.* As her heart slowed, she did manage to widen her airways. The whistling stopped, but the rattle of the bones sounded closer. All the time, *closer.* Now she could smell the Komodo. Then she heard a slurping sound and a glop of saliva landed on her shirt.

Cassie charged ahead, wheezing and stumbling barefoot over bones toward what she hoped would be the safety of the main cavern. She pitched onto the narrow path, taking a scary spill that scraped her up even more. It took seconds before she understood her good fortune and dragged herself to her feet. But then she set off on the ground at a much faster pace.

By the time she felt her way past the entrance to the main cavern, her wheezing had eased. But she still sounded terrified when she called out for Miranda and Steph. They'd said they would wait for her there, but didn't respond.

"Miranda!" Cassie screamed again, now trying to find her way to the narrow bridge without falling in the water.

"Run! There's a bad man down here," her friend shouted from far away in the darkness.

A bad man? She'd wanted to warn *them* about the dragon, which could be coming up behind her at any moment.

Then she heard footsteps hurrying across the bridge. Not a kid's. She pleaded with all her heart for whoever it was to stop and go away, but heard what sounded like boots landing on stone.

She backed up, still frightened almost senseless that she would walk right into the dragon's mouth.

"I see you," the man said.

How could he?

Cassie veered sharply, forgetting that the bank narrowed to nothing, and tumbled into the river.

She tried to find her footing in the water, worried that either beast or man would come in after her, then recognized she was in over her head—she'd fallen into the deep part that Miranda had warned her about. Realizing it, she panicked, almost swallowing a lungful of water.

Her arms and legs flailed as she fought ferociously to the surface, gasping for air once more.

Breathe, breathe.

Chapter Nineteen

Hundreds of pounds of maimed lizard raced through the dark tunnel, long steely claws ripping up the packed dirt. Jessie retreated two fast steps, bumping into Burned Fingers. The marauder was shoving the Mayor against a wall.

"Watch this bastard!" he shouted to Bliss, leaving the girl to rule the tyrant with a sword, as she had only minutes ago in the dragon's pen. Still, all their eyes—even the Mayor's—kept darting to the thundering darkness.

"Give me the gun," Burned Fingers demanded.

Jessie handed it over without pause; he was the killer of long repute. "Just don't wound him again," she warned above the din of the giant reptile's advance. Hacking off a chunk of his tongue had made the fierce creature even more dangerous. "Shoot him in the heart."

They smelled Chunga, heard him about to burst out of the dark, but the sudden sight of the reptile's gaping, bloody mouth was still startling. The beast reared away from the torch. Dust from its abrupt stop drifted over them, along with more of the creature's vile odors.

"Mom!" Bliss groaned.

Jessie pivoted, keeping the flame pointed toward the

dragon. Bliss clutched her stomach. The Mayor had kicked her and bolted when the girl glanced at the reptile's alarming arrival. He was disappearing into the darkness with surprising speed and agility for a man with his hands tied behind his back. Bliss, still gripping her gut—and slowed by her sword—set off after him.

"Get down," Burned Fingers yelled at her.

She looked over her shoulder. He pointed angrily to the ground and she threw herself down, opening a line of fire.

Chunga bugled as Burned Fingers fired blindly into the pitch three times, shifting his aim rightward with each shot. They could not hear whether the Mayor fell during his pet's raucous attempts to attack them.

Jessie turned back to the carnivorous beast. Chunga looked even more gigantic in the tighter confines of the passage. When he extended himself on all fours, his head smacked against a roof support. She could see that the ceiling would never allow the dragon to rise high enough for a shot to his heart. The lizard, hideous, lashed the air with his mutilated, yellowy tongue, then lunged at Burned Fingers, who had looked toward the darkness for some sign of the Mayor.

"Watch out!" Jessie yelled at him, and jammed the torch against the dragon's neck, then leaped back when the Komodo tried to bite her. Burned Fingers reeled away and fired twice. Both rounds tore into the reptile's face.

No! Sickened with dread, Jessie watched the lizard bash his jaw into a wall and gouge out a shovelful of dirt with his razory teeth—the behavior of a beast wholly deranged by pain.

She tried to fend off Chunga's fury with the torch, but he no longer found the flame as daunting.

Burned Fingers grabbed her, pulling her back so fast she tripped and fell. The beast lurched at her, and she stabbed at its face, searing a nostril. The dragon snorted loudly, flaring the torch, shooting smoke from his nose like the mythical beast of fairy tales and trilogies.

Jessie clambered to her feet. "Shoot him!" she shouted in panic.

Burned Fingers shook his head: "One shot!"

That's all?

As if reading her mind, the Komodo exhibited a bald impunity. Jessie had to hold the torch to his appalling face; stabbing the lizard with the flame didn't slow him anymore. Even using the fire directly had little effect. He simply shook, made loud guttural noises, and advanced faster, biting the walls, ground, and ceiling, biting with abandon, mindless and terrifying. His teeth found a beam and he ripped a roof support loose in a blink, spraying dust on everyone.

Burned Fingers swore. His sword no more useful than shouted threats, his gun only an instrument of incitement. Behind them, Bliss disappeared into the darkness.

Stay away, Jessie implored her silently. Nothing could be worse than this.

But she was wrong. Her daughter was headed to a land of horror.

Cassie sank slowly in the river, gripped by agony. Her chest felt crushed. She opened her eyes, as she had when she'd swam with Miranda, hoping to find salvation in some miraculous form; but no deliverance appeared in the inky depths that her friend had warned her about.

Her feet grazed the bottom, and she tried to push off on the tips of her toes. She remembered Miranda springing out of the river to her waist. But that was in shallower water, and Miranda had jumped with her knees fully bent.

Cassie's efforts lifted her only inches. With pain now clawing her chest worse than ever, she feared she'd missed her only chance to survive. So when her toes touched the rocky bottom, she had to resist an overwhelming, but useless, urge to spring right back up. Instead, she waited . . . and waited . . . to sink deeper, knees bending with almost unbearable torpidity.

When she felt light-headed, dizzy, about to black out, unsure whether she'd waited long enough—or too long—she leaped as high as she could, moving her weakened arms and legs to try to propel herself farther.

She managed to force her mouth from the river, stealing a single breath before the water claimed her again. But she had filled up with air.

Keep doing it. If the bridge was the deepest part, she figured the current would carry her to a shallower stretch soon.

With each jump, she forced more of her head from the water, and gained confidence. By the sixth or seventh effort, she bumped into the bank, never so happy to endure a bruise, realizing the flow had borne her to the cavern side of the river She grabbed rock and held it tightly, gulping large breaths.

But be quiet, she cautioned herself as she feasted on air.

She tilted her head to clear her ears, and heard the man again. He was scurrying along the bank. His steps sounded only feet away, and then he shifted so close she was afraid he was reaching for her. She was about to push off, but then *he* moved, stumbling in the dark and swearing quietly to himself.

That gave her hope. He was the one making noise, threatening her, but in a low voice, like he was scared, too. Twice she heard him say, "I see you," but he was a liar. He moved farther away each time, and she realized he'd never seen her. Who could see anything in such darkness? It kept her safe. For the first time in hours, she welcomed the night and hoped it wouldn't pass soon.

When she couldn't hear him anymore, she started to climb out, but thought better of it. Why not stay in the water? He hadn't found her when he'd been feet away. It was safe in there. She would move along the bank and get as far as she could from the dragon. The Komodo might have smelled her blood on land, but couldn't find her in the river, right?

She also hoped Miranda and Steph were okay. She felt horrible for not warning them about the Komodo, but she'd never had the chance because they were already hiding. *From him.*

She listened carefully, then drifted along the bank, handhold-to-handhold. The river began to burble, as if conspiring with the night to grant her cover.

The minutes passed. Moving along became almost effortless. She flattered herself into believing she'd grown at ease in water. Perhaps she had. But as she made her way, the current accelerated deceptively, taking her firmly in its grip as it narrowed. With a start, she realized she was about to be forced underground for the long passage deep into the garden cavern. Grabbing the overlapping stone, she tried to haul herself out, but it felt like the water had endless arms to drag her down.

"Stop," she blurted when the current swept her legs out from under her. She regretted her outburst immediately, but even her fear of the man couldn't compete with the terror of being sucked into the earth for hundreds of feet.

She held on with her armpits hooked around the stony edge. Facing upward, she stared into the blackness above—*like someone in a grave*—and clawed the smooth stone floor. She bloodied her fingers—panic much greater than pain—but inch by inch she dragged more of herself from the water.

She finally freed a leg, then rolled the rest of her body out, hyperventilating from the effort.

Cassie lay on her back, chest rising and falling to the hard pulse of her heart. It took minutes before her breath calmed so she could sit up. She looked ahead and noticed dawn seeping into the garden cavern. Then she saw him. Not well, but enough to know for the first time that he was Jester, the man who'd kneeled close to her on the desert only moments after he murdered Maul.

A door latch snapped shut. That was all, but Bliss knew somebody had left the tunnel's darkness. Somebody like the Mayor. Furious with herself for letting the tyrant escape—

furious at him for the blow to her belly—she wanted to bring him back to her mom and Burned Fingers at the point of her sword. Kill him, if she had to. But most of all she wanted to catch him before he got his hands untied.

She hurried, trailing her fingers on the dirt wall until she felt a door. Peering behind her, Bliss saw no sign of her mother's torch, not even a distant glow; but she had moved fast and the tunnel might have curved, leaving her beyond a bend. And she'd heard one of them firing the gun. No screams, no struggles, just gunshots. They should be okay. She was the one who'd screwed-up.

She left the door open so her mother would know where she'd gone. The Mayor had a two minute lead on her, but after stepping into a sepulchral, scary stillness, she gave up all thoughts of trying to reclaim the time by rushing. The faint scent of a Komodo slowed her even more, and she realized her most feral instincts had come alive. She wondered if the odor had been carried by the Mayor or by her own body. Or if the other dragon was lurking nearby, moving closer. She listened intently. An absolute silence ensued.

Bliss thrust her sword along walls, corners, and stabbed the length of a couch before concluding that she'd entered a room, and that the Mayor had fled deeper into his city. She paused, still sensing the uneasy emptiness clinging to the confines, like someone had died there. And then she realized that of course the room had witnessed death—and much worse. This was the City of Shade. Murder haunted every corridor, corner, and hideaway.

The loss of life felt so real and grisly that she feared for her sister and the other children. Her hand settled on another door. She opened it to check, setting off a loud *creak*. She flinched, knowing how exposed a single sound could leave her. In that same harrowing instant, much fouler odors assaulted her. She'd smelled them at the Army of God— burned skin, burned hair, burned clothes—and knew without question what had drawn her there: the scent of injury or death had slipped through the door and into her senses.

Covering her nose, Bliss forced herself forward. *Not Ananda, please. Not Jaya.* "Or any of them," she mouthed wholly to herself.

Inching along, she tripped on a body, put out her arm to break her fall and pressed down on a moist torso. She jerked away, wiping her hand on her pants, then forced herself to reach out again, more carefully.

Her fingers settled on a burned shirt and chest, and with a rush of relief she knew it was a man. But not the Mayor. The body didn't have his girth, and nobody could have sustained such an attack in so little time.

She moved her hand to the face. He felt tall, thin. No one she knew came to mind. Her fingers settled on strangely rippled and torn skin, before finding cuts on a bald head. She felt like a blind woman "seeing" a person's features. Nothing but the horror was familiar.

A discernible cooling of the body had taken place. Only a degree or two, but it seemed odd that a man so burned, whose shirt had crumbled at her touch, should feel anything but fevered.

She checked for a weapon, and wasn't surprised to find the victim unarmed. Then she stepped back, knowing she would venture no farther on her own. But before she could turn toward the tunnel, torches flashed as sudden as lightning—and more blindingly after so much darkness. Men seized her arms and grabbed her sword. She was surrounded by one-eyed slaves with guns, knives, picks, and shovels. The torch flames reddened their empty sockets, while their lone eyes looked her up and down with the rapacity of pack animals.

Sam laid the satchel of guns into a shallow depression that sat below the sight line of anyone looking out from the back of the City of Shade. She brushed sand on the old leather, just enough to cover it, as she and Yurgen had planned. If she were caught or killed, they didn't want the pistols to fall into the hands of the men who claimed her.

Weak torchlight spilled past the columns supporting the edge of the roof. She saw the pale glow on packed sand as she approached the rear perimeter. The flames encouraged her. She'd worried that guards had immediately mowed down the prisoners in retribution for the attack, leaving no need for surveillance or light.

But as she slipped behind a column, more than anything she hoped the guards had left the torches burning in their haste to defend the other end of the city. Linden had said two were assigned to the smaller pit, though they were supposed to patrol the entire area, so they could be anywhere. She'd rather die than fall into their hands.

Armed with a pair of pistols and a knife, she looked left and right, her range greatly limited by the faint light. Her eyes settled back on the sand. No footprints but her own. She chided herself for leaving them.

Sam crept about twenty feet into the city, taking cover at the next column. She peered from behind the bricks, absorbing her first view of the area around the pit. She did not have an angle to see into it. A small fire burned on the left side of the opening, near a guard sleeping on his back. From where she stood, she could see only his head, long black hair fanning out on both sides. He appeared oddly pretty. Then she saw torchlight on a flask a few inches away, and adored his dereliction of duty. She just wished she had a better shot at him; his head was a miserably small target at her remove. She studied him so closely she failed to hear an advance on her right. Had the shadow of a torch not shifted, she would have been taken by surprise.

She wheeled and fired twice at a tall, sinewy-looking guard stealing from behind a column. Brick chips exploded into the air inches from him. She ducked back, then peered out to see that he had done likewise, but without returning fire.

Glancing to her left, she saw that her gunshots were slowly rousing the sleeping guard from his stupor. The other man, behind the column, yelled at him to shoot her. But his minion looked too drunk or tired to respond to the command quickly.

Two of them. Maybe more to come, though she assumed the sentient guard would have called others, if any were nearby. She clung to the reasonable hope that her gunplay would fade into the periodic shooting that formed the night's deadly backdrop. Looking at the supine man, who appeared deep in slumber once again, she thought it might have happened already.

"You're outgunned." The man she'd missed spoke coolly from behind his column, evidently unable to see that the other guard had never reacted to his order. He didn't sound drunk, but knowing he hadn't moved gave her seconds to brace her left hand on the bricks that hid her. Then she rested her pistol on her forearm to steady her aim at the head of the man still lying by the fire, and held her breath to still herself even more. But before she could shoot, her target did himself an enormous disservice by sitting up. He looked alarmed, as if the command to kill someone had just registered. She gunned him down so fast he might never have fully awakened.

"Not anymore," she replied.

"Keep thinking that."

Reflexively, she cocked the hammer and shouted, "Anyone in the pit know how many guards are here?"

"Two," a man yelled.

"Thank you," she shouted back. "Now that we have that clear," she said to the sinewy guard, "do you know your men are getting wiped out by us over at Fight Night? We dropped the roof right on their heads. You must have heard the explosions. Huge packs of us are hunting you guys down. They'll be working their way here real soon." She inched one eye past the column and caught the guard looking at her. "You don't have to die," she lied.

"But you do," he snapped.

She sighed, louder and more theatrically than she'd intended, then heard movement at the city's rear, and once more regretted the footprints she'd left so stupidly on the dimly lit sand.

Was that another step? She was sure of it. *Where?*

A bead of sweat cold as the moon slid down her spine. It defied logic that the city would deploy guards to protect the smaller pit. By now all of the men at Fight Night had to know they were targeted for death, and wouldn't want to give up a single gunner.

She almost convinced herself of this when torchlight wavered for a beat. She pulled out a second revolver to try to cover both of her flanks. She even glanced at the long-haired guard, wondering if he'd miraculously rallied. Not at all.

A flurry of gunshots had her looking in as many directions at once. Then the tall guard was backpedaling into the open, firing at a shadow advancing from behind his column.

He glanced at her just before she shot him twice in the torso. He fell screaming, and she delivered a carefully aimed head shot that shut him up.

Yurgen stepped into the light, his gait hesitant. He might have been uncertain whether the guard was dead.

"He's finished," Sam said, stepping closer to her husband. That's when she saw him pressing the hand with his gun to his chest. A bloodstain swelled rapidly on his shirt. He dropped to his knees and pitched onto his face, setting off the round that killed him.

"**W**e . . . have . . . to . . . get . . . out." Ananda punctuated each pause by pounding her fist against the door of a big wooden box, or whatever the guards had thrown them into. Maybe it was a jail without bars or windows. They were pushed in so fast it had been hard to see anything, especially with the black guy waving around a torch like a maniac.

Leisha grabbed her arm. "Stop that. He said they're going to hurt us bad if we do that."

Kaisha had yet to say a word. Ananda thought she might be too terrified to talk. Supposedly, that had happened to tons of people, even grown-ups, when the collapse came and nothing worked anymore. Millions had walked around in a daze till they died. Her mom and dad had told her about it.

"They're going to hurt us real bad anyway," she said to Leisha. "Don't you know that? Let *go.*" She jerked her arm loose. "And start helping me."

She and the twins had been locked up for at least an hour. Maybe two. Ananda didn't know for sure. A long time. The guy who shoved them in there was white, strong, rough, and superscary. He'd grabbed the torch and put it so close to her face that she had to turn away, sure he would burn her. Then he laughed: "You see what I see? She's gotta be the porn queen's sister. I heard she had one."

"What?" she'd asked, thinking he had to be talking about Bliss.

He whipped the torch back at her. She had to duck. The heat still hurt bad. What he'd said was even worse: "I'll show you all about porn queens just as soon as I get back." Then he warned them about escaping and locked them up.

Moments later, Leisha had swatted her head and shouted, "Your hair's on fire!"

Seeing sparks flying in the dark, Ananda grabbed her braid, smacking and squeezing it while the twins beat out and smothered the flames on the back of her head. The burns weren't as bad as others she'd suffered.

Now, she needed Leisha and Kaisha to beat on the door. "Come on," she said to them.

The twins gave up after a fitful effort, but Ananda leaned against the rear wall and continued to bash the wood as hard as she could with her heels. In seconds the door flew open.

"See!" she exclaimed, although she could scarcely believe what she'd done.

But before she could straighten, she saw torchlight again, and the white guard reached in and dragged her out.

"I told you not to do dick, didn't I?" he snapped.

She was too frightened to say a word, then saw it wouldn't have mattered; he was already waving the torch closer.

Cassie tried to stay as still as possible as the murderer rose to his feet, knowing that if she could see him, he could see her. But he wasn't turning in her direction. He was heading toward the raised beds.

Her relief vanished the moment she looked behind her. The cavern she'd just left was still mostly dark; there were only two openings in the ceiling, and they weren't nearly as big as the ones above the garden. She realized the Komodo could be roaming around thirty feet away and she wouldn't know it, unless she got a good whiff of the beast. And she couldn't kid herself anymore about hiding in the water. The safer parts—if there were any—lay farther upriver, and she had no desire to backtrack along the bank, where the dragon could be waiting. No way. Besides, she was too cold to want to climb into the water.

She glanced toward the garden. The killer, Jester, had disappeared in there. What she wanted was to bundle up somewhere, hug her knees to her chest and hide.

For now, she huddled close to the wall and tried to review every step of Miranda's tour of the caverns. She couldn't think of a single good hiding place anywhere nearby. Then she remembered the punji sticks in the smaller cavern near the waterfall.

Not totally safe, but it was plenty dark in there, and she was skinny enough to make her way among those sharp points. *Just don't fall,* she told herself. She figured the lizard would stab itself a hundred times if it tried to run over those bones. Plus, who would even think of hiding in a place like that?

Me, she told herself with no little pride.

If the murderer did come in there, what could he do? Chase her? That would be hard for a grown-up. If he tripped, he'd die. Or get all bloody and turn into dragon bait.

Same goes for you.

A sobering thought, but the punji stick cavern was the best place she could think of. First, she had to get past the garden.

Moving so stealthily she couldn't hear her own footsteps, Cassie edged along the wall in the tall passageway that led to the cavern with the raised beds. When she reached the opening, she spied him rushing around the last of them on the far side. He'd covered a lot of ground fast, but the sky had paled to a light gray, which made it easier to see.

She crawled to the nearest bed, then scurried from one to another, checking behind her every few seconds to make sure the dragon wasn't tracking her. *He can't,* she reassured herself. *You stopped bleeding.* She doubted she even smelled after spending so much time in the river. Still, she kept looking back, unable to shake the fear that something was following her.

After reaching a bed in the middle of the cavern, she rested. The sky loomed above her, and gave her hope. She heard Jester's footsteps, but they didn't rattle her because he was heading back toward the darker cavern, the one he couldn't have searched during the night. She hoped Miranda and Steph weren't hiding in there, or had climbed out. And then she smiled—did she ever!—when she recalled what *was* in there. The biggest surprise of all because he didn't know anything about a dragon. But now he sure would.

The prospect delighted her, and she put off crawling to the punji sticks, figuring that the dragon would get him any minute now. *Just wait for the screams.* She peeked again. *There he goes.* She watched him head out, almost squealing with anticipation.

He stopped just short of the passageway. Maybe the dragon was already there, she thought. He was looking down. But not for long. He started back toward the raised beds, following the same path she'd taken, except she'd crawled and he was hurrying.

I'm not bleeding. How's he—

Her mind went blank when she looked down, too, and saw the watery trail she'd left. Something *had* followed her—her own hand, knee, and footprints. The Komodo might have ignored them, but not the murderer.

Jester started running then, and she raced off, fleeing from him. He was yelling something weird as she zigzagged around the beds, wishing they were laid out in a straight line, and doing all she could to keep taking air.

Now he was screaming the same weird words over and over: "Hey, iddy biddy bitch. Hey, iddy biddy bitch . . ."

She heard a sharp noise, and then again, and again. Looking back, she thought it might be Jester, and saw him closing in on her. He looked like a fiend. His face and neck were burned, nose squashed, and one eye was scalded shut, crusted with blood and yellow stuff.

The sharp noise got even louder. Only then did she recognize it as the telling sound of her own wheezing.

The slaves hauled Bliss over to Linden's body. X-ray held a torch over each of the grisly insults.

"Did you do this?" he asked her.

"No," she said, although who was he to talk? He'd strapped her and Ananda's legs into a harness with barbed wire, and was just as ruthless to the twins. "I don't even have a torch. I came from the tunnel. I had to feel my way in here." She hoped her mother and Burned Fingers would follow the same path—and fast. "I sure don't have a gun." She forced herself to look down and point to the dead man's legs.

X-ray nodded. "What happened to your mother and father?"

He's not my father! she almost screamed, but swore to herself instead. Maybe it was better if the slave thought Burned Fingers was her dad. She shrugged. "We got separated."

A hairy-faced man leaned close to Linden's body. "He wasn't just killed. This was revenge."

"Cuts both ways," X-ray said, without any apparent irony. "He was a good man. Let's go find the bastard."

"Who?" Bliss asked as they dragged her from the room.

"The Mayor. Who else?" X-ray replied.

Chunga advanced on Jessie and Burned Fingers, the reptile's attack was accelerating with every step. The two retreated ten feet, twenty. Burned Fingers jammed the gun
with its lonely bullet into his belt and tried to use his sword,
while Jessie jabbed the dragon repeatedly with the torch.

"Go for his eyes," he shouted. Only then did she see that
he'd been trying to blind the lizard with his thrusts.

"You want him even more insane?" she shouted back.

The dragon had continued to bite anything he slammed
into. He'd even taken a chunk out of the ceiling when he
tried to stand on his hind legs. Burned Fingers had pulled
out the pistol, but even Chunga's most maddening pain
couldn't drive the beast high enough for a shot to his heart.

Jessie spotted the open door. "Behind you," she shouted.
"On the left. See it?"

"Yeah." He looked back at the lizard, sank his sword into
Chunga's gum and then wrenched the tip out. Blood drooled
from the dragon's jaw.

Jessie kicked the door open. "Go on. I'll—"

"No, you first."

She didn't argue. Burned Fingers jumped in behind her,
banging the door shut so hard she worried it would break or
bounce open. The latch held, but the giant lizard smashed
his head through the wood.

Jessie and Burned Fingers spilled over furniture on their
way out another door on the other side of the room. She
slammed it, then saw they'd rushed into the Mayor's office.
She recognized the big table where the tyrant had held court
yesterday and Burned Fingers tangled with Pie, the frizzy-
haired marauder.

Her companion's scarred fingers tapped the door she'd just
closed. "That beast will come through this, too," he said, "in
nothing flat. It's hollow-core."

"I know. Let's go," she said, backing away. "But did you
see that couch? It looked like Bliss was searching in there."

"I did see—"

"Linden!" She held the torch over a dead, tortured body, and heard Chunga bash his way into the room with the chairs and eviscerated couch.

"We've got to get out of here." Burned Fingers knocked hard on the office's outer door. "This is solid. It could hold him. Those other two are crap."

Not just the doors: Chunga's burned, bleeding head exploded through the ancient drywall where the carpet with the presidential seal had hung. The creature's huge mouth opened a foot from Jessie, and its tongue smacked her in the chest.

"Out!" Burned Fingers yelled.

She jumped over Linden's body and grabbed his foot. "Help me."

"Leave him. He's dead. Let's just—"

"He was helping us. I'm not letting him get eaten."

Burned Fingers gripped the other foot, grumbling, "You're too goddamn sentimental." But he helped drag the body into the hallway, shutting the door quickly. "That'll have to do," he said.

Jessie agreed. "I better put this out. We're too visible." She looked for a way to smother the blazing torch, finding a guard lying facedown, legs splayed, about ten feet away. She checked his pulse—dead—and jammed the flame up under his crotch.

"Ouch," Burned Fingers said. "I take it back about being too sentimental."

With the cover of night, she checked the guard's body for weapons; he'd already been stripped of whatever guns or knives he'd carried.

They heard footfalls and saw distant torches.

"Let's keep moving," Burned Fingers whispered, taking out his gun. He still held his sword. Jessie had hers and the cooling torch.

"I've got to find Ananda, too," she said. In the darkness and chaos, the challenge of finding both daughters seemed almost insurmountable. Then she spied the first hints of daylight on the periphery, and heard Burned Fingers whispering again:

"If anybody's going to know where your kids are, it'll be that big bastard."

"Where the hell is he?"

"We'll find him."

"We've got to find him fast."

"I know," Burned Fingers said. "But these assholes will talk. I have my own means of persuasion, and I'm not as nice as those guards." He glanced back at Linden's body.

Sam cradled Yurgen's head, hoping for life, but the weight of evidence was brutal, final.

She kissed his brow and removed his spectacles, a prize so rare that even the most painful grief could not spare the obligation to save them. She also took his gun, sticky with blood, and his knife, hiding them beneath his body for now.

Sam stood and turned toward the pit. "You people down there, do you see or hear anyone?" she shouted. "There are two dead guards up here now, and I'm here to get you out."

As soon as she quieted, she recognized the foolhardiness of yelling, and wondered if she was so sick with sorrow that she wanted death's reprieve.

"We had just the two guards last night," answered the same man who'd responded during the gunfight.

More cautiously, Sam moved toward them, taking a torch from a brace on a column. Raising her gun, she peered into the opening, finding adults and boys on one side of the wall, girls on the other, including three young women holding babies.

"How'd you get in there?" she called to the group. "Did they make you jump?"

The African who had answered twice before told her there was a ladder. She spotted it lying against a column. When she lowered it, he lifted his hand for her to pause. "Thank you," he said solemnly, as if divining the cost of her mission. Or had she wept loudly without realizing it?

She acknowledged him with a nod, and asked, "Are you good with a gun?"

He shook his head.

"I—I—I am," a man stammered.

When he stepped off the ladder, she gave him one of her pistols. "What's your name?"

"B-B-Brindle."

"I'm Sam. I'll be right back."

All the caravaners had escaped the pit by the time she returned with Yurgen's weapons and the satchel. She opened it and held up a gun, calling out, "Who's ready to fight?"

Every one of them surged toward her, even the youngest child, a girl who couldn't have been older than ten. That felt tragic, too, the bitter reminder that vengeance was also blind to age.

Cassie raced past the last raised bed. Jester was so close she had to sprint straight toward the waterfall. Swerving to the punji sticks would have cost her a half step, and that could have meant her life. And her plan had not been to charge into the field of sharpened bones. She'd imagined easing her way past them, then hiding.

The distance to the waterfall shrank with agonizing slowness. She still heard herself wheezing, and the frightening rise of her respiratory whistle. Her chest was closing like a fist, and she felt as deprived of oxygen as she had in the river. But her legs pumped as if they had their own lungs—and a set of terrors that would never let them stop.

Jester lunged at her, his fingertips brushing her damp shirt. He swore, spitting out violent oaths. In the first shadow of morning, she spied his hand raised with a knife. She looked back—she could not help herself—and saw his lips twisting, rage stamped across his burned and beaten face.

The river rushed faster to her right, funneling toward the

waterfall. She thought of throwing herself in, letting the swift current carry her the last few feet. But she didn't dare because he might follow and carry her down to the depths with him. So she stayed on the stone. Another shadow showed him trying to stab her again. She leaped out over the churning whitewater, looking back one more time to see him stopping at the very edge.

The water looked soft and pillowy, but when she hit the foaming surface, the impact would have knocked the air out of her—if she'd had a breath to spare.

Cassie plunged deep into the pool, suspended for perilous seconds before drifting upward. With her legs kicking madly and her arms flailing, she felt the current nudging her forward and filling her with hope. Though far from any edge, and unable to grab a single breath, she thought that if she could last just moments more, the water—of all things—might save her.

The torch hovered right above Ananda's face, a bright instrument of pain that kept her back flat on the bed, head turned to the side. She heard the white guy stripping down, weapons clunking on the floor. He yanked her pants to her knees and pressed against her bare skin as the torch swung from them: someone had run into the room, yelling, "Cut me loose!"

The Mayor. "Help me," she pleaded

The big man glanced at the white guard, pushing himself off her and hurriedly pulling on his pants.

"What are you doing to the little one?" the Mayor demanded.

The guard slowed and lifted his chin, as if refusing to appear guilty. He walked toward the Mayor, boldly cinching his pants, like he was invincible and had nothing to be ashamed of. But Ananda knew better. He'd panicked at first because he'd been doing something really bad. But you wouldn't know it to look at him now. The guard rolled his shoulders, stepped up to the Mayor, and shocked Ananda by smacking the Mayor's face so hard it sounded like a gun-shot. Then he smacked him again, back the other way, leaving blood on his lips.

"Cut you loose?" The guard squared off like he was getting ready to punch the Mayor, and then he did—right in the stomach. "I got somebody to thank for tying your black ass up."

Still on her back, Ananda pulled her pants on. Slowly, she sat up.

The African guard moved the torch closer to the Mayor, who was hunched over from the punch and glaring at the white guy. Then the bound man straightened—his face looked tight—and turned so his hands could take a knife off an old wooden chest. The white guard watched him fumbling with the blade behind his back and taunted him.

"You don't have to do that all by your lonesome." He pushed the Mayor against the chest and seized the weapon. "Cut you? That's what you want?" He sank the tip into the man's back and dragged the blade all the way down to his behind before the Mayor could twist around. "I'm sorry," the guard said, now poking the tip into the man's broad belly, "did you want me to cut there instead?"

"You will die for this," the Mayor growled.

"I've been hearing that shit all night, but guess what? *I'm still here*. But Linden's not. Been to your office yet?" The Mayor didn't respond. "I burned him half to death before I used *his* knife on him. You want to know why?" The guard no longer paused for an answer, which scared Ananda more, like he couldn't wait to do whatever horrible things he had in mind. "'Cause he was with the assholes blowing the shit out of this place. But you were too fucking dumb to see that."

Without warning, he slashed the Mayor's stomach. Not deeply, but Ananda watched blood wash down over the big man's belt. The Mayor spun away, but the guard forced his face over the chest and sliced his back from shoulder to shoulder.

Ananda closed her eyes. *Not even the Mayor can stop him.* That's all she could think. She couldn't watch anymore and turned away. Her foot brushed something hard. She felt it with her toes. The guard's knife. She didn't want to touch it, couldn't bear the thought of what he'd do if she tried to fight him with it.

His gun, she recalled with an immediacy that shook her. There had been a couple of clunks. She glanced at him. Not in his belt. Not that she could see.

He's going to know, soon as you look.

So she searched with her feet, trying not to move her upper body. She didn't dare look back, not even to see if they were watching her.

"Burn him," she heard the guard say to his buddy. "Give him a good one."

Curiously, nothing happened. Quiet, except for the crackling torch flame. Then she heard a quick shout, and looked over her shoulder. The African guard was bent over, still holding the torch, though it had fallen forward, too, and the white guy had his hand down by the man's stomach. It looked like he was trying to jerk him up off the ground. But then he pulled out the knife and the African fell, squirming and groaning, but only for seconds.

The white guard picked up the torch, caught Ananda looking at him, and held the bloody blade near the flame. When he pointed the tip at her, the Mayor tried to dart away. The guard turned and grabbed him.

Ananda dropped to the floor, searching for the gun.

"Don't try to hide," the guard said to her.

That's what he thinks?

She peered over the top of the bed. He had the knife to the Mayor's neck now. She patted around blindly as a strange look appeared on the guard's face. He slapped his belt and stared at it, then forced the Mayor to the floor. "Move, and I'll cut your fucking balls off."

Ananda looked down. Still too dark to see. She moved her hands in frantic, wide arcs and hit the gun, sliding it under the bed. She cried out in anguish and reached for it, patting blindly again.

The guard rushed closer. She looked up and saw the raised torch rounding the far corner of the bed. Stretching as far as she could, she slapped the floor twice before finding the revolver. Rolling onto her back, she pointed the pistol with two hands, like her parents had trained her, and cocked the hammer.

The single-action clicked loudly in the silence. Ducking low, the guard bolted back across the room before she could aim. Ananda stumbled to her feet as he jerked the Mayor upright and ducked behind him, knife at his back. Then he jammed the torch in a metal stand.

Ananda felt her hands shaking, but *she* had a gun. They didn't.

"Get away from him," she yelled at the guard.

"Oh, no, you can kill your lover boy, but you're not killing me."

"He didn't touch me, not like you."

"And I'm not done!" He sounded gleeful, like he was enjoying himself.

"You are a stupid man," the Mayor said to him, voice taut with pain. "That is why you are a lowly guard, and why you will die."

"Stupid?" The guard pushed him toward Ananda. "Go ahead, shoot this fucking asshole," he said, driving the Mayor ever closer with piercing jabs to his spine; they were more than halfway across the room. "You get your shot, and then I get you."

Jester studied the plunge pool, hearing nothing but the pounding water, seeing nothing but a billion goddamn bubbles. Couldn't make hide nor hair of iddy biddy bitch. And just a few seconds ago he was so close he might have nicked her with his knife. But *she* wouldn't have noticed. That's how scared she was. Kids got so scared they wet their fucking pants. He laughed: *She got everything wet, didn't she?*

Where is she? He didn't know much about water, never seen more than a puddle at once before. Maybe if it got you, it kept you. Maybe you just sank when you died and never came up.

There she is. She was bobbing up like a fish. *'Cept she can't swim and can't get any goddamn air.* Nobody knew how to swim anymore. Him, neither. That's why he didn't go jumping in. *My mama didn't raise no fool.*

But he could swear. He stood there cursing her to holy hell and back. He'd been fixing to have his fun. Then he was going to take her sorry sack of bones to the Mayor, dump her on the floor and say, "There! She's all yours. Now give me my gun."

Not . . . so . . . fast. Look at that. She was popping up plumb in the center of that thing. Head above water. She could *stand* in it.

What am I waiting for? If she could stand, he sure as hell could. *I'm a lot bigger than her.*

If it had been him, he would have pretended to be drowning. *Help me, Jester. Help me.* That way nobody would have come in. Yeah, that's what he would have done, but that's because he was smart. There she was, giving him a big invitation, and she didn't even know it. *Come get me, Jester. I'm right here for the fucking.* But that was what made life so great—dumbass kids.

Jester sheathed his knife and ripped off his boots. "I'm coming to get you iddy biddy bitch."

He jumped, thrilled by the fall and eager to claim his prize.

Bliss didn't have a gun, so X-ray insisted she travel in the "middle of the herd." That was the reason she didn't see the head of a man protruding from a rubble pile until the slave stopped to check if he was alive. They'd found two other guards and two marauders trying to drag their broken bodies from the roof collapse. The slaves had dispatched them with a minimum of firepower.

"So is he dead or what?" asked a man with a spade.

"He's blinking," X-ray said.

"Our turn, then," said the man. Two slaves with picks pressed their way forward.

Bliss turned from the ghastly beheading, accomplished with powerful thrusts of the trenching tools and met with a single word of approbation—"Good!"—from one of the others.

Signaling for quiet, X-ray led them into a part of the city that looked familiar to her. Daylight seeped into the crannies, and she saw large canvas drapes about fifty yards away. She remembered the last time she'd been in the Mayor's bedroom: her attempt to reclaim her mother's M–16 from him had failed, but not before she tried to scratch out his eyes—and yanked his scrotum so hard he'd sent her to Section R.

Now, X-ray led a contingent of four slaves that stormed the chamber. Bliss, trailing behind, heard him yell, "Freeze or you're dead."

She rushed in to see the white guard holding the Mayor in front of him. X-ray and the others had stopped the pair only feet from Ananda, who pointed a gun at them. Bliss was so happy to see her sister that she could have wept. But as soon as Ananda saw X-ray, she pointed the gun at *him*.

"No!" Bliss shouted, jumping forward to block her sister's aim. "He's a good guy."

Ananda brightened at the sight of Bliss, but then said, "Good guy! Look at my goddamn legs. He hurt me." Her legs bore numerous cuts and were coated in dried blood.

Bliss moved toward her little sister as the armed slaves backed the guard into the bureau. With four guns pointed at him, he surrendered the knife. They tied his hands behind his back. Others dragged the dead African aside.

"You're right," Bliss said to Ananda. "He did hurt you. But he didn't kill you, and he's on our side. It's another one of those squirrely deals." She figured her sister would understand. After all, Burned Fingers had saved Ananda's life—after violently abducting her.

"I'm really sorry," X-ray said to Ananda as he checked the Mayor's binding. "I knew something was up, but I couldn't give anything away by giving you a break."

Bliss gently peeled Ananda's fingers from the gun, a nicely weighted Colt single-action revolver. A real prize. "Whose is it?"

"*Mine,* now," Ananda said pointedly.

"But before?"

"The guard's."

"Sweet." Bliss checked the load. Sweeter still.

"That's *my* gun," Ananda insisted. "I got it. Not you."

"How about you let me borrow it, and then I promise we'll talk to Mom, and whatever she says goes? And fix your pants."

Ananda looked like she would have argued more, but reddened when she saw that her drawers were stuck down around her crotch.

Bliss walked up to the guard.

"Is he the one?" X-ray asked her.

"That's him." As they'd made their way through the city, she told X-ray about Section R. The hairy-faced slave, Moore, had chimed in, saying he'd heard the guard bragging about turning her into a porn queen—a death that rivaled Wicca for cruelty.

Now X-ray directed the slaves to move themselves and the Mayor away from Bliss and the white guy. "Let her do this. The guard's got it coming. If she needs help, she'll ask for it. Right?"

Bliss nodded, turning to the man who'd made her life so miserable. "Why were my sister's pants pulled down?"

He shrugged. "Talk to *him,*" the guard said, glancing at the Mayor.

"That is a lie," the Mayor replied indignantly. "I told him to stop."

"Ananda?"

"The guard!" her sister said, pointing defiantly to him.

"Get on the floor," Bliss ordered the prisoner. The moment he hesitated, she shot out his knee. "Who the fuck do you think you're dealing with now?" she yelled at him. "Some girl you've got chained-up? Get *down*!"

The Mayor smiled, even with a rifle muzzle jammed under his chin.

Bliss watched the guard drop down.

"Let's try this again: Why were my sister's pants pulled down?"

When he didn't answer, she shot him in the crotch. He rolled screaming across the floor and crashed into the armoire. The chain hanging from the handle fell onto his face.

"I'll need that help now," she said to X-ray. "Can you guys grab his arms and legs?"

Four of them helped themselves to a limb and dragged him to the middle of the floor. Bliss pinned the guard's head between her ankle bones, bent over and shot him between the eyes, certain that she was treating him more kindly than he'd planned to treat her.

She looked up at the Mayor, who stopped smiling and shook his head rapidly. "You heard your sister. It was not me. I told him to stop."

"And that makes you a good guy? Because you didn't fuck a twelve-year-old? You just sell them to men who do?" Bliss shook with rage. "I hate you, you bastard." She wanted to shoot him, too, but couldn't. She'd made a deal with X-ray, and he had kept his word.

She turned around and walked into Ananda's arms. When her sister hugged her, Bliss saw that a big section of her braid had been burned away. She could not bring herself to ask about it. Not now. It was enough that her sister was alive and still sane after the City of Shade.

She gave Ananda another squeeze and nodded at the twins, who had not moved from the armoire. They appeared thunderstruck. "Are they okay?" she asked.

"Not really," Ananda replied.

The heavy chain on the floor caught Bliss's eye. "Did they lock you guys in there?"

"For a long time."

"We need to get them out. We've all got to stick together."

While they tended to the twins, the slaves surrounded the Mayor, drawing lots to see who would pluck out his eyes. There would be only two winners, and nobody wanted to lose.

"You guys do *not* want to see this," Bliss said to the younger girls.

"They shouldn't do that to him," Ananda said vehemently.

"Don't try telling them that," Bliss said.

The men wrestled the Mayor to the ground. His screams might have reached all the way to the wrecking yard.

"Now what are we doing to do to him?" Moore asked jovially.

"Kill him," several slaves shouted.

"Kill him," quickly became a chant, which X-ray quieted with a command.

"He's not getting off that easy," the slave leader said.

Bliss and Ananda led the twins away from the armoire, and everyone left the room. Two of the slaves gripped the Mayor's arms, guiding the moaning man brusquely. The slaves with guns walked point, or guarded the flanks. Bliss and a thick-necked, rifle-toting man covered the rear, with Ananda and the twins in front of them.

Morning had broken, but the torches were useful for peering into shadows. Moore spotted a man and raised his weapon to shoot. The target dropped down, but not so fast that Bliss failed to recognize Burned Fingers.

"Don't shoot!" she yelled. "That's— Wait, that's my *mom!*"

Jessie had stepped from behind the marauder at the sound of her daughter's voice. Bliss and Ananda raced to her and the three of them embraced. Bliss found herself crying as hard as when she'd heard of her father's death. She was thinking of him, too, feeling both relief and grief.

Bliss looked at Burned Fingers then. She kept an impenetrable wall between them. Her dad was dead because of him, yet she knew her mother had survived because of the marauder. Another squirrelly deal.

"Thank you," she managed to say. He nodded.

X-ray had stationed two guards to protect them during the reunion. Now, as they approached him, he was briefing the others about the new arrivals.

". . . and then they were both in the pit getting ready to fight the dragons when this one," he pointed to Bliss, "jumped in to help them." The slaves stared at her in open awe, which X-ray must have noticed. "That's right," he added with a touch of pride. "She jumped into that thing and grabbed a sword, and stood back-to-back with her folks. So don't go shooting up this family."

Folks? Family? Bliss wanted to scream, and at any other time she would have. Now, she just winced.

Burned Fingers walked up to the Mayor, staring at his empty eye sockets, then turned to X-ray. "What are you going to do with him?"

"I'd like to feed him to his goddamn dragons."

"I might be able to help you."

Sam assembled the caravaners behind a dune, out of sight of the city, and handed Bessie a .32 with a wooden grip. The big-boned redhead and her dark-haired friend, Teresa, had volunteered to escort the children to the wrecking yard. Bessie had said she knew how to shoot. She certainly appeared to know how to handle the semiautomatic, one of the precious few still working. Sam watched her pop the clip to check the load, snap it back into place, and rack the slide. Ready to shoot in about three seconds.

"On the fourth row," Sam explained to the two young woman, "you'll see a truck trailer. It's the only one in the whole yard. Knock three times, then twice. Helena's inside.

Tell her Sam sent you and that everything's going well. She'll take over from there."

They trooped off with the kids, and Sam turned to the adult caravaners, a few more of them women than men. "We're going set mines to bring down this end of the city. Then we're spilling gas everywhere we see or hear survivors in the rubble. We burn them to death," she said emphatically, waiting for any objections.

"Six of our people are in there," said another redheaded woman, who identified herself as Maureen Gibbs.

"If we see them, we'll help them. But we have to press this extermination forward until it's done. We're doing this one section at a time, and then we move to the next one. We'll meet everybody blowing up the other end somewhere in the middle."

Nobody had tried to flee the city since daybreak, but a squad from the wrecking yard still covered the perimeter.

"Why not just shoot the survivors?" asked Maureen's husband, Keffer.

"Because thanks to you guys, we have a lot more gas than bullets. And it's more effective. If one person's alive in the rubble, there's a good chance he's got a buddy or two down there with him."

"Four of our kids are missing," Maureen said.

"We're not shooting kids."

"No, they're too valuable," Maureen snapped.

Sam smacked Maureen's chest so hard she drove the woman backward two feet. "Get one thing straight: we're not them. We don't take kids to the Alliance *for any price.* And we're saving your lives *and* the lives of all your children."

"I'm sorry," Maureen offered. "It's been horrible. You don't know—"

"We *do* know. *I* know. That's why we're not taking prisoners, and the biggest mistake any of you can make is trying to stop us. They *all* die."

"Okay," Maureen said. "I'm really sorry."

Sam saw nods of affirmation from everyone but the gracious African, whose head never moved. But neither did he object. She spotted a small cross burned into his chest, and figured he was religious. Maybe he'd just have to find his faith again later in the day, because now was the time to put hell to rest.

Cassie waited, and waited, to see if Jester could swim. She didn't think so. He hadn't jumped till she lured him into the water by standing on the rise in the middle that Miranda had pointed out. But if she was wrong, she knew she was dead.

"Drown," she whispered.

But he surfaced in front of her with a gasp so shocking that she almost fell into the deeper water. He thrashed with a look of terror on his burned face. But she *could* see his face, which meant he could breathe.

Cassie pushed off the rise, swimming underwater, aided again by the current. But she ran out of air quickly—panic burned it up like a furnace—and had to struggle to take another quick breath.

In this uncertain manner, rising just enough to breathe when she had to, she moved away from the rise where Jester now stood. Had she looked back, she would have realized that the moment he jumped, she should have taken off, rather than marking so clearly where he could find footing. But she'd kept her head above water for as long as possible because she feared drowning—or getting sucked underground where the river disappeared for miles.

She felt the current strengthening, pushing her toward the gap that could kill her, and struggled mightily to a smooth round boulder just to the left of the dark opening. Hanging onto it, she glanced back and saw Jester hurling himself toward her, floundering right away.

"Drown, drown," she whispered again.

Cassie pulled herself onto the rock, feeling safer just as his hand rose from the water and gripped her foot. She jerked hard. He let go, but only because he needed both hands to keep from getting swept away himself.

She climbed halfway up the narrow chiseled steps, breath tightening as he pulled himself from the water with frightening speed and scrambled after her. She was so petrified at finding him gaining ground that for several seconds she didn't hear Miranda or see her outstretched hand.

When she did, she reached up, and saw Steph trying to help, too. She was so grateful she could have cried. They hauled her up as Jester tried to grab her again. Then the older girls rolled a lethal-looking boulder at him, but it bounced to the side and landed in the water, harmlessly splashing him.

While Cassie tried to catch her breath, the other girls hurled rocks at Jester, hitting him several times, hard. But to the terror of all three of them, he not only weathered the barrage, but scuttled up the vast steps even faster.

Miranda dragged Cassie to her feet and they all ran toward the garden cavern. Cassie felt like a sluggard compared to the older girls. Miranda stayed by her side, but urged Steph to run ahead. When Steph hesitated, Miranda shouted, "If you can do it, then *do* it."

Run fast? Cassie knew she couldn't have at that moment, but she saw Steph take off.

When they reached the cavern moments later, Miranda yelled at her: "Now *you* go! Run for your life."

The older girl turned toward the onrushing Jester, reached into a wide bed of tall tomato plants and grabbed two rocks.

"Come with me!" Cassie shouted at her. "Go!"

Miranda screamed without turning back.

She couldn't leave Miranda here, she thought. Not by herself, with nothing but a couple of stones. Dizzy with fear, Cassie ran to the bed, planning to grub for rocks, but found a small pile right away. They'd been left there in the meticulously tended garden. After retrieving as many as she could in two hands, she returned and stood, pale and trembling, next to Miranda.

When the older girl threw her rocks, Jester slowed and

ducked. She missed, but Cassie threw, too, and hit him in the leg. It didn't appear to have any more effect than stoning him back at the plunge pool had, but then he took another step toward them and Steph jumped from behind the tomato plants and drove a punji stick into his neck. She did it with such force that the sharpened bone went through Jester's body and stuck out on the other side.

He staggered, spun around and clawed at the wound. Spotting Steph, his eyes widened. "You! You!" he gasped at the mute girl.

She wasn't silent anymore: "Fucker!" she shrieked, pulling another sharpened bone from the bed and ramming it like a spear into his gut.

Miranda dragged Steph away from Jester when he started to fall forward. The girl kept screaming at him as he jerked on the ground, spasms that ended seconds later.

"He hurt me!" Steph screamed, sobbing so hard her whole body shook. "He . . . hurt . . . me . . . like . . . nobodyshouldev erbehurt," she finished in a furious torrent of words.

She dropped to the ground and curled up, wailing with such anguish that tears sprang to Cassie's eyes.

Miranda wrapped herself around Steph and rocked her, whispering, "It's okay now."

"No, no it's not," Cassie said, gripping Miranda's shoulder.

The girl sat up, staring at Jester.

"No, over here," Cassie screamed, pointing behind her to a Komodo dragon. The beast had a grotesque neck wound and mangled leg, but was dragging himself toward them.

"Oh my God! Get up, Steph." Miranda pulled the grieving girl to her feet, and the three ran.

But Tonga never even looked at them. The reptile trudged up to the meat that didn't move, stripping off most of Jester's back and a buttock with his powerful jaws.

A tortured cry rose in the cavern. The girls paused and looked back, watching Jester make a feeble attempt to push the Komodo away. The giant lizard ripped off Jester's arm with his teeth.

Morning sun burned by the time Teresa and Bessie led the children to the top of a dune that bordered the wrecking yard. Most of them remembered seeing the stacks of smashed-up cars on their march to the City of Shade. When they looked back now, only a middle section of the city still stood. Dark smoke billowed from all parts of a huge rubble pile that had been a massive structure just hours ago.

Several of the children said they could still hear screams, but Teresa gaily insisted they were listening to the souls of birds singing. Bessie agreed, whistling beautifully until none of the children heard any other sounds at all.

Hot and weary, they descended the dune to the fourth row. When Teresa spotted the trailer door hanging open, she asked Bessie to stay back with the kids.

"Only if you'll take the gun," Bessie said, trying to hand her the .32.

"You keep it. You have them," Teresa replied, casting a glance at the line of children.

Bessie shook her head. "We haven't see anything for two hours. *Take it*. It's ready to go. Or let me handle this instead."

"I'll go." Teresa took the pistol, feeling ultimately responsible, as she always had, for the safety of any children in her care.

She approached the trailer warily, slowly opening the door all the way. Bright morning light swept across the sand that had gathered over years on the wooden floor, exposing the body of a woman who had been savagely knifed to death.

Teresa backed away, then thought to latch the door to keep scavengers out. She didn't know the form they took in the desert, but there were always scavengers.

"We can't wait in there," she said softly to Bessie, handing the gun back. "Someone's been killed. It's really bad. We've got to find a safe place for these kids, as far from here as we can get and still be in the yard."

In an adventurous voice, Teresa said to the children, "Let's go all the way out to the end of these cars so we can see just how big this place really is."

"Why? What's wrong?" asked one of the three Gibbs kids, as flame-haired as her mother.

"Nothing's wrong," Teresa said.

"Then why did you jump away from that door like you got *bit*?" the girl asked, sounding as peckish as her mom.

"I just thought it would be nice to be outside after being cooped-up in that pit all the time."

"You're lying."

"Would you please just be nice?" Teresa said to the girl. She could have wept, after what she'd just seen, and now this?

They had started back up the row when they heard a loud engine. Teresa looked for a place to hide the kids, but it was too late: a motorcycle with a sidecar slowed at the end of the row. The driver looked at them and turned.

"You can put the gun down," Teresa said to Bessie. "That's Bliss's friend on the back."

The driver braked. His leg had bled through his pants, and Teresa glimpsed an S burned into his brow. She wondered what that meant.

"Who is he?" Bessie asked, the gun by her side.

Before Teresa could confess her ignorance, Jaya climbed gingerly off the bike. His leg was bloody, too, but he ignored her inquiring gaze and pointed in the direction of the city, asking what was going on.

"Who's he?" Teresa asked, glancing at the driver.

"Esau," Jaya replied. "He was a slave at the Alliance." Then he introduced him to her and Bessie and told them about the Russians.

"If they didn't get you, what happened?" Teresa stared openly at their wounds.

"The guy who owned this bike is what happened to us," Jaya said. "But we killed him. Now will you tell me what's going on over there? Is Bliss okay? The others?"

"Everyone in the pit got out, and they're fighting. But I

don't know about Bliss. No one's seen her. The people from here," Teresa glanced at the stacks of wrecked cars, "are blowing the place up."

"I've got to go there," Jaya said to Esau.

"Tell them we're in the last row, not the fourth one," Teresa said. Then she whispered, "We'll be hiding. A woman was murdered in the trailer. That'll mean something to them."

The Mayor, blind and bound and still moaning, tried to bolt when he heard Chunga. But without his eyes, he wasn't as agile or as fast as he'd been in the tunnel, and he never broke free of the furious slaves pushing him toward his office. The starving Chunga was still thrashing around behind the door, as if the beast sensed the meat just beyond the barrier.

"How the hell are we going to get him in there without getting eaten ourselves?" X-ray asked Burned Fingers.

"Chunga might do the work for us," the marauder replied. "He stuck his head right through a wall when Jessie and I were in there, and he would have eaten us alive if we'd given him half a chance. So let's give him an opening and see what he makes of it."

He and the slaves had escorted Jessie and the girls safely out of the city before forcing the Mayor to his office. X-ray told Jessie to alert the wrecking yard people about the men still fighting for them under the last section of roof.

"The only question I have," Burned Fingers went on, "is if you guys have enough firepower to kill the beast once he does his job. You'll never get a heart shot in that space. And keep in mind that I need some ammo from you."

"We've got plenty," X-ray assured him. "We've been collecting guns and bullets at every turn. We'll fill him so full of lead he won't be able to lift his mangy ass, plus he'll be weighted down with a couple hundred pounds of him." The slave nodded at the Mayor.

Burned Fingers found it notable that after trying to flee, the Mayor had not resorted to begging for his life, sparing them any maudlin speeches. The marauder liked to think that when his time came, he'd also handle himself with dignity.

Opening the wall, he realized, even a little, was risky, but not as dicey as opening the door. The tactic seemed to work: As soon as a slave pounded through the drywall, the dragon's head exploded into the hallway, craning his neck as far as he could.

X-ray and the other slaves pushed the Mayor toward his pet. The beast chomped the man's torso, ripping off a large chunk of his chest and back in a savage swipe. The Mayor fell bellowing to the floor in a flood of blood as the beast ate his flesh.

When Chunga's meal tried to crawl away, the lizard looked down, as if sizing up his prey in the most literal sense, and clamped his jaws fully around the man, lifting him up as Tonga had the young woman in the circus wagon.

The Mayor's head protruded from one side of the beast's mouth. His screams weakened; his lungs had been severely punctured. Burned Fingers thought the Mayor might catch a break with a quick beheading, but the tyrant wasn't that lucky. The reptile jerked him around in his mouth until the Mayor's head and upper body disappeared into the beast's long throat. His legs, like the young woman's, kicked, but not for long.

The slaves stared as if struck. Only Chunga's swallowing violated a daunting silence.

Burned Fingers leaned toward X-ray and said he'd be taking his leave. The slave handed him a pouch full of bullets.

"These work?" X-ray asked.

Burned Fingers eyed a shell. "Perfect. I'll bring you back whatever's left."

"Thanks." X-ray clasped the marauder's shoulder. "It's not going to be easy, but what you're doing is a good thing."

Burned Fingers headed off as the first shots tore into the dragon. A surprisingly charitable impulse had him hoping the Mayor was dead and wouldn't find himself half alive in the throat of a dead beast.

When he reached the large cell with the bone bars, he saw a staggering display of madness. The diseased women, undoubtedly incited by the violence all around them—and the virus's own demonic instigations—were brutalizing one another or themselves. Only the straggly-haired teen came forward.

She slipped her arms through the bars as rage boiled dangerously close and threatened to sweep her away at any second. But this time she wasn't begging for food.

Burned Fingers nodded and glanced at his gun. He had the one bullet left in the cylinder. He wouldn't reload just yet. He would give the girl something that had been saved, even if it was a lethal remnant of the long ago.

He cocked the hammer and raised the revolver. She gave him what might have been a smile. His burned index and middle fingers curled around the trigger, and he wept for the first time since finding the massacred bodies of his wife and son in a burned-out basement in Baltimore.

And then he did what had to be done, for the grateful girl and all the others, just as he had so many times before.

Chapter Twenty

Noon. Small fires still burned across much of the destroyed city, but the last wave of the extermination had slowed. The screams were quieting.

Jessie had not taken part in the systematic incineration of the wounded and injured. That task was directed by a woman named Sam, and carried out by people ruthlessly reclaiming the desert so they might survive in the caverns below it.

Instead, Jessie and her oldest friend, Solana, had spent the morning accounting for everyone on the caravan. Astonishingly, only Maul had been killed. The other losses—Erik's dog, Razzo, and a Pixie-bob kitten—paled so much by comparison that Jessie felt more gratitude than grief when she considered their absence.

The cavern people had not fared so well. They'd lost three men, and a mother who'd been murdered by a guard, who then tried to kill little Cassie. She said his name was Jester. Esau reported that a guard by that name had been ordered by the Mayor to find Cassie, under penalty of death. The guard had, indeed, died—at the hands of a cavern girl and a mortally wounded dragon.

What a way to grow up, Jessie thought.

As soon as Solana headed for the caverns, where all the children had been taken, a slave named X-ray ran up to Jessie.

"I have to apologize for something that happened with Bliss under my watch." He told her about letting Jessie's oldest daughter execute a guard who had brutalized her in Section R and tried to rape Ananda. "I had no idea she'd just turned fifteen. I just found out this morning. Your kid claimed the right to kill him, and I figured she was of age. I never would have—"

"It's okay," Jessie interrupted. "I'm just glad you were there to help her and Ananda." The guard who died was the same thug who delighted in bragging to her about what he'd done to Bliss.

"They're just kids," X-ray said, shaking his head.

He returned to the ruins, helping other freed slaves open a stairway to a huge supply of wood stored underground. Pyres needed to be built.

Jessie gazed at her daughter, carrying rubble to men who were building an open, cross-shaped tomb in front of the smoking ruins. It was easy for her to see how Bliss could be mistaken for an adult. Her older daughter was tall, strong, and deeply responsible. Nonetheless, Jessie waved her over.

Bliss jogged up, and her mother asked how she was doing.

"I saw X-ray talking to you, Mom. Don't worry. I'm fine. I wouldn't be if I'd let him live, but he wasn't my first kill. Remember that. And I got my hands on that bastard right after he tried to rape Ananda. No way I was going to let anybody else kill him."

Her father's daughter, a little voice said to Jessie. *Mother's, too,* it added a moment later. But it saddened her to consider how Bliss had come of age. Minutes ago X-ray had said, "They're just kids." Jessie wasn't sure that was true about Bliss. She feared her girl's youth vanished on the day she learned that her father had died, when she'd beaten her fists against her belly and might have pounded the last of her childhood to bits. Jessie wished she could soften her with love, but the loss of innocence seemed as irretrievable as the loss of life itself.

"So you're okay?" she asked.

"I'm getting by. I found out they gave Jaya to the Alliance." Bliss turned from Jessie. "I've got to stay busy."

But she never made it back to her work detail. A motorcycle roared toward them, and a young man on the back waved madly at Bliss. She started running, screaming Jaya's name over and over, abundant and fervent with a life she had thought was lost. She reached for him long before her arms finally embraced the young man she loved so fiercely.

Jessie didn't believe Bliss could ever remain unaffected by all that she'd endured, but this had to help: her daughter and Jaya pressed their foreheads together, as if to let their eyes reclaim the heart of the other, and then they kissed.

She'll soften, Jessie assured herself.

Her gaze settled on the men building the tomb. It was for the bodies of the Russians killed trying to escape the city. Sam's idea. Jessie agreed that it could put an end to the Alliance. For years, after a battle the zealots would gouge crosses into the skulls of their victims, then dump the bodies into cross-shaped tombs open to scavengers of all types. It was a final insult to an enemy—and the Alliance's most notorious signature.

The Russians had been just as merciless with the Alliance allies who resisted their recent takeover of the Strategic Petroleum Reserve. Sam figured the Russians would view the murder of their advance party—and the flaunting of their dead comrades in an open grave—as revenge, and launch an equally vicious attack on Alliance headquarters at the old military base. Who else could have murdered their men? Now that the City of Shade had been leveled, its inhabitants massacred, all the cavern people could disappear into their Eden. They no longer needed to turn the wrecking yard into a Potemkin village. And the Russians weren't likely to meet much resistance when they unleashed their vengeance at the base. The Alliance was short of fuel, food, and mercenaries, many of whom had been crushed or otherwise killed in the past eighteen hours.

"She's going to be all right."

Jessie started when Burned Fingers spoke. She'd been staring so intently at the transformation of rubble into a tomb that she hadn't heard his approach.

He nodded at Bliss, who was looking at Jaya's wounded leg.

"I hope so," Jessie said. "What she's been through—what all of them have been through—would be a lot for anyone, and they're so young."

"Not that young. They're not kids like we were. The world wouldn't let them. That's the biggest crime."

He always surprised her when he said something like that. Endeared himself, too, which amazed her most of all.

"How long do you think we can tempt fate by leaving our vehicles up here, if we take a break in the caverns?" she asked him. "We could all use some R and R."

"Three days. That would be safe, and that's assuming the Alliance could even muster a force at this point, which I doubt."

"The Russians?"

"Even longer. But they're definitely on their way. They didn't send an advance party this far for nothing."

"We'll have to wangle an invitation." Jessie looked at Sam, who was still overseeing the last of the extermination. "She's a real iron lady."

"She's had a tough go of it. Her husband was killed last night right in front of her. And her girl was taken by the Alliance a few years ago and murdered when she tried to escape. That's what I picked up from one of the guys on the work crew. To me, she seems like someone just barely hanging on."

"I didn't know." Jessie closed her eyes for a moment and took a steadying breath. Then she walked over to Sam, who was studying the small pitiless fires with an unwavering gaze.

"I just heard," Jessie said to her. "I'm sorry. I lost my own husband a few weeks ago."

Sam's face cracked, and then the woman who had appeared so stalwart—"a real iron lady"—crumpled.

Jessie caught her, but the sudden weight of accumulating grief brought them both to their knees. Jessie held her tightly, feeling Sam's throbbing pain as clearly as she saw the smoke horrors still clinging to the sky.

Sam and the others did invite the caravaners to stay for R and R, welcoming them to a wondrous world of whimsical rock formations and stunning colors sharply at odds with the blanched desert above them.

They flocked to the clear-flowing river right away, weaving through a forest of turquoise-colored stalagmites and stalactites. Jessie watched adults and children alike smile, most for the first time in weeks. They bathed and played in the water and ate fresh food, before helping to clear away the detritus of battle that had reached all the way down there.

They started with the engorged body of the dead Komodo, flushing it from the caverns through the opening in the plunge pool.

Then nine-year-old Denton announced that he knew something else "really big" that had to go. He led them to the punji stick cavern where he had hidden after being separated from Miranda and Steph in the dark. The black-haired boy pointed to a corner where a large man had crashed through the ceiling and died.

Burned Fingers identified the body as belonging to the frizzy-haired marauder named Pie. After he provided an unexpurgated obituary, that body was flushed from the plunge pool as well.

But a solemn service was held for Maul; Miranda's mom, Helena; Yurgen; and two other cavern men. Each body was laid on a separate pyre.

Sam, still reeling from grief, spent most of her time with

Miranda. Without a word having been spoken, the girl blended into Sam's family, along with Cassie. Both girls had lost their mothers to murder.

The littlest caravaner felt torn by her decision to stay with the cavern people, and cried at the prospect of never seeing Ananda, M-girl, Teresa, or any of her other friends again. But with Maul's death, Cassie's last strong link to her annihilated home camp near the Gulf had been severed; Miranda, wounded by her own loss, became an older sister to her. Steph, as talkative as any other child now that she'd killed her abuser, Jester, rejoiced openly when she learned that a new playmate had joined their pack.

None of the other caravaners were invited to make their home in the wonderland beneath the desert, but neither Jessie nor any of the adults begrudged their hosts' resolve to keep their community small and sustainable; it could not have withstood an immediate doubling of its population without risking its survival. The cavern people did take in the seven slaves who had survived the attacks on the city and killed the Mayor, while the travelers accepted Esau into their ranks.

Only Ananda felt sick with envy over Cassie's good fortune, and only because an endless supply of freshwater to slake her thankless thirst seemed like the greatest bounty of all.

Sitting on the riverbank, Ananda told her mother that the Mayor said she had diabetes. "The kind that kills you."

Jessie nodded and allowed that she and Hannah had also talked about that possibility. "But Hannah said those symptoms could be caused by other things, and she's a nurse. We just can't test for it anymore."

"But he was sure, Mom."

"He was sure about a lot of things, hon, and look at his city now."

But Ananda never saw the rubble on the desert again. A day later Jessie and Burned Fingers consulted with Sam, and decided that sending the children north through the caverns, with the river's promise of water, would be safer than having them cross the Great American Desert—the Bloodlands, as the Mayor called it when he first took them captive. The caverns ended where the old Lake Michigan, now barren, once lapped at the shore. Even if the Alliance were defeated by enraged Russians, Jessie and Burned Fingers had heard from Esau that the mysterious Dominion was the real force that wanted all migration north stopped. The desert might prove treacherous yet again. Better to keep the children far from harm, even if it meant having them travel paths through millions of human bones.

So each boy and girl was outfitted with a rudimentary pack of dried fruit, vegetables, and smoked snake. They would have to hike about five miles each of the next forty days to rendezvous with the caravan at what had been the U.S.-Canadian border before the collapse. That would be a rigorous pace for the children, dictated as much by the caravan's speed as the amount of food the kids could carry. But it was feasible, according to Sam, who had debriefed two young men who had explored the entire length of the underground passage several years ago. She casually noted to Jessie that the pair had never returned from a second exploratory mission, though she added, "They probably moved on to the Arctic. They'd talked about that. You know how guys can be, especially at that age. They're always looking for something better."

Jessie could not imagine what could be better than the caverns surrounding them.

Sam's only cautionary note concerned several stretches of darkness in the cavern route—one that extended for more than ten miles—where the hikers would need torches. But the cavern ceilings had split apart in numerous places, assuring natural light for much of the journey.

"They'll be a lot safer down here," Sam advised.

Safer, in no small measure, because they would not be

anywhere near the fuel in the tanker truck, a nearly priceless prize for any takers.

Jessie, Burned Fingers, Bliss, Jaya, Esau, and Brindle would stick with the vehicles. Burned Fingers planned to ride the old Harley. Jaya would take over the wheel of the van, which would still ferry the three blind girls and the babies, along with most of the foodstuffs. Brindle would move up to the helm of the tanker.

Jessie, Bliss, and Ananda experienced a wrenching good-bye. The three hugged as tightly as they had after Bliss rescued her mother and sister at the Army of God by gunning down the sect's tyrannical leader. It agonized Jessie to let go of Ananda and watch her march off, but she consoled herself knowing the child would not suffer the hardships of the sun or have to fret over water for the duration of her trek. Hannah promised to keep a close eye on her health, and Augustus and the twins would also be nearby. M-girl and Imagi always stayed by Ananda's side, too. She would be watched over with great care by people who loved her dearly. And, though only twelve, Ananda had already proved her amazing mettle in battle.

An hour later Jessie and the other caravaners climbed the rope ladder to the blistering desert, prepared to resume their journey to the promise of verdant land, fertile farms, and freshwater in the Arctic. She eyed the ruins and tried to tell herself that the City of Shade would be the last terror they'd have to face, that the desert would yield peaceably to them from now on. But she could not put aside Esau's warnings about the Dominion's vicious determination to stop anyone from crossing the Bloodlands.

What the hell is the Dominion, anyway? she wondered.

Esau knew only what he'd overheard from His Piety and the Chief Elder, but he didn't think the Dominion was another cult, at least not a religious one.

Burned Fingers had certainly prepared for the worst. He had salvaged a .45 revolver from the rubble, along with ample ammo, and plundered the Mayor's office for the despot's bolt action rifle and bandoliers. The marauder looked ready for war.

That's what he knows best.

Jessie assumed her perch on top of the tanker trailer. The truck's engine rumbled to life, and the twin stacks on either side of the cab belched black smoke into the air. She still thought they looked like the smoldering horns of a demon— but a demon they needed desperately; after they arrived at Lake Michigan's cracked bed, they would still have to travel almost 3,500 miles to the Arctic.

Bliss climbed on top of the van as a lookout for Jaya at the wheel. Exigencies, as much as love, had brought them together.

The girl's shotgun, like her mom's M–16, had been taken by the Mayor and his minions and lost in the destruction of the city. Bliss was now armed with the Colt single-action pistol. By edict of her mother, she would have to surrender the handgun to Ananda on her sister's fourteenth birthday. The young warrior was the rightful owner, under rules that still governed the spoils of war.

Jessie carried a pistol, too, the Mayor's chrome-plated Smith & Wesson .45. She was also armed with an AK–47 the slaves had taken from a guard and given to her. The venerable rifle had outlasted most all the nations that once treasured it.

The cavern people had donated canisters, giving the smaller caravan crew enough water to see them beyond the desiccated lake that was their initial destination.

With a satisfied smile, Burned Fingers fired up the old Harley, signaling the caravan forward with his scarred hand. He raced ahead of the van, point man for any menace, a role he clearly relished. The van followed him, and the tanker truck—with Jessie scanning the vast landscape—fell into line.

She could see nothing in the Great American Desert but

rubble, wrecked cars, and the cross-shaped tomb made of broken bricks. But if she could have viewed the cross from above, she would have spied scores of vultures that had come to scavenge in the open grave, teeming so thickly that they draped the moldering bodies in black as they stripped away the skin.

Only bones in time.